LEAGUE OF UNWEDDABLE GENTLEMEN

Books 1-3

TAMARA GILL

COPYRIGHT

League of Unweddable Gentlemen
Books 1-3
Tempt Me, Your Grace
Hellion at Heart
Dare to be Scandalous
Copyright © 2020 by Tamara Gill
Cover Art by Wicked Smart Designs
All rights reserved.

ISBN: 978-0-6450581-4-7

TEMPT ME, YOUR GRACE

League of Unweddable Gentlemen, Book 1

She was banished from England...and she banished him from her heart.

Upon her return to England following her father's death, Miss Ava Knight becomes the owner of one of the largest racehorse estates in the country. There's only one problem: the future of the estate requires a strong breeding program with the services of a stallion named, Titan. A shame that the horse is owned by a man she swore to never see again.

The Duke of Whitstone, Tate Wells, was heartbroken when Ava abandoned him on the night of their elopement, and he vowed to never lay eyes on Ava again. Despite Tate's unwillingness to forgive Ava, she comes to his aid during a deliberately lit fire at his estate. Someone is determined to destroy them. Now, the two are forced to work together to ensure the safety of their horses and their homes.

．　．　．

Will their previous feelings for each other rekindle their love, or will their feelings stall out at the starting gates?

PROLOGUE

Knight Stables, Berkshire, 1816

Miss Avelina Knight, Ava to those close to her, tightened the girth of her mount, and checked that the saddle wouldn't slip whilst hoisting herself onto one stirrup. With a single candle burning in the sconce on the stables' wall, she worked as quickly and as noiselessly as she could in the hopes that the stable hands that slept in the lofts above wouldn't wake.

Pleased that the saddle would hold, and that her mount was well watered before her departure, she walked Manny out of the stables as silently as possible, cringing when the horse's shod feet made a clip clop sound with each step.

Ava blew out the candle as she walked past it, and picking up her small bag, threw it over her horse's neck before hoisting herself up into the saddle. She sat there a minute, listening for any noise, or the possibility that someone was watching. Happy that everything remained quiet, she nudged her mount and started for the eastern gate.

There was still time and she didn't need to rush, now that she was on her way. Tate had said he'd meet her at their favorite tree at three in the morning, and it was only half past two.

She pushed Manny into a canter, winding her way through several horse yards that surrounded her home and past the gallop her father used to train their racing stock. Or what was once her home. From tonight onward, her life would finally begin. With Tate, she would travel the world, make love under the stars if they so wished, and not have to be slaves to either of their families' whims or Society and its strictures.

Tate and she would find a new life. A new beginning. Just the two of them until they expanded their family to add children in a few years.

Pleasure warmed her heart at the knowledge, and she couldn't stop the soft laugh of delight which escaped her.

In time, Ava hoped her father would forgive her, and maybe when they returned, happily married with children even, her father would be pleased.

The shadowy figure of a man stood beneath the tree. Yet from the stance and girth of the gentleman, it did not look like Tate. Coldness swept over her skin, and she narrowed her eyes, trying to make out who was waiting for her. Her stomach in knots, she pushed her horse forward unsure what this new development meant.

Ava looked about, but could see no one else. With a couple of more steps she gasped when she finally made out the ghostly form. Her father.

Her heart pounded a frantic beat. How was it he was here and not Tate? They had been so careful, so discreet. Why, they had not even circulated within the same social sphere to be heard whispering or planning. With Tate being the heir to his father, the Duke of Whitstone and Ava only the daughter of a racehorse notable, their lives couldn't be more different.

Ava rode her horse up to the tree. She saw little point in turning back.

Pulling up before her father, she met his gaze, as much of it as she could make out under the moonlit night.

"Ava, climb down, I wish to speak to you."

His tone was not angry, but guarded, and the pit of her stomach lurched at the notion that something dreadful had happened to Tate. Had he been hurt? Why wasn't he here to meet her instead?

She jumped down, walking up to him, her mount following on her heels.

"Papa, what are you doing here?" she asked, needing to know and knowing there was little point in ignoring the fact that he'd found her out.

She dropped her horse's reins, and her mount reached down to nibble on the grass.

Her father's face took on a stern cast. "The Marquess of Cleremore will not be meeting you here, Ava. I received a note late last night notifying me that, as we speak, his lordship has been sent to London to catch the first boat out to New York. From what his father, the Duke of Whitstone, states, this was the marquess' decision. Tate confided in his father the predicament he'd found himself in with you, and that he didn't know how to untangle himself from having to marry a woman who was not his equal."

Ava stared at her father, unable to fathom what he was saying. Hollowness opened up in her chest and she clasped her shawl as if to halt its progress. Tate had left her? No, it couldn't be true. "But that doesn't make any sense, Papa. Tate loves me. He said so himself at this very spot." Surely she couldn't have been wrong about his affections. People did not declare such emotions unless they were true. She certainly had not.

She loved Tate. Ava thought back to all the times he'd taken liberties with her, kissing her, touching her, spending copious amounts of time with her and it had all been meaningless to him. She had been a mere distraction, a plaything for a man of his stature.

Her stomach roiled at the idea and she stumbled to the tree, clutching it for support. "No. I do not believe it. Tate wouldn't do that to me. He loves me as I love him and we're going to marry each other." Ava stared down at the ground for a moment, her mind reeling before she rounded on her father. "I need to see him. He needs to tell me this to my face."

"Lord Cleremore has already left for town. And by morning, he'll be on a ship to America." Her father sighed, coming over to her and taking her hand. "I thought your attachment to him was a passing folly. His lordship was never for you, my dear. We train and breed racehorses and, in England, people like us do not marry future dukes."

Ava stared at her father, not believing this was happening. She'd thought tonight would be the start of forever, but it was now the beginning of the end. Her eyes smarted and she was powerless to hold onto her composure. "But I love him," she whispered, her voice cracking.

Her father, a proud but humble man from even humbler beginnings, straightened his spine. "I know you think you did, but it wasn't love. You're young, too young to be throwing your life away on a boy who would have his way with you and then marry another titled, well-connected woman."

"I'm not ruined or touched, father. Please don't speak in such a way." She didn't want to imagine that Tate could treat her with so little respect, but what her father said was worth thinking over. The past few weeks with Tate had left very little room other than to plan, to plot. Would they have thought differently, would Tate have acted differently if he'd been older, more mature? If his departure showed anything, it was certainly that what her father was saying was true. He had regretted his choice and had left instead of facing her. Letting her down as a gentleman should, had not been his course. It showed how little he thought of her and the love she'd so ardently declared to him.

She swiped at her cheeks, wanting to scream into the night at the unfairness of it all.

"I'm sorry," she said, looking at her half boots and not able to meet his gaze. *How could he have done this to me?* She would never forgive him.

He sighed. "There is one more thing, my dear."

More! What else could there possibly be to say! "What, papa?" she asked, dread formed like a knot in her stomach at her father's ashen countenance. She'd seen a similar look from him when he'd come to tell her of her mother's passing and it was a visage she'd never wanted to see again. Ava clutched the tree harder.

"I'm sending you away to finishing school in France. I've enrolled you at Madame. Dufour's Refining School for Girls. It's located in southern France. It comes highly recommended and will help prepare you for what's to come in your life; namely, running Knight Stables, taking over from me when the time comes."

Finishing school! "You're sending me to France! But Papa, I don't need finishing school. You know that I'm more than capable of taking over the running of the stables already. And I know my manners, how to act in both upper- and lower-class society. Please do not send me away. I won't survive without you and our horses. Don't

7

take that away from me, too." *Not when I've already lost the happiness of which I was so certain.*

He shushed her, pulling her into his arms. Ava shoved him away, pacing before him.

Her father held out his hand, trying to pacify her. "You'll thank me one day. Trust me when I tell you, this is a good thing for you, and I'll not be moved on my decision. We're leaving for Dover tomorrow and I, myself, will accompany you to ensure your safe arrival."

"What." She stopped pacing. "Father, please don't do this. I promise not to do such a silly, foolish thing again. You said yourself Tate was leaving. There is no reason to send me away as well." Just saying such a thing aloud hurt and Ava clutched her stomach. To have loved and lost Tate would be hard enough; nevertheless being sent away to a foreign country, alone and without any friends or support was too much to bear.

He came over to her, pulling her against him and kissing her hair. "This is a good opportunity for you, Ava. I have worked hard, saved, and invested to enable me to give you all that a titled child could receive. I want this for you. Lord Cleremore may not think that you're suitable for him, but we shall prove him wrong. Make me proud, use the education to better yourself, and come home. Promise me you will do so."

Ava slumped against him. Her father had never been flexible on things and once he'd made a decision it was final. There was no choice; she would have to do as he said. "I will go as I see there is little I can say to change your mind."

"That's my girl." He pulled back and whistled for her mount.

She couldn't even manage a half-smile as Manny trotted over to them.

"Let us go. I'm sure by the time we arrive back home breakfast will not be far away."

Using a nearby log, Ava hoisted herself up onto the saddle. The horse, as if knowing her way home, started ambling down the hill. Light shone in the eastern sky and glancing to her left, Ava watched the sun rise over her land. Observed the dawn of a new day, marking a new future even for her, one that did not include Tate, Marquess Cleremore and future Duke of Whitstone.

A lone tear slid down her cheek and she promised herself, there and then, never to cry over Tate again or any other man. She'd given him her heart and trust and he had callously broken them. That the tear drying on her cheek would be the last she ever afforded him.

And his precious dukedom that he loved so dearly. More dearly than her.

CHAPTER 1

So many miles separate us. I do not sleep with the thought of you. When did your love for me perish? I cannot fathom why you would not confide in me that your feelings had changed, maybe even moved on elsewhere...

— An excerpt from a letter from Miss Ava Knight to the Duke of Whitstone

KNIGHT STABLES, Berkshire, 1821

Ava pushed her newly purchased mare, a fine sixteen hands thoroughbred that had breeding to rival her own, into a blistering gallop. She smiled, sitting low over the neck of this precious girl, and they started around the corner and down the home straight of their family gallop.

Her stable manager and trainer, Mr. Greg Brown, stood watching from the side of the gallop, hearing his exuberant shouts as she went past him in blistering speed.

She smiled, impressed with her horse's unfathomable swiftness.

The early morning mist started to burn off the grass and trees, freshness in the air after a light shower of rain. Pulling up the mare, Ava kept her in a slow trot to return to Greg. The mare blew steam out of her nostrils with each breath and Ava patted her, giving her a congratulatory rub.

Ava breathed deep herself, marveling at the beauty of her life, the beauty of this place that was now hers.

"What did you think, Greg? Do you think she has a chance at Ascot?" Ava teased, knowing they had a lot ahead of them before they could even think to enter the mare into such a race there.

He chuckled, bending under the railing and coming out to pat the horse himself. "Maybe next year if she keeps performing as she is. She'll have to prove herself at Epsom before then, though."

Ava kicked her feet free of the stirrups and jumped down. She handed the reins to Greg and walked around the horse, checking to make sure she was sound after her run. "Gallant Girl will prove herself, just as her name suggests, you wait and see. And with the new yearlings in a year or so that we'll produce with Titan breeding with Black Lace, we'll have more beauties like this one."

"About Titan," Greg said, pulling off his cap and running his hand through his hair. "There may be some difficulty having him cover with Black Lace as you wanted. I got word today that Mr. Tuttle has sold him."

Ava paused in her inspection of the horse and placed Gallant Girl's front right hoof down. She met Greg's gaze and read that he'd not been making a joke. "Titan's been sold? But Mr. Tuttle promised my father that if we gave them the first foal off Black Lace two years ago, that he would allow us to have Titan to cover Black Lace this year.

My father held up his end of the bargain, and you're telling me that he has not?"

She started for the stables, yelling out to one of the young lads to saddle up Manny. Greg followed her as fast as he could while leading Gallant Girl beside him. "Wait, Miss Ava. Wait. I do believe there are options other than Titan that you should consider."

There was no other horse better than Titan and if Mr. Tuttle thought to swindle her and her late father, why, she would take back that little foal, Beatrice, and be damned the scandal in the racing world. How dare the man cheat them in such a way? He'd shaken her father's hand, damn it. Didn't that mean that the agreement was as waterproof as a ship's hull?

"There is no other horse as fine. I want Titan to sire the next generation of foals here at Knight Stables and there is nothing anyone can say to change my mind. You know as well as anyone that he's the best thoroughbred in England, possibly on the continent as well. His height, along with his strong blood lines and speed, makes him the only horse that'll do."

Ava thanked the lad who saddled up Manny for her and, clutching the saddle, she hoisted herself up.

"Where are you going?" Greg asked her, clutching the reins under her horse's neck.

She frowned at his impertinence. He let go. "I'm going to find out what Mr. Tuttle is about treating my stables with so little respect. I may be a woman, and my father may be gone, but we had a deal. I'll not stand for it."

She turned her mount and kicked Manny into a canter, heading directly for Tuttle Farm. When her father had been alive, nothing of this sort of underhanded business ever took place. They would never have thought to cheat her dearly departed papa. But here she was, a woman, and being treated with so little respect.

Anger simmered in her blood, and even by the time she trotted into Tuttle Farm's yard, her temper had not waned. She spotted Mr. Tuttle lunging a horse in the lunging yard and walked her mount up to the fence, waiting for him to notice her.

His look of contrition told her he knew exactly why she'd come.

"How could you, Mr. Tuttle? You had an agreement with my father that still stands with me," she demanded, forgoing all pleasantries.

The older gentleman yelled out for a nearby stable lad to take the rope and whip and walked over to the fence. He seemed to have aged in the last few months since she'd seen him. As she looked down at his gray, receding hairline and whiskers to match, a little of her temper eased.

"I had no choice, Miss Ava. In fact, if you do not purchase your foal back from me, you'll be buying her back at auction."

She frowned. "What is wrong, Mr. Tuttle? Has something happened to force you to sell Titan and Beatrice?"

He sighed, his shoulders slumping at the words. "It has, my dear. I don't mind telling you as our families have known each other for many years, but I made a bad investment last year and, well, it'll cost me the farm. We're preparing to move to Bath where my wife, Rose, has family. Selling Titan, at least, enabled me to pay off the most pressing debt. With the sale of the house, the land, together with the horses of course, we may have a little left over to keep us for a few years in reasonably comfortable conditions." He met her gaze, his eyes glassy with unshed tears. "I'm sorry, Ava. I know how much you wanted Titan's bloodline."

Forgetting about the horse, she said, "Can I help at all? Is there anything that I can do to ease the debt and enable you to stay? These stables have been in your family for three generations. I would hate to see you lose it all."

"Well," he said, looking about his property, the love he had for his land evident in his gray orbs. "When one makes a mistake, one must own it. I'm just sorry that my wife and my children will lose all that we've worked so hard to build. And I thank you, Miss Ava, but I cannot accept your generous offer. It wouldn't be right."

She nodded, wanting to press, but Mr. Tuttle had always been a proud man. To force him into anything had never worked before and she could not see it changing now. And she did not want to part having argued with him, even if she wanted so very much to help. "Very well, but do let me know if I can support you in any way. Or if there is something you do not want to be sold off to anyone else that maybe I can purchase. At least you'll know who has it and that it'll be loved."

"You're a good girl. And know that I would never have reneged on our deal if I could help it. There really was no other way around it."

Ava adjusted her seat, watching the horse that was being lunged who seemed quite interested in their conversation instead of doing what it was supposed to be doing. "May I ask whom you sold Titan to? Maybe I can negotiate with them."

He looked down at his feet, shuffling them a little.

"Mr. Tuttle," she ventured when he didn't reply.

"As to that, my dear. Well, that is to say…"

What was wrong with the man? "Mr. Tuttle, tell me. Surely, it is not a secret."

He met her gaze and, for a moment, she wondered if he had been sworn to secrecy. Surely not?

"The Duke of Whitstone purchased Titan, Miss Ava. I heard from your father, you see, all about your family falling out with them and, well, I'm sorry that for you to have Titan cover your mare you'll have to go through his grace."

Her hands shook at the mention of him and she clasped the reins tight, anger simmering in her veins at having heard his name. Even after all these years. "Why did you sell it to him? I could've matched the price you wanted."

He shook his head, again shuffling his feet like a naughty school child. "He came here only yesterday and offered cash. I've had money lenders down my back for weeks, so I took it without thinking. I'm sorry, Ava. But I had to think of my family."

Damn it! "I understand," she said, unable to hide the disappointment in her tone. The Duke of Whitstone could be a persuasive gentleman from what she understood. The stories she'd heard about Tate in London did not resemble the boy she'd once loved. If anything, he now sounded like a man who only sought pleasure and cared for little. In the year since she'd been back in England, he'd not once called to apologize for his treatment of her all those years ago.

Ava turned her horse, preparing to leave. "Do come by before you leave, Mr. Tuttle. Bring your family and we shall have tea and cakes. I am disappointed about the horse, but I'm more disappointed you've been placed in this situation. I wish it were not so."

He tipped his hat, bowing a little. "You're very generous, Miss Ava, and we shall call around to say our farewells."

"Very good." Ava waved and started toward home. She kicked her mount into a gallop and swore. Damn the duke and his interfering ways. If only she'd heard of Mr. Tuttle's struggles earlier, she might have been able to help him, or purchase the horse instead of the duke doing so. In her estimation, the duke was not worthy of such high standard of horse.

She could not face having to deal with him either for that matter. That he had not called was a blessing, for she certainly had not wanted to see him and his ugly, lying heart.

But it did not solve how she would gain access to Titan for her breeding program. It was a dilemma she hadn't thought she'd have to cross. But the stallion was paramount to supplementing her bloodlines, possibly siring future winners, and enabling the farm to prosper and never have to face the same fate that Mr. Tuttle has had to.

To give up on her dream to become the best and most esteemed breeding and racing stable in England wouldn't do. She'd given up previously on things she'd wanted, marriage and a family with a man she'd thought loved her, but she wouldn't in this regard. The duke would not take this away from her as well. She would send her manager, Greg, over to the ducal property and have him negotiate if at all possible.

And with any good fortune, the whole breeding program could be accomplished without his grace or her having to step one foot near each other. Just as she preferred.

Tate Wells, the Duke of Whitstone, leaned back in his leather-bound chair behind his desk and steepled his fingers as he listened to the Knight Stables' manager lay out the suggested terms for allowing Miss Ava Knight access to his prized runner, Titan.

Not that he would tell the old man, who was as loyal to Ava as her own father had been prior to his death, that hell would have to freeze over before he'd allow her anywhere near his property or Titan. It had been five years since he'd seen or thought of the woman, and he wasn't about to start now.

He shifted on his chair, his mind mocking him for the lie that was. Hell, he thought of her often. Hoped she was well and happy. Even when he went down to the local inn and had a tankard of ale, his ears would always prick up with the mention of Knight Stables and the mistress who ran the successful horseracing farm.

Even so, he would never forgive her for having him sent away. His being in America had stopped him from saying goodbye to his father. By the time news of his father's illness, two years ago now, had arrived in America his departure for England had already been too late. He'd arrived in Berkshire two weeks after his father had been placed in the family mausoleum.

Another hurt he could lay at Ava's door. Or Miss Knight, whose soul was as black as a moonless night.

"Therefore, you see, Your Grace, it would be beneficial if we were to have Titan cover our mare, Black Lace. Miss Knight is willing to pay handsomely for the service and I, along with your own head trainer, can organize all the particulars regarding the horses so you and Miss Knight need not be disturbed."

Tate met the older gentleman's gray gaze, his eyes a little watery with age. So, Ava didn't wish to see him, did she? Well, there at least was one part of the agreement on which they could concur. A small part of his heart ached at the notion that she wanted nothing to do with him. Her severing of their relationship, of leaving England had been so different from the girl he'd once known. There was a time when they could not be kept apart, when every hour, every minute was spent together.

Tate shook the unhelpful thought aside. "I'm not interested in breeding Titan at present. We're looking to have him race in Ascot next year, which I need not remind you is less than eight months away. I do not need the horse taxing himself if it's not necessary."

"I beg your pardon, Your Grace, but horses run and tax themselves daily. To breed the horse will be no more vigorous than training."

Which was true, not that Tate was going to abide by those rules. And he liked the idea of Ava not getting what she wanted. She had ripped his hopes for his future from beneath him. Marrying the woman he loved, respected and adored, not simply a woman who was considered suitable to become a duchess. "It is too much for my horse and I'll not allow it. Please tell Miss Knight to look for another stallion elsewhere for her breeding program."

The older gentleman wrung his cap in his hands. If this deal was so very important to Ava, why hadn't she come and asked him herself? He'd taken great pains in not running into her here in Berkshire and, so far, he'd been successful in his plan.

To know that she was back from France, had been for a year, it was nigh on improbable that they'd not run into each other thus far, even at race meetings and such. Tate thought on it a moment and wondered if she, too, was avoiding him as much as he avoided her.

He stood. "I'm sorry to have wasted your time, Mr. Brown, but my decision on this is final. Please let Miss Knight know." He held out his hand. "Good day to you, sir," he said, ending the conversation.

Mr. Brown stood his shoulders slumped. Tate felt for the man. He would now have to go back and face Ava. It was certainly not something even Tate would enjoy. At least, when he'd known her well all those years ago, she had been determined as much as opinionated. Two traits he'd once adored about her. They had been friends before he'd fallen head over boots in love with her. She had never backed down on a subject if she thought he was incorrect with his thinking, going to great pains to make him see the sense in her judgement. Her determination, her fierce brown eyes alight with fire when she spoke of making Knight's stables the best known in England and with Tate by her side. Ava had always expected the best of people. What a shame she was not able to live up to her own standard.

Mr. Brown shook his hand. "Thank you for your time, Your Grace. Good day to you."

Tate watched him leave. He sat back in his chair, leaning back, thinking on who Miss Knight was today. That she'd not come here and asked herself for the use of Titan was telling, indeed. It seemed all their association of years past meant very little to her. *That they were truly strangers.*

Not that such a realization surprised Tate. The day she'd sent a missive telling him she would not marry him had been enough to tell him exactly what Miss Knight thought of him. Of how much she'd lied and teased his boyish ideals.

Tate ran a hand over his jaw. Even with all that had passed between them, all the hurts, he couldn't help but wonder if she still looked the same. Did she still have long locks that were as rich as chocolate? Were her eyes as brown and wide? Were her cheekbones as high, or had they filled out a little with age?

The clock chimed the hour and, picking up his quill, he pulled the estate paperwork before him and started to check the finance ledgers for the stables and his tenant farms. What did it matter how much she'd changed? He'd changed, too, moved on.

The past two years as duke, he'd been lax in attending to the running of his estates, but no more. It was time he ensured the people who lived off his lands were well cared for. That his racing stable here in Berkshire grew and prospered as he'd always wanted. To make his stables better than the Knights' three miles from here was a good enough motivation to be here instead of town. And with Titan in his stables, he already had the upper hand in moving his plans forward.

Tate pushed thoughts of Ava from his mind, just as she'd thrown him away without a backward glance. No one who was so disloyal and self-centered deserved a minute of his time. Not ever again.

CHAPTER 2

A va pushed her horse into a gallop, the roofline of Cleremore Hall, named when the family only had the marquessate emerged from the trees. In only a few moments, she would see Tate again. Be once more in the hallowed halls of the Duke of Whitstone's home. It had been years since she'd ridden this close to his estate, and nerves pooled in her stomach at the thought of seeing him again.

Had he changed as much as she? Five years was a long time, and he'd been away in America for three of them. She supposed that could change someone very much, make them more *worldly*, knowledgeable even. Over the years, she'd secretly listened to the idle gossip about the great family whenever she heard it, wanting to hear if Tate had married or was engaged. Nothing of the kind had ever been mentioned but, upon his return to England, his antics in London certainly had been all that was on anyone's lips. In this county at least.

The man was a veritable rogue from all accounts and, somehow, the notion that he had many lovers, or at least took women to his bed on a regular basis, left the hollowness of his betrayal open like a gaping wound.

It was also not who she'd thought he was. Tate had certainly never been such a man when she had known him but they'd been a lot younger then, only nineteen in fact. His grace had also refused to marry her. So, she supposed, maybe if he had been legitimately attracted to her and loved her, he would've taken her to his bed as well. He had not.

She pulled Manny up on a small incline not far from the ducal horseracing stables, and from here she could see Titan eating grass in an adjacent paddock. Clicking her tongue, she pushed her mount forward in the direction of the stables, wanting to speak to the head trainer. See if she could get him to barter with the duke, who seemed to be a stubborn oaf, all of a sudden.

She tied up her mount to a nearby railing, leaving her with enough rein to nibble the grass. The stables were as large as hers, and yet the wood did look in need of fresh paint. At least hers were in better condition, much better than a duke's.

Entering the stables, she stood inside the darkened space and gave her eyes time to adjust. Men went about their business, some boys shoveling out days' old straw from the stalls while a couple of younger lads sat oiling the stirrups on the leather saddles.

"No oats today. He's getting fat," a familiar voice said and she gasped at hearing Tate again after all these years. The thought of fleeing entered her mind for a moment, before she raised her chin and faced the inevitable reunion that was bound to happen now that they were both back in England.

He walked out of a stall and she took the opportunity to drink in his form, his features, while he was unaware of her presence. The youth she'd once loved was no more. His soft brown hair looked sun kissed, longer on top than the sides and he'd pushed it back without thought giving it a ruffled appearance. His straight nose and chiseled jaw were as perfect as ever and, even now, she recalled the feel of it. Tate's lips were pulled into a half smile after talking to his workers, and she marveled at the fact that one man could be blessed so generously with good looks.

Certainly he was a good four inches taller, and as for his arms that once had been spindly, the current Duke of Whitstone's were muscular and strong. His thighs, encased in tan breeches, bulged with lean muscle and heat bloomed on her cheeks. She bit the inside of her cheek. Even after all that had passed between them, that her body betrayed her by longing for one more caress, a look, a kiss…

What a silly little commoner she was.

He turned and started when he spotted her. A flash of pleasure crossed his features before he blinked and it was gone, replaced with annoyance.

"I will not change my mind, Miss Knight. You're wasting my time and your own."

She sighed, lifting her chin. "I had an agreement with Mr. Tuttle before you forced him to sell you Titan. I deserve for that agreement to be upheld."

He turned, giving her his back. If he meant it to be a slight, he was sadly mistaken. Instead of infuriating her, her body simply had a mind of its own and her gaze dipped to his bottom. Biting her lip, she fought not to grin at how perfect he still was down there.

"By and by, Miss Knight, should you be dressed in such a way? You look like a man."

She raised one brow, still staring at his bottom since he was still looking the other way. "Like I care what you think, Your Grace. I didn't come here to discuss our clothing, but horse stock. What will it take for you to give me Titan so I can have him cover my mare, Black Lace? I'm willing to pay if its money you want. I remember well how much your family adores currency."

He did turn at that and she narrowed her eyes. Good. She wanted him annoyed. Annoyed as she was, that it was because of her lack of connections, of titled ancestors in her bloodline that had made her so ineligible for him. He'd left for America, abandoned her instead of telling her to her face that he'd made a mistake. That he no longer loved her and didn't wish them to marry.

She would've been hurt, to be sure. But that hurt would've healed knowing that he'd been honest and had acted the gentleman. The man before her was a coward who ran away instead of facing his responsibilities. He'd left her alone and vulnerable. Her school friends had been her salvation, but upon returning to England there was no one. With her father gone, she'd been alone, without protection and she'd paid for that lapse in the worst way possible. She would never forgive him for that.

"You would not have enough funds even if I were to ask that of you."

His words irked and she came to stand not a foot away from him. "I have plenty of blunt, duke. And I'm sure had your father still been alive, I could've bought Titan ten times over by now. So tell me, since the apple never falls far from the tree, what is your price? What will it take for me to have Titan?"

His attention moved over her face and her stomach fluttered at his inspection. What was he thinking? Did he think her much changed since he'd seen her last? Up close, Ava could see the slight shadowing of stubble on his jaw. His clothing, instead of buckskin breeches and superfine coats cut to perfection to fit his form, were tan breeches, knee-high boots, shirt and brown coat. No cravat or waist-coat, no highly starched shirt or polished boots. Ava glanced down at his chest where the tie had come loose on his shirt and the sprinkling of chest hair could be seen. Her fingers itched to feel it again. Once, when they'd been alone, they'd kissed with such passion that she had touched his person, and he too her.

The memory of it made her ache and she ground her teeth, hating that her body would deceive her with the enemy before her.

"He's not for sale," he said, staring down at her, his hardened words brooking no argument.

She narrowed her eyes. "Still stubborn I see, Your Grace." She turned about and started for the door, the click of his boots following quickly behind her. "America didn't cure you of that trait," she threw at him.

He clasped her arm and spun her to face him. She gasped, slapping his hand off of her as his touch left her burning for more. For five years, she'd not reacted to a touch as she'd reacted to Tate's and the hunger in his eyes told her he damned well knew what his presence did to her.

"What do you know of me or how I am? Do not throw insults, Miss Knight, simply because you've not got your way. I could say myself that your stubborn streak has not been trained out of you either. I would've hoped the French finishing school would've been more thorough in your education."

Ava fisted her hands at her sides. "Oh, do not worry, Your Grace. My education taught me a great deal. The most important of all was what type of gentleman to stay away from, vile lechers such as yourself." It had not taught her so very well though, and she pushed that ugly memory away, not wanting to relive that horror that had nothing to do with the man she was currently arguing with. Ava strode over to her horse and hoisted herself up. "Which I intend to do right now."

"Lecher?" he said, his eyes wide. He caught the reins of her horse and stopped her parting. "You know as well as anyone I was never a lecher."

She raised her brow mockingly. "Really, so the gossip in London about you is wrong? You're not a rake? A man who has too many lovers to count? A man who prefers folly to looking after his many estates? Tell me, duke, did the women of New York not satisfy you enough that you had to return home and sow your wild oats here? How very changeable you are from the young man I once knew." Ava shut her mouth with a snap. How had the conversation about Titan escalated into an slaying match between them? All of which was too personal, and too telling. She didn't want him to know that he'd hurt her all those years ago. Had broken her heart.

"I beg your pardon, Miss Knight, but I fail to see why you should care. Do not lob your insults at my head when you're no angel."

"What?" she said, aghast. "What do you mean by that?"

He glared at her. "And now you play me a fool. Good day to you, Madam." He stepped back, giving her leave to go. Throwing him one last glance, she kicked her mount into a canter and left. The ride home was a blur, her blood pumped loudly in her ears over a conversation about a horse that had turned into a fight about their relationship and broken engagement.

Not to mention her lack of manners in bringing up the fact that he'd slept with half of London. The rumors that his estates lacked attention, of which she had no solid proof, was true. She cringed. What was wrong with her?

Ava took a calming breath and nudged her horse into a gallop. She would not allow his boorishness to rile her. He wasn't worth it, and yet, the hurt that had been etched on his face when she left just now had opened an old wound she'd thought long healed.

TATE RAN a hand over his jaw as the delectable bottom of Ava's galloped off up his drive. What woman rode about Berkshire in men's breeches? It would seem Ava did so and with little care as to who saw her or what they thought.

The moment that she'd walked into his stables, his heart had jumped in his chest at seeing her again. He'd had to physically stop himself from taking her in his arms and telling her how much he'd missed her. Within a split second of the thought, the memory as to why they'd not married had reminded him why he would need to be wary of the woman before him. She'd pushed away his love for a chance to travel abroad and study. To run away from being a duchess as it was so very distasteful to her, or so her letter had said.

But, blast it, she was as pretty as he remembered her. Her long dark locks tied loosely at the back of her head, a delicate red ribbon the only article holding it in place. Her eyes were as fierce as ever, burning with passion, or loathing in his case, but still seeing her again had quenched his thirst after being thirsty for so long. He frowned when he lost sight of her, wanting her to come back and give him another set down if only to see her perfect little nose rise high in the air.

"Was that Miss Ava Knight?" his closest friend, Lord Arthur Duncannon said, looking up the drive and in the direction Ava had disappeared. His lifelong friend never missed anything he thought might be fodder for gossip. If it looked juicy and worth commenting on, he always had an opinion.

"Yes," Tate said, starting back toward the house. He didn't want to discuss Ava any more than he wanted to discuss why his heart wouldn't stop pounding in his chest. Or why her words cut him like a sword. She seemed angry at him, considering she'd pushed him aside for foreign shores.

Duncannon caught up to him. "The very one who jilted you? The same Ava Knight who runs the horseracing stables next door?"

Tate glared at his friend and hoped Duncannon would get the hint that this conversation and Ava were not up for discussion.

"Tell me, Your Grace. Or I shall have to find out another way."

"You will not," he said, his voice brooking no argument. "All that you need to know is that we're neighbors and certainly not friends. The past was nothing but a foolish childhood infatuation that is well over on my behalf. And from my conversation with Ava just now, so too it would seem is hers."

Duncannon threw him a disbelieving look, even so much as to scoff a little at his words. Tate halted. "What now, man? What is it that you're concocting in that minuscule mind?"

His friend grinned. "From watching you two from the stables, I would suggest that the feelings that are so very over between you two are not. In fact, I would lay good blunt down and say that, if anything, you both still care for each other more than you're willing to admit."

Tate fisted his hands at his sides. "I do not care for Miss Knight and you need to keep your opinions to yourself lest you're shuffled off to London to live with your mother."

Duncannon held up his hands in defeat. "Very well, I shall not say another word. But do tell me, what did she want to discuss? It seemed she wasn't very happy when she left."

Unhappy was calling what Ava was feeling lightly. She was mad as hell if he knew her at all. At one time, there hadn't been another person in the world who knew her as well as he did. In the past, after a disagreement such as the one they just had, Ava would ride home going over the fight. More than likely cursing his name and spitting fire. He could only assume she would've reacted today in the same way.

He half smiled at the knowledge of it. "A stupid thing really. She had agreed with Mr. Tuttle to have Titan cover her mare, Black Lace. By purchasing Titan, that deal is now void. She simply asked me to uphold the agreement, which I refused."

"Why did you refuse?" Duncannon asked. "Was it not your plan to breed Titan and race him? Why not breed with one of the best breeding stables in England? She owns Knight Stables, does she not?"

Tate started toward the house again. "She does, inherited it after her father died twelve months ago."

"So what is the problem?"

The problem was that he was being a stubborn bastard who didn't want to give her what she wished. Not even when she'd asked him so nicely at first. Seeing her again had exacerbated all the injuries of her jilting him. Of wanting something else, books of all things over his love. What type of woman turned down a future duke? Turned her back on the love he'd thought they'd shared? What kind of woman could be so callous with words of sentiments and matters of the heart? A woman who put her own ambition before anything else. And Tate would do the same. With Titan in his stables, the stallion was one step toward becoming real competition to the Knight Stables, to start his own breeding program and produce future horseracing winners. He would not give her the opportunity to best him again, not in business or on a personal level.

"I've changed my mind," he said, shrugging.

"You've changed your mind? Really? Seems to me you're basing your decision on what happened between you all those years ago. Maybe you should accept her offer, but put a stipulation in that should the mare birth a foal that looks promising for racing, any wins the horse might have during its lifetime you'd be entitled to half the profits."

Tate turned to face him. "She'd never agree to such terms. The stables have offered to pay for Titan covering her mare, they will not want to share the profits."

"The stables have bred fifty winners in the last ten years. You could get a piece of the pie. If she wishes for Titan to be used for her breeding program, she'll have to agree," Duncannon said, his business mind coming forth for a moment.

Duncannon was a shrewd man, and some of what he said made sense. It would certainly help financially should the mare breed a winner, and having a horse jointly owned by the renowned Knight Stables would only lift his own name within the racing community.

He thought on the prospect a moment. Ava would not be pleased by this development, and Tate grinned at the idea of annoying her further. If only to see her eyes flash fire at him. "I will think upon it," he said, entering the house. Would think about all the ways he could tell Ava these were his terms and watch the little hellion become further displeased.

Tate pushed the idea away that he'd offer such an idea simply to spend more time with her. She did not deserve his attentions, and yet, walking into his library, Tate's steps were somewhat lighter than when he'd walked out of the room earlier that day. He could not fathom a guess as to why…

CHAPTER 3

A s I look out over the French landscape, so very similar and yet different from where we grew up, I wonder if we'll ever see each other again...

— An excerpt from a letter from Miss Ava Knight to the Duke of Whitstone

A WEEK LATER, Ava lay on her bed, staring down at the unread book in her lap and thinking about a certain duke who had been thrust back into her life.

Three short miles was all that separated them, and yet it wasn't far enough. If only an ocean still kept them apart she would be well pleased. After their disastrous conversation last week, she'd not seen or heard from him. Not that she hoped to, but there was a time when she wouldn't go a day without being near him. If only to tell him how much she had missed him and possibly sneak away for a kiss or two.

Shouts down in the yard caught her attention and dropping the book on the bed, she raced to the window. Ava glanced toward the stables which she could see from her bedroom but couldn't see anything amiss. The men were running toward the barn where the carts were kept, and hearing them yelling orders to grab hessian bags and buckets, fear shot through her that the stables located on the opposite side of her home were on fire.

Ava raced to her closet and pulling on the clothes she'd worn that day, she stumbled into her dressing room, searching for her half boots when she saw an orange glow kiss the night sky. A sickening red radiance coming from the direction of Tate's property.

She stopped for a moment, stunned still at what she could see. Was it the stables or the house? Ava quickly finished dressing, throwing on her boots without stockings.

She ran down the stairs, calling out for the male servants to follow her and within minutes, those who could ride were hard on her heels toward Tate's property, the other men traveling as fast as they could in the carts and buggies.

The closer they came to the ducal estate, the larger the glow in the night sky became, and peeking at the hill she had ridden over only a week before her worst fears were realized. The stables were on fire and the men were fighting the flames, others trying desperately to axe through the side walls of the wooden structure to free the horses.

Leaving the horses in a nearby field, they ran toward the fire, her stable manager handing her a Hessian sack to help. The heat of the fire pricked her flesh as they came up close to it, and wetting the bag in a nearby trough, she started to bash it against the multitude of flames that were licking the wood of several buildings.

Horses were running wild and scared into the night, and all she could hope was that the horses had been spared. The buildings could burn for all she cared, but the life of the horses was paramount.

More shouts sounded from behind her and turning, she saw the second and larger stable catch alight, a pile of straw inside the double frontage doors smoldering and lighting to full flame. She shut her stinging eyes as the smoke blew in her face and opening them again, she could not quite make out who was the man who notified them as he took off in another direction.

"The second stable," she shouted, running toward it. From where she was, Ava could see several horses sticking their heads out over the stall doors inside, looking at the fire, some ran about their stalls, kicking at the walls.

Without thought she ran inside, opening the stall doors as quickly as she could. She covered her mouth with the hessian bag, stumbling and feeling her way along the stalls until she felt the second stall door. Unlocking that too, the horse bolted and sent her flying backwards.

"Ava," she heard Tate's familiar voice yell, and getting to her knees, she blinked as her eyes stung with the smoke that filled the space.

"I'm well. There are more horses back here," she said, getting up and heading toward where she could hear their fear. She would tell the duke after all this, that for a stable to be safe for animals and people, both ends had to have exits. A silly thought at such a time, but nonetheless, she had it. Ava released the last two horses on her side, and raced to the opposite, just as the duke met her at the last stall. He fought with the lock on the door, but it wouldn't budge. "It won't open," he yelled, coughing. "It's locked."

Ava turned about as the flames started to lick the walls of the stall doors opposite them. Looking about she spied an ax on a nearby wall, and running over to it, clasped it. "Here, Tate, use this."

He stared at her a moment, as if she'd grown two heads, before a wooden panel behind them came crashing down and brought him to his senses. "Thank you." He slammed the axe head down once, twice on the door lock and it broke away, allowing them to open the door and free Titan.

The stallion bolted outside, and as they were about to follow the horse, the front of the stable crashed down, trapping them inside.

"Tate," she said, clasping his shirt. "Is there a window or door in this end?" not that she'd seen one, but these were his stables after all, maybe in the smoke and fire she'd not seen any.

"No," he said, pulling her into a nearby stall and shutting the door. Not that it would keep the fire out, but it would halt the straw they were standing on from catching alight before it needed to.

"Stand back, Ava," he said, swinging the axe high and coming down on the stable wall. The smoke grew ever thick and Ava went to the wall, trying to breathe the air that slid between small cracks in the wooden boards. On the outside, she could hear men hitting the wall in the same location that Tate was smashing through. She tried to concentrate on the small amount of fresh air she was breathing, but the heat of the fire on her back made panic settle in her stomach.

"Quick, Tate. I cannot breathe."

A piece of wood smashed in toward them, then more, and with the intrusion of the men outside breaking through, so too did the fresh air. Unfortunately, with the fresh air, the fire behind them only increased its ire.

Her legs refused to move. She tried to crawl over to where there was escape, but her body wouldn't cooperate.

"Ava," Tate said nearby, before she was lifted into familiar, comforting arms. She coughed as he stepped through the hole in the wall, half running, and half stumbling them away from the stable before collapsing on the ground with her in his arms.

She rolled onto the ground, coughing and gasping for breath, and at some point someone passed her a cup of water. Ava turned to see Tate lying beside her, he too was trying to catch his breath. She went over to him and pushed his hair out of his face, waiting for him to meet her eyes.

"Are you well? Are you hurt at all?"

He reached up, running a hand across her cheek. The action brought tears to her eyes that he'd nearly been killed. That they both had. "You look like a chimney sweep."

She laughed despite herself and despite the situation was not at all funny. "You're making jokes, Your Grace? At a time like this," she said, her voice scratchy, her breathing labored, and with a wheeze.

He threw her a mischievous grin. "I think in times like this, amusement is needed." He struggled to sit up and she sat beside him. They were silent a moment as the stable burned before them, the first stable that she had fought to save was nothing now but a charred pile of glowing timber.

The duke's steward came over to them, kneeling down to their level. "All horses and workers are accounted for, Your Grace. They're in the holding pen down near the house. We're giving them some feed to try and calm them down."

The duke nodded. "Do any of the men know how the

fire started? There was no wind, no reason why the second stable would go up like it did."

Ava thought back to hearing shouts behind her when fighting the first fire but the face was as blurry as her sight was right now. "From what I saw, the fire started in the straw that had been piled in the center of the stable after cleaning out the stalls. I heard shouting, as if someone was alerting us to this new threat, but I could not tell you who it was. You don't think it may have been deliberately started, do you?"

And if it had been, where was the culprit? Fear shot through her at the thought. With all her stable hands here fighting the duke's blaze, her own horses were alone at her estate, without protection. She went to stand and Tate's steward pushed her to sit back down.

"Your manager and a couple of your stable hands have headed back to your estate, Miss Knight. I'm sure we would've heard from them should anything be amiss."

Tate sat up beside her and she studied him a moment, glad to see that he seemed to be breathing a little easier.

"We'll have to house the horses somewhere until the stables are gutted and rebuilt. They cannot stay in the fields."

The steward met her gaze, and without asking, she knew what he was hoping. "Of course your stock is welcome to be housed at my stables, Your Grace. There are more than enough stalls for them," she offered, never one to turn away and not help those that were in need. Even if it was the duke and they were hardly friends. But the horses needed homes and loving the animals as much as she did, she would not leave them out in the cold, even if it were not so very cold at the moment.

"Are you sure, Miss Knight. We have over twenty," the steward said, looking back over to where the horses were standing in the yard and watching the fire burn down what was left of the buildings they'd escaped from.

Ava sighed, watching the horses. "Of course all of them are welcome."

The duke reached out and laid his hand atop hers. Heat, similar to the warmth at her back from the burning stable filled her, and with it a longing for him to touch her like that again. She glanced down at where he'd left his hand and the urge to place hers atop it was almost too much to deny.

Ava met his gaze.

"Thank you," he said, studying her.

She threw him a small smile and, standing, brushed down her breeches and shirt as best as she could.

"I don't think there is much more I can do for you here, and so I'll head back home and let Mr. Brown know that you'll be bringing the horses over for stabling tomorrow."

"Thank you," the Duke said again, looking up from where he sat on the ground, "Truly Ava, thank you."

The steward headed off to oversee elsewhere. Ava turned to take in the devastation of what had happened here tonight. The men still fought to bring the fire to heel, even though it had destroyed all that it had touched. Smoke permeated the air, everyone about them covered in ash and soot, some clothing singed from the flames. "No matter what has passed between us, Your Grace, I will never turn my back on someone who is in need."

Ava turned and started back to where she had left her mount, hoping the horse would still be there after all the commotion. As it was, a lot of the horses, those that weren't watching the goings-on, were running about the yards, tails high in the air and clearly spooked and uneasy.

The poor souls were lucky to be alive, and if this was a

deliberate act of arson, then that would mean everyone in Berkshire were in trouble and would have to be on the lookout.

She'd worked too hard, lost too much already in her life to have it all burned to a cinder due to a fool's desire.

And she would never go down again without a fight.

CHAPTER 4

The following day Ava was up early, even with the late night before. A few minutes after breakfast, the horses from the duke's estate started to arrive along with their grooms and trainers who would stay and help look after all the horses, to feed, and exercise them daily.

Luckily here at Knight Stables, Ava had her own gallop, and so it was an easy five-minute stroll over to where the horses could go for a run or race.

She sat on the wooden fence that overlooked the yard that her prized breeding mare, Black Lace, was being lunged within. She was a beautiful horse, with her ebony coat and white socks. She hoped the horse would also make beautiful foals.

The mare had good bloodlines, but the horse itself had not had good starts in the few races she had been tried in, and so she was going to breed a foal from her that possibly would. The sire and dam of Black Lace had mixed careers before she retired them both and placed them into her stud program. They had managed one first, but mostly seconds and thirds during their race meets, not great, but also not too terrible either. Such history didn't always mean that the foals of their union would suffer the same fate. If she wanted Knight Stables to survive, she would have to experiment, try expanding and testing breeding theories.

A letter with her father's last wishes had been for her to keep the stables going, to push forward with their plans to make it one of the most prestigious and admired stables in the land. Such a promise had not always been easy to keep, and there were times she was excluded from racing invitations, or her horses were ignored as breeding opportunities simply because she was a woman, but it would not stop her. If anything it had made her more determined to succeed and now nothing would stand in her way of making Knight Stables a household name. As well-known as Tattersalls even, at least in regards to its prized horse stock.

She'd wanted to make a life with Tate all those years ago, leave this life behind, but it was not to quit the racing world in its entirety. Tate and she had simply wanted to make their own stables, become trusted and sought after in their own right. Her father's death had offered her the chance to take over his role, as a woman and an unmarried one at that. She would not let Society's opinions or protocol for a woman to stand in her way and she would not marry simply to make her role here more acceptable, more respectable to the male-dominated world she lived in.

Ava glanced over toward the stables and was glad to see the grooms and stable hands seemed to be greeting each other affably, but even from here she could tell they were tired and in need of a good night's rest, uninterrupted by disaster.

"The duke's coming now, Miss Knight, leading Titan with him," her stable manager said, coming to stand where she sat.

Shading her eyes, Ava looked up on the hill that the

duke was riding down. In all the years since she'd seen him, even now his muscular form when atop a horse was on full show and a delight to watch. How well he looked, the years having turned the boy she'd known into a man. A man even she reluctantly agreed was still as handsome as sin.

Ava thought back to the evening before when they had been laying on the ground after escaping the burning stable, the glide of his hand against her cheek when he checked to see if she was well. The look he'd given her had stripped the time away, all the hurts that he'd caused her, and all that she'd cared about in that moment was if he was well, uninjured.

She reached up and touched her cheek, unable to deny that his touch made her yearn for things long buried. He'd been so careful, so kind and gentle that she'd not been able to conceal what he'd always been able to make her feel.

Alive…

Had he noticed her yearning? She could only hope that, in the chaos of last evening, he had not.

"Put Titan in the western stable. It has the larger stalls for horses of his size. He'll be more comfortable there."

"Right away, miss," Greg said, starting toward the duke who had stopped and was talking to both her staff and his own near a watering trough.

He glanced over to her and nodded in acknowledgement and Ava did the same before turning her attention back to her mare who continued to lunge in a canter.

She supposed she would have to go, speak to him, and discuss his own sleeping arrangement now that all his horses were here. Knowing the duke as she did, she did not think he'd want to return to his estate. Not that she could offer him a bed under her roof, being unmarried and without a chaperone as she was. But there was a cottage that she'd had refurbished the previous year that sat down near the natural running stream on the property, and wasn't far from the stables.

The duke could stay there and still be close enough to keep an eye on his horses and the continuation of their training while his own stables were rebuilt.

"Wash Black Lace after her workout and ensure she gets a good rubdown. I think she's earned her oats this evening."

The stable hand dipped his hat and pulled Black Lace into a trot.

Ava jumped down and started toward the western stable. No time like the present to discuss how they would go on, now that the duke was here. By the time she'd walked over to the stable, the duke and Titan had disappeared into the building. She went inside and coming up to the stall where Titan was standing, patted the stallion as he came over to her and nudged her hand.

"He likes you," the duke said, coming to stand beside her, a biscuit of hay in his hand. He reached over the stable door and placed it in the feed bin.

With food on offer, Titan left her and went to nibble on his hay. "He's such a beautiful horse and loving, by the looks of it. Spoiled perhaps," she said, grinning at the duke who smiled back. Oh, how she'd missed that smile…

"I do spoil him, and he's settled in quite well at home, or at least he had until the fire. I'm not sure what type of issues we may have, going forward, with the horses being frightened so much last night. Some of the mares may miscarry."

Ava nodded, knowing only too well that horses could be easily spooked after such a traumatic event. She could only hope that it wasn't the case with any of the duke's horses. "They'll soon settle and know they're quite safe here, and I've instructed my stable hands to take shifts in watching the stables and barns about the property."

"I have sent for a Bow Street Runner to look into the fire at the Hall. I cannot help but think it was deliberately started."

Ava remembered back to the man who shouted out behind her, notifying them of another fire. Was that the man who'd started such destruction and if so, why. Why would anyone wish to hurt horses that were locked away in stalls and defenseless against such actions?

"Do you have any idea who may wish to injure you and your horses? Have you quarreled with anyone of late?" she asked, meeting his gaze.

The duke threw her an amused glance. "Other than you, no one."

She chuckled at his attempt of a joke and reached into the stall to run her finger across Titan's shoulder. "Well you know I would never do such a thing, so someone has a grudge against you, Your Grace. You need to find out whom?"

"Hmm," he said, turning about to lean against the stable door and crossing his arms against his chest.

She glanced back at the horse, as the action only accentuated the muscles on Tate's chest. Oh yes, he'd changed and for the delectable better.

"I did have to let go of a stable lad who'd become too close to a maid in the house, had started to harass her somewhat and was trying for liberties that were not his to have. It could be him, I suppose, but I have not seen or heard he's still in Berkshire working elsewhere, so I do doubt that is a lead."

"I would tell the Runner in any case, and let him look into any tips. In this business, we may be civil and act as if racing is a gentleman's sport, but really, we all have many enemies, jealousy being the foremost." Lord Oakes flittered through Ava's mind at the mention of jealousy, and she dismissed the notion instantly that he might have been involved.

He wouldn't dare.

"I would've thought your stables to be in more danger than mine on that score. Yours have certainly won more races recently than mine. I did fear, when everyone was fighting the fires at the Hall, that your own livelihood might also be at risk."

It was a fear that Ava had herself, and thankfully her stables and horses had been fine upon their return. To think of losing the animals which she loved so dearly, who had been her company and salvation through so many troubles in her life, filled her with dread. If what the duke was saying was true, then they needed to find the culprit and have him thrown away into a cell where he couldn't hurt anything or anyone again.

"When I saw the glow of the fire at your estate, I did not even think to leave someone here to keep an eye on my horses. A foolish mistake I'll not make again. We are very thankful that none here were put in harm's way. And we're happy that your horses are here too. It will give me time to convince you to allow me to breed Titan with Black Lace."

At the mention of the horse's name, the stallion lifted his head out of his feed bin and glanced in their direction. Ava laughed, reaching out to pat the horse's soft velvety nose. "What a mischief maker you are," she cooed to the horse, overlooking for a moment the duke was still beside her.

"I forgot this." He glanced down at her and Ava fought not to meet his gaze. To become lost once again in his dark, gray orbs that were like a stormy, swirling sea.

"Forgot what, Your Grace?" She shouldn't ask, but

where the duke was involved, there was little she could do to stop herself. Like a moth drawn to the hottest part of the flame, so too was she drawn to hearing what he wanted to say about them. About their past, when the only things worth fighting for were each other.

"How you were with horses. How much you love them."

"I do adore them." She sighed, stepping back from the stall. "But it was not all that I loved."

"You're still reading gothic novels then, and sneaking out in the middle of the night to count the stars?" he asked, smiling.

Warmth spread through her, comforting and familiar, that the man before her knew her as well as anyone in the world. "Of course, although I no longer have to sneak out, I can simply walk out the front door."

"True," he said, glancing at the blue sky above them. "Do you remember when we met down by the lake on my property in the dead of night? You were so determined to draw the full moon that I almost froze to death waiting for you to sketch it."

"I'll have you know that my father, even though he never questioned me as to how I came to own such a sketch, was very fond of that drawing. He even framed it. It hangs in the library." Ava sighed, thinking on that night. It had been the first time they had kissed, not as an acquaintance and friend, but as lovers, as a couple who longed for more than mere familiarity.

Meeting the duke's gaze, the banked fire she read in his eyes told her he remembered the night as well as she did. Ava cleared her throat. "We should probably discuss what you're going to do now that all your horses are here. I have a cottage that I've recently repaired that is separate from the staff quarters, but it's still close enough to see the horse yards, barns and stables if you wanted it. I would invite you, of course, to stay at the main house, but well, as you know that wouldn't be proper."

His eyes darkened at the mention of the word proper and what her meaning implied. "Is that the old cottage where your cook, Mrs. Gill, used to reside?"

"Yes, that's right. She left our employment some years ago, and the new cook preferred to stay at the main house." She started toward the stable doors. "Come, I'll walk you down there now and you can decide if it'll suit."

They made their way through the yards, walking across the meadow that sat at the back of her home, and they soon came to the small cottage that sat overlooking the stream. Ava turned and gestured toward the view. "Here, you can see the entire layout of the property, except the front of the main house."

He took in the situation and nodded. "This will do very well." He turned back to her. "What happened to Mrs. Gill. I always adored her—"

"Rout cakes?" Ava answered for him. "Yes, I remember." Ignoring the familiarity they had. She opened the door to the cottage and stepped inside the three-room home. "Her daughter who worked for a family in Kent married a baker and offered her mother a place with them. Mrs. Gill lived with her daughter for two years or so, but became ill last autumn and sadly passed away."

"I'm sorry to hear that. She was a lovely woman, much liked by the staff, from what I can remember."

Ava smiled, thinking back. "She was lovely and is sorely missed. I do not believe the rout cakes have ever tasted as good as when she was here."

The duke ducked through the doorway and inspected the modest kitchen, the bedroom and washroom that ran off of it. Ava considered him for a moment, having

48

forgotten how well they had known each other. How much time they had spent in each other's company over the years.

The cottage was tidy, with wooden flooring, a large woven mat sitting beneath the small table that was placed not far from the fire. In the bedroom there was a large unmade bed, along with a small window with blue velvet curtains. The washroom comprised a jug and bowl, a washstand, a small hip bath and chamber pot that sat on the floor.

"This will do very well, thank you."

"I'll have the maids come through and make up the bed daily and get you some fresh linens and water. Of course, you do not have to eat here, you're more than welcome to dine with me each night and break your fast in the morning at the main house." Ava wasn't sure where her failure to leave him well alone and keep their distance came from. The duke did not fit in with her plans for the future. For years, she'd schooled herself to move on, to not need his opinion or support. The fire and smoke inhalation had obviously muddled her mind.

Ava shut her mouth with a snap and busied herself inspecting the oven. She was being too kind to the duke, and they were not even on the best of terms with each other. Why was she going out of her way for him? A terrible little voice whispered it was because she still cared for him, even after all this time and all the pain he'd caused her.

Taking one last inspection of the cottage, she started toward the door. "I'll leave you to it," she said, not taking one step before he clasped her arm, halting her.

"Truly, thank you Ava, not just for taking my horses or giving me leave to use this cottage, but for last night. For coming to my aid, not leaving my side or my horses, when by staying, put you in extreme danger. I shall not forget your kindness."

She stepped away from his hold, not liking the fact that her body refused to remain indifferent to him and his touch. If they were to be on the same property with each other for some weeks, she had best start to learn to be around the duke and not show her emotions like an open book waiting to be read.

"It was nothing, Your Grace. Nothing that you, your-self, would not do for me in return, I'm sure." She started toward her home, needing to get away from the expression of devotion that was written all over his visage. The last thing she needed was for him to start looking at her in such a way. The way he used to when they were young.

TATE LEANED against the doorframe of his cottage as Ava strode back to her home. With her wearing breeches, not a dress, it gave him the perfect opportunity to admire her from behind. He fisted his hands at his sides, as longing for what was lost washed over him like water.

Had he stayed, had she not rejected him all those years ago, they would be married by now. Possibly even be parents and raising their children to take over the great racing estate they wanted to forge on their own. To have a son who would inherit his title and maybe if blessed, a daughter who would be as wild and unmanageable as her mama.

He closed the door and leaned against it. He didn't have to stay at Knight Stables, but the thought of going back to the Hall did not appeal to him either. His horses were here, and he could have his steward send his paper-work over regarding his estates. If what his stable manager had said this morning was right and the evidence he'd found in the rubble of the fires was correct, there was an arsonist on the run.

It was best he was near Ava in case she was the fiend's next victim. His steward would keep watch of Cleremore Hall until the stables were rebuilt and he could return. In truth, he was here at Ava's home because this was where she was and now that they were at least on pleasant turns with each other, he was loath to leave.

She'd always had the ability to draw him in. Make him long even to hear her voice or see her across a field. Tate pushed away from the door and opened it, needing to tell his valet where to bring his bags. At least, such a task would keep his mind occupied for a time and not so obsessed with a woman who'd ripped his heart out of his chest that felt like only yesterday.

CHAPTER 5

I *have no hopes that we can be anything other than passing acquaintances in the future, but know that I shall always care for you. That you were my friend and will always be part of me.*

— An excerpt from a letter from Miss Ava Knight to the Duke of Whitstone

THE NEXT MONTH kept everyone busy at both Ava's farm and the rebuilding of the duke's stables at his own estate. A couple of times, Tate had asked her for an opinion on the layout and design of the new stalls and stables, and together they had come up with what would be modern and practical solutions to any issues they'd had in the past.

And most importantly, the stables were brick instead of wood and all would be built with a second access door in case one is blocked, as what happened at the fire.

Ava sat behind her desk in the library and leaned back in her chair, looking out over the grounds. The day had come in stormy and so a lot of the activities she'd had planned for the day had been put off until tomorrow.

She stood and walked over to the window, looking in the direction of the small cottage that the duke had made his own these past weeks. Most nights he came to dine with her and, unfortunately with each night, Ava was reminded of what could have been. Of what she had lost when Tate had chosen a different path than the one they had planned.

They had not spoken of what had happened between them, in fact, they both seemed to be at pains to never bring up their past. She did not mention France and he did not mention New York. It was no surprise that they could not go on in such a way. There was a glaringly taboo subject they needed to talk about. Ava especially needed to know why. Just why he'd lied and not loved her as she'd thought he had.

How he thought that after all the time they'd spent together, she only deserved a letter to tell her all her dreams were crushed. A letter delivered to her father, not even herself. Why could he not have done the deed himself?

With the rain pelting against the window pane, the small glow of candlelight at the cottage became blurred, a small wisp of smoke floated into the sky from the chimney. Dinner was not so very far away and then he would arrive…

She turned and started for her room, bathed quickly, then had her maid help her dress. Most days she wore men's breeches, paid little attention to her hair or how clean her boots were. But tonight she would wear one of the new gowns she'd ordered from London when she'd traveled there last month to ensure her manager had purchased a yearling from Tattersalls she'd wanted. Madame Lanchester had accommodated her without trouble and her abilities as a seamstress were better than Ava had hoped.

Over the years they had been apart, the thought had crossed her mind more than once that the reasoning behind the duke's crying off their elopement had been because she was too rough about the edges. Not ladylike enough or educated in the arts of a lady as most duchesses would be. For months she'd lain awake, wondering if her wearing of breeches, and unfashionable straw bonnets had put him off. That, in time, he'd come to realize himself that she would never make a good duchess.

Which was perfectly correct, she would not, not now at least, too much had happened in the five years since they'd parted. She was certainly no duchess material now, but that did not mean for herself she could not dress up, show the duke that one ought to look past the outer shell of a person to what they were inside. Maybe he'd forgotten what it was that had drawn him to her in the first place.

Ava stared at herself in the mirror. Her embroidered muslin shift was simply the prettiest undergarment she owned and it was almost too pretty to cover up with a dress.

"Which gown, Miss Ava, would you like to wear?" Her maid opened the armoire and started inspecting the few gowns that she owned.

"The bronze silk with lace and pearl edging, and I'd like my hair placed in soft curls atop my head, if you can tonight, Jane."

Her maid smiled, busying herself preparing the gown. "Oh, you'll look lovely this evening, Miss Ava. And I've been practicing with some new French designs for your hair. It'll look right pretty with the cut of the dress."

Which, Ava had to admit, looking over the gown lying on her bed was very low about the breast. A delicate lighter bronze ribbon ran beneath the chest line, and a delicate fleur-de-lis pattern in pearl and silk lace ran along the hem.

"Thank you, Jane." Ava smiled at her maid, eager for the night to commence.

Over the next hour Jane fussed with Ava's hair, pulling it up into a semblance of style, not simply tied back with a ribbon that she always sported, and she was ready for dinner.

The sound of male voices came from downstairs and Ava caught her maid's eye. "I'll go downstairs, Miss Ava, and tell the kitchen staff to start serving upon your arrival downstairs."

"Thank you, Jane." Ava turned back to the mirror and studied her appearance. Her maid had done wonders with her hair and somehow the woman who trained racehorses, wore breeches and mucked out stables as well as any of her staff had vanished. Instead, reflecting back at her was a woman who was the master of her own life. Tate had broken her heart, he had not broken her spirit. And the little devil in her wanted to show him what he'd lost. What he would never have again.

Winking at herself, she grinned and turned to leave, snatching up her shawl, laying it across her shoulders. The dress shimmied about her, cool and soft, and she had the overwhelming feeling of being almost naked.

It had been so long since she'd been to a ball or party, or even dressed up for dinner. Here at home she never followed the strict rules of the *ton*, and she supposed it could be one of the reasons Tate had fled to America instead of marrying her.

Ava checked her gown as she made the stairs, and her steps faltered at the vision Tate made waiting for her at the bottom. Gone were his tan breeches, and soiled shirt she'd seen him in over the last few weeks. Gone was the man who exercised the horses, helped build his new stables, and ran about both her and his own estate daily keeping up with all that he had to. Ruffled, dusty or muddy depending on the English weather.

Before her stood a duke. The boy she'd loved and the man she'd come to respect in a lot of ways again. In his buckskin trousers and glistening black knee-high boots, his silver waistcoat, his perfectly starched shirt and tied cravat. Well, words failed her a moment.

Never had she thought he could become more attractive than he did right at this moment. She had pictured him dressed so when imagining their Gretna Green wedding, before he hightailed it to America. She pushed the thought aside, not wanting it to dampen her mood.

She moved off the last step, and he dipped his head a little in greeting, but not before she saw the flare of awareness that entered his eyes.

Did he like what he saw too? Did he regret his choice? Ava, at least, certainly hoped so.

TATE TOOK THE OPPORTUNITY, as he bowed to Ava, to school his features to one of indifference and not what he really felt each and every time he saw the woman before him. The overwhelming desire to fall to his knees and ask her to tell him why she'd turned away from his love all those years ago.

She'd not married, which was the first thing he had expected to hear while away in America, but no such news had reached him and it only muddled his mind with the need to know the truth. Why did she not love him anymore? Why had she sent him that cold, unfeeling letter the night before their elopement.

His parents had only gone so far as to update him that she was away at school and seemingly enjoying the continent immensely, not missing her home or those she left behind. The change in her character had been so altered from the Ava he'd known, that he couldn't help but wonder if it were true. Could people really be so false?

He gestured for her to take his arm to walk her into the dining room. The intoxicating scent of roses filled the air and left him with a longing for a time long past. He closed his eyes a moment to compose himself.

How a scent could bring back so many memories he'd never understand, but it did.

She sat herself down at the table, and he took in her silk gown that was adorned with lace and gold thread. The gown was the height of fashion, and her figure was most pleasing within it. Gone was the body of a girl on the brink of womanhood. Seated across from him was a woman who would please even the starchiest of men.

Her long russet brown locks were pulled back into a delicate coil of curls, accentuating her perfect shoulders and neck. Her eyes, wide and clear, sparkled with pleasure and her lips shone with the lightest touch of rouge, and playfully quirked into a smile. Seeing Ava tonight, feminine and all soft curves, hell and damnation, she was beautiful.

A nearby servant poured them glasses of wine and taking his seat, Tate waited for the first course to be served.

Ava adjusted her seat, placing the napkin on her lap before meeting his gaze over the highly polished mahogany table.

"Thank you for coming tonight, I did wonder if you would since the weather has been dreadful today…" her words trailed off as a hot, steaming vegetable soup was placed before them.

"I do not mind the walk, although with the rain this evening I was grateful for the carriage Mr. Brown sent for me. As short as the ride was, it made the hike a lot less wet underfoot." Tate almost rolled his eyes at the banal conversation. There was a time when they would share every thought, dream and desire. That they had lost their way, lost each other, maddened him. He frowned, turning to a servant.

"Wine for us both. Thank you."

The young man bowed, quickly going about his duties. "Yes, Your Grace."

Tate waited for the wine to be poured. "We will call when we're ready for the next course. Thank you," he said to the servants, not speaking again until they had all shuffled out the room and he and Ava were alone.

Finally...

"There is something that I wish to discuss with you, Ava and it's probably best that this subject is discussed while we're alone. And forgive me, but I cannot wait any longer to know what has been vexing me for quite some time."

She looked at him wide-eyed, and placed down her glass of wine after taking a sip. "Of course. What is it you wish to say?"

He leaned back in his chair, idly playing with his soup with the spoon. After a time, he willed himself to speak the words that had been locked inside him for too many years. "Why did you not elope with me?"

She laid down her spoon, her face ashen. "Why did I not elope with you?" She laughed the sound mocking. "Are you really asking me that question?"

He nodded, once. "Why?"

Ava studied him a moment and he could see her trying to understand why he was asking such a question after all these years. But if he didn't know the truth behind her decision, it would continue to drive him mad.

"I snuck out of the house in the middle of the night and made my way to our tree. You were not there, but my father was. He informed me that you'd left for London where you were catching a ship to America. He said that you had written and cried off, saying that the understanding that you believed I harbored was a mistake. That I was hoping for a connection that would never eventuate being that you were heir to a dukedom and we were not a family with connections or nobility."

A punch to his gut would've caused less pain. Tate thought back to that night and the situation that led to his parents coming into his room.

He'd been packing not five minutes before and had been thankful that they had not seen his small luggage case that was sitting in his dressing room. His mother had sat before the fire on the leatherback chair he'd often read in, his father standing behind her.

Tate reached into his coat pocket and pulled out the missive that they had handed to him, having retrieved it earlier that day from his ducal estate, determined to find out the reason behind their parting.

He handed it to Ava, and she reached across, taking it without question before unfolding it and reading the note.

Horror crossed her features.

"I, ah…" she bit her lip, gasping as she read the last of the note. "I didn't write this, Tate." She looked up at him, shock etched on her sweet visage. "Our parents must have worked together on keeping us apart. My father," she paused, her eyes welling with tears. "I cannot believe he would hurt me in such a way." For a moment they stared at each other in silence before she said, "I can only gather from this that the letter your father sent per your favor was not from you either." She refolded the letter, sliding it across the table to him. "I do not have your father's letter on me, but I have kept it. I will show it to you tomorrow."

"I need to see it now," he demanded, pushing back his chair to stand. He went around the table and helped Ava out of her seat and, taking her hand, pulled her toward the dining room door. It had been years since he'd touched her in such a way. To have her silk-gloved hand within his own brought back all the longing that he'd had to endure knowing she didn't want him. A lie that he now believed his parents had fabricated.

A lie he would travel to London and ask his mother about and see if she could explain her despicable actions.

He wrenched the door open and the footmen who waited for instruction started, standing to attention.

She'd not scorned him. Did that mean she'd been as heartbroken as he had been all these years without her? The memory of how he'd tried to forget her. The many women he'd bedded, had on call for his desires, all a distraction for a heart that called out for another thought lost. How would he ever make it up to her…?

Entering the hall, they quickly made their way upstairs. Tate ignored the shocked and inquisitive glances from the staff who viewed an unmarried woman lead a duke into her private quarters.

He didn't give a damn about what proprieties he was breaking. The anger that thrummed through his veins at what their parents had done, pushed away any thought of what was right and wrong at this present moment.

She came to a room at the end of the hall and, casting him a nervous glance, entered.

Tate leaned against the door's threshold, not willing to

completely breach her private space and yet, for the first time, he glimpsed into her most private of places; her bedroom. Where he'd imagined a more masculine feel for a woman who rode horses and mucked out stables like the best stable lad in Berkshire, her room was all soft tones of blue and pink. The furniture was white and looking about it reminded Tate of a field of flowers on a summer's day.

Ava walked over to a small bedside cabinet and opening the drawer, pulled out a folded missive. She came back to him, handing it over.

He opened and scanned the note quickly. His stomach churned. His mother's writing. So she had been involved in this scheme to separate them, a scheme that had worked for too many years. But no longer. Not if Ava would have him back.

"My mother's writing, I'm afraid." He folded it and handed it back to her. "I don't know what to say other than I'm sorry, Ava. I did not think our families could be so cruel as to play such a trick on us both, but alas, it seems that is what has happened."

She walked slowly over to her bed and sat on its edge. "I said to papa, on the night he told me that you were not going to arrive, that he was wrong. That you would come because it was so out of character for you. I could not believe that the boy I loved could play such a cruel joke on me. Lie to my face about what he supposedly felt for me, only to turn about and say it was all in my imagination."

He went over to her and knelt, taking her hand. "I could not do that to you because I did not do this to you. Our families did this to us. I'm sorry Ava and I promise you that I'll find out why."

Tate had a small idea as to why his parents disapproved of Ava. Their social standing was as different as the horses' temperaments they owned between them. His mother had never approved of their friendship and, now that these letters and who was actually behind them had been revealed, he would confront his mother and demand an apology. One for himself and one for Ava. He was no longer the Marquess, he was now the duke, and he would damn well marry whomever he pleased.

She squeezed his hand in return. "As much as this shocks me, Tate, I'm glad we know the truth and we can go on without any animosity between us."

The years fell away and he wanted to take her in his arms, surround himself with the smell of roses that always permeated the air around Ava. Certainly, he didn't want any animosity between them to continue, but he also didn't wish for them to be distant. Ava had once been his best friend, his heart, and he would give anything to win her back.

She pulled her hand free and he stood, giving her space.

"You should probably leave. We both have a lot to think about. I'm sorry to cut our dinner short, but I think its best."

"Of course," he said, heading for the door. "I will bid you goodnight." Tate closed the door behind him and leaned on it a moment to catch his breath. It was hard to know what to do from here, how to begin again. As young as they both had been when they'd both declared their love, and it had been love, true and as pure as air they breathed. A lot of things had happened since, a lot of time had passed. His own life in London wasn't something he was proud of. He cringed knowing news of his antics had reached Berkshire and Ava. He'd been a distant landlord after his father passed, wishing to bury himself in the amusements of London than to grow up and return home, take up his role as he should have. All because he was angry, not just at himself, but at the cards life had dealt him regarding Ava.

Tate started for the stairs, needing to return to his estate to organize travel to London. He needed to return to town and confront his mother over her cruel meddling in his life which meant he had lost the one woman who truly knew and loved him for him, not who he was or what he offered.

He clenched his jaw. Due to his earlier careless actions, his trip to town would also mean he would have to visit his leman, not that anyone knew such a thing about him, and part ways from her. The confrontation might not go well and he would have to provide a monetary lump sum for the congé.

Then, he could return to Berkshire and win back his lady. His duchess, as Ava always should have been.

CHAPTER 6

After sending a missive to Ava, telling her of his plans to travel to town, he arrived in London late the following day just as the little season was starting. Tate jumped down from his carriage as the lamplighters walked the streets and lit the pavement lamps.

Tate went straight round to Whites to catch up with his good friend, Lord Duncannon, whom he'd asked last month to return to London to hire a Bow Street Runner, even though for the past month there had been little evidence come to light nor any further attacks on the estates other than his own.

He went into the foyer and before a footman could take his coat, he was handed a missive from Lord Duncannon telling him he'd been held up elsewhere and would be joining him later than they'd planned.

Tate turned and stared out toward the street, debating with himself if he could put off seeing the woman who'd warmed his bed regularly during the past year in town. Having sent a missive the previous day of his impending arrival, he knew his arrival would be met with her believing all was well and expecting a night of passion would commence.

Girding his loins, he left, calling out the road to his driver and hating himself for the fact that he was going to hurt her. Fleur, Lady Clapham and the widow to Viscount Clapham, did not deserve such treatment. Not that she had ever aspired to be his wife, but he had promised not to make a fool of her in Society, and they were often seen together at events and balls. She had been a friend, a comfort during his flashes of weakness and the loneliness that had plagued him sporadically since arriving back in England.

The carriage rocked to a halt before the portland stone townhouse in Mayfair and he stared at the building a moment before his groom opened the door. Tate jumped down and walked up the stairs. The butler let him in without question or delay, and automatically Tate started toward the front parlor where Fleur always liked to meet prior to their rendezvous.

The parlor was his least favorite room in the home, having been decorated in the most vile shade of pink that hurt one's eyes.

The butler opened and shut the door without comment, and taking a step further into the room, Tate couldn't help but smile at the pose Fleur had positioned herself in as she awaited his arrival.

Her ladyship was sprawled on a pink settee, one arm lazily lying behind her head while the other sat atop her stomach that was visible through the transparent silk shift she wore. Her nipples, a pink that suited her surroundings, stood erect beneath her garment, and the darker patch of curls at the apex of her thighs was visible.

Even with the knowledge that he would never have the woman in the way she expected again, he could not deny that she was beautiful and deserving of so much more than life had given her, himself included. Her father, a country gentleman had fallen on hard times, and with his downfall, so too had his children. Lady Clapham had been married off to a rich viscount without a moment's thought. It was now left on her shoulders to support her siblings and find grand matches when their times came, and so Lady Clapham had married a man twice her age and with a rumored temper as hot as Hades.

"Tate, my darling, where have you been? The little season is almost over, and we have not seen you these past months. I truly despaired that you would never return to town again. I've been so lonely," she said, her gaze raking him with unsated lust.

He sat on a chair opposite her, and sensing that he wasn't going to sit beside her and take her in his arms, Fleur sat up, pulling her dressing gown about her front. "Is something the matter?" she asked.

"There is something that I need to speak to you about and I'm afraid that you may not like what it is." If he knew Fleur at all, and he did, very well, she was not a woman to cross and he didn't want for them to part on bad terms. What they had was enjoyable while it lasted, but he'd never given her false hope. Had never offered more than what they had agreed to before any liaison had started.

"I'm going to be spending a great deal of time in Berkshire, at my estate. As you may be aware, there was a fire at my stables last month—"

Fleur gasped, leaning forward. "There was a fire? Was there much damage?"

"I lost two stable blocks that I'm in the process of rebuilding. All my horses have had to be stabled at Knight's. I was extremely fortunate not to lose any of my cattle."

The viscountess leaned back in her chair, a knowing look in her eyes. "Is not Knight Stables owned by Miss Ava Knight? Was she not the girl who jilted you all those years ago?"

Tate didn't want to tell Fleur the whole truth, for as soon as he did the whole of London would know and no one here in town needed to have any participation in his life.

"She's home from France and is doing an excellent job keeping her racing stables profitable and successful. What happened in the past between us I'd prefer to leave in the past. We are neighbors, and due to our mutual love of horseracing, we need to get along."

"Well," she said, her tone having a disbelieving edge to it. "I'm glad you've been able to put the past behind you, but that does not mean that we cannot still be together when you're in town. We get along well enough, and you know we always have fun. Do not be a bore and tell me that we can no longer go on as we have been."

Tate was gambling on the idea that in time and with patience, he could possibly win Ava's love back. Make her see that together they could make both their estates the best racing and breeding stables in the land. That under no circumstances would he try to clip her wings and force her to change, to suit his title. They had both longed for children, and a marriage built on a strong foundation of love. He would not give up on such hopes now that the possibility of them was perhaps an option once again.

He stood. "I'm sorry, Fleur, but I can no longer be your lover. I will, of course, always be your friend and should you need anything at all, you know that I will always offer assistance. But what we've had must come to an end. It would not be fair to you to keep you for myself when we've always been in agreement that this was only ever temporary and a fun way to pass the time during the Season."

She studied him a moment before she stood, coming up to him and wrapping her arms about his neck. "I shall miss you, Your Grace, and all the delectable things we used to get up to. I look forward to seeing you next year in town."

Tate untangled her arms from about his neck, but leaned down and kissed her quickly on the brow. "Good night, Lady Clapham." He handed her the congé.

He left without another word, and reaching his carriage called for Whites. Lady Clapham had taken the news much better than he'd thought she would have. Perhaps she already had someone else in mind to keep her occupied. She was a widow and many gentlemen had taken an interest in her, which she was always amenable to.

And now they were both free to do as they pleased. And it pleased Tate very well to win Ava's love. He'd won her heart once before, surely that meant he could do it again.

CHAPTER 7

T wo years have passed since I saw you last. Sometimes I wonder if we shall ever meet again...

– An Excerpt from a letter from Miss Ava Knight to the Duke of Whitstone

TATE'S CARRIAGE pulled up before his London townhouse, the lights blazing from within and the sound of music playing made his steps cautionary as he walked up to the front door. A footman in red livery, clothing that they only used when hosting a ball, made his steps falter. Of all the days he would return to London would be one of the days that his mother was hosting a party.

This would make it the third for the year. Did the woman not have anything better to do with her time? He handed his great coat to one of the servants that came upon him in the entrance hall and said hello to the few people who mingled outside the ballroom.

Not in the mood for such entertainments, he started up the stairs. Not only did he not want to socialize, but he was far from dressed for a ball. Come morning, he would discuss his mother's excessive hosting and try and rein her in a little. Not to mention the letter she wrote to Ava being foremost in his mind made him less than willing to allow her little follies.

Halfway up the stairs a gentleman's voice yelled out to him and Tate paused, turning to see the Earl of Brandon, his good friend whom he'd met during his first year in New York.

"Scott," he said, coming down the stairs and pulling him into an embrace. The man was one of his closest friends, and he'd missed him when he'd left to return home to England. Scott had traveled to England as well, but had gone on to Europe to see the sights. "How have you been, my friend?"

"Very well. Very well, indeed," Scott said, grinning. "I remembered the dowager duchess was holding a ball tonight to bid farewell to the little season and thought to catch up with you while you were in town."

"May I say congratulations? I will admit to being quite surprised when receiving your letter that you were engaged, but I'm happy for you. Is your betrothed with you? I would love to meet her," Tate said, glancing about to see if any one young lady was waiting to be called over for an introduction.

"Yes, you are right. I'm engaged. We're to marry next June. Her family will be traveling over from Italy as they wish to prepare and plan the wedding with Rosa. Of course, I'm all for allowing Rosa to have whatever she wants."

Tate smiled. "I'm happy for you, my friend. You will make a wonderful husband and I am sure Rosa will make you a wonderful wife if she's the one you've chosen. I count the days until I can meet her."

"They're on their way now from Rome and will arrive by Christmas. I will be sure to introduce you. She is simply perfect."

Tate clasped him on the shoulder, happy for his friend. "You're a good man. You deserve this bliss."

"Thank you," Scott said, turning toward the ballroom. "Shall we have a glass of champagne to celebrate?"

Tate could not refuse and so started toward the ballroom doors. In no way was he dressed for the occasion, but being the Duke of Whitstone did give him some leave to wear whatever he damn well pleased.

He caught sight of his mother across the other side of the ballroom, her eyes widening in shock. Tate wasn't sure if it was because he was here, or because of what he was wearing, possibly both.

Scott took two glasses of champagne from a passing footman and handed one to Tate. They made the congratulatory toast and took a sip before looking about.

"When are you returning to Berkshire. I heard from Duncannon that you've had some troubles at the Hall."

Tate nodded. The mention of home brought up the memory of Ava and how much he missed seeing her, even for a day. He had become accustomed to being near her again, and now that he was in town, he itched to rid himself of the city and get back to the country. How he had put up with living here for the past two years, never leaving for the country, was beyond him.

"I have some business to attend to here, but no more than a week, and I'll return to Berkshire. As for the trouble, yes, I've had some of late."

The Earl gave him his full attention and Tate debated whether to tell Scott all he was thinking. They had never held anything back from each other before and Tate could not do so now. He needed to discuss Ava with someone or he'd go mad. "Do you remember a lady I once spoke to you about, and the reason why I was in America in the first place?"

Scott nodded. "Of course. Miss Knight, was it not?"

"Yes, that's right," Tate said, warmth seeping through his veins at the mention of her name aloud.

"She lives in France I understand, but her father owned one of the best racehorse stables in England."

"Yes, you remember correctly, but alas, she's not in France. She's back in Berkshire."

His friend studied him a moment before he raised his brow, his mouth twitching in amusement. "She's returned? How very interesting." He paused. "And does this have anything to do with why you're now living in Berkshire instead of London?"

"Not entirely," Tate said, not wanting to look like too much of a lovesick puppy, but then he'd never been able to lie to Scott. "I will disappoint you in telling you our reunion was not my finest hour, but then as you may have heard my stable block was burned down, which I will go into later with you, but on that night, Ava saved my prized stallion and me to an extent."

"And so you've formed a truce."

Tate shrugged. "I have had to move my horses over to her estate, and over the last month, since the fire, we've come to know that she never jilted me five years ago. In fact, both our parents played us for fools and removed us from the other's life. It is also another reason why I'm in town. I want to confront my mother about her involvement in such an underhanded scheme."

Scott whistled, his eyes wide. "The dowager never approved of Miss Knight. Did you know?"

"Mother never said such a thing to me directly, the letter, which I've read is in her hand. Her distaste for Miss Knight as my wife was clear in every word. I did not think her capable of such treachery, but I was wrong. It was no wonder Ava never reached out to me over the years. The letter was very cold and offensive."

Tate shook his head, hating that they'd been ripped apart all because someone else thought it best for them. "We had dinner the other evening and during the conversation, I could not stand not knowing the truth as to what happened. Why she sent me the note crying off our understanding. It was then that she asked about my letter in turn. Both of which neither of us had written. We had both been played and by the people we were supposed to trust most." Tate looked across the room and watched his mother a moment with her friends, laughing and lording it over others simply because she was a duchess. A cold, hard lump formed in his gut and he turned back to Scott, not wanting to look a moment longer.

"I've returned to town in part to confront my mother about her despicable actions. I had meant to do it tonight, but returning home I found she's hosting this ball, so our conversation will have to wait until the morning."

"What other business brings you here?" his friend asked.

Tate adjusted his cravat and cleared his throat. "Well, other than some business in town regarding my other estates, and my issue with my mother of course, the other reason I was back in town was because of a delicate subject."

Scott raised his brow. "Really, care to elaborate?" His friend finished his champagne and summoned more from a footman nearby.

Tate ground his teeth, not liking the fact he'd

succumbed like so many men of his sphere and taken a lover. Lady Clapham had not been his mistress, she was free to do whatever she like and with whomever she choose, the fact he could call on her when it pleased him, did make her seem like a mistress, although he did not want to use that term.

He glanced about to ensure they were not within hearing of nearby guests. "Not my finest hour, but I have been sleeping with a woman this past year. No one knows, and I'm sure she took other lovers during that time, but if I want any sort of future with Miss Knight, I had to be honest with her. I just came from her home here in Mayfair."

"Did she take the news well?"

Better than Tate had thought she would, but then they both had always been honest and Lady Clapham had said many times that she did not want to marry again. "She did. In fact, she was hardly bothered at all." A lucky escape if Tate was being honest with himself. Lady Clapham was a complex woman and one never knew which way she could twist.

He sighed. "Even tying up all my loose ends may serve me very little. I'm no longer certain that Miss Knight will have me. After finding out the truth, she remained distant." Tate ran a hand through his hair, unsure what Ava felt. "It did not seem like she was sure any longer what she wanted in life, whether she wanted me or not."

"How so?" Scott asked.

"I've come to think she no longer wishes for that institution to be part of her life. She is so very independent, runs her racing estate with expert precision, is thorough and fair, and is beholden to no one. Becoming a duchess brings with it new responsibilities and pressure, and I'm not sure she has room for that in her life." There was a time when she'd not wanted anything else but to be his wife. But time had a way of forcing people into situations that they might not have thought of before and being separated for so long…Tate wasn't so sure Ava cared for him any more than as a friend.

"You must speak with her and see. Maybe she will surprise you and have room for you and your hefty title. Yes, you are a duke, a man with multiple estates and people depending on you, but Miss Knight was willing to be mistress of all that before your parents became involved. If she loves you, and there is always a chance that two people destined for each other can make their way back to be with one another, she will make room for you in her life as well."

Tate grinned at his friend. "You've become a romantic since meeting Rosa."

Scott laughed. "That, I have, and I'm proud of it too. But you'll see I'm right. If you're patient and as you once were with Miss Knight, there is no reason why she would not fall in love with you again."

If only that were so and he would hope for such a thing. Once he returned to Berkshire, slowly and with caution, he would try to ease his way back into her affections. It wouldn't be easy, even if they were on friendly terms once more. A lot could happen in five years, people changed and so did their goals and their dreams.

His certainly had. After idling his time in London over the past two years, rumor reached him that the thorough-bred Titan would be sent to Tattersalls for sale, and his disregarded dream of owning and running his own horse racing and breeding program burst back to life. He'd returned to Berkshire, even with the knowledge that Ava was only three miles from him, but he had wanted to fight for what he'd once imagined doing. Not being just a duke, but a man with interests, a profession that he not only enjoyed, but loved.

He drank down the last of his champagne. He would succeed in winning her, he would succeed in joining their estates and making all their dreams come to fruition. "You make excellent points, Lord Brandon."

"Well, if Miss Knight is your future, then yes, the past must be dealt with and moved on from. I'm happy for you and I wish you well with your lady. I remember how broken you were. You may disagree with me, and I can see from your face that you do," Scott said, chuckling. "But when you speak of this Miss Knight, you shine. She is a light for you, bright and true. I hope you're able to win back her love."

Tate smiled, clasping his friend on the shoulder. "Thank you. I shall take your good wishes and hope for the best as well. A lot has happened in the past five years, it may take some time for us to find our way back to each other, but I'm determined."

"I hope you do, and be sure to bring Miss Knight to my wedding if you're successful. Rosa would love to meet her, I'm sure."

"That my friend is something I shall promise you," Tate said, hoping that in turn he would soon be able to invite Lord Brandon to his wedding also.

❧❦❧

TATE SAT at the breakfast table the following morning, thankfully alone. The smell of hot brewing coffee permeated the air, the Times was freshly pressed and his breakfast of bacon, poached eggs and sliced ham sat before him. He leaned back in his chair, enjoying this quiet time, eating breakfast in solitude.

The door to the room opened and in bundled his mother. He folded his paper, sighing at his moment of peace would now be short-lived. "Good morning, Mother," he said, picking up his knife and fork.

His mother sat herself at the table, asking a nearby footman to serve her tea and her usual breakfast of toast and butter. "I did not know you were coming back to London, my dear. What has brought you to town, since I'm soon to join you at Cleremore."

"I had business in town." At his curt answer, she merely raised her brow and turned back to her meal.

Tate ate for a moment, thinking over all that he wanted to say to her. Fighting to remain calm and not lose his temper. "Did you enjoy your evening last night? How many balls would that make this year? Three?"

His mother threw him a sweet smile. "It was, in fact. How wonderful you're keeping tabs on my parties. And I'm glad you arrived in time for last night's entertainment, since you disappeared before the Season and have not returned these past ten months!"

"I think that is an exaggeration. I have been to town sporadically for different matters pertaining to the estates."

"Do not vex me, boy, for I am very annoyed. How can you leave London when so many eligible, wealthy women are here for the taking? All ready to dip a curtsy and marry a duke. Might I remind you of Lady Clapham who is more than eligible, a widow who seems to enjoy your company, or so I hear. But no, you run off to Berkshire and your silly horse hobby never to return. I despair of you."

Tate would've loved nothing more than to tell his dearest Mother that Berkshire too hailed some very sweet and perfectly acceptable women who could be his bride. Well, one in particular.

"I need to be in Berkshire as I've recently acquired one

of England's most treasured racehorse. And if it has not missed your attention, you do remember me writing to you regarding the stables. You know," he said, gaining her attention, "the ones that burned down."

She waved his statement away. "I do remember you mentioning both those things, but I fail to see how this is so important enough to keep you from town." She paused, taking a sip of coffee. "How are the stables coming along?"

"They are being rebuilt as we speak, and they didn't simply burn down, as I said in my letter, I believe the fire was started deliberately. I have hired a Bow Street Runner to investigate, but be sure not to repeat that. I do not want anyone to know I harbor suspicions."

"Very well," she sighed, picking up a piece of toast. "I will not say a word."

"Good, which brings me to another matter for which I'm in town, and that concerns you."

His mother placed down her toast, complaining it was cold. A servant picked up the plate and took it away before his parent bothered to look in his direction. "Really. What is it you wanted of me?"

Tate placed down his cup of coffee. He wanted to see her face when he confronted her with this truth. "Why did you fabricate the letter that Miss Knight supposedly sent me all those years ago? Allowed me to believe that her affections were false, that she wished for a different way of life? That she did not want me?"

His mother's eyes went wide before her face paled to an awful shade of gray. In that moment, Tate knew without any doubt she had been behind the calculated way of separating them. He had hoped that possibly it was not true, but that did not seem the case.

"I don't know what you're talking about," she said fussing with a napkin. "Now let me eat my breakfast in peace. I have a busy day, many calls to make all afternoon."

He ground his teeth, better that than yell at his mother before all the staff. "You have plenty of time for your calls, I want to talk about your underhanded, cruel scheme."

His mother seemed to accept her defeat in this regard, lifted her chin, her lips pursed in a tight line. "Yes I wrote it and I would do it again. Your father and I thought it was best considering both your young ages. You had not even had your first Season and you were thinking of marrying a girl who had no rank, no nobility. A horse trainer's daughter, of all things." His mother shrill voice lifted at her last point and he cringed as pain coursed through his temples. "I spoke to Miss Knight's father and he was in agreement, after we explained how we would never countenance such a union and his daughter would be ruined by being cut by society."

He shook his head. His mother's cruelty had no bounds. So she'd even brought Mr. Knight into her scheme by threatening his only daughter's reputation. "Miss Knight was more than a horse trainer's daughter to me. I never cared about rank, money, the title in the way you have. Miss Knight may have had humble beginnings, but she is equal to me in every way."

"Pfft," his mother spat. "She is not suitable for a duke's wife, nor will she ever be."

He took a calming breath. "You had no right to interfere in the way you did. Are you not ashamed to have played such a cruel trick on your son or the people who have been our neighbors for years now?"

"Mr. Knight, need I remind you, Tate, was also in agreement."

"You convinced the man he was, by threatening Ava."

"Do not tell me that you have offered for her hand yet again," she sneered. "I will never forgive you if you have."

"Not that it is any of your business, but no, I have not. At this time Miss Knight is no more than our neighbor and a woman who is housing all my horses after the fire. Even though there is no discussion of me and Ava being anything more than what we are now, it does not excuse what you did to us both. How could you do that to your own son? You knew how much I cared for her."

She shook her head, dismissing his words. "A childhood folly that would have ruined your life. You wish for me to be sorry at stopping such a union. Well," she paused, throwing her napkin on the table. "I will not and never shall."

"For years, you sent me away to a country that was not my own, all to keep me away from her. You could've been honest." Not that it would've changed his mind about Ava as his wife. Even now to the very core of Tate's soul, he knew that she was the right woman for him.

"My family treated you well in New York. They lavished you with everything a young titled man of great wealth wanted at his feet. Women, parties, social events mingling with the best my country had to offer. Do not say to me that your life has been so unhappy and despondent when it has not. Do you think I did not hear the goings on about London regarding you, when you first returned? Of the many lovers, the gambling and so on. Do not be so quick to judge when I could've judged you two years ago upon your return."

How could she be so blind? Yes, he had enjoyed America, but that was only because he was forced to stay and could not leave. He had thought the woman he loved did not love him. "I will not forgive you for such duplicity."

"I suppose you're going to tell me that your interest in

Berkshire these past months has nothing to do with Miss Knight being home from France. Please tell me that you've not taken up where you left off with that little nobody."

Tate fisted his hands on the table, his breakfast forgotten. "How dare you call her that? Do not *ever*," he said, making his mother start, "call her that again. Her name is Miss Ava Knight, and hear this, Mother. No matter what happens between me and Ava, know that I will not put up with your meddling. What I choose to do with my life or whom I select to be my bride is my choice. As head of the family if I wanted to marry a doxie from Soho I will." Tate stood, having had enough of this conversation.

"Do not threaten me. I'm still your mother and do not forget that I can make your life in Society easy or hard. Miss Knight hails from the lineage of servants. People who worked as our tenant farmers prior to purchasing a horse and racing it. Pure luck that it paid off for them and while I'm very happy they could drag themselves away from a life of servitude, that does not make her equal to the task of being a duchess."

He'd always thought his mother's light blue eyes pretty, but right at this moment they were cold and without an ounce of feeling.

"If you marry Miss Knight, make her the Duchess of Whitstone will be the laughing stock of the *ton*. I did not marry into nobility, sacrifice my life in my own country to live in England, just to watch my son marry a woman who would bring nothing but shame and a few mares to the marriage."

Tate clasped the table, leaning toward his mother. "Do not speak to me or about Ava in such a way again, mother. I'm warning you," he sneered. "I am the Duke of Whitstone and whomever I marry will be accepted by Society because if they do not, as a duke, they would rue the day they slighted her. That warning includes you too. If you wish to have anything to do with my future, you will not meddle in whom I choose as my bride."

His mother pushed back her chair. "There are many who are more suited as the future Duchess of Whitstone," she said, her voice shaking. "If you only gave them the opportunity, you would see that there are many who would be perfect for you. You must see that Miss Knight is not for you. She may satisfy some honor code that you think you're breaking by stepping away from the union, but it will not last forever. With people with backgrounds such as hers, there are always hidden skeletons that the *ton* is salivating to find out. It will be only a matter of time before her family and something that they have hidden in their past will come to light and ruin you. Ruin my future grandchildren's prospects."

"You talk rubbish."

"Do I?" she said. "Think of your male heir, away at Eton or Harrow. The bullying your children will suffer when they find out their mother bred horses. That the boy's grandparents were once tenant farmers. That, in itself, will be hard enough to bear, let alone some other scandal we do not know about yet."

He shook his head, not willing to listen any further. He strode to the door and then paused. "You're hysterical and I suggest you calm down. Heed my warning, Mother. I will banish you to the castle in Ireland if you do not obey and do as I want. You are no longer head of the family. Do not ever cross the line that will make me act upon my threat."

His mother glared at him, the little lace cap atop her head shaking with her temper.

"If you cared about the dukedom so very much, you would've come home when you heard about the fire. But instead, what do we find, merely more parties and balls for you to host. At least, Miss Knight cared enough to fight the fire alongside of me that night. Where were you, I wonder? Drinking champagne and enjoying the company you only believe are of value to you. It would not occur to you to think of others, but Miss Knight does and that is why she will always be suitable as my wife. There is not a selfish bone in her body."

"You have no idea what you're talking about or what you need. Just like your father. Easy to lead astray."

"I will be returning to Berkshire in a few days. I think it is best that once you've finished the little season that you re-locate yourself to one of the other properties other than Cleremore Hall."

"You would throw out your mother for a nobody?"

Tate glanced at his parent, disgusted by her words. "Because of your actions, of sending me away to America, I missed saying goodbye to my father. You allowed me to blame an innocent woman for that instead. Miss Knight may be a nobody to you, but she is everything to me. And always has been. No matter how many years you took to try and change that fact, it will never change." He left her staring after him and headed for the door. After such a confrontation, Whites sounded perfect right about now. Anything would be better than here.

CHAPTER 8

A few days later Ava looked up from the chair she sat in on the terrace when she heard the sound of wheels on the gravel drive. She shaded her eyes against the sun low on the horizon, and shutting the book she was reading, she tried to make out who was paying her a visit.

As the carriage came into view on her drive, she stood and started for the front of the house, her curiosity getting the better of her. The black equipage was covered in dust from its many miles of travel, and there was a range of traveling chests atop the vehicle. Her heart leapt with joy and she started to run when she recognized the dark head of curls peeking out the carriage window.

She waved. "Hallie, is that you?" Ava laughed, beyond happy to see her friend. Hallie had been one of the first girls to have befriended her at school in France. Her no-nonsense manner and outspokenness had redeemed her in Ava's eyes and she loved that she was so bold, so opinionated. Not that looking at her you would guess such a thing. She was all delicate softness at a glance. Her dark locks, with a natural curl, were the envy of all their friends and her fierce green eyes echoed intelligence far beyond Ava's comprehension. Hallie was simply an English rose, but one who loved far harsher climes than any such plant could tolerate.

"Ava," Hallie shouted back before opening the door and jumping down without assistance. Her dearest friend ran and pulled her into a fierce hug, one which Ava reciprocated. She'd not seen her friend in a year, and to have her here and now and in Berkshire was a dream.

"Hallie," she said, hugging her tightly. "Oh, I'm so happy to see you." Tears pooled in her eyes and drawing back, she noted her friend's eyes were too a little watery.

"It has been too long, my dearest. How is England? How are your magnificent horses doing?" Hallie asked, looking over toward the stables.

"They're all doing fabulously well." At least the horses were doing well, as for her life, well, that was up for debate. "How was Egypt and all those magnificent Pharaohs you love so much?"

Hallie laughed, pulling off her hat and looking up at the sky. "They are perfect in every way. And one day you must come and visit me there. I know you'd love it so very much."

The idea of seeing such a hot, ancient and cultured land filled her with jealousy that she'd not traveled as far and wide as Hallie had. The woman was so intelligent and worldly, and had arrived at the most perfect time. "I cannot believe that you're here. How long are you staying?" Ava led her indoors, dragging her toward her parlor, and ordered tea and lunch to be served in there today instead of the dining room.

Hallie looked about the room, picking up some of the old antiquities that Ava's father had collected, studying a vase or curio, before sitting them back down. "For a month or so, if you'll have me. I have some business to attend to in London at the museum. The new benefactor there is refusing to accept a stone tablet we found on the Egyptian plateau to be authentic. I do believe it's because a woman found it, namely me." Hallie sat her hat on a nearby chair and slumped into the seat, sighing.

Ava sat also, smiling at her friend's carefree and easy manner. How she'd missed her. "Congratulations on finding such a magnificent piece of history. I'm sure you will persuade the gentleman that it is what you say." She couldn't wipe the smile from her lips at having her friend here. "I cannot tell you how happy this makes me that you've come to stay. Not because of the trouble you're having, but because I'll have a month of your company. It'll be like old times."

"Talking of which," Hallie said, glancing inquisitively her way. "I heard a funny little rumor in town before I started toward Berkshire. Do you want to know what it was?"

Ava leaned back onto the settee and kicked off her slippers, folded her legs up on the seat beneath her. Did she want to listen to idle, silly chatter that floated about London on a regular basis? No, not really, but her friend's demeanor, the naughty twinkle in her gaze made her curious. "Very well, what is London all in a flutter about?" she asked, already dreading her failing at being drawn into tattletales.

"You're the neighbor of the Duke of Whitstone, are you not?"

The mention of Tate had her sitting forward and a pang of fear shot through her not knowing where the conversation was headed. "I've know the duke for some years, yes." Ava had not told a soul of his slighting of her when she'd started school in France. Hallie had been one of her school friends, and seemed content not to pry into her past. All of them, the five friends she'd made, had their own secrets to keep hidden, she supposed. To be jilted was not something any young woman of any social stature wanted to be reminded of, so Ava had tried to push it away and carry on with her life the best she could.

Now that she knew that Tate had never rejected her, well, it changed things somehow, and she was desperate to talk to someone other than the man himself about it. Her life here at Knight Stables had become her whole world. Being away at school had taught her to trust and rely on herself and no one else and, over the years, she'd become independent. She had the ability to carry on with her life content and happy without the bounds of matrimonial bliss. Not that Tate was the only other reason she had shied away from marriage, her disastrous run-in with Lord Oakes had cemented within her the decision that being a woman of independent means was preferable to being at the whim of any husband.

"Rumor has it he's returned to town and has quit his mistress's home. The whole town is in uproar, or at least Willow is saying so. Some were shocked that he had one at all, since it was so very discreet, but alas, it's been revealed and this is what is being said."

Willow Perry was another school friend Ava had met in France and resided in London most of the year with her titled aunt. "What did Willow say?" Ava asked, having not known the duke had a permanent lover. Of course, the mistake was hers. He'd been famous for his dalliances, his socializing and gambling ways since his return from America. It was only natural he would have such a permanent fixture to sate his needs. She steeled herself to listen, her stomach churning at the thought of him with another woman.

"Only that she is free to do as she pleases, even though some say there was never an agreement of exclusivity in the first place. That it was simply a mutually satisfying union and nothing else."

Ava swallowed the bile that rose in her throat. "Oh, well," was all she could manage.

Hallie continued. "When he returned from America two years ago, people stated that the moment he'd seen her at her husband's funeral no less, the mutual attraction was undeniable."

"She was married?"

"Oh yes," Hallie went on. "She's a titled lady. Lady Clapham, a Viscountess from all accounts."

Ava was lost for words. Tate's lover was a lady of his own class. Her mind whirred at the thought of it. Why had he not offered for her hand? Why end it now after so long...

"The *ton* is full of questions as to what has occurred between them and without most of them ever knowing. When I heard that he was your neighbor, well, I simply had to ask." Hallie smiled, thankfully completely unaware her news threatened to tear Ava's heart out of her chest.

"I had not heard. Just because we're neighbors does not mean that I have anything to do with his personal life. He may do whatever he pleases, as I shall."

Ava looked away, staring at nothing in particular. Her stomach churned at the idea of Tate sleeping with another woman. Up until this, point she'd purposefully not imagined such a horror of him marrying or loving someone else. The duke was his own man. Responsible for his own actions and could do whatever he liked.

"Of course, my dear." Hallie studied her a moment. "Did you know the duke when he was a young man? Gossip says he is one of the most handsome men in

England. Is it true? It's has been so long since I've been in this country, I no longer know a soul, other than you and our friends from school, of course. You'll have to enlighten me on all of this, Ava."

"Well, I hate to disappoint you, Hallie, but your little tidbit of gossip is the first thing I've heard in months from town. I've been so busy with the horses and getting the estate up and running, keeping the racehorses fit and healthy that I don't have time to socialize." And it was how it ought to be. Ava couldn't think of a more delightful way to spend her time than outdoors, riding horses or grooming them. Being a successful woman in a man's business. "I find myself very content with this sort of life."

"Really?" Hallie asked, scrutinizing her for a moment. "Are you really content? None of us are getting any younger and most of the girls we went to finishing school with are married with children. I had thought you wished for such a future." Her friend settled back in her chair, crossing her legs. "I must admit, as much as I love being an historian, traveling to foreign lands, I do wonder what my life might have been like had I returned to England after completing our studies and married. My parents, God rest their souls, would've loved nothing more, and I feel I let them down a little bit by following my own path."

Ava, too, had let her father down. Before his death she had known he'd longed for grandchildren to see them grow up and eventually inherit his racing dynasty. For a time she'd thought to give him his wish, a path that had almost brought on her ruin. After that, Ava had been determined to ignore Society norms and expectations, had let it be known that Miss Ava Knight of Knight Stables was in no way looking for a husband.

Even so, with all her independence, and guarding of

that status, one man still had the ability to haunt her dreams when she slept at night. *Tate*.

Ava stood and strode over to the mantle and rang to find out what had happened to delay luncheon. She moved over to the window pulling back the blue and cream velvet curtain to look out onto the lawns. "You will get an opportunity to meet the Duke of Whitstone. He is staying here at present. His stables, you see, where destroyed in a fire and all his horses are being stabled here until his own are rebuilt. I'm sure once he returns from London you, will meet. Maybe by then there will be a new rumor about his grace, and his proclaiming of a new lover."

Hallie chuckled. "You do not fool me, Miss Ava Knight. When I mentioned the duke and that he was removing Lady Clapham from his life, I did not fail to see that your face fell at the realization he had a lover. You say you knew the duke for many years, but I wonder how well did you know him? Because to me, I cannot help but think that you knew him very well indeed."

Ava refused to glance in her friend's direction. Hallie had always been so good at reading people. It was a trait they'd used often at school, have Hallie determine the mood of their teachers so they'd know if they could be a little naughty or needed to be nice. Now, in her parlor, her friend's insight was not welcome.

"Knowing that he had a lover has hurt you and I'm sorry, Ava."

She sighed, not wanting to lie to her friend anymore. For years she'd kept the pain hidden, but there was no more reason to do so. Hallie was her friend and she should've confided in her years ago. "To hear such news is shocking, I'll admit, but nothing that isn't happening all the time within the *ton*," she admitted quietly. A little part of her still dreamed of them, longed to go back and fight for what she'd wanted five years ago. But as much as it hurt to have lost him, through no fault of their own, Ava had come to realize that it was for the best.

She was not made to be a duchess. To attend balls and parties, to be a hostess of the highest caliber of the *ton*. Such a life simply wasn't for her. So, in a way, their parents had done them a favor by lying and separating them. For there was no doubt in Ava's mind that she would've failed at being a duke's wife and eventually Tate would've become frustrated and disappointed in her lack of social graces. She could never have borne his disappointment. And no duchess should be anything but proper, undamaged, perfect in every way, and she was none of those things.

"I've never met a duke before," Hallie said, changing the subject. "Will I like him, do you think?" she asked, smiling a little.

"I think you will," Ava answered, nibbling her lip as she thought about Tate. "He is nice enough and is pleasant to all his staff." A knock on the door sounded and bidding them enter, a servant carrying a silver tray of tea, cold meats and bread into the room. He placed it on the wooden table before the settee before bowing and leaving them alone.

Ava busied herself pouring the tea, placing one spoon of sugar into Hallie's cup, as she remembered she liked it, with a dash of milk, and she held it out to her friend. Hallie took the tea and met Ava's gaze over the cup's rim. "Why do I get the impression that you're not telling me something? Does the duke's parting from Lady Clapham have anything to do with you, Ava?"

Ava shut her mouth with a snap. She sat, hoping that the heat proceeding up her neck wasn't noticeable to her friend. "How should I know what the duke's thoughts are on his mistress?" Ava said, sipping her tea.

"I think you know a great deal more than you're saying," Hallie grinned mischievously.

She sighed, running one finger along the side of the porcelain saucer her tea cup sat on. "The duke is here merely because of the circumstances that have happened at his estate. An unfortunate circumstance that was very dangerous. He's hired a Bow Street Runner, you know. When they looked into the fire at his Cleremore Hall they found that it was possibly started on purpose. That someone actually wanted to hurt innocent horses, of all things."

Hallie frowned at Ava's words, all mirth gone. "Although I do not enjoy riding the animals myself, to think that someone would try and injure so many horses must be terribly upsetting. Please tell me that all of his cattle survived."

"Yes, thankfully," Ava said. "We were able to get them all out in time, but his two stables were unsalvageable." She thought back on the night, when they had collapsed onto the ground after exiting the stable that burned behind them. She could still smell her singed hair, the pain that occurred with each breath. Seeing Tate lying beside her, gasping for breath was a sight she never wished to see again. The crippling fear that he could've died had been telling, and she'd known in that moment that she still cared for him. When Tate had reached up and wiped the dusting of soot from her cheek, even now her heart fluttered in her chest.

"And so now, he's here to stay," Hallie grinned once more and Ava fought not to roll her eyes. "And you are friends. I am not ashamed to say as your friend also, that I would love to see you make such a grand match. Do you think you'll ever marry?" Hallie asked."

"Not now," Ava said quickly. "I think that time has passed for such an event, and I am well on the shelf. I'm four and twenty do not forget."

Hallie narrowed her fierce, green eyes. "What about taking a lover? You would not be the first woman to do so, or the last."

Ava shuddered at the thought. The idea bringing back memories she'd rather forget. "No, I would not like that."

Hallie sighed, sitting back on her chair and resting her head against its back. "I had one, you know, in Egypt. He was a Major General or Liwa' as they term them. He was deadly handsome just as his sword skills were, but it wasn't enough to save him. They went on patrol just outside of Cairo, a small skirmish in an outlying village, and he was killed by locals."

Hallie was quiet a moment and Ava didn't know what to do, having no idea her friend had been in love. "His skin was so dark and beautiful, like copper under an Egyptian sky. His dark hair and features even now make my heart beat fast. He had the longest eye lashes I've ever seen or ever will see on a man, I'm sure."

Hallie met her gaze, her eyes overly bright. "It was one of the reasons why I have returned home to England. Everywhere I looked in Cairo I saw him, had memories of our times together." Hallie shook her head, sighing. "It was too hard to stay."

Ava stood and went to sit beside her friend, pulling her into a tight embrace. Having had no idea her friend had been through so much. So many secrets between them all. "Dearest Hallie, I'm so sorry for your loss. If you gave your heart to him he must've been a good, honorable man. I'm glad that you came home and you are more than welcome to stay here as long as you need to heal your heart."

"Thank you, Ava. I knew you would understand. You know that I no longer have any family, that I'm an orphan in fact, and so I need my friendships at this time."

"I wish I could've met him," Ava said, wiping a tear from her friend's cheek.

Hallie sniffed and Ava reached into her pocket and took out her handkerchief, handing it to her friend. "I do not know how it happened exactly, only that some of his men returned bloody and almost dead themselves. Omar never returned and some days later, more soldiers went out to find him and found him where he'd fallen. They buried him and that was all the closure I received."

"Oh, Hallie." Ava rubbed her back, trying to give comfort where there was no comfort to be given for such a thing. To lose one's love was not a severing that one could get over easily. Ava knew this as well as anyone, for it had taken her years to get over Tate and his abandoning of her, if she ever did. "Tell me what I can do, Hallie, to make it better for you." How could she not see under her friend's laughter and good humor that she'd been suffering from a personal loss? She cursed her own feeble troubles that paled in comparison and her blindness to them.

"Just being here with you is good enough for me and I will get over my pain eventually, I'm sure. But I shall never forget him, he was the loveliest man, even if our backgrounds and religions were so very different."

Ava hugged her again. "If you gave your heart to him, I have absolutely no doubt that he was a wonderful person. As you are and only such people have amazing things happen to them."

Hallie smiled through her tears and Ava promised she would be here for her friend for as long as she needed her.

"Now that you know my sad little story," Hallie said, reaching to pour more tea, "will you tell me the truth of yours."

Ava gave a self-deprecating laugh. How intelligent Hallie was to see through her words and demand the truth that lay behind them. She shook her head in awe of her wiles. "Very well, since we are both telling each other the truth of our lives, our sad pasts, I will tell you the truth of mine.

She settled back on the settee, folding her hands in her lap. "Five years ago, the duke, who was a marquess then, and myself thought ourselves in love. Looking back at the time now, I have no doubt that I did love him, wildly in fact. We were willing to run away and marry. It has only come to light recently that our parents put a stop to that plan that neither one of us knew about. We were dispatched oceans apart. I, for France, and the school that I came to know you at. The duke to America to his mother's family. We believed each other indifferent. We believed that the other had broken trust. This is not the case and now that we know the truth, well…"

Ava stood and started to pace, the percale cotton of her gown swooshing with each determined step. She stopped at the mantel, holding onto the polished marble and hating the fact that they had been deceived so. Lied to by the people they loved and trusted above all else.

"Now, I don't know where we're at. I don't know what I feel anymore. I love my life. I love the horses and the races. I can ride astride and I can gallop across the fields whenever I wish. I don't have to go to town and I don't have to take part in the Season. I'm not at the beck and call or an ornament to a husband's whim. I like this way of life, to be my own master."

Understanding dawned at how difficult her life had

become with Tate's return. How messy it was all of a sudden. When did that happen? A month ago she hadn't had any of these concerns, now it was all she thought about. Could she give up her life here and become a duchess? Would that be something Tate would expect of her? Ava bit her lip, not sure now that she'd tasted freedom that she could ever become someone else's property again. That Tate did not know her as well as he once had, when he found out the truth, even if she wished to be his wife, he might find her lacking.

Hallie picked up her tea and took a sip. "Do you think that the duke still likes you in that way? You are friends, you said, could you wish for more and still enjoy this life here in the country? Even as a duchess?"

Ava didn't think this life would be possible if she became Tate's wife. A duke was one of the highest of the peerage. Society loved nothing more than to have them at their parties and events. Tate would want her by his side in town every Season, and she would be a nobody, new money perhaps but little else. A woman who had married above her station. Talked to yes, and then talked about behind closed doors.

"I confess that I do still think of him when I'm alone. I think about what it would be like to be taken into his arms once more. Trapped against his hard chest where I might run my hands up over the corded muscles that I know lie beneath his clothing." To have the touch of his lips against hers, to have him make her his haunted her dreams. Ava opened her eyes and turned back to her friend. "I don't know what's wrong with me. I thought myself past all this silly infatuation."

"I think," Hallie said, leaning over and buttering a scone before placing it on a small plate. "That you still like the duke and that maybe you need to find out if he likes you as well."

Ava sighed seeing the logic behind her friend's plan, but the nerves that pooled in her belly at the thought of being so bold would make the fruition of it hard to complete. "That is the problem. I know I like him. But it is not what I thought my life would be like and I'm not sure I want him enough to give up everything that I have now. I would have to give up this life if I were to become a duchess. And can you really see me at balls and parties, dressed up in silks and chiffons, wearing the height of fashion and jewels. That is not who I am."

"I think you would make a wonderful duchess," Hallie said with some gumption. "Even so, it sounds to me that you have a lot of thinking to do. And you do not need to make any decisions now. I'm assuming the duke's stables are being rebuilt and he will return home very soon."

"Yes the stables are coming along very well. In fact, if you want, I could show you tomorrow. We could ride down to the Hall and look them over. It will fill in a little of our time, at least."

Hallie smiled. "That sounds simply perfect."

Ava, content for now to talk about other things, pushed her musings about the duke out of her mind. She would dwell on him when she was alone. "You must tell me what you would like to have for dinner. What is your favorite meal? I'll have cook prepare it for you."

Hallie leaned back in her chair, seemingly a woman without a care in the world. How very wrong everyone would be to make that assumption.

"I would simply delight in having anything that is not a goat or sheep. I don't think I could stomach another bowl of rice either."

"Consider it done," Ava said. "And I will go and organize this now and confirm that your room is ready for you too. I'm sure you're very tired after your travels today."

"Thank you, Ava." Hallie leaned over and taking her hand, squeezed it a little. "I'm so thankful that we are friends."

Ava laid her hand over Hallie's. "As am I, dearest. As heartbroken as I was, my traveling to France for school was worth it, in the end. You, Evie, Willow, and Molly made it all better again and I am so glad that it was so."

⚜

THE FOLLOWING day Ava and Hallie made their way to the duke's estate. The sound of hammering and sawing of wood, the gentle hum of male chatter as they worked carried toward them. They stopped atop the small hill that overlooked the estate, watching for a moment and allowing the horses to catch their breath. A highly polished black carriage sat before the front of the estate. Footmen swiftly carried in a siege of traveling trunks.

"Do you think the duke's back?" Hallie asked, casting a glance in Ava's direction.

Ava took in the details of the horse that was being led toward a nearby holding yard. "I think he may be, but I do not think he is alone. Dread pooled in Ava's stomach with the unfortunate thought that his mother had returned with him from town. The woman was the only surviving parent who separated her and the duke all those years ago, and Ava was not the forgiving type. Not for such things as decisions borne out of spite and social pressure.

They walked on, halting not far from where the new stables were being built. A nearby builder tipped his cap at them, greeting them warmly. He spoke to them for a short time, detailing the progress and explained how the new design would differ from the old. It looked marvelous. The new building of red brick construction, and almost all the walls were completed, while some men were on the roof fixing the tiled shingles. The smell of freshly cut pine permeated the air.

"It is coming along well," the duke said, walking out of the stable and greeting them with a smile. "Do you not agree?"

Ava glanced down from atop her horse, taking in his Hessian boots and the tan breeches that highlighted his form for their visual pleasure. His hair, again, was mussed from travel, but otherwise his bright gaze was warm and inviting. Ava smiled, thrilled to see him again. She bit back a sigh. If she were to remain indifferent, merely friends, she would have to curb her appreciation of his handsomeness.

The week that he'd been gone had dimmed her memory of how very attractive he was. How the sight of him made her long for things, which she had not desired for five years. How was she ever going to continue on with her life as an independent, strong woman who did not need a husband to make her life complete when men like the duke walked about Berkshire?

The clearing of one's throat reminded Ava of her manners and she gestured toward her friend Hallie who threw amused glances at them both.

"Forgive me, Your Grace, this is my best friend Miss Hallie Evans. She's newly returned from Egypt. She's a historian."

The duke bowed. "It's a pleasure to meet you Miss Evans. Any friend of Miss Knight's is a friend of mine."

"Thank you, Your Grace, how very kind of you." Again Hallie threw her an amused, knowing smile before sliding down off her horse.

Ava did also, and handing the horses off to a waiting stable boy, started toward the main house.

"I was about to have tea." Tate caught Ava's gaze and, for the life of her, she could not look away. Much to her annoyance she would have to admit to having missed him the past week. Even knowing that he'd been in town, meeting with friends and one of which was Lady Clapham, did not lessen that feeling. Was she possibly the reason he'd broken with his lover?

"We would not like to intrude. I wanted to show Hallie the stables, and did not expect to find you home," Ava said, slowing her steps.

"Thank you for the invitation, Your Grace," Hallie replied, clasping Ava's arm and pulling her toward the house. "I, for one, would love a cup of tea."

"If you have somewhere else that you wish to be, that is fine also," Tate said, no doubt sensing Ava's reluctance.

"We have nowhere else to be," Hallie answered before Ava could get a word in. "I see the carriage is being unloaded with a great deal of luggage. Do you bring company back from town to Berkshire?"

The duke cleared his throat. "Ah, no I have not, but it would seem my mother has returned to stay for a time. I had thought she was traveling to one of my other estates that's located in Surrey, but I find her here..."

The thought that it was indeed his parent left a sour taste in Ava's mouth and for a moment, it was almost impossible to look pleased and polite for him that his Mother was back in Berkshire. The woman was a viper, and now knowing she'd separated them via lies and deceit... well, she would be lucky if Ava ever changed her opinion of the woman.

They continued toward the house before Tate turned to her, catching her gaze. "My mother's arrival will mean that my stay at Knight Stables will have to come to an end. But be assured I'll leave my best stableman at your disposal and my staff will continue to train my horses, and keep vigilance to ensure that what happened here does not occur at your own estate."

Ava was thankful for his help, but knowing that he would no longer be so close to her sent a pang of melancholy to swamp her. Over the month that he had been at her estate she'd grown used to seeing him about. Working the horses, wearing buckskin breeches and shirt and nothing else. The lovely, delightful glimpses of him had been were pleasing indeed.

With the lack of cravat and his shirt often out of his breeches, he could've passed as any one of her stable staff. Except for the fact that he held himself with years of ducal breeding behind him, the perfect straight aristocratic back and broad shoulders and thin waist. The intelligent mind that was always working behind gray eyes, made him stand out from anyone else.

Had always made him stand out...

A woman came to stand outside the front door, and the scowl on the dowager duchess' face told Ava all she needed to know. If she'd silently prayed that Tate's mother had mellowed over the years, the hope was eliminated in an instant, along with any hope that she felt even the tiniest fraction of remorse in separating her son from the woman he'd loved.

"Perhaps it is better that we return home, Your Grace," Ava said quickly. "You and the dowager duchess have traveled quite a way today and we don't want to intrude."

"Do not go." His words were softly spoken, so much so that Hallie continued on unaware of his whispered plea.

"I think it is best. Your mother does not look pleased to see me again."

Tate took in his mother's appearance before turning back to Ava. "I never had you down for a woman who cared for what others thought."

If he was baiting her into going inside...well, it was working. If there was one thing Ava disliked above anything else, that was being beaten by a foe. And the dowager Duchess of Whitstone was certainly that.

USHERING everyone indoors and toward the back parlor that captured the warm afternoon sun, Tate ordered tea and refreshments and reveled in the fact that he was home. It had only been a week and yet to be back in Berkshire, his main country seat, and only a few short miles from Ava was a pleasure indeed.

He'd missed her while away in town, and having seen her inspecting his stables today along with her friend, had brought a burst of joy unlike any he'd known for many years. He supposed it was somewhat similar to what he'd felt upon stepping foot on English soil after his years away in America.

His decision to remove Lady Clapham from his life had been a decision he was well pleased with too. He hoped, in the weeks to come, he could prove to Ava once more that she would be perfect as his wife and future Duchess of Whitstone. As independent as she had become, to have her beside him in town, to be his duchess, to have her caring, thoughtful, guiding hand within his life was what he wanted most. He'd idled away his time for so long, in a way lost without her. Being a duchess did come with responsibilities, but he was certain Ava was up to those obligations.

They sat before the bank of windows overlooking the

outdoors. The silk floral pattern on the settee and other furniture suited the feminine feel of the room and its location overlooking a rose garden.

Choosing to stand, Tate waited for his mother to initiate conversation with their guests, but at her continued silence, her steely gaze as they waited for tea, he stepped in and introduced Ava once more, along with Miss Evans.

"Miss Evans has recently returned from Egypt, Mother," Tate said, trying to dispel the tension in the room.

His mother's expression remained unimpressed. "Egypt, you say, pray explain what a young woman such as yourself is doing in such a remote and harsh environment. Quite an odd location for you, one would think."

Hallie smiled all sweetness and yet the look in her eyes told Ava that her friend was not fooled by the dowager and her calculating ways. "I have been in Egypt for the last two years studying tombs, pyramids and some locations along the Nile. I suppose you could say I have been digging in the sand and trying to find ancient graves and artifacts. Although that is probably too simple an explanation for what I do."

"And you intend to return? Do you not wish to marry?" The dowager looked over Hallie with a studied air. "You are quite on the shelf, if I may say so, Miss Evans."

Tate had to give Miss Evans points for not outwardly showing offence to his mother's comments. He threw his mother a warning glance which she turned her nose up at and ignored.

"I'm in England for only a short time, to see my friends, Ava included, and to finish some business in London. But I shall return to Egypt or some other place that offers such a rich historical locale, you can be sure."

"Are you staying long in Berkshire, Your Grace?" Ava

asked, smiling a little at his mother and gaining nothing but a cold, calculating stare back.

"I will be staying here for some weeks. There are some friends that I would like to catch up with in the county and, of course, my son."

Tate didn't believe that for a moment and he didn't bother to mention to his parent that they had seen each other only this week in town. Or that she wasn't supposed to be here but at the dower house.

"I was telling Miss Knight and Miss Evans that the stables will be ready soon. It'll mean my horse stock will not have to impinge on your time any longer, Miss Knight." Not that he wanted to bring them back. With his horses at Ava's home, it gave him the opportunity to see her often, to talk and have privacy.

"That is good news, darling," his mother said. "A duke should be at his estate if he's not in town attending to his many duties there."

Hallie gasped and turned it into a cough. Tate sighed at his mother's thinly veiled insult.

"Miss Knight, I can tell you now that I'm back from London, I'm more than happy to allow Titan cover your mare. As soon as she is in heat, we shall try them together."

His mother mumbled something under her breath, but Ava beamed at him. "You will? Oh, thank you, Your Grace. I'm very happy you've changed your mind."

He smiled at her and could see she wanted to hug him, a trait she'd often partaken in when they were younger and she was excited about something she cared for. He had missed her pretty face and beautiful soul. Her fine features were without fault, her skin like alabaster, except for her nose where a skimming of freckles ran across her cheeks. Her eyes sparkled with excitement, her dark lashes and perfectly arched brows would be the envy of town when she arrived on his arm. How his mother could think her common was beyond him. She was far superior to him in every way that mattered.

"Do we really need to discuss such things, Tate, my dear? The conversation is not really appropriate, don't you think?" His mother said, her tone full of censure and aimed at Ava.

"What would you prefer we talk about, Mother? The latest town gossip, or what scandals are going about your set? Neither of which interest me."

"They interest me and that's all that matters, is it not?" The dowager smirked. "I did hear some gossip about a certain gentleman of the peerage who was being foolish and willing to bring scandal upon his family. Now," she said, tapping her finger against her chin. "Let me think while I try and remember who it was about."

Tate glared at his mother who was walking a very fine line.

He turned his attention back to Ava. "Talking of my prized stallion, how is Titan, Miss Knight? I hope he's been behaving himself at your stables, not prancing around too much in front of the mares?" The horse as fast and brilliant as he was, was also vain, if horses could have such a trait.

"All your horses are in the best of health, and some of your grooms have had them out on the gallop this morning doing some time trails. I think you'll be pleased with how some of your yearlings are coming along."

What a marvelous woman she was, intelligent and passionate. She had a love for the same activities as he. In fact, it was Ava's father who'd sparked Tate's passion for racing, and he really owed the direction of his life outside of the ducal holdings to her father.

"You still enjoy running about and mucking out stables, Miss Knight. I see the finishing school in France has not cured you of that." His mother bore a self-satisfied smile and without an ounce of remorse at her inappropriate words, met Ava's gaze.

Tate glared at his mother. "There is more——"

"I find, Your Grace," Ava said, interrupting him, "that you are right. Finishing school did not cure me of my passions, any of them, and now that I'm back in Berkshire I'm well pleased with what's before me." Ava threw Tate a look of pure devilment, and unable to stop himself he chuckled. His mother's mouth puckered into a line of displeasure.

"I suppose we should hire your services, Miss Knight, and have you work in our stables since you're so fond of such pastimes. What does a stable hand earn these days, Tate dear?" his mother asked him, her voice dripping with innocent sweetness.

"Miss Knight is a successful businesswoman, Mother. She does not seek employment here." Tate threw his parent a warning glance, at which she tipped her nose up and ignored. If he had to, he would escort her out of the room before she insulted Ava anymore.

Without missing a beat, Ava said, "You know as well as I, Your Grace, that I inherited my family's business, property and land. In fact, if I wanted, I could waltz about London and take part in the very same events as you, so unfortunately in this case, you're unable to afford what it would cost you to have me work here."

The dowager narrowed her eyes. "You are wrong, Miss Knight. The spheres in which I circulate do not have young women from trade among their set. Which surprises me as to why I'm having to host you here at all for tea."

"Well' I suppose' that's because your son the duke

invited us, not you. So technically you're not hosting us anything," Ava said, taking a sip of her tea as if the conversation were about the weather.

There was a light knock at the door and a footman came in carrying tea and pastries before any more words could be spoken.

Tate had heard enough though, and walking over to his mother, he took her hand and pulled her to stand. "Please excuse us a moment," he said.

His mother smiled, but did not say another word as he towed her out of the room. Once safely out in the hall near the stairs, he rounded on her. "What has come over you? How could you be so rude? I warned you in London about such behavior. I will not stand for it."

His mother's face mottled in anger, her eyes flashing ire. "Do not bring that woman here again. She is not welcome and it's not fit for the likes of us, a Duke and a Duchess, to have to sit and have tea with a horse trainer."

Tate fought to rein in his fury. He took a step closer, pointing a finger at her upturned nose. "I will not have you speak to anyone that I invite into my home in such a way. You have a choice, Mother. Either go back into the parlor, apologize to Ava and be civil, or you can leave this estate."

His mother gasped. "You would oust your own Mother? The woman who gave birth to you for some servant who threw herself at your head before you were old enough to understand the implications of your foolish, youthful actions."

Tate ground his teeth, having heard enough. "Instruct your maid to repack your bags, if she's even finished unpacking them. You're leaving first thing tomorrow for London."

His mother stormed up the stairs. "I will not be going

anywhere, Tate, and do not force my hand or I'll never forgive you."

Tate took a moment to regain his composure before re-entering the parlor, only to find it empty. He went back out into the hall, and opened the front door and in the distance, up near the stables he could see Ava and her friend getting back upon their mounts.

"Damn it," he swore, watching them a moment before closing the door. This was not how he wanted his time with Ava to end today after being away a week. His mother's presence here was going to make his time with Ava difficult and he would have to be on guard when she was present. For if one thing was for certain, his mother was up to no good and was hell bent, it would seem, in keeping them apart with any means possible, even blatant rudeness.

CHAPTER 9

I *trusted in your love, your words and still I cannot understand how I could have been so wrong. That all that time you were trapped in an understanding you did not want. I'm sorry that you felt you could not be honest with me.*

– An Excerpt from a letter from Miss Ava Knight to the Duke of Whitstone

AVA PUSHED Gallant Girl as fast as she could go down the gallop they trained the horses on. Today they were testing to see if the horse would make good time in a sprint and with any luck, win a few races leading up to Ascot.

"Great work," her head trainer said as she slowed the horse into a canter and eventually a trot. The horse's breathing was rapid, and in the crisp morning air, steam rose from both her body and out her nostrils.

Ava's heart gave a little flip when she spied Tate standing beside her manager. He was taller than those about him, and today he was dressed in a large great coat with a gray fox fur collar snuggled close about his neck and keeping him warm. His wool cap finished off his casual look, and yet each time she saw him, he drew her in, tempted her like no one ever had before. Tempted her away from the life she had worked so hard to secure herself within.

She checked her face for any mud from the few horses that had been riding ahead of her and hoping she didn't look a sight, smiled. "What a pleasant surprise, Your Grace. I did not expect to see you here this early in the morning." She gave the horse one last rub and pat on her neck before sliding off. A young groom came over and took the horse's reins from her, before leading Gallant Girl back toward the stables where she'd get a well-earned rubdown.

"I was up early," the duke replied. "A little issue with the stables back home and thought to come and oversee my horses since they're still stabled here."

Ava had hoped he'd wanted to see her, but she nodded glad to see him no matter what reason. "Very good then, Your Grace."

Greg held up his pocket watch, smiling. "Good run today, Miss Ava. We may have a chance yet."

"Chance?" the duke asked, looking between them.

"We want to run Gallant Girl in Ascot next year. We think she has a chance of placing and she's never been more fit."

"Nothing ventured, nothing gained," Greg said, tipping his hat. "I'll be off then. I shall see you later, Miss Ava."

Ava nodded and turned her attention back to Tate who stood watching her. His intense inspection of her left her breathless and she hoped he did not notice the heat infusing her face right at this moment.

"If you have Gallant Girl racing at Ascot we may be up against each other." His deep voice made it hard to concentrate on what he was saying.

Ava pulled herself together and focused. "I have no hopes of winning, certainly not up against Titan, but I do hope to place. I think my Gallant Girl is capable of that."

"I would never doubt it." He gestured them to walk toward the house. "Can I escort you back to the house? There is something that I wish to discuss with you."

Ava studied him a moment and noticed his brow was furrowed. "Is there something the matter, Your Grace?" she asked.

He frowned, his mouth downcast. She didn't like seeing him so and she had an overwhelming urge to comfort him. A reaction she'd not had these past five years, not for anyone. "There has been another fire. This time it was at Lord and Lady Morton's estate in south Berkshire. The blaze started in the middle of the night, and sadly they've lost two horses and a stable lad." Tate rubbed a hand over his jaw and Ava realized he'd not shaved this morning.

"Oh dear God, no." Ava blinked back tears for the young stable boy's life which had been cut short and that of the poor horses. "How are Lord and Lady Morton?"

"Devastated, I would presume. I'm heading over there now and I wanted to know if you would like to come with me. Lady Morton may need a friend at this time, and I know she's very fond of you."

Ava was very fond of both Lord and Lady Morton in return. Lady Morton in particular had helped her through her troubles only last year, a support during a time that she'd prefer to forget. A cold shiver ran down her spine and she pushed the alarming memories away.

They were an elderly couple, and reminded Ava often of her own father who'd loved horses and country life and who hadn't been looking for anything grander than what was outside his front door. Her ladyship had been only too happy to give up Society and settle in the country and Ava had always loved that about them. They had done what made them happy and forgot what everyone else thought of the fact. A dream she and the duke once held themselves, but now with his many responsibilities away from Berkshire, she wasn't so sure he could leave London for months on end and bury himself in the country.

"Of course I'll come with you." Ava called out for her mare, Manny and within minutes they were cantering over the fields heading south toward the Mortons' estate.

With dew still on the ground and the birds tweeting their morning song, the sun rose to the side of them, warming the land and bringing forth a new day. Ava couldn't help but think of the terrible tragedy that the Morton's and the young stable lad's family would be going through right at this time.

"Do you think this fire has been started deliberately as well, Your Grace?"

Tate, riding beside her glanced her way and his look of contempt told her without words that he believed so. "The missive I received from Lord Morton stated a worker had witnessed a dark figure running from the stable where the first fire took hold. The worker raised the alarm straight away, and yet the stables took hold very quickly and it was out of hand before much could be done."

"You'll inform the Runner about this new incident."

Tate nodded. "I've sent my letter along with Lord Morton's for evidence about the fire. I'm sure the Runner will be in Berkshire in the coming days. I've asked him to stay, incognito of course, and see what he can find out."

"I think that is best," she said. They rode for half an hour, the entire trip should not take them any longer than an hour in total. Tate slowed his mount as they came to a copse of trees and Ava followed suit. Her mind had been a whir of thoughts over the fires that were oddly circling her own estate. There was one other neighbor close by and she would send a note around to them to be on guard. Better to be safe than sorry.

"We shall rest the horses for a few minutes and continue on."

Ava pulled up beside him, and giving Manny some rein, allowed her to nibble on the grass at her feet. She took the opportunity to look around their surroundings. A flash of movement in the valley beyond caught her attention and she narrowed her eyes trying to see what it was that had moved.

"What is that over there in the trees?" She pointed toward where she'd seen the movement last and Tate followed suit. "Is that a man riding a horse along the base of the meadow?"

The person riding unawares that Ava and Tate were watching, came out of a wooded area and she caught sight of him. He was dressed in dark clothing, a long great coat and hat that was pulled low over his face, covering his features. He was headed north and seemed to be coming from a southerly direction. Odd, considering a man who was similarly dressed had just burned down the stables south of here…

"We should ride down and see who it is. Considering there has been a fire only hours ago, and now we see this gentleman riding north, it would only be right to question him. He may have seen someone or something," the duke said, continuing to watch.

Or he could be the culprit. Ava didn't say the words aloud, but she couldn't help but wonder. There was somebody in the area that was starting these fires. It could be anyone of their acquaintance or a stranger. At this point in time they could not exclude a soul.

Tate picked up his reins and kicked his mount forward. Ava did the same and they cantered toward the man, all the while the rider heading north had not noticed them. As they neared, the low thud of hooves on the damp sod beneath them made the gentleman aware of their presence.

He looked up, clearly surprised, and Ava pulled up her horse when she noticed he had a scarf tied about his face, covering his mouth and nose. Only his eyes were visible, but at this distance she still would never have been able to make out who it might be, if they knew him at all.

Without hesitation the man kicked his mount hard, and pushed the horse into a hard gallop. That his intention was to flee made the hair on the back of her neck rise, and Tate took chase, urging his horse in the direction the rider had gone.

They raced after him. The rider continued to push hard to get away from them, and Ava followed Tate over a small hedgerow, weaving their way through trees and across fields that didn't seem to slow the questionable man in the least.

The rider looked over his shoulder, and Ava heard him curse. Knowing Berkshire as well as she did, Ava realized they were coming to a part of the area that had a stream running through up ahead, some parts of it deep enough to swim in while others were shallow.

"He'll have to slow to pass the stream," she shouted out to Tate, pointing to the waterway that was now coming into view.

Tate nodded. "We'll get him there and find out what he's about."

Coming out of a small wooded area, a tree branch

flicked back and hit Ava in the cheek, bringing tears to her eyes. She swiped at the sting, bringing her gloves away to see a little blood on them.

They followed him to the stream, and when Ava thought the man would halt and answer for his flight, he merely pushed his horse into the water to wade through. The horse's footing slipped and the man grappled for a moment, trying to keep his seat.

"Halt," Tate yelled, which the rider ignored, coming to the other side of the stream. "Why are you running?"

The man didn't bother to answer them, merely headed up a small hill. They lost sight of him a moment before Ava, studying the trees, found him again. She stilled at the sight of a flintlock pointed directly at them.

Tate pushed his mount forward, and Ava reached over, grabbing his arm. "He's armed, Tate, look," she said, edging her horse backwards.

"Damn," Tate mumbled, doing the same. It was too late to run and they were both out in the open, sitting targets, when one thought about such things.

The man raised the flintlock and she quickly turned her horse, knowing they needed to get as far away as possible. A shot rang out through the area and Ava's horse reared. She grappled for a hold, but couldn't, and then she realized it was not only her that was going to fall. Flying backwards, her horse lost her footing and toppled as well. Ava came down hard and a searing pain tore up her arm from her wrist to her shoulder.

Manny thankfully didn't land on her, but rolled next to her before regaining her footing again and standing.

The sound of a retreating horse echoed in the trees and then the comforting arms of Tate about her person as he kneeled beside her, his eyes wild with fear as he looked her over for a bullet wound or some kind of injury from her fall.

"I'm well. I merely fell, that is all." Ava went to stand and grimaced in pain when her arm rejected the movement."

"You're hurt," he said, helping to support her.

Ava tried to move her shoulder and found it well enough, but when she tried to move her wrist, pain shot through the joint. "My wrist, I think," she grimaced.

Tate ripped the cravat from about his neck and wrapped it about her wrist, attempting to limit movement. Ava couldn't help but glimpse Tate's exposed neck now that his cravat was about her wrist and for a moment she forgot about the man on the hill and the danger they could still be in.

She glanced over her shoulder to where she'd seen him last, but no one was there.

"He rode off the moment the gun went off. I'm so sorry to have put you in danger, Ava. I should not have had you chase him with me."

She shook her head as he helped her to stand. With her good arm she dusted down her riding attire and picked a few leaves and twigs out of her hair. "No one is to blame but him for what happened here today. Neither of us knew what he was going to do."

Tate did not look persuaded, but he helped her over to her horse, checking over Manny quickly, and giving her the all-clear of any wounds.

"Do you think you can ride?"

"I think so, but I'll need help getting up in the saddle." Within a moment of the words being spoken aloud, Tate scooped her up as if she were as light as air and sat her on the saddle.

He whistled for his own mount and adjusting her arm

to be against her chest for the ride home. He hoisted himself up on his horse, giving her a lovely view of his bottom. "Thank you," she said, tearing her gaze away, but not before he caught her ogling his rear end.

"Come, we'll head back to your estate and I'll have a doctor sent for straight away. If the wrist is broken, he'll know what to do."

Ava hoped it wasn't so, and was merely a sprain. The ride home was uncomfortable, but the bandage about her wrist did help in some way to stop the hand from moving and jerking the joint.

Tate glanced at her often, his eyes shrouded with concern, and her heart warmed that he cared. It was nice the two of them being friends again. She had missed him more than she admitted even to herself. "You were always looking out for others. Even now, so many years since we first met and you're still a caring soul, no matter how much you may try to dissuade me of that fact."

"Not caring enough since you're injured." He frowned. "This is my fault," he said again, glancing at her hand that rested against her chest. "I should have gone after him by myself. Not placed you in danger as I did."

"What good would that do?" Ava retorted, not wanting to hear him blaming himself in the least. "We did not know the man was armed, or that he would run. I do believe we can agree that the gentleman was up to no good and could possibly be the man starting the fires."

He sighed, leaning over and supporting her back as the horses worked their way through an incline in the field. His warm hand against her spine sent shivers down it and she shut her eyes a moment, reveling in the feel of him again, of having him as close as he now was.

"I think you may be right. I suppose I shall be writing to the Runner again this evening."

Ava threw him a smile. "I think so." The ride home was slow. The weather took a turn for the worse, and when the sunlight disappeared behind a cloud, Ava regretted not bringing her heavier riding coat along with them.

"Are you cold?" he asked, pulling his horse to a stop. Ava did the same, looking up at the sky, it now looked like imminent rain.

"A little, but we should be home soon." Not that such a thing helped since in truth she was quite chilled. She shivered again and Tate jumped off his horse, walking over to her and hoisting himself up behind her.

She stilled at the movement as his body came to sit hard up against hers. They'd not been this close since the day before the planned elopement and she swallowed, unsure of a sudden, what to do with herself.

Tate was quiet a moment and she wondered what he was thinking. His body was tense, hard and broad, shadowed hers to a point, and she smiled as he leaned forward, taking the reins from her and kicking the mount forward.

His own horse followed.

The scent of sandalwood permeated the air about her and brought with it a flood of memories of when he had courted her. Of how she'd kissed his neck one time in the large hay barn at his estate and how she'd loved the woody, earthy scent ever since. He shifted behind her with each step of the horse and heat bloomed on her cheeks.

Using one hand to guide the horse, he wrapped his other arm about her waist, hoisting her harder against him. She gasped, and she could hear his rasping breath against her ear. Her own breath was ragged as if she'd run a footrace. In years past she would've turned, kissed him as they walked along, but now she could not.

As much as she hated to admit, Tate's mother was right. The man behind her needed a woman fit for the role of duchess and Ava, with her breeches and half boots covered in mud, her love of horses and racing would never suit the role. He needed a lady in the truest sense. She would never be one of those. Not really.

And yet, damn it all, a part of her wanted him with a fervor that chased any chill away. She was not suitable as a duchess, but that did not mean they could not come to some other kind of arrangement. One that was pleasant for them both.

Ava placed her hand over his and squeezed it a little. "I know you're worried, but truly, I think it's a sprain. I've had worse injuries coming off horses before, as well you know."

He growled his displeasure and surprisingly she felt the slightest touch of his lips against her hair. "I cannot lose you again. When I saw you fall, I thought you'd been shot, or that the horse would fall on you."

She rubbed his gloved hand, liking him comforting her more than she ought. This was bad. She should not allow such liberties, such intimate touching, but how could she refuse.

"I do not think he was a good shot."

He chuckled and the movement seeped into her soul, lighting it up in ways it had not for many years. This time he did kiss her hair and tears sprung in her eyes. Ava put it down to the pain in her wrist, but it was not the reason. The man, his care, and sweet nature had always made her defenses crumble.

How would she deny herself him when she wanted him so very much? Just not the role of duchess.

Ava bit her lip, torn about it all.

The pull of Tate whenever she was around him grew stronger each day. More so than ever before, now that they knew the truth as to why they were separated in the first place. To ignore that pull was a battle she fought daily, and sometimes she didn't want to anymore. Sometimes she wanted to walk into his arms, lean up and kiss him like she used to and see where he would carry her.

To a future she'd once dreamed of, but had learned to live without.

❀

TATE WAS in as much agony as Ava who now lay slumped against his chest. The sweet scent of rose wafted up from her hair and he breathed deep, the smell bringing up memories of days lazing about in the sun, simply talking or reading together.

Soon they would be home and he would have to move her. Have her shift from his arms and the thought did not bring comfort, only annoyance. He didn't want her to ever leave his arms again if he could help it, and the thought of how close she was, how both of them could have been killed today, made his muscles ache with tension.

The bastard who had shot at them could have killed her. He would not stop until the fiend was brought to book for doing such a thing. Tate was certain above anything else that the man who ran from them had something to do with the fire at his own estate and that of Lord Morton's.

No one innocent ran away from anything. They faced the issue and dealt with it, then and there.

"Tell me about France," he asked, needing to distract himself from having nearly lost her.

She looked over the land surrounding them, lost in thought a moment. "Southern France was beautiful, and the school had a small vineyard and we helped with the making of the wine sometimes. The headmistress was stern, but accommodating and as much as I missed Papa and home, I did make some wonderful friends, Hallie being one of them."

He pulled her closer to him, holding her against his chest, loving the fact she did not pull away or tense at the action, but simply melded into his embrace and welcomed it.

"What about you?" she asked, turning to look up at him. "What did you do in New York?"

Tate inwardly cringed at his antics in the great city. The nights of unlimited imbibing, the many ladies that had graced his bed, the horse races and gambling. The over-indulged future duke that was acting out against a girl he thought guilty of playing him the fool. When in truth, she had been as miserable as he. "I hate to remember what I was like, both in New York and London upon my return. I'm ashamed to think how I acted out against my circum-stances that I wholly laid at your door." Tate met her gaze, her wide brown eyes watching him with no judgement. She should judge him. He'd been a rogue of the worst kind. "I'm so sorry," he whispered. "If I could change the past, I would."

She threw him a tentative smile. "It was not your fault and nor was it mine. We were tricked."

Tate lost himself in her gaze, the pull of her, the need that coursed through his blood at having her in his arms once more was too much to deny. Her eyes grew heavy, slipping to look at his lips and he leaned down, just as the shouts and laughter of someone nearby caught his atten-tion. He glanced up and realized with a great deal of annoyance that they were back at Ava's estate.

Cursing the fact, he'd missed an opportunity to kiss her, he walked the horse on before stopping before the front door of Ava's home. A servant ran out with a candle now that the sun was dropping in the western sky. He jumped down and then helping Ava do the same, didn't give her a moment to walk, but simply scooped her back up again and started for the doors.

"Have Doctor Bradley sent for in Ascot immediately. Miss Knight may have broken her wrist."

The servant followed them indoors and bowed. "Of course, right away, Your Grace."

Without thought, he started up the stairs, ignoring the knowing giggle from Ava as he made the first floor landing. "I'll take you to your room and ensure you're tended."

She grinned, nodding without opposition. A maid came out of a room further along the corridor. She bobbed a quick curtsy, her eyes widening in shock at seeing Tate carrying her mistress.

"I can walk perfectly well, you know, duke," Ava said, the only person in the world he allowed to call him that. Even though the first time she did they were arguing with each other, but it did have a sweet, private notion about it, something just for them. "Do not worry, Jane," Ava said as they passed her maid. "The duke thinks I have broken my leg instead of my wrist."

He glanced down at her, not amused at her teasing. "Are you laughing at me, Miss Knight?" he asked, raising his brow.

"Always," she said. He placed her on her feet beside the bed, his attention not on their surroundings or the staff bustling about them, but Ava, only ever Ava.

Miss Evans rushed into the room, coming over to them. "What happened? I saw the duke carry you upstairs and I didn't know what to think?"

From her knowing look Miss Evans gave them both, Tate would wager she knew exactly what to think. He masked his amusement. "Miss Knight fell off her horse and landed heavily on her wrist. It may be broken."

"Oh, my dear," Miss Evans said, calling out instructions for the maid to prepare a cold compress and tisane for pain.

Another maid bustled into the room, pulling down the bedding for the night and going into the dressing room and coming out with a shift.

Miss Evans met his gaze and she smiled. "We will take care of Ava from here, Your Grace. Old friends you may be, but propriety must be upheld. Once she's settled and the doctor has called, I shall send word to you about her condition."

He nodded, looking back to Ava. "Miss Evans is right, but I will not return home. I'll wait downstairs until the doctor has left, and please do not hesitate to ask me for anything that you need." Her sweet, angelic face looked up at him and he had the overwhelming urge to clasp her cheeks and kiss her. Damn he longed to taste her sweet lips once more.

How many times while away had he dreamed of her, of being just so, alone in her room. No one to interrupt them or stop them from what they'd both desperately wanted before they parted. A couple of times they had both almost lost control of their emotions, but thankfully they had not. And yet now, five years later, the emotions she wrought inside of him, it only felt like a matter of time before they both combusted from them.

He lifted her uninjured hand and kissed her glove. "Good night," he said, walking from the room.

Tate strode down the passage heading for the stairs and the library below. He had to get hold of himself. There was no certainty that Ava even wanted him in the way that she had all those years ago. He might be dreaming up all her reactions to him, seeing and feeling things that were no longer there for her. His own yearning for more might be wholly on his own behalf and not be reciprocated.

He entered the library, which also acted as Ava's office, and slumped down in the leatherback chair before the well-stoked fire. A decanter of brandy sat on a table beside his seat and reaching for the crystal, he poured himself a glass.

Sipping his drink, he thought back over the day, all that had occurred. Once he knew of Ava's condition he would write to his Runner and also to Lord Morton to notify him as to why they had not arrived this afternoon. He would ride over there tomorrow and see how they fared, talk to the older gentleman and see if he could give any more details on the fire and if anyone saw anything not yet mentioned.

The thud of horse's hooves on the turf outside sounded and Tate stood, looking out the window to see the doctor pull up his horse before the door, Miss Evans going out to greet the elderly gentleman.

Tate stayed where he was knowing Miss Evans would have everything in hand. The fact he could not go into Ava's room, in any case, meant his presence was unwarranted. There was little doubt Ava would be dressed for bed and it would not be appropriate for him to attend.

He pushed the thought away, not needing to imagine what she looked like lying on her bed, hair cascading down her shoulders, her eyes heavy with sleep and reminiscent of what they looked like when she was thoroughly kissed.

Tate went back to the chair before the fire, sat, and settled in to wait for news.

When Ava had been hurt, the crippling fear that he could lose her had been telling indeed. If there had ever been any doubt that trying to win her love once more would be a mistake, today proved otherwise.

The moment she fell, Tate knew at once that he could not live without her. But could she live without him? That was a question he could not answer.

Certainly she reacted in his arms as she always had, and if he kissed her, there was little doubt in his mind that she would respond favorably. But that did not mean Ava wanted him for a husband.

There were certain times of the year that they would need to travel away from Berkshire to Town. Mingle and be seen, and of course he needed to attend the House of Lords. Upon marriage Ava, would become responsible for managing his many households, a mistress to hundreds of employees across all his estates. It was no mean feat, but Tate was certain she was capable. An intelligent, forward-thinking duchess was what he'd always wanted, if only she would give him a second chance.

With his hand in marriage, came responsibility. A duty that he wasn't convinced she wanted. Not now that she had tasted independence, and was answerable to no one but herself. Not that he would curb or box her into any sort of life and keep her under strict rule, but that didn't mean that Ava did not believe that being a duchess meant that anyway.

And if she did not have those worries before, his mother's words the other day to her would've most certainly placed them in her mind. Tate frowned, drinking down the last of his brandy. He had a lot of work ahead of him, and not including the rebuilding of his stables or catching the culprit who had burned them down, but winning back the love of his life…

CHAPTER 10

The next two days were a blur of pain and restless moments of sleep. No matter which way she moved in bed, or walked about the house, the action caused her hand to shift and therefore her severely sprained wrist to ache.

Ava rolled over in bed, the morning sunlight streaming into her room and pulling her from sleep. The sight of a male form sitting in a chair beside her bed pushed all sleep from her body. She sat up, cringing as her wrist protested the movement. "Tate, what are you doing in my room?" she looked about quickly, noting they were alone. "You should not be in here," she whispered.

Tate sat on a chair, a discarded book laying open in his lap. He leaned toward the bed, reaching for her hand. "I came early to watch Titan on the gallops and wanted to be here when you woke. I brought you up some breakfast," he stood and walking to a sideboard in her room, picked up the tray and placed it beside her on the bed. "How are you feeling?" he asked.

Ava adjusted herself on her pillows. "Other than my

wrist aching, the rest of me feels very well. The tisanes Hallie has been having made for me work very well. I'm not sure what she's having put in them, but whatever herb she's found is very beneficial. I'm thankful for her company." She glanced down at the bandaging about her wrist, her shift gaping a little at her throat. Ava clasped her blankets and pulled them up over her chest. Tate stared at her a moment, before he sighed, coming to sit on her bed.

"I was so scared there was more to the injury and I cannot tell you how thankful I am, you were not shot. The doctor says you will be fine, after a week or two of rest."

Leaning back on the pillows she could imagine what she looked like. A woman who'd been unable to do a lot for herself these past three days, and having just woken up, her hair would be askew, her eyes puffy from sleep. And yet, the look of utter adoration that she read on Tate's face reminded her of how he used to look at her when they were courting.

"Do you remember when you taught me how to swim?" she asked, watching him.

He smiled, nodding a little. "I do. You had me showing you all these different strokes that I was so worldly and knowledgeable about and all the while you already knew how to swim. I discerned in that instant you were trouble."

Ava chuckled, remembering he'd gone as red as a beet when she'd told him the truth of her ability. "You were so embarrassed and thought I'd tricked you. Which in a way I had, I suppose?"

He looked down at the bed, his finger following the line of the embroidered flowers on her bedding. "What made you think of that time?" he asked, looking up and catching her gaze.

The urge to run her hand over his jaw, shadowed with the smallest amount of stubble was impossible to deny.

He'd always been there for her, wanting to please and be her friend, a protector. "I don't know." She shrugged. "I've been thinking of our past a lot lately and that is but one of many memories that makes me smile."

"As good a swimmer as you professed to be, you were lucky I was there the day you had a cramp and went under, flailing about, if I recall." He grinned and she chuckled, although at the time it was far from amusing.

"There are going to be times in our lives when accidents or situations occur where we'll not be together. I wanted you to know that what happened to us three days ago was completely out of our control. You don't have to stay and keep watch over me, Tate. I'll be fine." Ava reached out and placed her hand over his, reveling in its warmth and that he turned his palm up and clasped her hand in return. "And anyway, is it proper that you're in here, Your Grace?" she asked, smiling mischievously.

His intense stare, loaded with too many emotions to deal with at this time bore into her. "Do you want me to leave?"

She thought on it only a moment. Ava shook her head, going against her better judgment, against her own promises, that she would forever be her own person. Answer to no one and be owned by none.

"I don't want you to go, no," she said at last, meaning every word.

"That is good, then," he said, leaning down and placing a soft kiss on her cheek. "Because I do not wish to leave," he whispered into her ear.

Ava shivered and turned, placing her lips close enough to kiss him. Her injured wrist forgotten, her attention snapped to his lips, still as soft and as tempting as they ever were. A fierce longing tore through her at having been denied him for so many years.

She wrenched back as the door opened and her maid came in with hot water and fresh linens.

Tate did not move for a moment, and then with a heavy sigh sat back. His intense stare left her breathless and she could feel her cheeks burning. What was he thinking after their almost kiss? Was he waiting for the maid to leave? Or was he simply debating whether to wait at all and kiss her anyway, spectators or no.

He leaned over and picked up her breakfast tray, placing it before her. "Thank you," she said, picking up her cup of tea, and taking a sip. Ava dismissed her maid, and also ignored Jane's startled visage at being asked to go. "I must admit that I feel ravenous this morning."

"So do I," he murmured, no mirth in his tone. "I will call on you tomorrow, Ava. There are some things that I need to discuss with the Bow Street Runner about the fire. He arrived today from London. Apparently there is the possibility that it's Lord Matthew Oakes, the viscount who's been starting the fires."

A cold shiver tore down her spine at the mention of Matthew, a man she never wanted to set eyes on again. A man she'd promised herself that she would never be a victim to again.

Ava reached out and clasped Tate's arm, halting his departure. "No wait, Tate. I mean, Your Grace. Are you sure it's Lord Oakes that you suspect? I thought he was in Spain."

"He was, but he returned only a week before the fire at Cleremore."

Ava gasped and he frowned, studying her a moment. "What do you know of Lord Oakes?"

Sickness pooled in her stomach at the thought of telling Tate what a fool she'd been only last year when she'd returned to England only to hear that Tate was in

London, living life to the fullest with a bevy of women, all of whom were not her. That she'd acted out of jealousy and with her foolishness, a mistake that had almost cost her life and reputation.

"He is not to be trusted, that is all I know of him."

"You're lying, I can tell, Ava," he said, using her given name that startled her a little. "And please, allow me to call you by your given name and you in turn mine. I think we've known each other long enough to be on such terms when in private."

She met his gaze, liking that idea. "Very well, we shall go by our given names." Her answer was in part a way to stall answering the question he asked. How could she explain that town gossip had been like a knife to her heart and had made her foolish and blind? That she'd made a mistake that she could never take back again.

"I know Lord Oakes somewhat. Rumor has it he's in financial strife, but to start fires in the same county he resides in makes no sense. I do find it hard to believe that he would have anything to do with this matter. He never showed such cruelty towards animals that I ever saw." But she'd certainly seen his temper toward people, her in particular when he did not get his way.

The duke sat beside her again, and she shuffled back a little, his size and presence overwhelming her, muddling her mind, and she needed to keep her wits about her. Needed to remind herself that she didn't want a husband, that he didn't fit into her perfectly planned future as an old maid.

Ava picked up a piece of toast and took a bite, busying herself as much as she could in the hopes that he'd forget this line of inquiry and go home.

"If you know anything about Lord Oakes, you need to tell me. I have not seen him since he was a boy in short coats and from what I can remember he was never any bother. But if you know anything that may explain why he's been possibly seen at Cleremore and now Lord Morton's estate, you must tell me."

Thinking back to the night of the duke's fire, the gentleman who'd yelled out notifying them of the second fire certainly sounded similar to Lord Oakes... Ava shook the idea aside. She was imagining things now. There was so much going on that night, so many people about, it could've been anyone, even one of the duke's own employees.

"I do not know anything," she said, pushing away her breakfast. Tate picked up the tray and placed it on the small table beside her bed.

"Ava," he said, tilting up her chin so she would look at him. "You can tell me anything. Please, it's important."

His beseeching pulled at a part of her only he had ever been able to reach and she sighed, ready to fall on her disgraceful sword one way or another. "This is only what I know of Lord Oakes' character. I have no knowledge or reason to suspect him of starting the fires about the county."

"Of course," he said, waiting patiently for her to begin.

Ava bit her lip, trying to find the right words to tell Tate of her shame. "Upon my return to England I returned to Berkshire to take over the estate here. I had heard you were living in London and what a life you were having."

Tate shifted on the bed and she smiled when a light blush stole over his cheeks. Of whom he was enjoying and how many they totaled. Ava wanted to tell him how the news had ripped out her heart for a second time, but she could not. He could never know how much she'd missed him when she was not deluding herself. "I made a dreadful mistake, and one that I shall never be able to repair."

※

TATE WAITED PATIENTLY for Ava to tell him what she knew of Lord Oakes and the shame he recognized in her eyes gave him pause. He could not help but wonder what it was that she knew about the man that made her so uneasy. He'd not known she was well acquainted with his lordship at all, but her uneasiness when talking about him and her avoiding telling him what happened chilled his blood.

He shut his eyes a moment, hating the thought that she'd been courted by the gentleman. That she'd possibly cared for another person, enough so to form an attachment, even if that attachment was merely friendship. He didn't want her to be with anyone else. All his time abroad the very last thing he had thought of before he slept at night was her.

"Tell me, Ava." *Please* hovered on his lips but he bit the word back. She would tell him when she was ready.

"We met through the stables. At the time Lord Oakes had a thoroughbred, Majesty, that he wanted us to train up for racing. Prior to the gelding breaking down and being retired soon after, we formed a friendship. Well, at least I thought it was a friendship."

A hard knot formed in his gut, but he schooled his features, not wanting to scare her. "And he believed it to be more than benign friendship?"

She met his gaze quickly before looking away. "He did, he thought that there could be more. He asked me to be his mistress. Said he was courting an heiress who would soon solve his financial troubles, but that she was a woman who preferred Town. A mistress in the country, not far from his estate would be favorable."

"Not his wife?" Tate clamped his mouth shut, lest his voice betray his disgust and loathing for Lord Oakes. The bastard wanted to use Ava as his whore. Rage consumed him and he clamped down on his temper, knowing it would not help in having Ava tell him the whole truth.

"No, not his wife." Ava fiddled with her blanket for a moment, lost in thought. "I thought myself for a time capable of such a thing. He is certainly handsome and seemed genuinely sweet, and as I had no intention of marrying, the idea of taking a lover wasn't wholly abhorrent to me. And so I agreed."

Tate stood, running a hand through his hair, a multitude of visions running through his mind. His head thumped and he thought he may be sick. "You gave yourself to him?" The words came out strained and he wasn't sure what he should do.

Ava remained silent a moment, her face pale. "No, it never went so far, but he did get very close. If it were not for my maid walking in after hearing an odd noise, he would have."

Shock and revulsion shot through him like a bullet and he went to her, sitting on the bed and taking her in his arms. "Ava, no." He held her tight, wishing he'd been here to protect her. She was stiff in his arms a moment and he sighed in relief when she relaxed and wrapped her arms about his waist, melding against him. "I'm so sorry, my darling."

He felt her shudder in his arms and to his shock he realized she was crying. "I'm so ashamed, Tate. I led him to believe that I wanted such a relationship, but when one afternoon he pressed for more I realized my mistake. I tried to explain, to apologize to him that I was mistaken, but he became so mad, so violent. The words he yelled at me were unlike any I've ever known and when I went to leave the room, he wouldn't allow it."

Tate rocked her slightly in his arms. All this time he had been in London, sleeping his way through the willing ladies of the *ton* and the woman who'd always had his heart, his beautiful, caring Ava had been assaulted. And he'd not been there to save her.

"I'm so sorry. I wish you had sent for me. I would've been here for you." And he would've killed Lord Oakes for his actions. And even if the blaggard was not proven to be the arsonist, he would still have his revenge on him regarding Ava. That, he could promise the bastard. He would call him out if he had to.

"No one knows," she said, pulling back a little, her eyes swollen and red. "No one can ever know. I've had to keep this to myself, a dirty, nightmare-inducing secret that could ruin all that my father and I have built. If any of the peerage found out that I even contemplated being his mistress…it could ruin me."

His heart ached for her that he could not fix her pain. He held her close, not ever wishing to let go. "I made my maid swear not to tell a soul and to this day she has not."

He wiped the tears that slipped down her cheek. "You have nothing to be ashamed of, Ava. His actions toward you were his own and say everything about what kind of man he is and what type of moral code he abides by. You had nothing to do with his choices. People are allowed to change their minds there is no law against that."

She smiled through her tears, reaching up to lay her hand over his that still touched her cheek. "Thank you for saying that. I do try and think that way, to push down the horror of that afternoon, but sometimes it is hard."

"Never give in to such thoughts for they only give Lord

Oakes power over your mind. And if there is one thing I know about you that I admire and adore equally, it is your mind and the fierceness that simmers in your soul. You're a good person, Ava. What happened to you was not."

Even as children she'd been the kindest person he'd known, and it was possibly why from the moment he'd met her down by the river where they had swum together from that day forward, he'd gravitated toward her.

His parents' marriage was amicable enough, but his mother was a hard, often cold and unforgiving duchess. His father was simply never there and so the family life, the connection between parent and child that Ava had with her papa had been new and amazing to him. He'd wanted that himself, and as soon as they were friends, Ava's father had enfolded him into their pack of two and made them a pack of three.

"This happened after your father had passed?" Tate couldn't believe what he was hearing. He stood and walked over to Ava's desk near the window in her room, and poured himself a glass of water. His stomach churned and threatened to cast up his accounts. He ought to call him out. Put a bullet between his eyes and let him rot in the woods. To know Ava had been carrying around this burden on her own brought such guilt to course through his body that it near crippled him. After loving her as wildly as he did, he should've returned to Berkshire and ensured she was cared for after her father's passing. He should've ensured her safety, no matter her choice regarding her future whether it be with him, someone else or no one at all.

"I had no one to call him out, you see. As you know I have no siblings, and with father gone I simply had to live with the torturous memory of how close I came to being ruined. To hear that he could possibly be the man who is starting the fires about the county, well," she shook her head, her eyes downcast. "I never wanted to see him again, you see, but I fear, with this new development, that may change."

It was more than despicable and Tate couldn't help but wonder why Lord Oakes would act out in such a violent way. Was he ill of mind, or simply angry at his neighbors and their successes that he had not gained himself in the racing world? Or was it Ava and her refusal of his lord-ship's proposition.

"The selfish part of me does not want to face him again. Do you think I'm a coward for saying that?" she asked, meeting his gaze. Fear lurked in her dark, brown orbs and his heart went out to her. He could understand Ava not wanting to see Lord Oakes. It did not mean that he could not face his lordship. Call him out, put a bullet through his head, and solve all their problems. "I'm going to kill him," he mumbled to himself.

Ava gasped and Tate cringed, knowing she'd heard what he'd said. She pushed the bedding back and came over to where he stood near the windows.

Ava clasped his arm and pulled him to face her. "You will do no such thing, Tate. It's illegal to duel to start with. If he is the man that has been causing all these fires, then we will deal with him through the law and we need to do it without him knowing. There is no proof of what he did to me and although he tried, he did not succeed with his assault. If he finds out we suspect him of the crimes at your estate and Lord Morton's, he will ruin me in Society and he'll take pleasure in doing so."

"I cannot let him get away with what he did to you."

Her grip eased and she slid her hand down his arm to clasp his hand. "And we won't. I know financially he has very little left. He's had to sell off land around his estate to the point that all that remains is his home and an acre or two that surrounds it. Seeing him go down for this crime as a fire starter and murderer is good enough for me. He can do no harm to any property, stable hands or woman again if he's in Newgate."

"It's not good enough for me though, Ava." He stepped toward her and clasped her cheeks in his hands. "He tried to take what was not freely given. I cannot allow him to get away with such a heinous crime."

Her eyes filled with tears and his loathing of Lord Oakes doubled.

"I know you want to defend my honor, and I'm thankful for that. I truly am. We've known each other for so long, Tate. But it's not your job to save me. I will not let you put yourself in harm's way for something I prefer to forget. Please, leave it in the past, where it belongs."

The physical scars may have healed for Ava, but the mental scars still remained after what the viscount had done to her, and so no, he would get his revenge on this bastard, whether or not he was the culprit behind the arson attacks.

He sighed, letting the conversation drop. She was still injured and didn't need to be thinking of her attacker or Tate's actions against him at this time. "Come," he said taking her hand and pulling her back towards the bed. "You need your rest. And I promise I shall not do anything until we have a chance to talk about all this further, when you're better."

Tate helped her back under the covers, puffing up the pillows behind her head and pouring her another cup of tea before handing it to her. "I will leave you now and let you get your rest. I will return this evening, maybe we could dine together in here."

She glanced at him mischievously. "Do you think that's

wise, Your Grace? Your reputation as a libertine is well and truly fixed in London. You really shouldn't be dining in my bedroom."

He shook his head at her ability to be sweet and funny, especially now that he knew she'd been hurt. In all truth he should not be in her room now, no matter later to dine with her, but first and foremost they were friends and if she were too sore to come downstairs to eat, well then, he would come upstairs instead. "I will be back to dine and be damned what Society says about that."

He left her then, heading downstairs and out the door, needing to get on horseback as fast as possible. Within a few minutes he was galloping back toward his estate, but he wouldn't return too soon. Tate needed to clear his head, calm his blood, and plan on the downfall of Lord Oakes. He pushed his horse on, jumping a hedgerow before slowing to cross a small stream. Ava would have justice and he would make sure she did.

If he enjoyed meting out such justice, then all the better for it.

CHAPTER 11

I'm free from what I once felt for you. I wish you all the very best in whatever direction your life takes you and hope that no matter what, that you are happy...

— An Excerpt from a letter from Miss Ava Knight to the Duke of Whitstone

A WEEK LATER AVA, with her wrist still bandaged, met Hallie in the hall who was taking the mail from a servant.

"Anything in there for me?" she asked, ordering tea and going into the library where there was sure to be a pile of letters and work that she'd neglected the past week after spraining her wrist. Considering how sore it was only two days ago, she was surprised today it was feeling reasonably well. Of course she didn't have full movement back yet, but it was definitely a marked improvement.

The daily visits from Tate had also aided her healing, both of her injury and her heart, making her self-inflicted tenet to never marry, to never seek a partner in life even more difficult to abide. So many times she'd caught herself contemplating them. Caught herself watching as he read to her poetry and gothic novels that they both enjoyed, wondering if marriage to him, being a duchess, would still allow her the freedom she had now. Or would she have to compromise somewhat on her independence? Would Tate in turn allow her to do the same for what was expected of her as a duke's wife?

"There is a letter from Willow," Hallie said, breaking the seal and scanning the note quickly. "She wants us to come to London for a week or two. To attend some balls that she's been invited to by her great-aunt through marriage, the Viscountess Vance." Hallie sat on a nearby settee and continued to scan the note. "She says something here about the little season coming to an end and wants us there with her before they leave for the viscountess' country estate."

Ava went to her chair behind her desk and sat, rummaging through her letters that were neatly piled before her. "I forgot Willow had a titled aunt. Does it say if her ladyship is happy for us to attend with them?"

Hallie scanned the note further. "Yes, it states here that she looks forward to meeting Willow's friends from school, and that we're welcome to stay at her townhouse in Berkley Square." Hallie glanced up, her eyes bright with excitement.

It was a lovely invitation and one that even Ava would never turn down. Not that she particularly wished to attend London events over a week or two, but Willow was one of their best friends in the whole world, and if she'd asked for them to come and keep her company, well then, Ava would do so of course.

"I will inform my maid to pack our things and ready us for departure next week."

"What about your wrist?" Hallie asked, folding the letter away.

Ava shrugged. "It'll be healed more so by next week, and gloves will hide the bruising that remains. If anyone does see the injury I will simply tell them the truth that I fell off my horse. No one will question me further on it."

Hallie leaned back in her chair, studying her a moment. Ava picked up the letters and busied herself sorting and opening them. When Hallie went quiet, like she was right now, it only meant that her mind, sharp and all-too-knowing, was churning to ask something.

"What about the duke?"

Ava shrugged, reading a letter from her feed supplier in Ascot. "What about the duke? I'm sure he's more than capable of keeping himself busy while we're away." Ava smiled at her friend, determined to evade her questioning.

"You know that's not what I meant." Hallie raised her brow, nonplussed.

"He's just returned from town and you're mistaken if you think he'll return to London simply because we've been invited down for a few days."

Hallie chuckled, shaking her head. "I think that if anyone is going to be mistaken it'll be you. The man is smitten with you, and you know it. Why, the day he carried you into the hall after your fall, well, he looked like a man about to have an apoplectic fit. The fear etched on his face over your injury wasn't merely neighborly concern, he was panicked that it was possibly more severe than it turned out to be, thankfully."

The mention that the duke was so very worried for her left a warm, comforting feeling to settle in her soul. She bit her lip, unable to hide the smile that formed on her lips.

She shook the thought aside, reminding herself that she didn't want him courting her, forming an understanding with her again. He needed to marry a woman suitable for a duke. A woman who actually wanted the position and all the trappings that came with it.

A WEEK LATER, Ava stepped out of the viscountess' carriage with the help of her ladyship's coachmen and followed Viscountess Vance and her friends up the steps of Earl Tinley's townhouse. The ball this evening was rumored to be a most sought after event in London due to the fact that their host was distantly related to King George IV. Everyone who was anyone wanted to be in attendance, Viscountess Vance and her friends were no exception.

Not that the King would attend such an event, even for distant relatives, but it did make for an interesting conversation. The ballroom was alight with hundreds of wax candles, giving the room a golden, magical glow. The musicians were situated on a small balcony that overlooked the ballroom. They played a minuet and some of the guests already present were dancing while others watched on, chatting and mingling with their set.

Tonight Ava wore a gown of gold silk, and her mother's pearls that her ladyship's maid, a master with the latest designs that Ava's own maid had been happy enough to learn from, had artfully woven the jewels throughout her dark locks. Thankfully her silk gloves hid her hands and bruised wrist, not to mention her nails that were not as well kept due to her constant horse work.

She smiled when Hallie placed her arm through hers, her friend all but bouncing with expectation.

"How exciting this is, Ava. It has been so long since

we've been in such company, if we ever were. I can tell you that they do not have balls such as these in Egypt."

They did not, Hallie was right about that. Keeping pace with the viscountess who was heading for the opposite side of the room, Ava noticed a few curious looks from those present, and nodded hello to those she knew through the racing world.

Interestingly enough, some of the glances they gained were appreciative and curious, and for the first time ever Ava set out to enjoy her time in London.

They stopped beside a well-lit hearth, a gold embossed mirror the size of the chimney sat above the mantle and reflected the light and the guests. Everything about the room screamed privilege, and looking about she couldn't help but think of Tate.

This was his world, his life. Such furniture, excess and wealth that was on show, the jewels, imported silk dresses and men's finery, the *ton*, and manner of speech, were all part of a life he was used to living within.

Ava glanced across the room and spied the dowager duchess of Whitstone talking with a group of matrons, no doubt all of them titled and married to some peer. She hadn't realized the dowager would be back in town, considering she'd only recently arrived in Berkshire. Her grace spotted her and turning her nose up into the air, gave her the cut direct.

Ava shouldn't have expected anything less, but still, the affront stung.

"Here is a glass of champagne for you, Ava. Drink it, it's all deliciousness."

She laughed, taking the flute from Willow. "Thank you," she said, turning away from the dowager and the few women about her that had looked over toward her at the same time. Ava wasn't naive enough not to know Tate's mother was spreading her vicious lies about her. She pushed the disappointment away that they could not even be civil toward each other and set out to enjoy the ball instead.

The years she'd spent in school in France had not allowed for such outings. They had not been able to partake in dances and balls that the peerage living in France partook in. Quite often they had only each other for company. Their isolation from the outside world, only ensured that their friendships had morphed into something stronger than stone.

It was a shame that Evie and Molly were not here. They would enjoy a night such as this.

A gentleman bowed before Ava and the viscountess. He was an attractive man, of Ava's age, she would presume. His hair, even though quite short, suited him. He was a little shorter than Tate, but still taller than Ava, which she liked, but it was his eyes, they were amused and kind-looking, a feature Ava often looked for when meeting new people. You could tell a lot by looking into the soul of a person.

"Lady Vance, may you do me the honor of introducing me to your friends?"

The viscountess smiled, gesturing toward them as she made the introductions. "My niece, Miss Willow Perry, and her friends Miss Ava Knight and Miss Hallie Evans. This, dear girls, is the Marquess of Harlan."

Ava dipped into a curtsy and his lordship looked each of them over with an appreciative glance. "Pleased to meet you all. And Miss Knight, if you're not otherwise engaged, would you care to dance a cotillion with me?"

Ava glanced at Hallie and with her nod of approval, she held out her hand. "I would like that very much. Thank you, my lord."

He took her hand and placed it on his arm, leading her out onto the ballroom floor. "You're from Berkshire, I understand. Is there not a very well renowned racing stable there that goes by the name Knight?" he asked, maneuvering them expertly through the throng.

"I, yes, there is. My father had bred and trained horses prior to his death. I now run Knight Stables."

His steps slowed and he chuckled, looking down at her again. "Ah ha, so it is the famous female horse trainer that everyone is talking about. You're highly recommended. Did you know that?" He pulled her forward and it took Ava a moment to dampen down the pride that filled her, knowing their stables were so well regarded.

"Thank you, my lord. I'm happy to hear it is so. We certainly do our best to breed and train up the best racehorses that we can." Of course, some horses would never win any races, but with their breeding it did not mean that they could not produce one. A mistake some trainers had made by selling off horses that could very well produce a champion. Something Ava and her father refused to do unless they had tested the horse on the racetrack.

They settled into their positions for the dance and Ava looked about, taking in the grandeur. It was highly unlikely she would return to town after this week, certainly not to partake in the Season, and so she would enjoy this opportunity, if only so it gave her more contacts within the *ton* so they might use her stables, should they like to own a thoroughbred in the future.

The dance was pleasant and even though Ava hadn't taken part in a cotillion for some years, the steps she had learned from her dance master as a young woman were something she'd not forgotten. Over the next hour she danced two more dances with other gentlemen, and stood with the viscountess when Hallie and Willow too danced.

The evening was surprisingly enjoyable, considering she disliked such events and had never gone out of her way before to participate in them.

Ava sipped her wine while she waited for her friends to return from their dance sets when a cold shiver stole down her spine. Looking to her left she spied Lord Oakes staring at her with icy amusement.

Her skin prickled and she shivered having hoped to never see his face again. The image of him, pushing her down into the settee's cushions, his painful, punishing grip on her arms as he held them behind her back, holding her still bombarded her mind and she fought not to be sick.

What was he doing here? He started toward her and she fought to pull all her defenses around her for the forthcoming confrontation. He bowed, smiling, the perfect gentleman for all Society to see. But Ava knew what lurked behind his cool, pretty visage. It was as ugly as the devil himself, and just as cruel.

"Miss Knight, how lovely to see you here in town. I have missed our rendezvous."

She glanced back toward the dancers, wishing the set would be over already so she would not be alone with him. "I fear, Lord Oakes, that your pining has been misplaced, for I have not felt the loss of your presence in any way." If anything, she'd hoped that he would be hurt in some carriage or riding accident. But alas, he was as healthy as the last time she had seen him.

He clasped his chest in mock injury. "You have not? I thought you would've missed our last joining most of all." He leaned toward her, closer than he ought and she stilled, fear spiking through her. "I know I still think of that time. How hot you made me. Why even now I grow hard at the thought of you compliant and beneath me, mewing and writhing in pleasure."

Ava refused to look at him and she let out a breath when he pulled away. She would not answer his taunt. He was not worthy of anything from her.

"Come now, my dear. We're friends, are we not? Come dance with me." He took the liberty of grabbing her injured wrist, spiking pain up her arm. She gasped and tried to pull her arm free without causing a scene.

"We are not friends and I do not wish to dance, my lord." When he let her go, she started back toward the viscountess, hoping she'd reach her presence before Lord Oakes caught up to her.

He clasped her wrist again, sensing an injury and squeezed, hard. Ava took a furtive glance about the room and heat stole across her skin when she noticed a few guests watching their every move. Lord Oakes, sensing the same, let her go, smiling sweetly. "Do as you're told, Ava darling. I would hate for London to find out that you contemplated being my mistress."

She rounded on him. "How dare you?" she whispered fiercely. "It would be wise to keep away from me, Lord Oakes, before you are the one that London turns their back on."

He laughed, throwing back his head as if she'd told an overwhelmingly amusing tale. "You're nothing but a horse trainer. Who do you think the *ton* will believe? A peer of the realm, or a whore from Berkshire."

"They will believe me."

The sound of Tate's voice brought tears to her eyes and she blinked quickly, not wanting Lord Oakes to see how relieved she was that Tate had rescued her. That Tate had seen Lord Oakes' treatment of her and had come to remove him from her presence vanquished her misery, and she was glad of his company. She threw him a tentative smile, always her protector.

The duke took her hand and placed it on his arm. "You come within an inch of Miss Knight again and I will call you out," the duke said, taking a step toward Lord Oakes and making him step back, "and put a bullet through your thick skull. Do you understand?"

Lord Oakes' eyes widened, and glancing at Ava nodded once. "We are in agreement, Your Grace," he sneered.

Tate pulled Ava out onto the dance floor as the first strains of a waltz started to play. "Are you all right, Ava? When I saw Lord Oakes starting toward you I could not get to you fast enough. I'm sorry you had to listen to that bastard."

The steps of the waltz allowed them to speak intimately, and not for anything could Ava take her eyes off him. He was such a good man, even with his ducal title and all his lands and money, he was still better than anyone she'd ever known. Her friend, first and foremost, and tonight he'd been her hero.

"Thank you, Tate. Dreadfully embarrassing to admit that had you not come I think I would've broken down in front of everyone."

His thumb brushed her shoulder through the silk of her gown and she wanted his touch elsewhere. Wanted to feel his strength, his security that he always made her feel more than anything in the world. Under normal circumstances she was a strong woman, capable of running a successful business within an industry that was wholly male. She was accepting of her own company and that she would never marry or have children. A decision she was content to live with.

But being in Tate's arms again, under his protection also had its advantages. She'd forgotten what it was like to be loved, cared for and protected. Not that she believed

Tate still in love with her, but he certainly cared enough to seek her out. His appearance in town could not be for any other reason other than that she was here. The knowledge left a warm, a safe feeling washing over her. Ava threw herself into the dance, wanting to enjoy every moment she could in his arms.

"I will never allow him to hurt you again. You have my word on that."

TATE DREW AVA CLOSE, hoping that his face did not betray the seething rage that boiled inside of him. He would kill Lord Oakes if it were the last thing he did on this earth. Having walked into the ballroom, greeting guests, he had spotted Ava almost immediately.

She was like a spike of summer sun, glowing brightly within a sea of gray skies. He'd been caught by some acquaintances, but the moment he'd seen Lord Oakes sidle up beside her and the despair on Ava's visage, he knew his lordship was being inappropriate.

He'd left his group without a word and started for her immediately. Typical of a bully's character, Lord Oakes had scuttled off when Tate threatened him. But he would have him pay. A man such as Lord Oakes was a menace, an untrustworthy, vicious man that had he been a dog would've been put out of his misery long ago.

Without care, he pulled Ava closer than he ought, wanting to hold her completely and ensure to himself that she was well. "Do you wish to speak about what happened?" He met her gaze and was thankful that she seemed a lot calmer than when the dance first started.

"Not particularly. All I'll say about Lord Oakes is that I do not wish to see him again, in Town or in Berkshire."

He nodded, wanting that for her as well. "I have a meeting with the Bow Street Runner tomorrow morning. Would you care to sit in on the meeting? He has some information to impart apparently. His letter I received yesterday was quite adamant that I meet with him as soon as may be."

"Do you think someone has seen who has been starting the fires? Even if it is not Lord Oakes, I would, of course, like to see whoever is the fire-starter be brought to justice."

"As would we all." They were quiet a moment as he maneuvered them around some other participating couples. "Ava, I need to speak to you about what happened at Cleremore regarding my mother. After the dance, would you be willing to take a turn about the terrace with me?"

A small frown marred her brow but after a moment she said, "Of course. I think we need to discuss that as well."

He nodded and set out to enjoy the dance. Every so often he caught glimpses of Lord Oakes skulking about the room and Tate's temper notched ever higher. How dare the bastard show his face in Society? Now that Tate knew what he'd done, and what he could possibly be doing in relation to the fires, the fiend deserved to be ostracized from London Society forever, from England, for that matter.

The dance came to a regrettable end and taking Ava's hand, he led her toward the French doors that were open for the evening and escorted her outside. The air was not cold, considering the time of year, and yet the sweet, fresh country smells that assailed them in Berkshire were not to be found. Here, the air had a hint of coal dust in it, along with the smell of burning wood from the indoor fires. Surprisingly and with some relief, there were no other couples on the terrace to interrupt their discussion and

Tate didn't want to share Ava with any of London Society, in any case. He wanted her all to himself, now and forever.

He took Ava's hand and placed it on his arm, walking her toward the steps that lead down onto the lawn and garden beyond. From here, he could see a small wooden structure in the garden that, in the moonlight, revealed it was covered in ivy. They ambled without haste, happy to be in each other's company.

"I want to talk to you about what my mother said the other day that I know you heard." It had bothered him the moment he'd returned to the parlor to find Ava gone. That his mother had made her feel unwelcome was not something he'd allow her to feel. Not without her knowing that he did not feel the same.

She flicked away a stray strand of hair that had fallen over her eye, placing it behind her ear. "You have nothing to apologize for, Your Grace. It is no secret your Mother has never liked me and I can understand that she wants someone suitable for you to marry. If I were titled, had multiple properties that I had to produce heirs for, I too would be concerned if my son who had inherited a dukedom had been showing an unwavering preference to a woman of no rank who has little to recommend her but for the horses she breeds."

He pulled her to a stop, meeting her gaze. "You must know that I think more of you than someone who trains and breeds racehorses. I do not care what my mother thinks. All I care about is that I right the wrong committed against us five years' ago and that you give me some indication that you might possibly be mine again."

She walked ahead of him and he followed her, unsure of what she was thinking. They came upon the structure covered with ivy and Ava went inside, seating herself down on a small wooden bench that was placed in the middle of the space.

"My thoughts on marriage have changed, Tate. Surely you've seen that I do not need the sanctity of marriage to be happy, a successful businesswoman?" She glanced at him, her eyes troubled. "It's not something I need in my life. Do not make me deny you. I don't want to hurt you."

Her words drove panic to course through his blood and he came to sit by her side, willing her to see that had their parents not separated them all those years ago they would've been married right now. Possibly parents to a horde of children, running two great racing estates, happy.

"Being near you again has been like waking up from a nightmare. My life has been nothing but meaningless nothings and mistakes. I don't want to live like that anymore. I want you in my life as my wife, my lover, and my best friend."

"Tate," she whispered, shutting her eyes for a moment. "There are expectations for a duchess that I cannot rise to. I'm so set in my ways now, the racing stables that alone take up most of my spare time. As your wife, we would be required to travel to Town, entertain, be present during the sitting of Parliament. When will any of that leave room for my responsibilities? It would not."

"Of course, being my wife, a duchess comes with responsibilities, but you never shied away from them before, do not let what others say, what you believe will occur to dismiss the possibility of us together entirely."

She bit her lip, her brow furrowed. "Can we not be as we are, with no pressure and we'll see what happens? There is much that I need to consider, to think about."

Tate ran a hand over his jaw, wishing that they'd never been parted. That the time had not given way to Ava having to face things alone. He'd wanted to be there with her when she made decisions, support and push her in her endeavors. He would do as she asked, give her time, prove his loyalty, his love and he hoped to win her heart back?

"I will do anything that you ask of me," he said, meaning every word to the very core of his soul.

She turned toward him on the bench, her beautiful innocent eyes searched his gaze for a moment and heat spiked through his blood at the resolve he read in her dark brown orbs. She reached out and clasped the lapels of his jacket running her hands up his chest. He shut his eyes reveling in her touch and yet it was not enough. He wanted more, so much more. "More than anything right at this moment I want you to kiss me, Tate."

His body roared with need and he was desperate to kiss her. The years fell away and clasping her jaw in his hands he tilted her face, leaned down and took her lips. He sighed at the taste of her again, her soft, pliant lips that he remembered and had craved for so long.

Her hands fisted into his superfine coat, holding him firmly, but he wasn't going anywhere. He would never leave her again if she'd only choose him. Tate lost himself with each brush of her tongue, her soft sighs and little nips upon his lips that teased and hauled him back into her life.

The kiss was as if they had never parted at all. As if time had stopped. He hauled her hard against him, and her soft moan set alight his desire. The kiss deepened, changed, became more savage and raw. No matter what Ava told him, her kiss told him something completely different. She still wanted him with as much fire and need as he did her, and that gave him hope.

She belonged in his arms, his life.

"I've missed you so much," he said, kissing her neck, paying homage to her earlobe, knowing how much she enjoyed it.

She shivered in his arms, wrapping her arms about his neck. "I missed you too," she whispered against his lips.

He kissed her again and she moaned, and Tate took the opportunity to pull her closer still. They had never been so intimate before, but somehow now that they were older, wiser perhaps, such a closeness seemed natural, the next step for them.

Tate reminded himself Ava was an innocent, a woman who had already been through so much, and the last thing he wished to do was frighten her, or push her to a point that she was not ready for. And then she moved, placing herself all but in his lap and fire burst through his blood. He stilled a moment, at a loss to what she was doing and then she moved, undulating against his rigidness and he fought not to lose himself like an untried lad of eighteen.

"What is it that you're making me feel?" she asked, clasping his nape and meeting his eyes. Hers were glassy, bright and full of longing.

Tate's lips lifted in a half smile. "Desire, need."

"Ah," she said, nodding a little and undulating a little harder against his engorged member. He clamped his jaw, fighting the temptation to hike up her skirts and take her out here in the garden. "I like it," she whispered against his ear, the breath of her words firing his blood even more.

"I like it too," he growled, his hands flexing on her hips and helping her in her exertion.

The sound of laughter and clinking of glasses floated to them through the ivy and she stilled. It was all the warning they needed to know they were no longer so alone. Tate reluctantly untangled them, and set Ava away from him. In the little moonlight they had in the pergola he checked that her gown was back to rights, and that her hair was not mussed from the kiss. She grinned up at him as he took one last inspection of her appearance and his heart squeezed. He adored her and he could not lose her a second time.

"Do I look like I've been well kissed, duke?" she asked. She did look like she'd been kissed within an inch of her life in fact, and it made him only want to kiss her again. He would of course, but the next time it would be in a more private setting.

"I think we should stay here for a few minutes until we're both less conspicuous." And hopefully the few minutes' away from the ball would allow Ava's lips to return to their normal size, not a little swollen and ruddy from their exertions.

She reached up and settled his own hair back into place, before adjusting his cravat and waistcoat, ensuring all sat exactly as they should on his person.

"There," she said, nodding once. "That is better. Now you too do not look so ravished either."

The sound of the couples on the terrace quietened and Tate took the opportunity to look out through the ivy, pleased to see that they had gone back indoors. "Come," he said taking her hand and pulling her towards the terrace. "I think it is safe to return to the ball now." Without any trouble he returned Ava back to Viscountess Vance and greeted her friends who waited patiently beside her ladyship when Ava introduced him to them. He had not met Miss Perry and her widened eyes at the sight of him led him to believe she'd not met many dukes in her life. "When are you returning to Berkshire?" he asked, before taking his leave.

"We are here a week, Your Grace," Ava replied. "Willow was kind enough to invite us to town to take part in the few events left during the little season. I must admit it's been a nice distraction from the troubles we've been having in Berkshire."

Which reminded Tate of what he needed to appraise Ava before he left the ball. "The meeting with the Bow Street Runner is at eleven tomorrow morning at my home in Grosvenor Square. Do you think you'll be in attendance? As a landowner in the area, I think it is important if you attend."

"Ava told us of your troubles, Your Grace," Willow said, lowering her voice to ensure privacy. "If there is anything that you need me or Miss Evans to do, please do not hesitate to ask."

"Thank you, Miss Perry. I will keep that in mind."

Ava smiled at her friend before turning back toward him. "Of course I shall attend. We're staying with her ladyship and I shall ask if I can take a maid with me."

"You can take Betsie with you, Ava. She is my maid," Miss Perry said.

Tate liked Ava's friends more and more. They both seemed level-headed, intelligent and loyal. All traits he himself looked for in his own lifelong friendships.

"Thank you," Ava said. "You're being very kind."

Tate clasped Ava's hand and bowed over it. "Until tomorrow then, Miss Knight."

She threw him a secretive little smile that made him count the hours until he saw her again.

"Until tomorrow Your Grace."

AVA RAPPED with the brass knocker on the door of the duke's residence at 11 o'clock sharp. A footman answered the door, his red livery coat and breeches adorned with gold buttons were a beacon of the wealth and power which resided inside these great walls.

Ava had never been to Tate's London residence, and its imposing, large size made her feel insignificant and common. Of course Tate's Berkshire property was large, but not as imposing as this home. Here the floor was marble and polished so much so that one could almost see their reflection. A wide, winding staircase stood center in the entrance leading up to the many rooms above. This floor too had multiple doors opening onto it, each one framed by two pillars that too looked to be made of marble.

So much grandeur and expectation sat on the shoulders of whoever lived here. A position she hesitated to accept. She took a fortifying breath, and shuffling out of her pelisse handed it to the waiting footman, along with her bonnet.

"The duke is expecting you, Miss Knight. If you would follow me, please," a butler said, stepping out of the shadows and startling her a little.

His severe frown and disapproval at her arrival made Ava dared not do anything other than what he requested. Two chairs sat inside the door to the library. He pointed at them as if she could not see them well enough on her own. "You and your maid may sit there," the butler said, his severe countenance not budging an inch.

Ava took in the room as she entered. Tate's desk was situated central in the space. At one end, banks of mahogany shelves were full to the brim with books and scrolls, all of various shapes and sizes. The front windows overlooked the street, and carriages and people bustled by on their outings.

"Your Grace." Ava stood, dipping into a curtsy when Tate strolled into the room. His steps faltered a moment before dismissing the butler, he came over to her, smiling.

Tate nodded in greeting, pulling her toward the chair

that sat opposite his desk. "Thank you for coming," he said, squeezing her gloved hand a little.

All thoughts of keeping her distance, of reminding herself that this was not the life she longed for any more vanished as he grinned down at her. Now there was nothing she'd like to do more than to kiss him again. The only thing stopping her was her maid and that the Bow Street Runner was due to arrive at any moment.

He leaned forward and kissed her cheek instead, and heat bloomed on her cheeks knowing Willow's maid would've seen his affection. The maid cleared her throat and Tate merely chuckled, giving her a devilish grin as she sat.

"I would be perfectly happy to kiss you fully, my dear. I no longer care that servants might see my regard for you. I will not hide my affection any longer. I have already spent too many years doing what others thought was best for us and I will not do it anymore." Ava glanced up at him as he stepped back and leant against his desk, arms folded over his chest.

Today Tate was dressed in tan breeches and knee high boots. His waistcoat, shirt and cravat were expertly tailored and his coat fit him like a kid glove. In this setting, this grand home and perfectly attired clothing, Tate was duke to his core. Powerful, charismatic and so above her reach, or at least he should be. He was too aristocratic for her common blood and deserved a woman who brought fortune and connections to his family. They had been so young, so immune to what was expected of them when they had planned to run away. Ava could see now that although there was a spark between them, a fuse that ignited each time they touched, that did not mean they were suitable to become husband and wife. As much as it pained her to admit, she was not his social equal, and should she marry him, the *ton* and Society at large would let him know that his choice was considered beneath him.

"While I will not put your reputation in jeopardy by declaring my intentions, but here in my office away from the prying eyes of meddling family members and matrons of the *ton*, I will kiss you if I want. I will kiss you for as long as you wish me to," he whispered, so the maid did not hear.

Ava bit her lip. How on earth would she deny him anything when he spoke to her in such a way? After last night and their kiss she'd thought of little else but doing it again, but that did not help either of them. Her life was in Berkshire, and his life was London, the House of Lords, Society and overseeing his many estates. A duke would expect his wife to be by his side, a pillar in Society, a hostess during the Season. How could a woman who bred racehorses and trained them to be champions do everything that was expected of her? She could not.

"Tate, I need your opinion on a subject that has been troubling me."

"Of course," he said. "Ask me anything, Ava?"

She met his gaze and forced the words she dreaded to know the truth of through her lips. "If we were to marry, what would be expected of me?"

He frowned, kneeling before her and taking her hand. "I would want to show you off. Bring you to London and shout it from the dome of St Paul's Cathedral that you're mine and no one else's. I would cover you in jewels, diamonds and gifts that would bring out the stunning color of your eyes and sweetness of your soul. And we shall dance, and make love until we no longer have the energy to do so. And that is to start."

His words sent panic through her of all such a promise

would mean to her. "You would want to spend the Season each year here in town?"

He nodded. "Of course, we would have to travel to London often as I'm a member of the House of Lords and so Parliament brings me here regularly. As the Duke of Whitstone, it's expected that I'm seen during the Season, to attend balls and parties. My friends, which will become our friends will expect and want us to attend their gatherings."

He smiled, his eyes full of hope and unable to tell him how much his words dashed all her optimism, she smiled a little, running her hand over his jaw. "Tate..."

A FAST RAP at the door brought Tate to his feet before the butler entered, introducing the Bow Street Runner and thankfully stopping Ava from having to reply to Tate's words regarding their future, of what she would expect should they even contemplate marrying.

"Ava, this is Mr. Shelly the Runner I was telling you about. Mr. Shelly this is Miss Knight, my neighbor from Berkshire, and who came to my aid on the night of the fire at Cleremore."

The man bowed in her direction. "I'm pleased to meet you, Miss Knight."

Whatever Ava had pictured the Runner to look like it was certainly not what stood before her. This man was as tall as the duke and just as broad across the shoulders. His face, although not as pleasant as the duke's, in her opinion, he was certainly still very pleasing to the opposite sex with his dark, short locks and vibrant emerald eyes she'd not ever seen the like of before.

They all sat, and once settled, the duke said, "You have some information for us I understand."

Mr. Shelly threw her a curious glance and Ava smiled,

knowing exactly what the poor man was thinking. What was a woman doing here in what should only be gentlemen's business?

"You may speak freely in front of Miss Knight. She knows of everything that has been occurring in Berkshire, and I do not hide anything from her."

Ava couldn't help the warm comforting feeling that engulfed her at the duke's words. He was such a very good man. She would be a fool indeed if she did not contemplate a future with him, but she would not if it meant sacrificing all that she'd worked so hard for.

But now was not the time to muse over what she wanted with the duke, or he in turn. Now was the time to find out if Lord Oakes was behind the awful attacks and if there was a possibility that he could be brought to justice.

"Of course Your Grace." The Runner reached into his pocket and pulled out a black notebook ruffling through a few of the pages. He stopped when he came to one page that Ava could see had points written upon the paper.

"The day you chased a gentleman in the woods and when he shot his flintlock in your direction, where unfortunately Miss Knight was injured after a fall." The Runner met her gaze. "I do hope you're feeling better, Miss Knight. I was quite distressed that the culprit had acted in such a way and toward a woman, no less."

Ava thanked him, knowing that if the culprit was indeed Lord Oakes that he was capable of worse deeds than shooting someone. Ava would rather go up against a gun any day, than be forced into a situation that she could not get out of or escape from. Just as Lord Oakes had tried to do to her.

"A farmer was working nearby and heard the shot. Within moments of the gun firing, the rider in question raced past where the farmer was standing. He does not believe he was seen. The culprit's bandana however by this time had slipped down to his neck, exposing his face. The farmer recognized this man as none other than Lord Oakes."

Ava met Tate's gaze and read the hope in his eyes that his lordship would soon be locked away and incapable of any more damage. To think she would not have worry about him ever again, be scared he would turn up at her door in the middle of the night and force himself upon her, finish what he started, sent hope soaring through her blood. He would be punished once and for all.

"I have men following Lord Oakes wherever his travels take him. We are watching where he goes, what business he deals in while in London and if he travels outside of the city, we'll know about it."

"This is encouraging news," the duke said. "Can we prove Lord Oakes was not in London on the day of the Cleremore fire or when Miss Knight and I were shot at?"

"We can," the Runner replied, "On both counts. We called at his lordship's London home and had a very insightful chat with his cook. The woman was quite willing to talk since we gifted her a crown. It also became known that his lordship is behind by a month on the servants' wages. The cook stated that although she didn't know where his lordship had gone, he had indeed traveled out of London. Of course, this is a commoner's word against a lord's, and that goes for the farmer as well. It is not enough evidence to prove his guilt, and if this did go to trial we would surely lose. But it is a start.'"

Ava frowned. This was all good information but it was not enough to bring Lord Oakes down. "What is your next step?"

The Runner grinned. "Lord Oakes will slip up at some stage and when he does, we'll be ready and waiting for him. In my experience, when they think they have outsmarted everyone, they do something that's not part of their original plan, and the knot they tie about themselves starts to unravel."

The duke nodded, seemingly pleased. "He's in London right now, and I've not been notified of any other fires from our home county. When we return to Berkshire, and if Lord Oakes too departs to his country estate, it will be interesting to see if any more incendiary attempts occur."

"I'm sure they will," Ava said. "He must enjoy inflicting such pain and suffering on others, and if I may impart an observation about his lordship."

Both the duke and the Runner glanced at her. "Please," Tate said, gesturing for her to speak her mind.

Ava cleared her throat, heat rising on her cheeks. "Mr. Shelly, I need you to know that Lord Oakes wished me to be his mistress some months ago. At the time he was courting a woman in town of substantial means and wanted to have a mistress near his country estate. I refused when I realized his intentions were not honorable."

"Ava, you do not need to tell…"

"Yes, I do," she said, interrupting Tate. "All of this needs to be known, at least to Mr. Shelly."

Tate sat back in his chair and Ava turned to the Runner. "It has not escaped my notice that the fires have been at properties that surround my own racing stables in Berkshire. I cannot help but think he's targeting those closest to me, my friends and neighbors, and leaving me till last."

The Runner's eyes widened with understanding and now having said her worries aloud, they did make sense. Lord Oakes had proven himself a selfish, mean human being. It would not surprise Ava if he wished to pay her back, torment her in this way before targeting her own home last.

"He would not dare," the duke said, murder in his tone.

The Runner looked between them before writing something in his note pad. "Your concerns are warranted, Miss Knight, and I shall have men stationed at your home to keep extra vigilance. Lord Oakes seems to have a sickness that is not curable," he said, blandly. "With an illness such as this, we do not know what he plans or when."

Ava could well believe that. "I suppose now we must be patient and wait, although it worries me where he'll strike next. If he's successful in his endeavors, what it will mean for those people? I know his cruel character. He is capable of inflicting pain on others and caring not at all that he has done so."

The Runner studied her a moment, seemingly thinking over her words. He folded his little black book closed and slipped it into his coat pocket. "There is no reason why someone will act out in such a way. Some people are inherently evil, wish to do harm to others for no other reason than it pleases them. We know Lord Oakes is in financial difficulties due to the woman he was courting having married someone else. Her father, you see, caught wind that his lordship had pockets to let and refused his suit. You turned down his advances, and those about him in Berkshire are prosperous, successful estates, nothing like his own."

Ava thought on the points. "And so, are you saying that you think he's targeting these estates, these families, simply because he's envious?"

The Runner shrugged. "People have murdered for less. I see no reason why Lord Oakes would not seek revenge for misdeeds concocted in his own feeble mind."

"This is disturbing," the duke said, thoughtfully. "I cannot deny that I shall be glad when Lord Oakes is behind bars or possibly sent to the colonies to never darken our doorsteps again."

"That is what we aim to do, Your Grace. It may take some time but he will make an error, they all do at some point or another and when he does, we'll be ready."

Ava thought over the Runner's words. To wait was all well and good but Lord Oakes' desire to hurt people, his desire to see animals burn in their stables was not something she was willing to gamble with. Not something she was willing to allow Lord Oakes to do again. This time, no matter how many runners were following his lordship, they might be too late just as they had been too late to save Lord Morton's stable lad and horses only a few weeks ago.

"What do you think of the idea of saying something to Lord Oakes? Not that we have runners after him, simply hint that someone saw a gentleman riding off the day I was injured. Let his lordship's mind fester with the fear that someone had recognized him. If we were to say something such as that to him, it may scare him enough to stop him from starting any more fires ever again. I know we have to sit back and wait. I understand why you would do such a thing, but we risk so much with that plan. My stables, for instance, house horses that are worth hundreds of pounds. The prized thoroughbred Titan currently resides under my stables' roof. If we allow Lord Oakes to strike again, then we risk our livelihood, my staff and the horses' lives. What are your thoughts on that, Mr. Shelly? Do you think such a plan is worth a try?"

The Runner rubbed his jaw, pursing his lips in thought. "I see your dilemma and I understand the frustration behind it. We do risk a lot by waiting for him to strike again. But I think in this case we need to wait. My men have been instructed to hold off until the very last possible moment before they seize Lord Oakes, so if he does attempt to start a fire we will be there and we will stop him, but we need to catch him in the act. If he finds out that he is being watched or that you suspect him, he may bolt. The man is a coward at heart, and by running, well, we will never be able to prove his guilt if that happens."

Ava leaned back in her chair. She could understand his opinion but it still didn't make the prospect of letting him carry on any easier to stomach. "Very well," she conceded. "I will not say a word." Ava read the understanding in the duke's warm gaze and it gave her comfort. They would catch Lord Oakes and then they would be done with him. She would be done with him forever and maybe for the first time in an age, she would be able to breathe again.

"Very good," the duke said, "we're in agreement and that is settled. We will wait."

After discussing some miscellaneous items in relation to where the Runners will be housed between the duke and Miss Knight's estate, and who they were pretending to be so not to cause suspicion if Lord Oakes came upon them, the Runner bade them a good morning and left.

The duke, after bidding the man farewell, came back into the library, shutting the door behind him. Ava stood, knowing she too should leave. Even with the maid present, she was still risking her reputation by being there.

"I should be going too," she said, not moving. The duke reached out and took her hand, leaning over her gloved fingers and kissing them. His touch sent a frisson of awareness through her body and she squeezed his hand a little in return.

"Are you attending the Yorks' ball this evening? I understand that we're to attend with the viscountess."

The duke ushered her toward the door. "I'm attending now."

She chuckled and seeing the maid waiting patiently beside the door, she gestured for her to stand. "Until tonight then, Your Grace." Ava stopped at the library door threshold, drinking in the duke, as much as she could. She loved being alone with him. He was never the lofty peer of the realm with her. To her, he was simply Tate.

Whenever they were together her body never felt like her own. It shivered and craved his touch and she was powerless to stop it.

"Oh, how lovely," a cold, disinterested voice said from the stairs. "If it isn't Miss Knight. I thought my eyes were deceiving me last evening when I saw you at the Tinleys' ball. I did not think you were invited."

Ava took a calming breath and turned to smile at the dowager who leisurely strolled down the staircase toward them. Behind her stood a woman of striking beauty, all ethereal elegance and goddess-like with blonde flowing locks.

Ava curtsied and couldn't help but glance down at her own modest morning gown which was from last year's fashion plates. She steeled herself to ignore the word dowdy and plain that flittered through her mind whenever being around women who were fashionable, the *haut ton* and titled. She lifted her chin, determination straightening her spine.

She glanced at Tate, his face an awful shade of gray. He caught her looking at him and he shut his mouth with a snap, his lips thinning into an annoyed line. Toward her or his mother, Ava was uncertain, but she certainly hoped the latter.

"Tate, my dear, you remember Lady Clapham. She's

my new companion and will be returning to Berkshire with me next week."

The woman dipped into a neat curtsy and something akin to jealousy shot through Ava at the sight of the striking beauty. She threw the duke an amused half smile, which only made her look prettier if that was even possible. For a moment Ava stared at them all, trying to place the name of her ladyship. Where had she heard it before?

Tate, seemingly remembering his manners, bowed slightly. "Welcome, Lady Clapham. I'm sure you will support my mother very well."

The dowager laughed. "Oh, indeed I do think she will."

Ava studied Lady Clapham and with sickening dread she remembered. She had been Tate's mistress. "Thank you again for the meeting, Your Grace. Good morning to you all." Ava collected her pelisse and bonnet from the footman who stood in the entrance hall, she didn't bother pulling it on, simply walked out as soon as the servant opened the door, her maid quickly following behind.

The way the duchess' companion looked at the duke was predatory. Were not companions supposed to be spinsters, women shy of nature, not interested in marriage or too old to catch the eye of a man? This Lady Clapham wasn't any of those things, but was perfect if the dowager had designs on her son keeping his distance from a woman of no rank and a business-woman too.

"Miss Knight," the duke called, coming down the front stops of his home and meeting her at the door of the carriage. "I will see you tonight, will I not?" he asked, taking her hand and helping her up the steps of the vehicle.

She nodded, but wanting to go before he saw how

jealous she was of the woman who would now live under his roof. She called out to the driver her directions.

To think Lady Clapham would have breakfast and dinner with Tate. Spend evenings before the fire in the parlor, playing games of cards and entertaining the dowager, like a little happily married couple. "I will see you then. Good day, Your Grace."

She didn't look at him as the carriage pulled away and she bit back the tears that threatened. This was why she was not made for this life. She was not a woman who played games, not like the dowager, or Lady Clapham who willingly took part in them too. This life was not who she was or wanted to be, something she needed to remember if she was to keep her head around Tate.

TATE STOOD on the footpath and watched the carriage rumble down the street until it turned a corner and went out of sight. He frowned knowing full well why Ava was upset with him, or more to the point, with his mother.

He turned on his heel and started back into his home, heading up to the first floor sitting room, where his mother had her private entertaining space. He found her with Lady Clapham, his former lover, no less, taking tea and smiling from ear to ear. No doubt their little coup that they had pulled off against Ava had gone very well.

"What," he said, pointing at Lady Clapham "is she doing here? And as your companion I might add. Are you mad, Mother? Should I call for the doctor and have you locked away at Bedlam before the day's end?"

The dowager narrowed her eyes, all amusement wiped at his words. "Lady Clapham is my companion and is dutifully keeping me company, amusing me as one's companion should. But if she also reminds you that you have a past, one that Miss Knight does not know about, well, all the better." His mother picked up her tea, taking a sip. "Whatever will Miss Knight say when I tell her that the woman who used to share your bed is now my companion?"

Tate didn't think his blood could boil any more fiercely than it had done when thinking about Lord Oakes, and yet, somehow his mother seemed to manage it very well. He fisted his hands at his side lest he try to strangle some sense into her. "You cannot make Lady Clapham your companion. Most of the gentlemen I know have been seeking out her attentions for months." Her ladyship gasped at his crassness, and Tate was sorry to offend her, but his mother and her schemes would help none of them. "No matter what you believe, Mother, Lady Clapham was not my mistress, she was simply a woman who warmed my bed for a time, a mutual agreement that is now over. If you do this, you will make yourself look ridiculous."

"I have every intention of doing so. I am the dowager duchess of Whitstone. No one would dare naysay me. Lady Clapham will be escorting me about Town and coming with me back to Berkshire. I, for one, am very excited about it all." His mother smiled, and yet only cold calculation was evident in her eyes.

"Why would you do such a thing? I always knew you were unloving, but I did not think you were so unkind to stoop to such levels. You ought to be ashamed of yourself." Tate glared at his parent.

His mother remained aloof and unmoved by his words. If he expected her to look even a little contrite, he was sadly mistaken. If anything she looked very well pleased with herself. "I am not, and I will not be. Lady Clapham is now working for me and we shall go about Town as much as I like. When I return to Berkshire, she too will come with me and we will make such a jolly party."

"You're not to return to Cleremore. I will send notice to the servants to have your things packed and moved over to the dower house. Your time as my parent who resides under my roof is over. As for the London home, you may remain here until you have organized alternate accommodation."

His mother shrugged, unfazed "Do what you wish, my dear. I shall see you at luncheon."

Tate stormed from the room. He fisted his hands to stop their shaking and fought the urge to strike out against the potted palm that sat against the passage wall.

Though he could not control his mother, he could control who lived in his houses. He started down the stairs. He would write to his steward at Cleremore at once, and have him pack everything up of his mother's and have it moved. He would not risk losing Ava again, no matter what underhanded schemes his parent came up with.

As for Lady Clapham, well he would talk to her about her conduct and what she thought she was up to, but without his mother being present. He thought he'd done the right thing by her, apparently she did not.

He shook his head, entering his library and locking the door behind him. Why, he'd even heard that she had a new lover already.

Tate didn't know that her ladyship's new patron was his mother. It wasn't to be borne.

CHAPTER 12

Later that night, Tate stood beside his friend, Lord Duncannon, and watched as Ava danced with another gentleman of no importance. It was her fourth dance she'd had this evening, and upon his arrival not two hours before he was informed that her dance card was full and she would be unable to step out with him.

He took a sip of his wine, wondering how to explain to her that what she'd thought she'd seen at his house this morning was nothing to do with them. He might have found Lady Clapham attractive at one time, one would have to be blind not to. But how could he tell the woman who held his heart in the palm of her hand that she was the only woman who turned his head? The only woman to capture his heart and soul.

He'd not had a chance to talk to Lady Clapham as to why she was in cahoots with his mother, but he would. His bigger issue right now was how on earth was he to explain this situation to Ava without her being hurt by the truth.

"How is the hunt for the fire-starter coming along,

Tate? Has the Runner any leads as to who he thinks it is?" Lord Duncannon asked, sipping his wine.

Tate turned to his friend, having forgotten for a moment that he was even standing there. Duncannon was as tall as he was, but a little less wide across the shoulders. Even so, with his cutting jaw, blond locks and zest for life, he was often a favorite among the ladies.

"We do have a lead, and right at this moment the gentleman in question is talking to Lord York." They both glanced across the ballroom to where his nemesis stood. Anger spiked through Tate's blood and he restrained himself from storming across the few feet of parquetry floor that separated them to crack the bastard in the face. He watched him a moment, hating that he'd hurt Ava, terrorized and tried to rape her. Tate shook his head, thankful for Ava's maid who'd walked in and stopped him.

"Lord Oakes. You suspect him?" The shock in his friend's voice brought him out of his musings of how to torture the bastard if he ever had him alone.

"The day Miss Knight and I were shot at, although…"

"Wait. Stop," Duncannon said, clasping his upper arm. "You and Miss Knight, the very woman you wanted to marry all those years ago, were shot at? How do I not know of this?"

Tate shook his head. "Need I remind, you were not in London or England for that matter, at the time. How is Paris by the way? Still as decadent as ever and only too willing to put on a show for a wealthy viscount?"

His friend grinned. "Of course, but never mind that," he said, frowning. "Were either of you injured? What happened?"

"Look for yourself," Tate said, nodding in the direction Ava was still dancing with the Baron.

"That is Miss Knight?" Tate heard the appreciation in

his friend's voice and chose to ignore it. Ava was very beautiful, even if she was unaware of the fact most of the time. And beauty, both in and out, which Ava had plenty of. It was no wonder she was quite sought after at balls and parties. The *ton* would miss her when she returned to Berkshire, even if Tate's mother did not.

"It is, yes."

Duncannon looked at him askance. "And she's dancing with someone else because?"

It was a question Tate had asked himself, but after Ava's hasty departure from his home earlier today, it wasn't hard to work out why she was avoiding him. She was angry and possibly hurt, but such emotions led to another thought. Ava cared for him, more than a friend and that in turn gave him hope.

"My mother has hired a new companion for herself. But the companion is Lady Clapham, a previous lover of mine."

"What!" The volume of Duncannon's statement had people turn in their direction, even Ava on the dance floor glanced over, catching Tate's eye before looking away.

"Shush, no one knows and she's only hired Lady Clapham so she can put a wedge between Ava, I mean Miss Knight, and myself."

"So you do care for her still. I thought as much when I saw you were not listening to me and your mind was elsewhere. While I did not know it was Miss Knight in particular that troubled you, I knew it had to be someone from the opposite sex."

Tate sighed, gesturing a footman over to deliver them some more wine. "It was not long after I returned to London. Miss Knight knows of some of the rumors that circulated Society about my shenanigans, but not all. Lady

Clapham is one of them, but somehow my mother has found out and is setting out to cause trouble."

"You will have to put your mother in her place," Duncannon said, taking a glass of wine from the footman and smiling his thanks. "I care for the dowager of course, but she cannot rule your life as she is setting out to do. You're a grown man, Tate. You must let it be known you'll not have anyone in the family treat you with so little respect."

Tate clenched his jaw, knowing everything that Duncannon said was true. His mother had overstepped her bounds, and he would ensure she was settled in the dower house before he returned to Berkshire. But that did not mean she would not cause mischief between himself and Ava even located there.

He glanced to his left and inwardly swore. Lady Clapham strolled toward him, her best friend and one of the biggest gossips in the *ton* lodged firmly by her side. Feeling all the *ton*'s eyes on him, he looked back to where he'd seen Ava last on the ballroom and found her watching him with her group of friends.

"Talk of the devil," his friend said, bowing to the two ladies who joined them momentarily.

Tate had never wished to be anywhere else in the world than right at that moment. He did the right thing as was expected of a duke and bowed slightly to the ladies as they stopped before them. Lady Clapham smiled up at him, all sweetness that he knew was only skin deep. The woman had ice running through her veins if she had chosen to join forces with his mother.

He could only thank Providence that he'd learned this now, and had not offered for her last year when he was muddled and lovesick for a woman he'd not seen for a half a decade.

"Your Grace. Lord Duncannon." Both women curtsied and Tate fought not to glance back toward Ava to see if she was watching this all play out. Hell, he hoped she'd looked away, was once again dancing with another gentleman.

"Are you enjoying the ball?" Lord Duncannon asked, sipping his drink and seemingly enjoying Tate's awkwardness over the situation.

"We are," Lady Clapham smiled, sidling up closer to Tate. "We were just saying that the next dance is to be a waltz."

If that was an attempt by Lady Clapham to suggest that Tate to dance with her, she would be sorely disappointed. There was only one woman he wanted to dance with and that was Miss Knight. Unable not to, Tate sought her out once more and watched as the Marquess of Boothby bowed before her, taking her hand and placing it on his arm as he led her out onto the floor.

Tate drank down his wine, placing the glass on a side cabinet behind him. Damn the man. Anger spiked through his blood at the genuine smile that played on Ava's lips. Not to mention his lordship's hold was too low upon her back, and he was holding her far closer than he ought.

Bastard.

A hand clasped his upper arm, and he'd not known he'd taken a step toward the dance floor. "Let it go, Tate," his friend whispered. "She's only dancing. I think you have bigger issues at play right now than Miss Knight."

Duncannon's words doused his temper somewhat and he nodded, willing himself to trust in what he and Ava felt for one another, even if she were so very put out with him at present.

"Well, since I'm a widow and quite scandalous already, I shall have to take matters into my own hands. Will you dance with me, Your Grace?" Guests turned, some gasped at her ladyship's words. Tate narrowed his eyes, hating the game she played to his cost.

He clamped his jaw shut, before pulling his temper into line. To save her blushes and be a gentleman how could he not dance with her now? He held out his arm, smiling through gritted teeth. "Of course, Your Ladyship. Shall we?"

She took hold of him and lifting her chin, strolled beside him as he negotiated their place within the already waltzing couples. He did not enjoy the dance, his troubles only doubling with each moment Lady Clapham was in his arms. The music continued, people floated about them, swirling and laughing, and all he could see was Ava. Her attention engaged with the Marquess, not a moment spared for him.

How could she not leave one dance open for him? No one knew that he and Lady Clapham had been lovers, unless she'd been told more gossip than he was aware. The thought did little to calm his unease. It would certainly explain why she had left his London home so eagerly.

Damnation.

AVA FOUGHT NOT to look in the direction of Tate dancing with Lady Clapham, the very woman who had once been his lover and now resided under his roof. They made a striking pair as they waltzed about the room, the duke's steps effortless and perfect, making her ladyship look like she floated about like an angel.

The night had turned into one she'd sooner forget. With Lord Oakes' presence, it had started the night off on a downward spiral, but to see Tate dancing with a woman who was beyond beautiful, titled and liked by his Mother, left her less than pleased to be in Town witnessing it all.

When she'd heard that Tate had returned from America, his flouncing about in London hadn't affected her as much as it did now. She'd distanced herself from caring about what he was doing, and who he was associating with. Ignored it as best she could, or at least her heart's reaction to such news. Eventually she'd hardened, learned to rely on herself, look out for her workers and her horses and forget the duke who'd once claimed her heart.

But now, seeing him among his set, as the ladies fawned at his feet like some Greek god was unsettling. She took a calming breath, well it wasn't to be borne, and certainly not something she would put up with. Not if the tears that threatened, each time she glanced in his way, was anything to go by.

Ava tried to concentrate on what the Marquess was talking to her about, but her mind was engaged elsewhere. Namely, the duke who now gazed down at Lady Clapham, deep in discussion. Thankfully the dance came to an end, and swinging her to a stop, she curtsied and thanked his lordship for the dance.

He bowed, and Ava didn't stay long enough to hear his final words, as she was already heading toward the retiring room. The last thing she needed was the *ton* to see her physically upset over a man that she herself had said she did not want to marry. Had not wanted that life for herself any longer, so why the upset? She shook the thought aside, angry at herself for being weak. For caring more than she'd wanted to.

Tate could dance with anyone he wished. He was free to court and marry and she'd made it as plain as day that she was happy with her life as it now stood. So why did the thought of him making someone else his wife bring out the worst of her character? The part that seethed made her stomach churn with dread, wonder what he was up to and with whom. The part of her that was jealous. So jealous that she could not act rationally or think clearly when that jealousy was baited, as it had been with the duke dancing with Lady Clapham.

"Ava," the duke called from behind her. She glanced over her shoulder, not altering her pace and certainly not willing to stop, lest she argue with him in public, where anyone could come upon them at any moment.

"Go back to the ball, Your Grace," she said, slipping into a room that had its door ajar and finding a vacant sitting room of some kind, the only light guiding her way from the bank of windows that ran the opposite length of it.

"Ava," he called again, following her into the room and closing the door behind him. The snip of the lock was loud in the space and she lifted her chin, meeting his gaze.

"Why did you lock the door? Actually, for that matter, why did you even follow me? Are you not supposed to escort your dance partner back to your Mother's side where she belongs?" She cringed at the envy that tinged her tone that would be evident to anyone listening.

He sighed, his shoulders slumping a little at her words. "I could ask the same of you. Why did the Marquess not take you back to your friends and the viscountess? You seemed to enjoy your dance very much, from what I could see."

Her temper soared and she growled, actually growled at the duke, before rounding on him. "Tell me what role Lady Clapham holds in your life? Your mother seems to like her very much and from her triumphant glances my way during your dance with her ladyship. I can only assume that she thinks you will be thrown together enough that you'll fall in love with her."

He frowned, shaking his head. "I do not care for Lady Clapham in any way other than a mutual acquaintance of my Mother's. If you must know she asked me to dance. I did not wish it."

Ava scoffed. "It did not look that way to me. In fact, you seemed quite happy to have her in your arms. I suppose I should not expect less since it's rumored you enjoyed having her in your arms very much last Season." Tate flinched but Ava stood by her words. She was not blind to how attractive Lady Clapham was, and why nearly every gentleman present sought her out.

"You're jealous." It was a statement of fact, and one Ava had to deny, even though it was as true as the sun rising in the east each morning.

"I am not jealous," she stated, the falsehood making her words come out thick and strained. "You may do as you please."

"Really?" he said, taking a step toward her. Ava stepped back. "Anything at all?" he asked again. He took another step.

She stopped moving knowing it was futile to try and outrun Tate. "Anything," her whispered word broke what restraint she held, and if Tate thought that it would be he who would decide what happened next, Ava would lay that thought to rest.

She closed the space between them, reached up and took his lips in a searing kiss. The moment they touched a wave of rightness swamped her and she knew this was where she wanted to be. Not dancing with anyone else, or alone in Berkshire training horses, but in the arms of the boy whom she'd always loved, had lost and found once again as a grown man.

His arms wrapped about her and he hoisted her up against him, his lips as insistent as her own. She could sense the desperation and need in each stroke of his tongue, of his hands against her back that couldn't seem to get her as close as he'd like.

Not that there was very much distance between them. For Ava could feel every line, every curvature of his body, including what strained against her belly and made her all shivery inside.

He walked her backwards until the settee hit the back of her knees. But not stopping there, they collapsed onto the cushioned seat, Tate's weight pinning her to the chair. Their kiss didn't stop, and nor did she halt Tate when his hand slid down her leg to lift the hem of her gown.

Cool air kissed her ankle, her calf and finally her thigh. Tate lifted himself a little, adjusting to lie fully between her legs and liquid heat swamped her core. Being here with Tate in such a way did not bring forth the fear she thought it would. To be held down beneath him with their intentions clear, she thought that maybe panic would assail her, but it did not. Not with Tate. Delicious desire and never-ending need that only he could sate, was all she felt and longed for.

He glanced down at her, his breathing ragged, but even so Ava trusted that should she say stop, he would do as she asked.

"Is this what you want, Ava? You know, I would never do anything that you did not desire."

She reached up, running a hand over his cheek, the faintest growth of stubble prickling her palm. His dark hair flopped over his forehead giving him a wicked air, and she sighed, her heart full with the affection that she felt for the man before her.

"I don't want you to stop."

He kissed her again, deep and sure and she lost herself within his arms. Let herself go to enjoy all that he could give her tonight. He sat back and reached beneath her gown, sliding her drawers out of the way. Tate's eyes darkened and Ava shivered as the soft cotton slid over her legs, leaving only her stockings and silk slippers on.

Not willing to deny herself him any longer, Ava reached across and clasped his breeches. With fingers that shook, either from nervousness or expectation, she wasn't sure. Ava flicked the buttons open wanting this for them, to lie in his arms and be the woman who brought forth all the desire and need she could read in his eyes, in his touch and every kiss.

Flipping the final button open on his breeches, Ava reached inside and clasped his hard member. She sucked in a breath at the softness of the skin that encased steel. His eyes met hers, dark and swirling with an emotion that left her heady and drunk on expectation. That is was her who made Tate react so. That it was her he desired and no one else.

Not the beautiful Lady Clapham or any other woman he'd been linked with over the past five years, but her.

"Kiss me," she asked.

She need not ask again. Tate took her lips in a searing kiss and Ava wrapped her legs about his hips, wanting him with a craving she'd never felt before. His sex slid against hers, teasing and torturous. She moaned as warmth rushed between her thighs. Tate reached down between them to guide himself into her.

"You're ready for me," he growled against her lips. "Tell me you're sure."

"Mmmm," she said, wiggling a little to try and get him to finish what they'd started. "I want this." She could not wait too much longer. She'd already waited years to have him just so, his delaying tactics, his teasing was not warranted. "Don't make me beg, Tate," she said, pushing against him and eliciting a need to pulsate through her abdomen.

"Oh, I won't make you wait at all."

❦

TATE RAN his fingers over the cleft of her cunny, soft and wet and ready for him to make her his own. She undulated against his hand and his cock twitched, hard as stone and dripping with his own need to have her.

Their location was not ideal, and vaguely Tate could remember snipping the lock on the door, but nothing and no one would move him from where he was right now. He'd waited so long to have Ava. He had dreamed of them being together in such a way.

She glanced up at him, her eyes dark with unsated need and trust and his heart gave a thump in his chest. How he adored her. She was everything he wished for in a wife, a lover and friend and there was no chance in hell that he'd let her go now that he had her back.

After today, after they gave themselves to each other in this way, he would marry her. Love her and ensure that Miss Ava Knight became the next Duchess of Whitstone.

"You're so wet," he said, slipping a finger into her hot core. He groaned when she tightened her inner muscles about his fingers, pulling on him, drawing him in.

"I am," she gasped, clutching at his shoulders while he pushed a little further inside. "I want you, Tate. I want you so much."

Unable to wait a moment longer, he pulled out, hoisted her legs higher on his hips and guided himself into her.

She lay back, closing her eyes and sighed her pleasure

that only made his cock harder. There was little resistance, and he was thankful for it, not wanting to mar this time with anything painful that could tarnish her memory. Their joining was something to celebrate and relish and he would make it everything she'd ever hoped.

"Oh, Tate," she sighed, leaning up to kiss him. "You feel so good, so right."

Tate pulled out a little before thrusting forward and her words had never been more true. Hell, this did feel right and good and everything else he could think of. They moved into a synchronized rhythm and he fought not to lose himself before she found pleasure. He wanted to see her shatter in his arms, to clench and spasm about his cock that would pull himself into climax.

Their movements became more frantic and Ava's breathy moans and sighs of pleasure were too much. He would spill himself if he did not do something to bring Ava to climax and soon.

Tate pulled out and kneeled between her legs, pushing her knees apart.

"What are you doing?" she asked breathlessly, trying to close her legs a little. He clasped her hands and placed them behind her head. "Hold the settee's arm rest. I want to taste you."

"Taste me? Whatever do you mean?"

He didn't answer, merely leaned down between her legs and licked Ava from core to clit. Her sweet musky scent made him moan, and licking her again he settled to tease the little nubbin that begged for release.

"Oh, my," she gasped.

Oh, yes… Tate looked up to see her place her hand across her mouth. He slid his tongue back and forth over her sex, loving the taste of her, that without guidance she undulated against his lips, seeking release. He didn't let up his assault on her sex, wanting to give her pleasure before he made love to her. She gasped his name and letting go of the settee's arm rest, spiked her fingers through his hair, holding him against her.

Tate felt the contractions against his fingers and smiled, kissing her fully, enjoying the moment as she climaxed against his mouth.

When he'd followed Ava into the corridor he had never dreamed this is where they would end up, but by God, he was thankful they had. The last thing he wanted was for them to be at odds over other people's reactions or plans.

He kissed her mons before coming up to settle between her legs once more. She opened for him, her eyes half closed and sleepy with satisfaction.

Tate guided himself into her heat, and she merely closed her eyes, sighing. "Are you well, my darling," he asked, lifting her chin with his finger so she would look at him. He slowly pumped into her, wanting to drag out his time with her as much as possible.

She met his gaze and smiled dreamily. "Oh yes, I'm more than well. Don't stop," she said, wrapping her arms about his shoulders and lifting her legs to sit about his back.

Her acceptance of him, her willingness broke what little control he had and he thrust into her, wanting to make her his and his alone.

She gasped, pulling him down for a flagrant kiss.

He kissed her deep, his tongue mimicking his strokes and within a few minutes he wanted to lose himself within her. But not yet, it was too soon. He had to hold off a little longer.

She reached down with one hand, clasping the cheek of his ass and pulled him deeper. With a tilt of her hips Tate sheathed himself fully and his restraint fractured. He thrust into her, once, twice, three times and came with such force that he forgot their location and called out her name.

Ava gasped, moaning his in turn and the sound of her enjoyment was a match to his flame. She was as perfect for him as the day he'd asked her to marry him all those years ago. He'd wanted nothing more than to bundle her up, take her home and keep her in his bed and life for forever and a day.

He collapsed to the side of her on the settee, pulling her to lie in the crook of his arm. The clock on the mantle clicked, marking the late hour of one in the morning. "I do not ever wish to move. I would be quite content to stay here with you forever if I could."

Ava ran her hand over his chest, playing with the buttons on his waistcoat that he'd not even removed in their haste to have one another. "And I too, alas, we cannot. We must return to the ball before we're missed."

Tate sighed, not wanting to do anything. "If I agree to take you back to the ball, will you dance with me?" He turned to meet her gaze. "Do I warrant a place on your dance card now?"

She grinned, raising her brow. "I think you do," she said, turning to look up at the ceiling and growing serious of a sudden. "If you want to know the truth for my displeasure, I know your history with Lady Clapham and I couldn't stand it. A woman who is titled, beautiful and elegant, of your social sphere. Well, I'm not fool enough not to know I was jealous."

He turned her face to look at him, beseeching her to believe his words. "I'm not looking at Lady Clapham to be my wife." *I want you as my wife, to be by my side always.* He didn't say the words, not yet at least, but he would. Everything that lay between them needed to be discussed and soon. "She is merely in the dowager's employ and nothing more."

When it came to Ava, there was no one who occupied his heart as much as she did. She had always been the one. A realization he'd come to know the moment she confronted him at his stables after five years of not seeing her.

"When we return to Berkshire we will discuss what this all means. What we want." He wanted her. As his wife, his confidant and partner. Nothing else would do.

She smiled, leaning up to kiss him quickly. "I think that would be best."

CHAPTER 13

I realized today that *I have moved on in my life. That although marriage is not something that I desire any longer, know that I'm happy.*

– An Excerpt from a letter from Miss Ava Knight to the Duke of Whitstone

THE FOLLOWING morning Ava woke late and rolled over on her mattress to stare out of the window of her room. She'd heard a maid come in earlier and open the blinds, carrying in some fresh water and wash cloths, but Ava had fallen back to sleep.

The ball the previous evening had turned out much better than Ava had thought it would. Certainly after being a jealous little swine over Lady Clapham and all but storming out of the duke's home earlier that morning, she'd not thought he would explain her ladyship's situation.

How wrong she'd been. Not that it changed much

about their predicament, but it did make her feel some-what better knowing his attachment to the lady was over. Still, she thought the best course for her was to keep her independence. The duke was so very revered within Society, people looked up to him, he was kind and a lot was expected of him. The role of his wife would be a massive undertaking, and Ava wasn't convinced she wanted it.

One thing she was sure of however was that she wanted Tate. The fire that burned, licked and charred their resolve whenever they were near one another could not be ignored. But there was another option they'd not contemplated, that of them becoming lovers.

Making what had occurred at Lord York's ball a permanent arrangement between them.

No marriage, no contracts, no expectations, simply time together, enjoyment and pleasure.

Nerves fluttered in her belly at the memory of what they'd done in that private room. Ava grinned, biting her bottom lip. She wanted to do it again and soon.

She pushed back her bedding and went about her morning routine before dressing in a light blue morning gown. Before she headed back to Berkshire she'd gone into Hatchards and ordered some books on horse breeding and lineage and they were supposed to be in by today. She would call in the bookstore before heading over to Hyde Park to meet with Hallie and Willow.

With the viscountess living in Mayfair it was only a short walk to Hatchards, and at the early hour when most households would still be abed after a late night at balls and parties about London, Ava had little trouble making it to the store within reasonable time.

The little bell above the door chimed as she entered, and saying hello to the clerk behind the desk, she walked about to see if there were any other books she would like.

The comforting scent of leather and polish permeated the air, the quiet, hushed tones of other booklovers in the store as they walked about made her smile.

For a time, Ava lost herself within the rows of books, the variety on offer, before one book in particular caught her eye. Opening the tome, she gasped, shutting it with a snap.

Looking about Ava checked that she was alone, and seeing that she was so, opened it again to see images of men and women, sometimes more than two in all sorts of bed play.

She stared as one image in particular that showed a woman lying in the opposite direction to her lover and Ava couldn't imagine such a way was even possible. How would that even work?

She shut the book, placing it back and determined to read it further when she was in next. Right now if she did not leave she would be late meeting her friends in the park.

It didn't take her long to pick up her books, and thanking the clerk, she walked out onto Piccadilly, turning toward Hyde Park and running head on into a wall of muscle that was standing before her.

For a moment Ava thought it might be Tate, until she looked up and all hopes for such a reunion was dashed.

"Miss Knight. How opportune it is to meet you here. Are you in a rush to be somewhere else by chance?"

The answer was a resounding yes. Yes, she was in a rush to meet her friends, but even more so now she was in a rush to get away from him.

"Excuse me," she said, moving past Lord Oakes. She started when he clasped her hand and wrapped it about his arm, joining her on her walk to Hyde Park.

Panic tore through her at being alone with him again. She'd sworn after the day he tried to assault her that she'd never be alone with anyone she did not trust and she certainly did not trust Lord Oakes by any means.

"So," he said, all joviality. "Where are we off to in such a rush? Are you going to meet the Duke of Whitstone again, or someone else?" He grinned down at her and his attempt to be amusing came off as nothing but a sneer.

Never did Ava think she could loathe someone as much as she hated the lord beside her, but alas, here she was with the one man she'd prefer to be dead than be with alive.

"If you must know I'm meeting my friends, Miss Evans and Miss Perry in Hyde Park. Not that it's any of your business." She tried to pull her hand free to no avail.

He tsked tsked her, smiling at a passer-by as if their little tête-à-tête was normal and commonplace. "Come now, Miss Knight. We know each other on a personal level. Do not be cold with me. There was a time you were all too willing and quite hot to touch."

She wrenched her arm free, rounding on him and bedamned where they were. "I was never willing. And you may think whatever you like, but if you come near me again, I will make you pay." She wasn't sure how she would accomplish this, but she would, even if that meant swallowing her pride and asking Tate to help her with his lordship. Not an option she relished since she was so very determined to keep her independence, but still, sometimes a man was required to pull other men back into line.

Lord Oakes lifted his hand and ran his finger over the wrist she injured. Very few people knew of her being wounded and why her horse had reared, causing her to fall. So how did Lord Oakes know of such a thing unless…

She narrowed her eyes and he grinned before pushing against her healed wound harder than one ought and she gasped, stepping away.

"I do apologize, Miss Knight. Are you sore there?"

She stared at him a moment, not believing he would be so brazen. "You ought to know, Lord Oakes," she said, seeing if he understood her words.

His eyes widened and then, throwing his head back he laughed as if she'd said something extremely amusing. People walking down Piccadilly glanced in their direction but continued on without comment. "Oh, you're a true beauty. I know now why I wanted you so much, if only to try and tame the little beast that rumbles in your soul."

"You have no soul," she said without thought. "So it would only make sense for you to try and take it from someone else." His admittance of being there that day was an odd thing to do. He may not have said the actual words, but he all but admitted to knowing of her injury and how it came about. Lord Oakes was the fire-starter, of that she had no doubt, but still, it was her word against his lordship, a female voice against that of a man's. A powerful man even if his pockets were to let by all accounts.

"You cannot prove a thing, my dear, beautiful Miss Knight. And your word against my own is moot, worthless, so if I were you, I would not try and sully my name. Even so, looking at you now, knowing what a fine piece of flesh you are, it does make me hard with want of you."

She recoiled, starting toward the park. He caught up to her, keeping to her quickened pace. "Does the duke know of our rendezvous? Does he know how you moaned my name that day in your parlor when I stroked your cunny?"

Tears pooled in her eyes and she blinked them away. "Leave, you've said enough and I will not listen to you a moment longer."

"Oh, but you will listen, you little whore." He pulled her to a stop, his grip on her upper arm painful, yet she refused to cringe, to buckle under his assault.

"I saw you last night with the duke. I saw everything…" he smirked. "I want you in my bed. I think I've waited long enough to have you."

A tremor ran through her, leaving her cold. She swallowed, looking about and thankfully seeing that the people on the street were paying them little mind. "You will never have me," she whispered fiercely.

"If you do not comply," he continued, "I will ruin your little horseracing business and breeding program and you'll be left with nothing, no income, no customers, and no duke," he whispered sadistically against her ear. "How sad you will be then. As sad as you were when the duke was abroad and you returned home to Berkshire. Or when he finally returned to England and decided to remain in London, fucking who knows how many women. But," he shrugged, "it is the way of my society. Lords take lovers and wives wait at home."

She flinched, hating the idea of such a marriage. Hating the thought of Tate making love to anyone else but herself. "You may threaten me with whatever you choose. I will not do what you ask." Her mind reeled, wanting to leave, to get away from Lord Oakes.

He chuckled, letting go of her arm. "We shall see, Miss Knight. Good day to you," he said, bowing before walking off in the opposite direction.

Ava turned for the park, not slowing her quickened pace until she spied Hallie and Willow. Her friends had always been a place of comfort and safety and right at this moment she needed them more than ever.

Willow waved to her as she came nearer to them, and Ava schooled her features to hide the turmoil that twisted and turned within her.

"Ava, we're so glad you're here. We're discussing the ball and the Marquess of Boothby's home. You know the gentleman, you danced with him at the Yorks' ball. It's this evening, and we're deciding on what to wear. We thought we may all dress in matching pastel colors so to look like a set. What do you think of our idea?"

Ava nodded, smiling and mumbling her agreement while her mind whirled with what to do. Could she tell the duke of Lord Oakes' threat? If she did tell Tate what had transpired today, he would call him out. Lord Oakes had already proven himself as a man who didn't shy away from firing upon innocent people. The thought of losing Tate in such a way made bile rise in her throat.

No, she would keep this to herself, go back to Berkshire and deal with Lord Oakes in the country, away from the prying eyes of the *ton* if she could manage it. He would trip up soon enough in all his nefarious dealings and threats, and then the law would take care of him for them all.

❧

UPON HER RETURN HOME, Ava could hardly remember how the past hour had gone by, what she and her friends had discussed or whom they had run into. All she knew was that she wanted to be alone, away from all the noise of London and back in Berkshire.

"If you'll excuse me, I think I'll lie down for a time. I have a sudden headache."

"Are you well?" Hallie asked, taking her hand and halting her steps in the foyer of the viscountess' home.

"I think not, unfortunately. I do believe that my megrim will stop me from attending the ball this evening. I hope you don't mind," she said and meaning it. Above all else she wanted to see Tate again. Just being in his presence would calm her nerves, but she could not face the *ton*. Lord Oakes undoubtedly would be there. Not tonight.

"Of course, my dear," Willow said, coming over to her

after she handed her shawl and bonnet to a waiting footman. "I shall have a tisane made and sent up to you directly."

"Thank you," Ava said, undoing her bonnet and starting up the stairs. "That is very kind of you."

TATE STOOD beside Lord Duncannon and his gut churned at the absence of Ava at the ball. Where was she? Her friends were here and were dancing and conversing happily, but Ava was not.

He bided his time, and seeing them partake in a glass of punch between sets, strolled over to them. "Good evening, Miss Evans, Miss Perry. I hope you're enjoying the night's festivities?" His banal conversation bored even him, but he would do the pretty so to ensure if Ava was well.

"We are thank you Your Grace."

They stared at him with knowing, amused visages and yet ventured nothing further. He couldn't outright ask about Ava, but dear God, he wished he could. These social rules and expectations really were a bore at times.

"Have you attended the marquess' ball before or is this your first time?"

Miss Evans considered him with a studied air before she said, "This is my first time in London for some years. As you know I attended school in France with Miss Knight and Miss Perry. Miss Perry attended this ball last year, as Viscountess Vance is her aunt."

Finally, Tate had his opening to enquire about Ava. "And Miss Knight, is she not here this evening with you? I thought she was a guest also of the viscountess?"

Miss Evans raised her brow, her lips twitching. "Alas no

Your Grace, she's indisposed at home this evening unfortunately."

He stepped toward them, about to enquire further and then thought better of it. "Well, that is a shame. I do hope she's better by tomorrow."

"Oh, so do we," Miss Perry said. "We have a night at Vauxhall Gardens planned and we'd sorely be disappointed if Ava is unable to attend."

"You're attending the masquerade?" Tate had thought it was an event normally for those of low morals and pastimes that took place more on their backs than on socializing with the *ton* looking for a little distraction.

Miss Evans shushed her friend, catching her gaze. "I do apologize, Your Grace. My friend is mistaken. We're not attending Vauxhall at all. We're staying in tomorrow night."

Tate watched the play between friends and understood that Miss Perry had misspoken. He bit back a smile at her lapse and schooled his features. "I hope Miss Knight is not so very ill. I would so hate for her to miss out on the pleasure gardens."

Miss Perry chuckled. "It is merely a headache, Your Grace, but I misspoke before. We're at home tomorrow evening."

"And are you attending any more balls this evening? Or is Lord Boothby's ball enough to satisfy you both."

Their cheeks blossomed into a light shade of pink, making them as pretty as the women about them who stood adorned with diamonds and silks.

"Tonight we have two other balls to attend after this one, Your Grace. The viscountess' good friend Lady Southerton is expecting us next and has promised some fireworks for her guests.

"That sounds most exciting." Tate bowed. "I wish you

an enjoyable evening. Please send my regards to Miss Knight when you see her next."

Tate turned on his heel, heading toward the ballroom doors. He made a hasty farewell to Lord Duncannon before calling for his carriage. The journey to Berkley square was quick and telling his driver to park in the mews, he started for the front door, knocking twice before a footman bid him entry.

He handed his card to the butler. "Please have Miss Knight attend me in the library at once."

The butler studied his card only a moment before he guided Tate toward a room at the front of the house. "This way Your Grace. I shall see if Miss Knight is available, she was unwell this afternoon."

"Your Grace?" A female voice said from atop the stairs. He glanced up and his apprehension at hearing of her illness abated a little at seeing her again.

"Miss Knight. I do apologize for this intrusion. I have news from Berkshire that I thought you might be interested in hearing. Being a fellow land owner as you are," he lied. Willing to say anything to have her come downstairs to talk to him.

"Thank you, John. I shall see the duke in the library. We're not to be disturbed."

The servant bowed and left them. Tate waited at the base of the stairs for Ava before he escorted her into the library. He went ahead as Ava closed the door behind them, and grinned at the snip of the lock that sounded loud in the room. "What are you doing here, Tate? If you're caught by the viscountess we'll both be ruined."

"I noticed your absence at the ball this evening and when your friends mentioned a megrim, I was concerned. I could not rest before I saw for myself that you were well."

Ava joined him before the fire. "You were worried about me?"

He smiled, pulling her against him and holding her close. "You know I would be."

She clutched him back and looking up, Tate's heart did a little thump in his chest. She was so beautiful in her day gown, no ornaments or rouge upon her cheeks that a lot of the women of the *ton* were so fond of. Ava looked like a woman who'd been enjoying a night at home, reading or simply relaxing in her room. Her long dark locks sat about her shoulders and he itched to run his hand through them, feel their softness and sweet scent.

"Are you feeling better?" he asked, pushing a lock of her hair behind her ear.

She nodded. "I never had a headache, I wanted a night to myself, but I'm happy to see you."

Tate liked hearing such words. He liked seeing her as well. Could imagine many nights such as these, together, alone where they could talk, simply enjoy each other's company, just as they had as children.

"You said you had something to tell me about Berkshire and Lord Oakes?"

He grinned. "I don't have anything to impart. I simply wanted to see you again."

"You did?"

"I did," he said.

Her sweet voice did odd things in his chest. He leaned down and kissed her, took her lips and tried to import with all his heart how much she meant to him. Ava went willingly into his arms, her fingers slid over his shoulders to wrap about his neck. Her breasts pushed against his chest, her pliant, womanly curves drawing him in as they always did.

Tate leaned down and swooped her into his arms,

picking her up and carrying her to a nearby chair. He sat, placing her onto his lap so she straddled him. He kissed her hard, licking her bottom lip, tracing the sweep of her mouth, unable to get enough of her. So soft and willing and the word *mine* reverberated about in his head. She opened for him and he deepened the kiss. His tongue slid against hers, and he moaned, fire igniting his blood.

Ava broke from the kiss, her breathing as ragged as his and for a moment they stared at one another. Emotions crashed through him watching her wide brown eyes stare at him in wonder, realizing that they affected each other the same. It should not surprise either of them it had always been like this. The first time they'd kissed under a large oak tree, they had both come away from that embrace forever changed, linked by some invisible tie that, even as young as Tate had been at that time, he'd known. She was meant to be his, forever.

He ran his thumbs across her cheeks, holding her face before him. Ava shuffled on his lap, placing her heat hard upon his. She sighed, rocking against him, her hot core tempting him to rip open the front of his breeches, and seal them together.

Tate shook with his denial to do exactly what they so obviously wanted. Somewhere in the recesses of his mind he reminded himself where he was. That he'd entered the room, and had not locked the door. An oversight on his behalf.

"I should go. If the viscountess comes home there will be hell to pay," he said between kisses. "I do not want trouble for you." Not that he would not marry Ava tomorrow, but she did not need the *ton* to shun and talk about her if they did find out about their tryst. His marriage to Ava would be because they wished it to be so, not because the *ton* thought he'd ruined her in some way and was forced into the union.

"I don't want you to go," she protested, in a tremulous voice. Taking his hand, she pushed it down to lie against her sex. Her wet cunny greeted him and he hardened to steel. He would not deny her, them both, not when she wanted this as much as he. Tate ran his fingers along her core, eliciting a sweet gasp from her lips. She pressed down on his hand, her eyes turning deep amber with flecks of fire in them.

"I want you, Tate!" She kissed him hard. "You make me crave you so much."

Tate moaned as her hand slid down his abdomen, taking pains to caress the contours of his stomach before delving further and wrapping itself around his engorged cock. "You make me want you too," he rasped, breathless.

Her fingers made quick work of the buttons on his breeches and then she was touching him, sliding her clever hand about his cock, a steady stroke that sent stars to flicker behind his eyes.

Ava shuffled closer and kissed him. "I saw in a book a position like we are now. Do you...do you think," she continued, "that such a position may be possible for us?"

What types of books was she reading? He wanted to know more. He left that question for another time, too distracted with her movements upon his lap. If he were at all a gentleman he would give her some days' grace before they made love again, but such an option was impossible when her penetrating stare all but begged him to fulfill her.

And he'd do exactly as she asked.

"You only need to ask." He grinned and reached between them, gathering her gown and hoisting it about her waist. She lifted herself a little, helping him with his endeavor. Their movements were quick and desperate. The need to have her, fuck her and lay claim to the woman in his arms was too much. He positioned himself at her entrance, catching her sultry gaze.

Tate thrust hard into her as she slid down over his length. Her tight core wrapped about him and he sucked in a breath at the sheer exquisiteness of having her again. They rocked together, her arms circling his neck, her fingers clawing into the skin on his back. He pumped hard and deep, wanting her to shatter in his arms, to come apart with him.

She was his, now and forever, just as he was hers. How could it not be so when each time they came together it was simply right? After all the years apart, still, they had found each other again.

Ava pushed him against the back of the seat, her hands clasping the chair. Tate reveled in watching her take control, finding her own pace to take pleasure from him. She was utterly marvelous, and he clamped down his need to spill inside of her. He reached between them, sliding his fingers against the little nubbin at her core. A half gasp, half moan escaped her lips and he gasped.

"Come for me," he begged, so close that temptation licked his every thrust.

Her movements became desperate, and he clasped her hips, guiding her deeper, harder each time she came down upon him. Her fingers clasped his nape, sliding up into his hair and he knew she was close. Her eyes fluttered shut, the slightest perspiration on her upper lip that he ached to lick.

"Oh, Tate." She threw her head back as spasm after spasm clenched about his cock, pulling him along into climax. Tate came hard, following her into bliss where he wanted nothing more than to do it again. He fought to catch his breath, to come back to reality after taking his fill. She slumped against his chest, her breathing warm upon his shoulder. She turned her head, kissing his neck and he shivered with renewed need.

He would never tire of the woman in his arms.

"However are we going to stop?" she giggled and he wrapped his arms about her, holding her close.

He kissed her forehead, catching her gaze. "I have no idea," he said, truthfully. And he did not, but nor did he wish to.

"I should feign a megrim more often, if you're my remedy."

Minx! He chuckled, holding her still and with little desire to move her from his lap. "It is only fair that I'm your cure, for you've always been mine."

CHAPTER 14

Some days' later Tate rode hard on the road out of London heading toward Berkshire. He'd finished up his work with his steward earlier than he had anticipated and with any luck he would catch up with Ava's coach.

He smiled at the thought of her. How much he missed her when they were apart.

The Ugly Swan Inn came into view a little way ahead, and he slowed his horse's pace as he started through the outskirts of the small village. People milled about the town going about their business. The Inn was busy with an array of carriages and people unloading and loading the equipages.

Halting in the Inn yard, a young stable lad ran out, and getting down, Tate handed the boy a shilling. "Tell me lad, is a Miss Ava Knight and her party still here or have they moved on?"

The young boy's eyes widened and nodding excitingly, he said, "Aye, they're still here, my lord. They're inside this past hour and have taken rooms so me pa says."

"Thank you," Tate said, dismissing the boy and his use of my lord instead of your grace.

He opened the Inn's front door and entered what looked to be the front tavern area of the establishment. It was filled to the brim with travelers and local folk from the looks of their dusty, crinkled and workworn clothing. Tate walked up to the counter and slid a sovereign across the bar. "I need a room for the night. I also need to know where Miss Knight is located within your premises so I may make my presence known."

The barman, a rotund, graying sort of man raised his brow, crossing his arms across his belly. "And who may you be?" he asked. Tate had to give him credit for asking instead of telling anyone of Ava's whereabouts when money was offered.

"I am the Duke of Whitstone."

The barman's eyes widened and he straightened, attempting to bow to him. "The party that ye enquire about is currently having a repast in the front private parlor, Your Grace. I will have my best chamber prepared for ye at once. 'Tis the first door on the left as ye go upstairs."

"Thank you," Tate said, starting for the room.

He knocked twice and opened the door to find Ava alone at the table. She sat in the sunlight with the Times paper open before her. She looked up and surprise registered on her face, before she placed the paper down and started toward him.

"Tate, whatever are you doing here?"

He shut the door and caught her up in his arms. "Two days was too long."

She smiled and kissed him and he took her lips, drank from them as if she were his last hope of quenching his thirst.

Ava melted against his chest and the feel of her breasts, her nipples hardened peaks through her soft cotton traveling gown made his blood race in his veins. He kissed her deep and long, hoisted her up against his person and left them both breathless.

"Damn, I want you," he gasped through the kiss.

"Are you staying the night?" she asked him in turn.

He'd stay forever if only she'd allow. "I have a room." He held her close, not wanting to let her go. "Would you care to join me?"

She threw him a wicked look that sent his blood to boil. "I will have to tell Hallie what I'm doing or she'll worry. But I'm sure she won't mind."

The door opened and in walked her friend as if by saying her name aloud Ava had summoned her. She started seeing the duke holding her friend in a most inappropriate way. She entered quickly, before closing the door just as fast before anyone saw them.

Tate gently set Ava away from him and smiled at the light blush that stole over her cheeks. Ava went to sit back at the table and Hallie joined her not saying a word. Tate sat also, and picking up the pot of tea he poured himself a cup.

Hallie glanced back and forth between them, before sighing. "What are you two doing? You're not married or engaged and yet I walk in here, in the middle of a busy country inn and find you both in each other's arms." Miss Evans reached for the bread and cheese, placing a good portion on her plate when neither of them ventured to answer. "Oh, and by the way, the dowager duchess has just arrived."

"What?" Both he and Ava said in unison. Tate stood and walked to the window, looking out onto the Inn yard. He inwardly swore at the sight of his mother and Lady

Clapham organizing help with their luggage, a bevy of servants doing the duchess' bidding.

He looked down at Ava just as she caught his eye and he read the wariness that entered them. "I'm sorry. I didn't know that my mother was traveling home today."

She clasped his arm, squeezing it a little. "You have nothing to apologize for, Tate."

His mother entered the inn, and within a moment there was a quick knock on the parlor door before she walked in with her companion. His mother took in the room and the occupants and gave a dismissive sniff.

"Tate, my dear, why didn't you tell me that you were leaving for Berkshire today, I would've ensured there was room for you in the equipage." His mother sat at the table after the servant who opened the door for them pulled out a chair for her grace.

"I did not know you were traveling for one. Second, I have my horse."

Lady Clapham caught Tate's eye and smiled up at him all but ignoring Ava and Miss Evans who sat at the table across from them.

"Will you escort us to Berkshire in the morning, Your Grace? With the man terrorizing the county lighting fires, or so I heard, it would settle both mine and your Mother's nerves if we had a protector at our side."

Miss Evans smiled and Tate understood very well as to why. Lady Clapham's tone oozed sin, even with his mother's presence, and Tate didn't miss that Ava's hands had fisted about the paper she was holding.

"Of course, I shall escort you to the dower house, Mother. I had word only yesterday that it is ready for your arrival, fully staffed just as you like things. And if I may be so bold, Miss Knight, Miss Evans, I can escort you also if you'd like to travel with us."

Ava looked between him and the dowager. His mother's mouth had tightened up to a small pucker of distaste and it was not hard to know what she thought of the idea.

"We would like that, Your Grace," Miss Evans answered when Ava remained quiet.

"If you'll excuse us, Your Graces, Lady Clapham, we've traveled a long way today and I think I'll rest before dinner."

Tate moved out of the way to allow Ava to move past him. He reached down and slid his hand against her fingers as she walked past. She didn't respond, merely left him alone with his vexing parent.

He ground his teeth for the forthcoming discussion to be had. Damn he was sick of his mother's interfering, rude ways. He'd warned her to keep her tongue in check, and yet still, she persisted to be insolent.

"I see Miss Knight is still chasing your coat tails, Tate dear. She'll get a reputation if she's not careful."

"Miss Knight was already lodging here when I arrived. So maybe it'll be I who gains a reputation." His mother threw him a quelling glance and he raised his brow. "You don't agree, Mother?"

"I care not what Miss Knight does in her own time, so long as it does not impinge or bring scandal to the Duke of Whitstone's doors."

"Like it almost did five years ago? You do realize, do you not, Mother, that I was the one who proposed to Ava and begged her to run away with me to Gretna? It was not the other way around, no matter what you may think."

Lady Clapham's mouth gaped open, and Tate took a calming breath, knowing that what he'd just declared would be all over London before the month was out, thanks to Lady Clapham. Not that he cared. All of the gossiping vipers could go hang.

"If you aspire for me to marry a woman of rank, such as her ladyship present, you are sadly deluded. The woman I marry will be of my choosing. Apologies, Lady Clapham for the bluntness of my tongue, but my mother has an uncanny ability to ignore people's wishes and decrees."

The dowager placed the teacup down with a clatter, spilling a little of the contents over the side on to the saucer. "Ava Knight will never be the Duchess of Whitstone. I forbid it."

"Why are you so against her?" he asked, truly baffled. "Mr. Knight was a gentleman and therefore his daughter is a lady. There is little to dislike from your perspective, I would think."

His Mother rolled her eyes, not something he'd ever thought to see a duchess do before. She stood, rounding on him. "They're common. Her great-grandfather lived in one of the ducal tenant farms before he started horse breeding as a hobby. Please think about that. If you were to have children with this woman, your future son and heir would have a great-grandfather who was a servant in your own home."

Tate had heard enough. He ran a hand through his hair before walking to the door. "How fortunate for father that he did not care for such rules, considering your own heritage, Mother. Common Americans who had money. That was your only claim to some sort of greatness, was it not? In my eyes you're no different to Miss Knight in that sense, except with Ava, she has a heart beating within her chest. I highly doubt you have one at all."

His mother gasped, and Lady Clapham paled. In time Tate might regret the harshness of his words, but today was not that day. "I shall come and see you the day after we arrive back at Berkshire to ensure you've settled in at the dower house. Good afternoon, Mother. Lady Clapham."

CHAPTER 15

*F*ather is unwell, but has insisted I stay in France. He says it's just a trifling cold, but there was something in his written words that sent a shiver down my spine. I feel like he's hiding something from me. Dread has curled in my stomach today and I cannot shake it.

– An Excerpt from a letter from Miss Ava Knight to the Duke of Whitstone

Two DAYS after arriving home from London, Ava stood at the stable doors with her stable manager, Greg, as Titan's groom walked the stallion around the mare they wanted him to cover. Today was the day they would see if Titan liked what he smelled when it came to Black Lace.

She hoped it was so. Over the last fortnight when they'd been stabled across from each other the two horses had seemed to get along reasonably well, and had neighed once or twice over the stable door, or so the stable boy had informed her, all good signs for a promising union.

"Very good of the duke to give you the approval for the breeding of Titan with Black Lace, Miss Ava. Even if they do not produce a champion, they'll certainly produce pretty foals."

Ava chuckled, supposing that would be true. "And yet that isn't quite what we're hoping to achieve. I'd prefer a champion to a pretty horse." Which wasn't entirely true. Horses, no matter their age or ability would always have her heart. To her, they were truly the best animal on earth.

"The duke mentioned yesterday that there was a break in at old Mr. Rogers' farm, although nothing was stolen, there was evidence that someone tried to light a fire, but it never took. The Runner seems to think it's connected to the fire-starter, but the local magistrate does not. Hard to know what is going on in these parts with all the trouble we've had."

Ava frowned, having not known that another neighbor of hers had been targeted. In fact, she'd not seen Tate at all yesterday. Why did he not call on her? She'd not seen him since they had stayed at the same inn on their way home from London.

Terribly crass of her, but the day she'd excused herself from the dowager in the parlor, she'd dallied in the hall, listening to the duchess' words. Scathing words really, derogatory in fact, and all about her and her unsuitableness as a duchess.

The loathing she'd heard in her voice gave her little hope for friendship. The woman hated her common blood, and as Ava could do nothing about such things, there was little chance of a reconciliation.

She had thought on the prospect of them during the carriage ride home, watching Tate who rode alongside the vehicle all the way back to her estate. Each time she looked at him her heart squeezed and there was little point denying what that reaction meant.

It was the same that she'd known it when a young girl. She loved him. In all truthfulness, she'd never stopped loving him, no matter how angry she'd been.

But that did not mean they were suitable. That the role of duchess was more important to the role she had here at Knight Stables.

"The duke was here?" she asked, keeping her eye on the horses and feigning an uninterested air that was only skin deep.

"Oh yes, Miss Knight. Came over before luncheon but couldn't stay as he was having luncheon with her grace and Lady Clapham over at the dower house."

"Of course." Ava was quiet as Titan mounted Black Lace. The joining was short, with little fuss, but hopefully successful. "Very good, thank you gentlemen, for your assistance. Now we wait," she said to the yard hands that stood around watching.

"I had thought the duke said he would be here for this, but alas he's been held up, I guess." Greg said, watching the horses.

Ava nodded having thought the same. After all the fuss he'd made about her not having Titan breed with one of her horses, she thought he would not have missed this.

"You may have Titan returned to the ducal farm this afternoon. Their stables are now rebuilt and I know the duke would wish him stabled there. No need in keeping him here any longer." Ava walked over to the stallion and ran her hand down his neck. "Even though he is such a handsome beast." She cooed to the horse for a moment before letting the groom take him back to his stall to prepare him for his walk back to Tate's estate.

"Right you are, Miss Knight. We'll do that directly."

Ava stayed outdoors for the remainder of the afternoon, watching some of the fillies learn how to lunge in the lunging yard, viewing her two hopefuls for the Ascot races do time trails on the gallops before looking over the books for the feed and grain.

She thought on Tate's absence. They had been home two days now, and not a word from him. Was something amiss? Had his mother's wicked tongue finally soured him against her? Ava leaned back in her chair, twisting the quill in her hand as she glanced out the window. Perhaps this was for the best. Their lives were so very different now, both of them had people relying on them, his as a duke and she as a horse breeder and trainer. Their social spheres could not be much further apart, even if one of her friends was a viscountess' niece.

Being home these two days had solidified her dislike of town. She'd missed the stables, of being around her horses, feeding them, simply watching them run about the yards or graze in the meadows. London life was not her forte and being a duchess, a woman of immaculate fashion sense and impeccable friends would not suit her. Why, all her friends from school were as common as she was, besides Willow of course.

Ava sighed and throwing down her quill, stood and started back toward the house. Dinner would be served soon and she'd promised Hallie that she would attend this evening since last night she'd been held up in the lower holding yard after one of her mares had gone through a fence.

Walking up the front drive, she moved out of the way as the rider who delivered mail cantered from the house, tipping his cap a little as he rode past. Entering the front hall her servant came out of her office, the silver salver in his hand. "Were you looking for me, William?" she asked.

He bowed. "Yes, Miss Knight. A missive from the dowager duchess of Whitstone just arrived. I've placed it on your desk."

"Thank you," she said, going into her office and closing the door. She'd always loved this room, even when it was her father's space and sanctuary. Now it was hers she'd decided not to change a thing about it. The dark mahogany desk, along with bookshelves that lined the walls and two leatherback chairs sat before the hearth ready for anyone to pick up a book, sit and read to their heart's content.

She broke the duchess' seal and scanned the note. The more she read of the missive the more she could not believe the impudence of the woman. How dare she, but then how dare she not? Ava scrunched up the note in her hand and then re-opening it, scanned it for a second time, not believing what she was reading.

Miss Knight,

I'm having a small ball at my dower house in coming weeks. I know we've had our disagreements in the past, and I do hope for the sake of our small county that we may become more agreeable to one another's presence in time. But unfortunately that time is not now. I am therefore sending this missive as a courtesy, as a small explanation as to why you have not received an invitation. Please do not attend, even at the behest of my son. The dower home is my own and you will not be allowed entrance.

Warmest regards,
Duchess of Whitstone

FOR A SECOND TIME, she screwed up the missive the blood in her veins thumping loud in her ears. How dare the woman? A light knock sounded at the door and Hallie popped her head around the threshold. "Ah, I see you received one as well. I'm so glad that you have. Maybe the dowager has seen that the duke is in love with you and has finally come around to embrace you as a future daughter-in-law."

Ava slumped onto her chair wishing that were so. "No, nothing of the kind, I'm afraid. This is a missive from her grace, but it's a letter telling me not to attend, that I won't be allowed admittance."

"What!" Hallie came into the room, leaving the door ajar. She came over to the desk and snatched the missive from between Ava's fingers, reading it quickly.

"Oh, my, I knew the dowager was cold and cutting, but this is beyond offensive." Hallie met Ava's gaze. "I'm so sorry, Ava. She seems determined to drive a wedge between you and the duke."

That was an underestimation. "Yes, so it would seem."

"What are you going to do? Are you going to tell the duke about this?" she said, waving the note.

Ava shook her head, sick of it all, tired of the constant barbs and bitter looks. The cuts direct in town and nasty notes delivered in the middle of the day. "No. He doesn't need to know about this, it would only make things more awkward."

"But the duke loves you, I'm sure. He's sent his mother to the dower house after all and she was living at Cleremore before."

That was true at least, but it did not change the fact that his mother hated her. A little voice whispered that perhaps their time had come and gone. That they should part now before any further damage to their hearts and families was done.

"Did you receive an invitation?" Ava enquired.

Hallie waved the piece of parchment that was in her other hand. "I did, but I will not attend if you're not going. The dowager inviting me and not you is unreservedly rude and I shall not give her the pleasure of such a slight. We shall stay here together and forget about her grace and her schemes."

Her friend's eyes sparkled with fire and Ava loved her for her loyalty. "You must attend, for if you do not she'll think I had a hand in it. Restricting my friend's outings. Go, enjoy yourself and mingle. Show the dowager duchess of Whitstone that we do not care who she does and does not invite."

"I cannot go without you. I do not care what the dowager will think. I shall stay at home and keep you company."

Ava smiled reaching for her friend's hand. "You will attend, and you will enjoy yourself and tell me all about it when you return. I'm quite content to stay home and I promise you, what her grace does, does not affect me in the lightest. She's interfered and been rude to me for as long as I have known her. She no longer has power over him and she loathes the thought."

Hallie sighed, seemingly unconvinced. "If you're sure, but I do not feel easy over this."

"All will be well, Hallie. Do not concern yourself with me. I'll be quite well at home."

A knock at the door sounded and her butler walked in, announcing the Duke of Whitstone.

Ava stood, her body warming to the sight of him. She schooled her features, meeting Hallie's startled gaze.

"Good afternoon, Your Grace," Hallie said, dipping into a curtsy. "If you'll excuse me, I have some letters to write."

The door closed softly behind her friend and the duke

strode over to her, pulling her into his arms and kissing her soundly. She leaned into him, taking all that he would give, relishing his touch, each stroke, touch, kiss that he bestowed on her.

He was impossible to ignore and had always been so.

Tate pulled back, his eyes ablaze with unsated desire. "I've missed you." He pulled her over to the hearth and seated them on the settee. "I've been meaning to call, and I wanted to come here today because we never managed a chance to finish the discussion we started in London."

Dread spiked through her and she sat up straight, folding her hands in her lap. "Our conversation," she queried, stalling.

He nodded. "About us."

"Oh," she said, light-heartedly. "What about us?" The hope that flashed in his stormy gray eyes vanquished her hope that it was about anything but them. She wasn't ready for this conversation or what his reaction would be to her words.

He reached for her hand her own swallowed up by his strong capable ones. "You must know that from the moment I found out that you had not jilted me that all the hurt, the anger I carried with me vanished. I tried to move on from you, even as angry as I was, it did not work and I no longer wish to live without you."

Ava could not tear her attention from him. His words were a balm to her soul, and she wished she could give him all that he wanted, but she could not. Not because she did not love him, burn for him every moment of every day, but because of so many things that stood between them.

She squeezed his hand, adjusting her seat. "You don't have to live without me, Tate, but please don't ask me to be your wife." He flinched at her words and clasped his hand tighter. "Listen to me, please, before you say anything."

He watched her a moment, his eyes guarded. He nodded.

Ava took a fortifying breath, licking her lips. "We were so young when we first fell in love. And it was love, of that I have little doubt. But, having lived abroad for four years, then coming home to run an estate with very little support other than from my staff, I've grown quite independent. I'm financially secure and do not need to marry if I do not wish to." She kept her attention on him, hating the fact that he'd gone an awful shade of gray. "And I do not. To marry would mean the loss of my independence, to not do what I love, whenever I wish. I cannot become an ornament, a woman who talks nonsense and accomplishes little. It's not who I am and having grown up, I know that now."

Tate stood, wrenching his hands free. "I want you to be my wife, Ava, my duchess. What are you asking to be?" His voice was hard, immovable and she cringed.

"I would be your wife tomorrow, Tate, please know that, but I will not be your duchess. It is too much, I would be giving up everything."

"You would not have to give up your life." He ran a frustrated hand through his hair, walking to stand before the fire. He leaned upon the marble mantel, his back to her. "Of course being a duchess comes with responsibilities. Situations that would take you away from here for several months of the year. Is that too much to ask? Are you not willing to give an inch to have me?"

Ava stood, hating the desolated look in his eyes. "I want you, I do. I do not want anyone else. We can still have each other, but not as husband and wife. I will be your lover for as long as you'd want me."

He wrenched from her, disgust twisting his otherwise handsome visage. "I must marry. The family name alone requires me to try for an heir and I will not break my vows to the woman I marry. I will not do that to her, no matter how tempting you are."

Ava bit her lip, panic coursing through her blood. He stepped further away and she stilled. "I will not have you as my mistress. I will not have you at all if I cannot have you as my wife."

Tate turned and strode for the door. Ava ran after him, clutching at his arm. "Please Tate, I cannot lose you again. I simply want…"

"You want it all," he cut in, halting her words. "You want me to scratch your itch whenever it arises. You want to keep your independence and be mistress of your domain. You want me to break my marriage vows to keep your bed warm at night."

She paled, her heart twisting. "Your mother was right I'm not suitable to be your bride. My lineage will always be fodder for town gossip. Our children will be food for the vultures of the *ton* to rip apart and look down upon. I will be ridiculed, gossiped about and ignored. At least as mistress of Knight Stables I am treated with respect. If I became your duchess, all of that would change. They would look for you regarding my horses, the training we offer here. They would look to you for advice and guidance. I will become obsolete, what my family built from the ground up will be obsolete." Ava raised her chin, anger straightening her spine. "I will not have it. Not even for you."

He glanced at her, his eyes void of warmth. "You are wrong, Ava and you are blind to what I can give you. As my wife, my name alone will protect all those that I love, even a woman whose lineage may not be as grand as some, but was grand enough for me."

For a long moment Ava stared at the door that Tate had stormed though, breathless at his declaration. He loved her? Never in all the time they'd been together had he uttered the words. She had silently hoped she was not alone in her affections and now she knew she was not. Ava walked to the window, watching as he rode off down her drive as if the devil himself was behind him.

A cold shiver ran down her spine that perhaps she'd been wrong, had made a mistake, one that this time she would not be able to undo.

CHAPTER 16

A fortnight had passed and Tate had not seen Ava, or more truthfully he'd avoided her after their parting. He stared down at the whisky in his hand, reminding himself that no matter how many he imbibed, it would not make him feel any better, would not numb the hurt that coursed through his veins every minute of every day.

She had rejected him.

He clenched his jaw, looking up toward the door as the butler announced more of his mother's guests at her ball, another useless, non-essential evening. He glanced about the room. The people laughed, drank, took more wine and food from the waiting servants. Useless beings all of them. Spoiled and entitled.

Was it no wonder Ava did not want to be part of this life. He did not either.

Tate stood beside Lord Duncannon, his friend as quiet as he, and thankfully not trying to fill the silence between them. He did not wish to speak as it was, not to anyone here at least.

A rumble of chatter sounded and Tate again glanced

toward the door. Hope surged through him as he recognized Miss Evans. His eyes moved past her, searching for another set of dark russet eyes and hair to match and found her missing. He pushed away his disappointment, drinking down the amber liquid and watched as Miss Evans bustled her way over to him, literally repositioning people who stood in her way.

Miss Evans came to stand before him and he spoke before she got a word in. "Where is Ava?" he demanded. The two women were very rarely apart at such gatherings, and so Ava should be here.

"Dear God, I did not think I'd ever see you again." Lord Duncannon gaped at Ava's friend, his face paling.

"Hoped would be a better word I think, Lord Duncannon," Miss Evans retorted, her eyes blazing with fire, but not before a flush stole over her cheeks leaving them a pretty shade of pink. "Or at least it was, in my case." She turned her penetrating gaze toward Tate and he looked between the pair wondering how on earth they knew each other.

He dismissed the thought a moment, needing to know where Ava was. "Is Miss Knight here this evening, Miss Evans?"

"She did not receive an invitation, but I convinced her to come, Your Grace." His attention shifted to his Mother at this declaration and anger spiked through him. This time she'd gone too far.

Miss Evans pursed her lips, inspected him like one inspected a bug and found it wanting. "I'm going to speak plainly and forgive me if I overstep my bounds, but Ava is my friend and I need to say what I must."

Tate nodded, steeling himself for what was undoubtably a set-down to come.

"Your mother sent Ava a note telling her why she

would not be invited tonight and Ava is in no doubt as to what your mother thinks of her. Just now, in fact, she was refused entry, in front of all these people you claim to be your friends. What say you, Your Grace? What will your course be?"

"Where is Ava now?" Lord Duncannon demanded.

"She's returned home in the carriage." Miss Evans kept her attention on Tate even though she had answered his friend's question.

The public slight to Ava was unacceptable. Tate would not allow his mother anywhere near him or the ducal property again after this atrocious behavior. He shouldn't even be here for that matter. And he should've acted earlier on his emotions that drove him regarding Ava. He should have returned to her home, on bended knees, begging forgiveness, asking her to love him as much as he loved her. Tell her that he'd never wished to box her in, demand of her more than she was willing to give. Tell her that he loved her more than any title.

"Fuck," he cursed, not heeding those about him.

He started toward the ballroom door, leaving Duncannon and Miss Evans to follow close on his heels.

Duncannon caught up to him. "Where are you going?"

"To get my duchess," he said aloud, not caring who heard him. Gasps sounded about him, and he schooled his temper as his mother stepped in front of him, stalling his escape.

"Move out of the way, mother."

The room stilled, dancers halted and conversation stopped. Even the orchestra ceased to play. "There is about to be a waltz, Tate dear. Would you dance with Lady Clapham?" His mother gestured toward her ladyship who curtsied and smiled knowingly at him, her eyes twinkling with mirth.

"Your Grace, I would be honored," Lady Clapham said, ignoring the fact he was leaving.

"I will not," he said, causing more gasps and barely audible whispers.

His mother laughed a nervous edge to it. Good, he hoped she was uneasy. He'd certainly given up all hope of his last remaining parent supporting the woman he loved and wanted to marry. His mother would pay for being blinded by her hate and exclusivity.

"The ball has only just begun and as Lady Clapham is my guest of honor, you must dance with her. It's only right."

"You disinvited and refused entry to Miss Knight. Are you so full of hate that you cannot remember that you too were common born, rich yes, but the same as Ava. The duchess' coronet is all that separates you from her. You should not have airs when none are justified."

His mother narrowed her eyes, raising her chin. "She is not for you, Son. Do not make the mistake that would bring our family scandal and to its knees. She's a lowly horse farmer. Please, be sensible."

"Ava is more than that and you damn well know it." He stepped past her, Duncannon and Miss Evans following close behind. Striding through the front hall, he didn't wait for a footman and opened the door himself, calling for a carriage.

"Are you going to Miss Knight's estate?" Duncannon asked as a carriage came about the house.

Tate stilled as an acrid stench wafted across his senses. "Can you smell that?" He walked further onto the drive, looking out over the land now kissed by night.

"There is a fire somewhere." Miss Evans came up beside him as the carriage pulled up before the front doors. "It's nearby, or we wouldn't smell it."

"Come," he said to both of them, heading toward the carriage and giving directions to Miss Knight's home.

The closer they came to Ava's estate, the heavier the smell of burning wood permeated the air and as they came over the small rise where Ava's home came into view, the horrifying sight of her stables along with her home in full flame was revealed.

Through the haze of smoke, he could hear yelling and the sounds of horses' hooves as they were released from the stables. Some frightened horses bolted past them and Tate yelled out to the driver to go.

"I should never have let her leave the ball. I should have made her come with me."

"This is not your fault, Miss Evans," Duncannon said, his voice surprisingly soothing in a situation that was anything but calm.

Tate's throat closed in panic and he fought to breathe. Where is she? Madness was all about them and until he saw her with his own eyes, held her close, he would not rest.

The closer they came to the fire the thicker the smoke, and by the time they pulled up a little distance away from the main house, Tate could see one whole side of the home was alight.

Servants ran in and out of the house, grabbing as much of Ava's ancestral belongings as they could. Tate bolted from the carriage. He scanned each and every one of them and not seeing Ava he looked up at the house, praying she wasn't inside.

He threw off his evening jacket and clasped the butler by his arm as he was about to dash back inside. "Where is Ava?" he shouted over the noise of the fire and those yelling orders about them.

"We cannot find her, Your Grace. She returned from

the duchess' ball an hour ago, at the time that the fire commenced. She went to her room, but when we checked there we could not find her."

Tate searched the faces running about praying one of them was Ava. Miss Evans and Duncannon caught up to him, their breathing as ragged as his own.

"What can we do, Tate?" his friend asked.

Tate fought not to panic. He looked about again, praying, hoping that he would spy her. He looked back up at the house, half of which was well alight. Was she inside? If she were, he'd not rest until she was safe. She'd risked her life to help him escape his stable fire and he would not leave her alone in this.

"Search the grounds, the stables, maybe Ava is there. Come back here if you cannot find her. I'll check the house."

Duncannon clutched his arm, hard. "You cannot go in there, Tate. You're the last of the Whitstone line. If you die, the title reverts to the crown. Let us search the stable first, you have a look about the perimeter of the house, maybe Ava is fighting the fire with the men on the opposite side."

"I will check there first, but if I cannot find her, I will be going inside. Be damned the title." Ava meant more to him than what he had inherited. His title did not define who he was, it was his character which did that, and he would not be a man who left a woman, his woman to burn to death.

Lord Duncannon nodded, seemingly resigning himself to Tate's decree. "Very well." He paused for a moment. "Miss Evans, come, we'll check the stables."

She left without a word and taking another look at those about him and still not seeing Ava, Tate ran around the side of the house. Still, Ava was nowhere to be seen, and panic started to rise up in his blood.

Please be safe, my darling. Don't be in the house.

The doors to the kitchens were open, and Tate ran for them, moving out of the way as servant after servant came out carrying whatever they could save.

Tate ran past them all, up a smoke-filled corridor to stumble into the front hall of the home. Doors to the burning wing were closed, but smoke filled the space. He coughed, untying his cravat and tying it about his mouth and nose to help him breathe.

Taking the stairs two at a time, he called out for Ava, and yet only the crackling, the moaning of a house that would be ash by morning sounded in the night.

⚜

AVA STOOD inside the door to her room, watching as Lord Oakes paced her bedchamber floor, seemingly oblivious to the raging fire that was devastating her home.

Her *home*, the place she had been born, the house her parents had built through years of hard work was crumbling about her and there was little she or anyone could do. She blinked as the smoke thickened, clogged her lungs and stung her eyes. Her eyes flicked to the window, her only escape, but she was a floor up and a fall from this height would break her neck. She edged toward it, willing to take the risk.

"Don't even think about it." Lord Oakes stepped in front of her, his features contorted into raw hate.

"Why are you doing this?" He leaned toward her leaving little space between them. "What are you getting out of such deeds?" she asked, coughing with the effort to speak.

"I left the best for last," he seethed. "You were supposed to be my mistress, the woman who warmed my bed, and yet you spread your legs for that bastard Whitstone."

She gaped at him. The man was mad! "You were jealous! That's why you started the fires about our county." Ava could not believe what he was saying. Surely he was not so obsessed with her that he would act out in such a way. Her neighbors were innocent people, they did not deserve this.

"None of them were innocent," he said, gesturing toward the outdoors. "Whitstone had your heart, always has had, and those blasted Mortons, his wife supported and comforted you over Whitstone. I could not allow such deeds to go unpunished."

Ava shook her head. "I will never warm your bed, Lord Oakes. You have proven yourself to be the worst of men, not just this night, but from the day you tried to force yourself upon me in this very house." She tried to think of Tate, of how he warmed her blood, comforted and protected her. Not to freeze in panic over the thought of what Lord Oakes was doing with her in this room. What his ultimate goal was for this night.

He stabbed a finger at her chest. Ava raised her chin, refusing to wince at the pain it caused. "Before this night, I shall sample your flesh, and I will enjoy every second of it. My desire to have you blinded me and it was because of you that my betrothed broke our understanding. She sensed I was not committed, so you see," he said, running a hand over her bodice. "I lost the bride that would fill my coffers all because of you. But alas, I have a plan."

Ava schooled her features as panic licked at her skin, willing her to flee, to run, even into the flames on the other side of the door simply to get away from him. She swallowed her throat dry and sore from the smoke, and tears pricked her eyes.

The image of Tate flittered through her mind that she would not see him again if Lord Oakes had his way and a cavernous chasm opened in her chest. She'd been a selfish fool. A silly, little idiot who could not see the wonderful gift that Tate offered when he laid it at her feet.

His love.

And she loved him, everything else would fit in and around that love and they would make their difficult, busy lives merge. If she made it out of here alive, that was.

"Your obsession has killed people, you should hang for your crimes."

He shrugged. "The lad was a lowly servant. They're expendable and I care not at all what happens to anyone that gets in my way, or your precious horses."

Rage tore through her at the mention of her horses and Ava set upon him. They fell to the ground and she scratched at his face, anything to hurt him. "You better not have touched my horses," she yelled, hating him with every fiber of her being.

He wrestled to clutch her arms and she punched him, trying to hurt him as much as she could so to escape. Lord Oakes reached up and clasped her hair, pulling it hard. Ava came down on her side, pain ricocheting through her head as he pinned her to the floor.

"Bitch," he seethed at her ear, his spirit-heavy breath turning her stomach. "Shall I have you now, Miss Knight? We're both going to die, a good fuck before we do is just what I need."

Fear held her immobile for a moment, before fight took hold and she lifted her leg as much as she could, trying to hit him between the legs where men are especially sensitive to pain.

He sensed her thoughts and pinned her legs with his own. "You're going to hang for this, you bastard."

He chuckled. "I have nothing left, so what does it matter if they stretch my neck, but my darling, Ava." He leaned down, kissing her hard. His teeth knocked her lips and her mouth filled with a metallic taste. Ava leaned into the kiss and bit his bottom lip, hard.

He squealed and wrenched back, but she refused to let go before his hands came about her neck, squeezing the breath from her lungs.

Lord Oakes stood, clasping his mouth. Ava fought for breath, watching him from the floor as her mind raced to save herself. A loud crash sounded somewhere in the house and the smoke thickened, the room choking them both of life.

He walked around her and she sat up, wiping her mouth of both their blood. "I will fight you until my last breath, you bastard. I will not be your victim."

Lord Oakes rushed her, kicking her hard against her hip. She gasped at the pain of his attack but instead of rolling away, she clasped his legs, pinning them together and halting him from doing it again.

Then she bit him, again.

He swore and a sense of power ran through her blood. Damn bastard burned her home and stables down would he? Hurt her horses. Well, he too would hurt this night. She would not be the only one to come out of this bloody and bruised, if she came out of this at all.

He fell over and Ava took the opportunity to get up and run for the window. She glanced at the door, a red glow flicking beneath the wood. Smoke slithered along the cornice of the wall like a snake and there would be little time left to leave. She had to get out now or she'd die.

Ava reached to unlock the window, hoisting up the

pane. She screamed as he caught her about the stomach, wrenching her back. Instead of landing on the floor, this time she hit the bed and Lord Oakes came down over her, his eyes wild with hate and determination.

Blood dripped on her face from his bloody lip and she pushed at him, scratched at him to no avail. He was too heavy, too resolute.

Her throat closed in panic at the similarities to when he tried to rape her all those months ago. She fought not to panic, to freeze in fear. "Get off, you bastard," she screamed.

He wrenched her gown up and air kissed her thighs. His movements were harried and desperate as he tugged at his front falls.

No. No. No! This could not happen to her, this could not be happening. Her body shook and she brought her knees up, trying to wedge them between him and herself, denying him what he wanted.

The roof gave an awful moan, and dropped, exposing the flames beyond. She was going to die. She was going to die as he raped her.

No.

"You think I don't have time. I cannot think of a better way to die than deep inside your cunny."

"Noooo," she screamed, wrestling him, the thought of such a horror pulling forth the last of her strength. He would not win. He could not win. Life could not be so unfair.

Shock registered on Lord Oakes' face, and a yelp expelled from his mouth before he was dragged from her body and she was free.

Ava shuffled off the bed as Tate slammed his fist into Lord Oakes' face, the crunch of bone and teeth smashing rent the air. An endless drubbing of blows rained down on his lordship, Tate's visage one of deadly ire. She shivered, having never seen him so mad. He would kill him if he continued. Not that she cared about Lord Oakes, but she did not want his death to be a burden on Tate's conscience for the rest of his life. She went up to Tate, clutching his arm as he went to hit Lord Oakes yet again. "Stop before you kill him. Let the authorities mete out the punishment, not you."

His muscles beneath her palm were taut and his breathing ragged. The fire took hold of the curtains and she pulled him toward the window. "We need to go. This room will be full alight any moment."

Lord Oakes mumbled something and then sat up, stumbling toward the door. "I should've shot you both that day in the field. It is the one regret I shall live with for the rest of my life."

Ava looked out the window ignoring the mad man's words. A downpipe ran along the corner of the house. It might hold their weight... "Come, we need to climb down."

Tate stood between Ava and Lord Oakes and didn't move. "You're going to hang for this," he yelled. "That will be something that I will ensure happens to you."

Lord Oakes smirked, wrenching the door open. He stepped out into the burning corridor before running into the flames beyond. Ava stared as his clothes caught alight, his hair aflame, before he disappeared into the smoke and burning house.

"He's dying," she said, not believing what just occurred.

"Let him." Tate strode over to her and wrapped his arm about her waist, helping her to climb out the window. The pipe thankfully held both their weight and Ava climbed down, some of her staff waiting at the bottom, should she fall.

Tate followed her, jumping from the pipe at the last minute just as an almighty crash sounded. Ava stood back from the house as the roof caved in, destroying all that lay beneath it. She swiped at the tears that ran down her cheeks. The house now fully engulfed in flames, there was little anyone could do.

Tate came over to her and held her close. Uncontrollable shivers raked her body and she bundled against him, seeking his warmth and comfort. Tate called for a blanket, and a maid ran to them, giving him one. He wrapped it about her, stroking her back. "I'm sorry I didn't get to you quicker. Are you hurt?"

Her soul was hurt, and she was shaken, but thankfully Tate had arrived in time. "I'll be all right. I'm sad, that is all." She blinked trying to stem her tears, but to no avail. "My home…"

"I know," he said, holding her tighter. "We'll rebuild it."

She looked up at him, wiping her nose with the back of her hand. Not the most ladylike action, but right at this moment she did not care. "I know, but it'll not be the same."

"We'll make it the same, darling." He didn't let her go and nor did she want him to. Not now or ever. With Tate she was safe, loved and respected, he was an honorable man, a good man and her heart swelled with love for him.

"Your Grace," a voice rang out and Tate and Ava turned to see one of the undercover Bow Street runners striding their way.

The growl from Tate sounded beside her. "How did this happen? You were supposed to be watching Lord

Oakes' every move," Tate said, pointing a finger at the man.

The Runner sighed, running a hand through his already rumpled hair. "When Miss Knight left for the ball, we can only surmise that Lord Oakes used the opportunity to steal into her home. Lay in wait until she returned." The Runner turned to Ava, placing his hand over his heart. "We're truly sorry, Miss Knight. Tonight we have failed you."

"We shall discuss this further in a few days' time at my estate, and I suggest you find out where the lapse in observation has occurred. I want to know." Tate pulled her harder against him, his warmth and care serving as a balm. Her eyes drooped as a sudden rush of tiredness swamped her.

The Runner bowed, stepping back. "Of course, Your Grace."

Ava glanced up at Tate, clutching the lapels of his evening wear. "You saved me," she said, her voice wobbling at the admission.

His gaze shot to her, surprise written on his handsome face. "Always." A pained expression crossed his features. "You are everything to me. When I saw what Lord Oakes was attempting, what he may have already done. If the fire had not killed him, I would have. I promise you he will never hurt you again or anyone else for that matter."

"I'm so sorry, Tate," she admitted. Her heart hurt at how foolish she'd been. The time she'd lost by holding on to a life that only ever half fulfilled her. No matter what she'd told herself, there had always been a piece of her missing. Until that piece had stepped back into her life.

Tate.

"I was holding onto my past and couldn't see straight," she continued. "I let what others thought of me, blind me to what I wanted. I let prejudice against me make me believe I was not worthy of you. But not any longer. I can see clearly now. I want a future with you. I want our lives to merge in every way. I want to make us work and let everything else fall about us as it will."

He smiled, pulling her closer. "You're not the only one who has been blinded by their own dreams. Of course, I want you by my side, my wife, my duchess, but I do not expect you to be away from here for months on end and it was selfish of me to think you could be. London is not so very far away, and when Parliament sits, or the Season calls me to town, I do not expect you to leave your responsibilities for such frivolities. Here is what matters the most." He ran his hands over her hair, linking them at her nape. "What I said the last time we spoke I meant. I love you, so very much. I cannot live without you."

Her eyes smarted as his voice cracked at his last words and she stepped up to wrap her arms about his neck, holding him close. "I love you too," she whispered against his ear. He turned his head to look at her and she smiled. Ava closed the space between them and kissed him, heedless of those about them. Tate didn't shy away and ravenously took her mouth, making her forget all the troubles of the night and warming the chill from her blood.

A discreet cough pulled them from each other and they looked to see Hallie and Lord Duncannon standing at their sides, amusement written across their faces. Soot and dirt stained their ballroom clothing, their faces and hands.

Hallie stepped toward them, enclosing them both in a hug. "I'm so relieved you're safe," Hallie said, her eyes overly bright. "We got caught up trying to save the horses. With you not at the stables, we stayed and offered assistance and thankfully no horses have been lost."

"We will have to round them up though in the morning. Most have bolted from the grounds," Lord Duncannon stated.

All of which was understandable from the trauma the animals suffered, all because Lord Oakes had been a madman. A man so blinded with jealousy at not getting what he wanted and so he had acted out, punished those whom he assumed to be at fault in hindering his ends. Ava shook her head. How could anyone be so evil?

"Come, there is little we can do here. We'll travel back to Cleremore and you both will stay with me for the duration of the rebuild of your home and stables."

Ava nodded. There was little she could do here, everything was gone. They would return in the morning and look for the horses, which hopefully had not run too far away. They made their way over to the ducal carriage, and Ava gave her thanks when Tate helped her inside, her legs threatening to give way beneath her.

She glanced out the carriage window and looked at what was left of her home, and despair swamped her. How could Lord Oakes do such a thing? A question she would probably ask herself for many years to come.

"Are you ready?" the duke asked, coming to sit beside her and taking her in his arms, pulling her close to his side.

Ava nodded, not wanting to see any more of the destruction of her home before she was prepared to face it. "I am more than ready."

CHAPTER 17

F*ather has died and I'm on my way home. I have lost everything it seems, you, my father, but at least I have my horses. I suppose that is some comfort in a time when I have none.*

— An Excerpt from a letter from Miss Ava Knight to the Duke of Whitstone

A MONTH LATER, Tate stood outside Ava's ruined home, and watched as the first lumber arrived for the new structure to be built. Last week carts arrived filled with stone, and now the builders were salvaging whatever they could of the old house's building material to use again.

The estate was a flurry of work, and Tate glanced across the yard and watched as Ava discussed things with the man they'd hired to rebuild the home and stables.

A smile lifted his lips. She was so beautiful, capable, and his heart ached at the sight of her. She caught sight of him staring and she gave him a knowing smile. Somehow she'd always know what he was thinking, feeling. Ava Knight was truly his perfect match.

He turned back to the house, shaking his head at the destruction. Lord Oakes had ensured nothing would survive and it had not. Except for the few pieces of furniture and valuables the staff had been able to carry outside before the fire took hold too much.

The local magistrate had declared his death an accident, and knowing that the man had admitted his crimes to Ava before his demise, the authorities were willing to let the case close and be done with it.

Tate was happy for this outcome. After what he'd seen Lord Oakes trying to do to Ava the night of the fire, he would've gutted him on the lawn had he escaped, the bastard deserved nothing less.

Ava sidled up to him, clasping his arm and holding him close. "It's going to be like the fire never happened when we're finished with it. Don't you agree?" she asked, looking up at him.

He tweaked her sweet nose. "With one little difference," he said, smiling, indulging himself with a kiss from her charming lips.

She glanced at his expectantly. "And what would that be?" she asked.

Tate chuckled. "After tomorrow, you'll return here a duchess and my wife." At the words, contentment settled over him, soothing his soul.

Her hand shifted from his arm to wrap about his waist. "Yes, and you will return as my husband."

He wrapped his arms about her and kissed her heedless of the workers about them. And even when whistles and laugher penetrated his brain he did not stop. Would never stop loving the woman in his arms, no matter where or who they were about.

They would be the Duke and Duchess of Whitstone and they made their own rules, made their own decisions and that would never change.

EPILOGUE

Two years and four months later.

A va shouted out from the ducal box at Ascot as Titan flew down the straight, the other horses hard on his heels and yet the stallion showed no signs of slowing down. She stood, yelling out across the swarm of heads before her in the stands, Tate by her side, laughing and yelling with her as their horse crossed the line the winner.

For a moment they stared at each other in amazement, before Ava jumped into his arms, tears smarting and her heart beating loud in her chest. They'd won! They'd won Ascot!

"I don't believe it," Lord Duncannon said beside them. "I've won a fortune."

Ava laughed, not believing it herself. "You must go down, Tate. Collect the cup and ribbon."

He glanced at her, clearly still shocked at what had

occurred. Ava glanced back at the racetrack and smiled as the jockey riding Titan trotted him back toward where they would receive the prize.

Tate kissed her cheek quickly before running down the stairs, heading toward their horse. Many people about them congratulated them and Ava thanked them in turn, wanting to remember every moment of this day for the rest of her life.

During the first two years of their marriage they had worked hard to get both stables back up and running, and thankfully the horses had not suffered too much from the trauma Lord Oakes had caused.

"If only Hallie was here to see this. She would love this so much," she said aloud. Lord Duncannon's smile slipped a little at the mention of her friend and Ava couldn't help but wonder what had happened between the pair. "She would be happy for you. I have no doubt."

Ava glanced to where Tate stood his smile wide, making him look like the most handsome man in the world. He shook the jockey's hand before giving Titan a big pat on his neck.

"Have you heard from her?" Lord Duncannon asked.

Ava's attention snapped back to him, having not expected him to be so forward. "She arrives back in London next week if the ship from Egypt is not delayed."

His lordship did look at her then and Ava didn't miss the unhidden interest in his eyes. She grinned at him, wagging one finger. "One of these days you're going to tell me why you both look sheepish when around each other. Tate and I know you are both not telling us something."

He chuckled and she shook her head. Even Tate did not know what had passed between the pair, but by God, Ava would dearly love to know. When they traveled to

London next week to collect Hallie she would demand to know. Not that Hallie would probably tell her anything. The woman was like a safe that secrets never escaped from.

Ava clapped as Tate took possession of the Gold cup and she smiled down at him as he lifted it toward her. Pride seized her, for them both at their day's success.

"I'm sure you're looking forward to seeing Miss Evans again."

Ava nodded. "Of course," she replied. "There is an artifact they wanted brought back to the British Museum. They surmised that because Hallie had contacts here, that she would be best to travel with the artifact." Ava shook the hands of a trainer who came to congratulate them. "I, for one, cannot wait to see her again. I do hope she stays a little longer this time."

Lord Duncannon nodded, smiling and Ava turned back to follow Tate's progress back to them through the bevy of congratulations and well wishes in the crowd.

"You do realize we'll not hear the end of this win for years to come," she said, laughing when Tate kissed the Gold cup in his hands.

Duncannon chuckled. "I do believe you are right, duchess."

Tate made it back to her and he handed her the cup. Marrying the duke had been the best decision she'd ever made, and even though his mother had never forgiven them and still refused to apologize for her atrocious behavior, the past two years had been the happiest of her life and she couldn't imagine a time any longer when they were not married.

"Congratulations, darling. You should've come down and received the cup with me. This is yours as much as mine."

She looked over the prize, smiling. "I will, next year when one of my horses race and wins."

Tate laughed, kissing her and not caring who saw, an action that he did often. If there was one thing Tate loved to do was scandalize the *ton*. Which, she had to admit, she enjoyed also.

HELLION AT HEART

League of Unweddable Gentlemen, Book 2

Sifting through the sands in the Middle East while learning of ancient cultures and buried civilizations is all Miss Hallie Evans dreams about. But when an impending scandal forces her back to England, her hopes and dreams are destroyed. Now, as a hired archaeologist for the rich, Hallie explores and studies the ancient ruins excavated on their properties.

The Viscount of Duncannon, Arthur Howard, was beguiled after a chance encounter with Miss Hallie Evans several years ago. She left an impression on him that never faded. But when their paths cross again, Arthur is determined to win Hallie's heart this time around--at all costs.

But as Hallie's buried secrets begin to surface, neither can stop society from unearthing the truth. Now, Arthur must choose between love and family duty. Can Hallie cease those who threaten her livelihood for a real chance at true love?

CHAPTER 1

Surrey 1813

Hallie sat at the breakfast table with her papa, reading over the latest articles that had come out of Egypt and the wonderful finds of the ancient land that had been buried for thousands of years.

She sighed, looking out the window at the dreary, wet morning, dreaming of the heat, the sand and culture. Where spices floated in the air and invigorated the soul. Not like her life here in Surrey, where she did little except tend the garden and read in the library.

Her father cleared his throat, gaining her attention. "Hallie dear, there is something that I need to discuss with you. It is of great importance, so please let me finish before you say anything."

Hallie set down her paper, and turned to her papa. "Of course."

Her father, a gentleman, but one with limited land and fortune smiled a little and she frowned, wondering why he appeared so nervous. A light sheen of sweat formed on his forehead, and, picking up his napkin, he dabbed it away.

"My darling girl, this is not easy for me to tell you, and please know that I do this only because I have your best interest at heart."

She sat back in her chair, a hard knot forming in her stomach. "Of course," she managed, although she feared this conversation would be unlike any they had had before. Something was wrong, but what that was she partially didn't wish to know.

"I'm sending you away to a school in France. The Madame Dufour's Refining School for Girls is highly recommended and with your love of history, I think this will be good for you. You're never going to achieve your dreams by only reading the books in my library. All of which are sadly lacking and will be even more so in the months to come."

"You're sending me away? Why, Papa? I do not understand."

He sighed, reaching across the table to take her hand. His touch was warm and yet the idea of leaving Surrey, her papa, left her cold.

"I may have been born a gentleman, the fourth son of a baron, but simply being related to the aristocracy, no matter how distant, does not earn you funds. I have kept the house for as long as I could, but it was of no use and only yesterday I'm happy to say that I have sold it."

Hallie gasped, pulling her hand away. "You sold our home?"

Her father ignored her accusatory tone and nodded. "I did, and with the funds I have purchased myself a small cottage in Felday. It's a two-bedroom cottage that looks out onto the town square and it'll do us nicely I think. All our possessions that we can fit will come with us, the books also, and so I think we can make the cottage our own and be very comfortable there."

She shook her head, not believing what she was hearing. "Papa, our life is here. I was born in this very room. My last memories of Mama are here. Please, reconsider."

Her father pushed back his chair, scraping the feet against the floor. Hallie grimaced as he went to stand at the window, overlooking the hollyhocks and roses outside.

"Do you not think I know this, my dear? Do you not know that it broke my heart to sell our home, but it was either that, walk away with some funds, or walk away with nothing? I chose the former. The sale was profitable, and I have enough to keep me for the rest of my days, and to give you a small dowry along with your schooling in France."

He turned and strode over to her, pulling Hallie to stand. "You must promise me to use your time at school to better yourself. Arm yourself with so much knowledge that nothing and no one can stand in your way. That you will run with your smarts that I know you have and make a life from it. See the world, visit your beloved Egypt you're always reading about," he said, looking down at her article, "and live a full and happy life. Just as I and your mama always hoped for. You are always welcome at the cottage when you're home."

Hallie swallowed the lump in her throat, having never heard her father speak in such a way before. "I promise, Papa. I shall make you proud and before I go, together we'll ensure the cottage is just how we like it. Make it our new home away from this one."

Her papa pulled her into a fierce embrace and Hallie wrapped her arms about him, noticing for the first time how fragile and so much older he was than she realized.

She squeezed him harder, wishing life to just halt a moment, to pause and stay as it was.

"I'm glad you said that, my dear. For I have old Farmer McKinnon coming tomorrow with his cart to help us shift. It'll be a busy two days."

Her father walked to the door, heading toward the foyer. Hallie followed him. "Two days. Why two days?" she asked.

He turned, smiling. "Because we have to be out of the house in two days. I suggest you finish breakfast and start packing."

Hallie stared after him, shutting her mouth with a snap. The house was not small, and the idea of packing, picking what they would keep and leave behind left her momentarily stunned. However would they do it with one house maid, a cook and one groomsman who also acted as their butler?

Shaking her head, but never one to shy away from hard work, Hallie called out to Maisie, her maid, for assistance. If they only had two days, then it would only take her two days to complete the relocation of their belongings. She rolled up her sleeves, heading toward the stairs. "I think I'll start with the guest bedroom first and work my way through," she said aloud to herself. Determined to hit her father's deadline and roll with the stones life throws at one's self, dodging accordingly.

CHAPTER 2

1817 New Years Day – Felday

It was the worst way in which to start the New Year. Hallie stood beside her carriage at the church yard gate, hating the fact that she was now an orphan. Even if she was three and twenty, her age did not change the fact that other than her school friends, she was alone in the world.

Snow fell about her, damp and miserable, and she looked up at the sky, wishing to be anywhere but here. Someplace hot so that her bones would no longer ache and her nose wouldn't feel like it was going to fall off.

The coachman helped her into the vehicle and she called for home. The small cottage that she would now close up and leave behind. Her father had always wanted her to live her life, use her education to explore, learn and enjoy the world that waited for her.

Now she would fulfil his wish and live. Not survive in this cold, wet England.

The journey into Felday was of short duration, and

Hallie stared out the window, thinking of her papa in his final days. By the time he'd passed, he'd been but a shell of his old self. A tumor in her father's kidney the doctor believed, the telltale yellowing skin and eyes of her father a sign that something was not right within his body.

Her only consolation through the ordeal was that he'd been happy. Her father accepted help when help was required, read and talked as they always had during the last few weeks. At times Hallie could even imagine he wasn't riddled with a disease, but those times were fleeting.

The carriage came to a quick halt and she slid off the seat, landing with an *oomph* on the floor. Scrambling to get up, Hallie heard a commotion outside and opened the door, wanting to see what the trouble was about herself.

She jumped out, the snow under foot crunching with each step. Hallie came about the front of the equipage to see a man, or better yet, a gentleman standing and talking to her driver. He was tall, his clothing much better made than her own, his greatcoat was cut to suit his muscular frame, and his legs were long and well-defined from hours on the back of a horse. Clean-shaven, his jaw was cutting, his lips full. A breath expelled at the sight of him. Heavens, Felday didn't sport men such as he. Hallie pulled her cloak about her, lest he see her own unfashionable clothes that had seen better years—her mourning gown that had been handed down from her mother.

"Oh, miss. I must impose on you to use your vehicle if you would not mind. Share it with you I should add. My friends, you see, have played a trick on me and have stolen my horse and I'm stuck out in the middle of nowhere not knowing which way to go."

Hallie stared at the Adonis as her mind scrambled to form a reply. He wore a fur cap and a large woollen scarf about his neck, but still she spied the hint of blond hair beneath. His eyes were wide and clear, a lovely dark shade of blue, his straight nose hinted at his breeding, not to mention his lips... They were full, fuller than perhaps her own, and for a moment Hallie thought she was looking at an angel sent to make her feel better on this sad day.

"Miss?" he queried again. "Do you think you could take me to the nearest town?" He hugged himself and she became aware of the chilling wind.

"Miss Evans, we dinna know who this man is. He could be a cutthroat, a highwayman." Her coachman pointed back toward Felday. "Walk in that direction and in an hour or so you'll make Felday."

"It'll be dark in half an hour," the gentleman said, turning back to Hallie. "Please, Miss Evans, if that is your name. Please may I hitch a ride?"

Hallie sighed. "What is your name, sir?"

He lifted his chin, bowing a little. "Arthur Howard at your service."

She lifted her brow, shaking her head a little. "Well, not really, it is I who's at your service, is it not?"

The Mr. Howard grinned and Hallie's stomach did a little absurd flip at the gesture. She adjusted her shawl, walking back to open the carriage door. "Back to Felday, John, and we'll drop Mr. Howard at the inn. I'm sure he can hire a horse from there on the morrow."

Hallie settled back on the squabs and pulled the carriage blanket to rest over her legs. Mr. Howard jumped in after her, shutting the door on the chill afternoon.

"Thank you again, Miss Evans for picking me up. I did have a horse, you understand, but I also have friends who think it quite a lark that they would leave with my said stead."

She studied him a moment, his articulation quite proper and correct. "Are you staying nearby?"

"I was staying at the Felday Manor and was returning to London with a group of friends when I stopped... Ah, I stopped for a moment and went into the woods and it was when I returned to the road that I found my horse and my friends gone."

Hallie shook her head at such absurdness. The man was not dressed to be left outdoors overnight and with the snow coming down quite heavily, he would've been dead by morning had he not reached Felday by foot.

"You are mistaken, Mr. Howard, for no friends would do such a thing, certainly not at this time of year."

He nodded, seemingly taking her point, before he sat back, crossing his arms over his chest in an effort to keep warm. "What brings you out on such a cold day, Miss Evans?" He smiled after his question and she pitied him her answer. Soon he would look at her with sorrow and sympathy like everyone else did in Felday village.

"I buried my father today, I'm returning home from the church."

His mouth popped open and she tore her gaze away from him to look outside. Soon, very soon she would be away from all this cold, this sadness and her life would start.

"Miss Evans, I'm so terribly sorry. Had I known I would never have intruded. You must forgive me. I am beyond regretful that my friends chose such an inappropriate time to play me a fool."

The carriage passed some outlying cottages of the county and Hallie turned back to the man who had turned as white as a ghost. "My father's passing was expected, Mr. Howard and he's out of misery now. Back in the hand of God and I'm happy for that. You need not apologize. On a night such as this, it would've been unchristian of me to have left you on the road."

He reached across and clasped her hand. "Even so, as a man who has also lost both his parents, I understand how hard today must've been for you. I'm wretched that I intruded at such a time."

She shook her head, swiping at a tear that warmed her cheek. "Thank you. That is most kind, but do not trouble yourself. I live in Felday and was returning here in any case."

The carriage rocked to a halt, and Hallie looked out the window. The inn had two horses standing out the front and oddly three carriages were being unloaded. It wasn't usual to see so many people at the inn and Hallie frowned. "Mr. Howard, this is the inn in Felday, you had best go indoors and see if there is a room available. I wish you well," she said, holding out her hand to him. He picked it up and instead of shaking it, lifted it to his lips and kissed it gently.

A shiver stole over her skin and she smiled a little to hide her reaction to his touch.

"Do you have far to go this evening, Miss Evans?"

She pointed out the window across the town green to a little thatched-roof residence. "I live just over there, Mr. Howard. I think I shall find my way home well enough."

He nodded, reaching for the door. "Thank you again and may I wish you very well."

Hallie caught his eyes, drinking in his beauty as he closed the door behind him. When he went out of sight, Hallie sighed her relief. To remain calm in the face of such a handsome man was worthy of a prize. Her father would've thought it such a lark that a handsome stranger would arrive on the day she'd said her goodbyes to him. Even though in truth she'd said her goodbyes to her papa weeks ago.

And soon, very soon she'd say her goodbyes to England

as well. And say hello to the Middle East and all that awaited her there. A life, as her father termed it.

A new start.

Egypt.

❧

Lord Arthur Howard, Viscount Duncannon would murder his friends when he arrived back in London. Not for only taking off with his prized gelding that had cost him more than five hundred pounds, but because their stupidity had forced him into the company of a woman who had just buried her father.

Of all the despicable things for him to do, Arthur did not think he would ever better such an inconsiderate, lowly action if he tried.

He turned and watched the carriage as it pulled out on the small gravel road around the village green until it pulled up before the thatched-roof cottage across the way. The door of the home opened and closed and the carriage moved off. Arthur pushed open the door to the inn, satisfied that Miss Evans had returned home unharmed.

He walked into the front taproom and found a scene of utter chaos. The room was full to the brim with people, and the bartender and his wife looked to be running around as if they weren't sure what to do.

Arthur went up to the bar, calling out to the bartender who stood pouring two beers. "Sir, can I press you for a room? I need one for just one night if you will oblige me and show me where I may go."

The bartender, a tall, muscular-looking gentleman glanced at him and grinned. "Oh aye yes, and everyone else by the looks of it. I'm full up. You'll have to find somewhere else to park ye ass tonight."

"I'm more than willing to sleep in the taproom if there is nowhere else."

"Taproom is full also. I have three carriages and two more wagons out the back. Full of the gentry and their staff who lost their way earlier today. I dinna have room for ya in here. You can sleep in the stables if ye like, but it'll cost ye a shilling."

"Thank you for your generosity," he said, doubting the man would hear the sarcasm in his tone. Arthur went back outdoors. It was now full dark, and he headed over to the stables that were down one side of the building. The chill air made his bones ache, and entering the barn, he sat on a nearby hay pile that was sheltered a little from the wind.

He sat there for a time, rubbing his hands together, but it was no good. He would never get to sleep and not only that, he doubted if he'd survive the night. Who knew Surrey could get so cold? How he would give anything right at this moment to be back in London, in his warm, comfortable home on Berkley square where he could stack his fire until it was roaring and no cold could seep into his bones.

He glanced out the stable doors, and from here he could see Miss Evan's little cottage, the candlelight flickering in the room behind her curtains. He stood, pacing and trying to warm his limbs. His mind whirred at imposing on her again. Arthur mumbled expletives. He could not disturb her for a second time in a matter of hours, especially after the day she had endured. He flexed his fingers, even in his kid-leather gloves, they were stiff and sore. His feet were tingling with lack of blood flow.

"Damn it," he swore. Arthur stood and started toward her residence. It was the most absurd, intrusive action he'd ever taken in his life, but it was either ask for shelter or freeze to death. Some men, strong men, may withstand a night in the stables, in the open without a fire or blanket, but he was not one of them.

He debated his choice all but a moment as he stood outside the green-painted threshold before rapping hard against the wood.

Miss Evans opened it, and now, without her black bonnet, black mourning gown and the large traveling cloak, she was unlike anything he'd ever beheld in his life.

She'd looked like a crow in the carriage before, but now... Now she was nothing of the kind.

He bowed, not sure what to do when one was at a loss for words, and so he fell back into that of a lord, remembering his manners when meeting a lady. "Miss Evans, I am throwing myself at your feet. Please pity me and allow me to stay here this evening. There are no rooms left at the inn, and having been sitting in the stable this past hour, I realize that I will not survive the night if I'm made to stay there."

Her eyes widened and she looked past him toward the inn before her attention snapped back to him. Her eyes, now that he could make out their color better, were a light green with the smallest fleck of blue through them. They were large, almond shaped, and her cheeks were the sweetest shade of pink. As for her hair, it was long and dark and he had the oddest feeling of wanting to see if it was as soft as it looked. Visions of it cascading over her bare shoulders in the throes of passion filled his mind and he cursed his wayward thoughts.

Miss Evans was not one of the many women in London who fell at his feet. She was an independent, honorable woman. His thoughts were dishonorable and not helpful.

At her continued silence, he said, "Please, Miss Evans. I will pay you handsomely if you will allow it."

His words caught her attention and she stepped back, allowing him to enter. "Very well, you may sleep before the fire, Mr. Howard."

Arthur headed straight for the fire, standing with his back to it and promising himself to kill his friends when he saw them again. "Thank you so very much. I shall pay you whatever you want, just name your price."

She raised her brow. "Any price, Mr. Howard? Are you a rich man?"

She came and sat on the settee before the fire and he chuckled. He was a wealthy gentleman, a viscount no less, and one with multiple estates and lands both in the country and London. She could name any price she chose and he'd pay it. Anything was better than freezing to death outside. For one, his grandmother would be very disappointed indeed should he die in Surrey before marrying one of the many heiresses of her choosing. A Duncannon married for wealth and connections. To freeze to death without fulfilling the family duty would be a catastrophe.

"Whatever you want, Miss Evans. The choice is yours."

She sat back on the lounge, and he looked down to see that she only had a pair of socks on her feet. The scene was awfully intimate, something a husband and wife may do late at night when all their staff were abed. She lifted her legs and placed them under her bottom and his lips twitched.

Arthur looked down at himself, his knee-high boots made by the best cobbler in London. His buckskin breeches and kid-leather gloves along with his riding jacket that was worth more than he would assume this small cottage cost. Not to mention his great coat and fur cap. He looked about, seeing a lot of books, but little else. The lounge Miss Evans sat upon was threadbare and worn, and the distinct smell of animal fat told him she did not use tallow candles.

"You have a lot of books here," he stated, matter-of-fact.

She glanced about. "Yes, they were my father's. We used to live in Felday House three miles from town. My father fell on hard times, and we were forced to move."

He frowned, not liking that so much pain and suffering had befallen the generous—and if he were not mistaken—intelligent woman before him. "I'm sorry, Miss Evans. That must have been a terrible blow to your family." He removed his gloves and slipped them into his pocket. "Another faux pas it would seem on my behalf since I was at Felday House just today. For what it is worth, the home was beautiful."

She shrugged. "It's been four years since I moved here, and I've been away at school most of that time. Soon I shall be going away again, closing up the cottage and starting my new life abroad."

"You are leaving?" Arthur pushed aside the odd twinge of regret he felt at hearing such news. Why would he be feeling such an emotion? It wasn't as if he knew her enough to be impacted by such information, and after today they would likely never meet again. And yet, the thought that he would never see her again made him melancholy. A state of being that he was not used to.

"I am. I've been offered a position as an assistant to Mr. Shelly, an Egyptologist from Cambridge University. He's traveling there to study the culture, the history and historical sites of course. I'm going to help him with those endeavours."

Arthur wasn't sure how to answer such a statement. To meet a woman who was going to embark on such a journey... Well it simply wasn't something that was done by the fairer sex. How splendid and intimidating at the same time.

"How extraordinary of you." He marvelled at her. "Are you not frightened? I would not think Egypt would be the easiest country to live, nor the coolest."

She laughed and her features lit up with the action. Not for the life of him could Arthur take his gaze from her pretty face and sweet nature. It was not every day one found someone on the road who would take a stranger into their home. Who was both beautiful and smart. Something told him the woman before him could hold an intelligent conversation that did not incorporate only discussions on current scandals or fashion.

"I should imagine not," she said. "But I think I shall like the warm. I'm so very sick of the cold." She shut her eyes, holding her face against the ceiling as if she already could feel the warmth of the sun on her skin. "I leave tomorrow for London to catch a ship the following day, so I had better like it, mustn't I?"

Arthur laughed. "I suppose you must." Warm now, he sat, but instead of sitting on the lone, leather-back chair to his left, he went and sat next to Miss Evans.

"May I know your given name, Miss Evans? You may call me Arthur if you please."

She turned and her inspection of him caused his blood to pump faster in his veins. How very odd. He'd never been so discombobulated with a woman before, and perhaps it was simply because the woman next to him was clever and soon to be more worldly than he as well.

"You may call me Hallie. Since you're staying here, I suppose it'll be all right." She leaned back on the settee and Arthur studied the fire.

"Have you thought about what you would like from me

in payment for letting me stay here? I meant what I said when I said you may have whatever your heart desires."

Hallie pursed her lips and he swallowed. Damn it, he really needed to gain some manners. Next he'd be spouting love poetry at her feet if only she'd bestow him a kiss with her pretty mouth. He studied her profile a moment, his body tensing at the sight of her biting her plump bottom lip.

Bloody hell. He cringed. What a cad he was. A typical London rogue with no consideration for others.

"I do require some funds for my trip. I have very little, you see. Father did not leave very much, and although the cottage will be let while I'm away, I will not have access to those funds while in Egypt." She looked him over, and heat licked up his spine. "So for helping you today on the road, and this evening, I should like fifty pounds, if you will."

Fifty pounds… Well, she did play a hard bargain, but one he was willing to concede to. He nodded, but he in no way planned on leaving her such a small amount. The woman beside him deserved a whole lot more than that, and he would give her double before he walked away on the morrow.

"Consider it yours."

Her eyes brightened with pleasure. "Thank you, you're most kind. I had worried how I would pay for things while away. The position with Mr. Shelly pays very little, and your money will stop me from having to sell some household goods and valuables that I have here." She stood, folding a small rug she had draped over her legs and placing it on the settee. "I do not have a lot left from Papa you see, so I was sad to have to sell things to do what I know he wanted me to do in my life. How favourable that your friends would play such a trick on you after all. How opportune for me."

Arthur stood, sensing she was going to leave him alone. "The honor has been mine meeting you, Miss Evans...I mean, Hallie."

She smiled and once again the vision of her threw him off balance. How was a simple gesture leaving him floundering? "I will see you in the morning, Mr. Howard."

"Arthur, please," he said, wanting to hear his name one more time on her lips.

"Arthur..." she repeated, turning away.

Panic seized him that their time together was coming to an end. He reached out, stalling her. "Before you go, may we have a toast, in honor of your father?"

She seemed to think about it a moment, before she nodded. Arthur watched as she walked into her small kitchen just off the room, the sound of a cupboard opening and closing and the clinking of glasses telling him that she had agreed.

He threw her a small smile as she came back in with two glasses of red wine, handing him one. "To my father. A man of wisdom and kindness." She saluted and Arthur did the same.

"To Mr. Evans."

He watched as she sipped the wine, one single droplet sitting on her lip. Without thought, he reached out, wiping it away with his thumb. Her gaze tore to him, her eyes wide and shocked. He expected to see reproach in her vibrant green gaze, but he did not. If anything, her gaze dipped to his lips and the hairs on the back of his neck rose.

Hell, she was a beauty. A hidden treasure out in the middle of nowhere.

Having had his fair share of women, he could read the signs of need as well as anyone, and his body stirred at the need emanating from her. Arthur leaned forward, clasping her face. He stopped, but a whisper from her lips. Their breath mingled, the scent of her, warm and sweet, intoxicated his soul. Never had he ever met someone so unique. A woman so unlike those he was expected to marry. She was intoxicating.

"I'm going to kiss you, Hallie," he said, brushing his lips just the slightest against hers. As he expected, they were soft, pliant beneath his own.

What he did not expect, however, was for Hallie to kiss him back. No maidenly kiss, but a deep and thorough exploration of his mouth. The axis on which his world spun, tilted, sped up and whirled into unknown territory.

And he was lost with her in the middle of nowhere and happily so.

CHAPTER 3

London season 1824

Hallie stood beside her closest friends in all the world at the Duke and Duchess of Whitstone's opening ball for the 1824 London season. Everyone who was anyone had accepted the invitation to the duke's London home, which was rarely opened these days due to the fact the duke and duchess ran a successful horse racing estate. Such a large enterprise kept them busy most of the year.

But, as with people of such high rank, there was at times a duty to the peerage and His Grace had responsibilities at the House of Lords.

"So many people here. I'm sure we'll not all fit in this room if people keep arriving like they are."

Hallie absently nodded at her friend, Willow's observation, thinking she may be right. The duke and duchess had planned well however, and there were other options for their guests. A large supper room had been opened all evening, along with a card room that Hallie could see from where she stood was full of gentleman gamblers already.

The four terrace doors were ajar, allowing a little of the outdoors to venture inside. The night was mild and a stroll or conversation outside would not be uncomfortable. To be in England and a society that she had never circulated within before was odd. Hallie watched the *ton* at play, her mind always divided these days. Part of her life meant she had to take part in this world. Be seen due to her friendship with Ava, the Duchess of Whitstone. But her heart also remained with her son, who right at this time would be sound asleep if her cousin, who was bringing him up, had stuck to Hallie's routine.

Hallie checked her gown, thankful her friend Ava had loaned her a dress suitable for the evening. She had very little, other than an education and a cottage in Felday, which she could not return to at present since it was being leased. But one day she would return home with her son. The thought of her upcoming dig in Somerset would help in achieving that goal, and if she could secure more work that was similar, her financial independence would be secure.

A footman passed with a tray of champagne and she procured one, needing fortitude to face the evening, or at least one person who would be here that she'd not seen in three years, not since the night of the fire at Ava's estate.

Lord Duncannon. The very man that had used her home and then before she was even out of bed the next day, up and left without a word. He was a rake, and a charlatan, both charges she could lay at his door. That the Duke of Whitstone was best friends with the gentleman made little sense, and she had more than once asked Ava how it could be that her lovely, charming husband could be friends with such an ass.

Hallie shook her head, shamed over her actions that night in Felday. What she had done was so out of character it made one think she'd lost her mind. Quite possibly so, considering what she did.

"Oh, look, Ava and His Grace are opening the ball with a waltz. How lovely," Evie said, watching them with both adoration and longing.

A gentleman came up to Evie, another of their school friends who had been sent to France and asked her to dance. Hallie smiled, glad her friend was enjoying herself. Even if she only danced once this evening, it would be enough for Evie and make the ball one to remember in her opinion.

"Stop squeezing your champagne glass, Hallie. You'll break the crystal stem off."

Hallie relaxed her fingers around her glass, unaware she'd been holding it so tight. "Sorry, I'm tired is all. The voyage from Egypt was long and I do not believe I've yet acclimatized to the cooler weather. Nor have I slept very well since I have to have so many heavy blankets on me just to stop myself from freezing."

"Or," Willow said, inspecting her as if she were inspecting a new pair of kid leather gloves. "You're nervous."

Hallie frowned, turning back to watch the dancers and ignoring her friend. Had she somehow found out about her and her child? Not one of her friends knew of her disgrace and nor would they ever, not if she could manage it. Her son was happy and living with her cousin in Berkshire and he would be raised without the besmirch of bastard clouding his name if she could help it.

"What do I have to be nervous about? I'm about to start my own excavation in Somerset. I will be away from the dreadful *ton* and will have no one but myself to contend with for the next three months. I am the happiest woman here, I am sure," she lied, preferring to be with her little boy, but she could not. She had to earn money to ensure he was safe. Nothing else mattered.

"So if I were to tell you that Lord Duncannon was staring at you from across the ballroom floor, you would not react?"

Her legs went weak at the idea of him watching her. As best she could, she glanced at her friend, feigning indifference. "Tell me it isn't so." She did not want to see him and certainly she did not want to speak to him. Mr. Arthur Howard indeed. He had fooled her all those years ago, but he would not fool her again. It had been bad enough upon her arrival in London that she'd learned he was the newly appointed benefactor to the London Museum, the location that she was to deliver Mr. Shelly's latest finds from Egypt. It was the last of her duties with the Egyptologist, who had declared this to be his final dig in Egypt and so her employment under the gentleman had come to an end.

Thankfully the day she had delivered the artifacts, Lord Duncannon had been absent and she'd not been unfortunate enough to have to engage with him.

"He is, and he's been staring at you for the past five minutes." Willow threw her a curious glance. "Whatever happened between the two of you? He seems fond of you, but you're very cold and distant. It makes no sense. A marriage to such a great man would enable you to do whatever you pleased for the remainder of your life."

"Except it would not," Hallie retorted hotly. The Duncannons were renowned to marry well. Ava had mentioned it when she'd first returned from Egypt that the Duncannons placed wealth and position above all else. She was a mother to a young boy, an illegitimate one at that. She doubted Lord Duncannon would be so very favorable to her should he know her secret. "I'm too low on the social sphere to be anything but a plaything for his lordship." As she'd already found out. "Nor do I wish to become anyone's brood mare or hostess."

"Not necessarily. Take Ava for instance, she is still a successful businesswoman. Marrying the duke has not stopped her from running her racing estate."

"The duke is an exception to the rule." There were few men within this society who would allow such freedom for their wives. Ava had been lucky in her choice. Hallie would be lucky in her own way. She had her boy, and he was her future. She did not need a husband so long as she was able to continue to work and source an income.

Willow reached out, touching her arm. "I hope you do not wallow away from life simply because you've loved and lost, Hallie. I know you loved Omar but he's gone now, and there is a possibility that you'll find that kind of love again. Please do not keep running away to archaeological digs so you do not have to have a life. We want you to be happy. To marry and be loved."

Hallie sighed. How to tell your friends that that is not what she wanted. Not really. She would be perfectly content if she did not marry at all, so long as she could keep up her work and make her son happy and safe. England was littered with historical sites, Roman one's mostly, and they were just waiting to be explored. Having a husband would only intrude on finding them and she doubted there would be many men who would want an illegitimate child about their coattails. That is why she'd taken an advance to dig up an old Roman fort that was supposably located at Baron Bankes Estate near Dinnington Somerset.

It was the next best thing to being in Egypt and Roman sites often turned up coins, pottery, tiles and even weaponry. Plenty of interesting things to catalogue and hand over to the British museum once the dig was completed.

"If I could find a husband who would be content to travel, spend all day digging up dirt and had an open mind I would be well pleased. But you know as well as I that isn't a possibility. All the gentleman here are too busy with their many estates. I grant you there may be a few who would enjoy a little adventure, but they would soon tire of it."

"Lord Duncannon does not seem to have ever tired of you. He speaks of you all the time, so Ava has said. She did not push him on the subject of his interest of course, but it was definitely marked. You may have an admirer there."

Nerves fluttered in her stomach at the idea that his lordship had spoken about her to her friend. When they had been thrown together three years before during the fire at Ava's estate, she had just about swallowed her tongue in shock at seeing him again. After the night he spent at her cottage in Felday she had assumed never to see the gentleman again.

She had been so angry with him, had not been able to put their past behind them and move on as friends. During the time they were thrown together just prior to Ava and the duke's wedding, she'd barely spoken two words to him. He deserved less than that as it was.

So many things had changed since the night they first met.

She had met and fallen in love with Omar, had borne his child. When she'd found out that he had died it was only a few weeks later that she'd come to realize she was with child. Luckily by then, the professor was wrapping up his expedition and they were soon to return home. Hallie had traveled with them as far as France and then she had made her own way home to Berkshire to her cousin's where she'd given birth and kept the notice of her child's birth secret from everyone she knew.

Shame washed through her that she had not married Omar like he'd wanted, regardless of what his family had thought. A mistake she would never be able to repair. She took a sip of her drink to quell the churning in her stomach.

"I do not care for his interest, as he well knows."

"Does he though, Hallie?" Willow asked as she looked out at the dancers before them. "He doesn't seem to."

Hallie wasn't sure if he knew exactly, but she'd certainly not shown interest in his lordship the last time they saw each other. An overwhelming urge to stomp her foot assailed her. If only he were not friends with the duke. If only she'd left him to freeze on the road in Surrey all those years ago she would not be suffering this introspection from her friend now, or the marked attention from the viscount across the room.

"I will remind him should he ask," she said. "I'm surprised he's not married in any case. Has he been linked to anyone romantically, do you know?" Why she asked she could not say, only that a man as handsome as the viscount was, left one to presume he would've been married off to a diamond of the *ton* years ago. It was certainly his family way of doing things after all.

Her friend watched her closely. Hallie fought to remain unaffected that one of the most sought-after men in London was staring at her. "Why do I get the feeling that you know his lordship better than you're telling me? Come, Hallie, we're best friends. You can trust me."

She smiled, forcing herself to remain indifferent. "I do not know him well at all, I promise," she said. One night in a cottage together did not give her any more insight than anyone else spending an evening with him in company such as this.

It was silly to imagine otherwise.

ARTHUR STOOD at the opposite side of the room and drank in the vision that was Miss Hallie Evans. Damn, he'd not thought he could miss a woman as much as he'd missed her. Their one night in Surrey had left a permanent imprint in his mind and he would not stop until she was as carefree and sweet to him again, just as she was that cold winter's eve.

The following morning, after his one night in her arms, their farewell should have been bittersweet, with promises of seeing each other again. He'd woken early and had walked to the inn, wanting to order a carriage for both himself and Hallie to London. Hoping to be able to spend some time with her before she left England.

That his rascal friends had been at the inn, looking for him, had forced him into their carriage and taken him back to town without his approval or without him having given Miss Evans the money he promised her, still irked. He'd not run with them since that night, and he knew it was the reason she'd frozen him out whenever their paths crossed since. She'd ignored all his attempts of explanation and apologies.

He'd not heard or seen her again, not until the night that the Dowager Duchess of Whitstone had hosted a ball. Whitstone had been furious Ava had been excluded from the ball, and he remembered glancing up to see the one woman he'd thought forever lost to him, storming toward them like a warrior.

His legs had threatened to give out at the sight of her

and it took some time before he could mumble anything coherent. Not that she'd wanted to hear a word from him, unless it was in response to her friend who had been treated unfairly by the duke's mother and as it happened, was in need of their help.

Arthur started toward her now, moving through the crush of bodies, all the while keeping a visual on her. *Hallie.* Even her name made his heart race. Tonight he would explain to her what happened, why he'd left and not returned. She had not wanted to hear anything from him when he'd seen her last, three years ago now, but no longer would he allow her to think the worst of him. She would know the truth and then she could decide if she wanted to continue to ignore his presence or at least be on congenial terms.

He bowed before her and smiled as her friend wished him good evening before she excused herself.

"Miss Evans, how lovely to see you here this evening. I did not know you would be in attendance."

She raised her brow, staring at him with a dismissing air. A little of his hope dissipated at her cold welcome. "I believe you knew I was back in London, Lord Duncannon. Of course I would attend my friend's ball."

He came to stand beside her and the scent of jasmine wafted from her skin and just like that he was transported back to Surrey and her little cottage. Did she still taste as sweet as the flower? He fisted his hands at his sides, knowing to think of her in such a way would not help his cause to make amends. To be friends at the very least.

"I hoped you would be here. I've wanted to speak to you for some time."

"Really? Do speak then, Mr. Howard...oh, please do excuse my mistake, Lord Duncannon," she amended.

He glanced at her, supposing he deserved that. Arthur

noted the lovely golden hue to her skin, the light sheen of freckles across her nose that was not there when they had first met. She was a well-traveled, independent woman now, more so than when they'd first met. He marvelled at her ability to put him to shame. He'd done very little in the few years they had been apart, except try to escape the many marriage proposals his grandmother hounded him to make to women she thought appropriate. He could only imagine what life the woman before him had experienced abroad. Sadly, he had not traveled past the Scottish border, while she had seen part of the world people only ever dreamed about.

"I wanted to explain why I disappeared that morning in Surrey. It has been playing on my mind these many years."

She waved his concerns away, but refused to look at him. "That was a long time ago, my lord. Best I think that we leave it in the past where it belongs."

"Please let me explain, Miss Evans. I do want us to be friends since we share mutual ones and there will be many occasions that we shall be thrown together." All true of course, but it was not the only reason why he wanted her to like him. He enjoyed her, more than anyone he'd ever met before and he hated that she thought the worst of him, not when in truth, his leaving had not been his fault.

She did look at him then and the slight slumping of her shoulders told him she had succumbed to his plea. "Very well, tell me what happened to you that morning."

Relief poured through him that he had the opportunity to tell her the truth. "I went to the inn to order a carriage for London. I had every intention of returning to you, but my friends, the very ones that had left me on the road the night before had arrived and were looking for me. They bundled me into the carriage before I could explain and refused to stop until we reached London.

"I do not need to go into detail of how very in their cups they all were, but needless to say, upon arriving back in town I tried to track you down at the docks knowing you were heading there. I watched the Ariande push off from its moorings. I was late and I missed saying goodbye."

She watched him a moment and some of the fire burning in her eyes dimmed a little at his explanation. "Thank you for telling me, my lord. I'm pleased to hear you're not so fickle and rude as I had assumed."

"I am not, Miss Evans." He willed her to believe him. "I often thought of you. What you were doing and how you were acclimatizing to the warmer country. Her Grace said that you're home now having finished working for Mr. Shelly. Do you have any plans for your future?"

A small smile played about her lips, lips he'd dreamed about kissing again for years now. No matter how many women he'd taken to his bed, he wasn't fool enough not to notice that all of them were of similar coloring to Miss Evans. All had the same almond-shaped eyes, and pouty, full lips.

Not that it ever helped as none of them had her mind. None of them were her.

Hallie.

How could one night be so altering to one's life? It made no sense. He'd fought to move on from his little infatuation, but he'd failed at every turn. His grandmother despaired that he'd never marry, but he could not help but feel that Miss Evans was the other half to his soul. The one whom he should throw all family duty aside for and marry.

If only she would toss him a little crumb, a little bit of hope that she didn't loathe and distrust him as much as he feared.

"I'm going to be doing an excavation in Somerset. I leave tomorrow in fact. Baron Bankes is the gentleman who's hired me and I must admit I'm a little unsure of who he is, although the Duke of Whitstone has vouched for his character so I'm sure it'll be safe."

"I'm sure it will be," he said, knowing the baron well. "I find it fascinating that you had a dream, you worked hard and set out to achieve it. Not many women do what you've done, Miss Evans. You ought to write a book on it. I'm sure it would be very beneficial to young women who wish to follow in your footsteps."

She chuckled and the breath in his lungs seized having drawn one from her. "No, I shall continue to do what I love, for as long as I can and be content with that. But I suppose I'm fortunate to have had a father who allowed me to first educate myself and then travel abroad. Mr. Shelly was also liberally minded, so that helped as well."

Arthur smiled, warmth in his veins at her thawing toward him. "I should imagine so."

The musicians held up their instruments, the sounds of a minuet on their strings. Arthur held out his arm. "Will you do me the honor, Miss Evans?"

She stared at his arm a moment and he wasn't at all certain she would agree to his request. Relief poured through him when she placed her hand atop his arm. "Of course, thank you, my lord."

He led her out onto the floor as the music started. They took their places in the dance, others lining up beside them. At least this was a start, a new beginning to a history that had plagued him for years. He hated the fact she thought ill of him, especially when it was his friends who had played him that morning and severed his contact with Miss Evans before he'd made good on his promise and said his goodbyes.

Hallie, as he'd always think of her, was the one woman who had gotten away. She would not escape so easily a third time. He promised himself that.

MR. ROBERT STEWART stood at the side of the ballroom and watched as Miss Hallie Evans circulated about the room with her friends, one of whom was the Duchess of Whitstone. The bitch who had killed his cousin some years ago.

The duchess was almost impossible to get near these days, but her friend and the other woman who had been part of that tragic event were a lot easier to circulate near. If he could not gain his revenge on the duchess, he would hurt her friend Miss Evans just as the duchess had killed his cousin. He would be content with something similar.

Already tonight Miss Evans had walked past him numerous times. So close in fact that he had been able to reach out and touch her gown. She had not noticed of course, he was particularly good at being unnoticeable. Even so, having Lord Oakes as his cousin enabled him to circulate within this sphere, even after all that his cousin had done to so many people of rank.

The *ton* were fools. The lot of them he doubted could form one intelligent person between them. Apart from Miss Evans, who he understood to be a very clever, well-educated woman.

But not clever enough for her to hide all that she was.

A mother…

Not only that, but a mother to a bastard child of mixed race.

He took a sip of wine, watching her over the rim of his glass. The man whom she'd borne the child to was long dead, but his family was one of influence and power in Egypt, Cairo to be precise and he knew they would pay quite handsomely if they knew their eldest son had fathered a boy child.

In or out of wedlock.

His only question was, what was Miss Hallie Evans willing to pay to ensure he kept his mouth shut? He smirked at the thought of all the things he could make her do. Oh yes, this season would be pleasurable indeed.

For him at least.

CHAPTER 4

Hallie looked about the room that she had been allocated. She had asked the maid who had directed her to the guest wing if maybe they had made a mistake. That she was certain being at the estate under the employment of Baron Bankes would mean he would wish her to be housed in the servants' quarters.

The maid had been adamant that wasn't the case, and had deposited her trunk, unpacked it quickly and efficiently and told her that should she require assistance to ring the bellpull and she would come immediately.

"Oh, and before I forget, Miss Evans. Dinner is at seven sharp if you wish to dine downstairs. However, you are welcome to eat in your room if you prefer." The servant bobbed a quick curtsy and was gone.

Hallie glanced about the bedchamber, the large, imposing double bed stood central in the room, and yet it was the only masculine piece of furniture she could see. Everything else was white, the cushions blue and pink, extremely feminine and pretty.

Not at all similar to how Hallie was in life, but she still loved it. It reminded her of her mother's room from Felday House before they lost it.

She had been told upon arrival that the baron was not due to arrive for several days, but from tomorrow she had the help of two stable hands who would do any heavy lifting or digging she may require up at the Roman fort site.

Hallie untied her bonnet, laying it over a nearby chair, before walking to the window and looking out over the grounds. There were several hills that she could make out. From her correspondence with the baron, she knew one of the hills had once housed a Roman fort and there were reports that it too had a Roman family living there at the outpost at that time. The possibility that she may discover footings to old living dwellings, pottery, coins, or military equipment made the blood in her veins pump fast. The funds she would earn would also help in her plan for a secure future with her son.

The little cottage her father left her in Felday would be their home. The village people would believe her story that her husband had died, and her son would be accepted there. Her father had been a well-respected gentleman and she had always helped out at church or for anyone in need. They would support and protect her, she was sure. This position at the Baron's estate was another step toward a life she had to procure for her son. The next few weeks here in Somerset were going to be busy and exciting and she could not wait to get started.

Hallie sat down at the little desk, and picking up a quill and parchment, set out to write a letter to her cousin and son. They would be eager to learn of her safe arrival and all the things she planned to do while here.

THE FOLLOWING day after breaking her fast, Hallie made her way out the servants' exit to where two stable hands— strong, young men of similar age she deduced—were waiting for her near the stable doors.

"Hello, I'm Miss Hallie Evans. It's a pleasure to meet you." She held out a hand and shook both of theirs in turn.

"I'm Greg and this is Bruce. A pleasure to be working with you, Miss Evans."

"Please, call me Hallie. We're going to be spending so much time together, I think it only makes sense that we forgo formalities."

They doffed their hats. "Of course, Miss... I mean, Miss Hallie."

Hallie gestured for them to lead the way. "If you would be so kind as to show me the locale of where this Roman fort was on the land I would be most appreciative."

The men picked up their wheelbarrows full of shovels and buckets and her equipment she'd had sent here a week past and started heading west of the property. The walk was uphill and they had to travel through a small woodland that circled the base of the hill before opening up to a cleared area of land. It took them half an hour to reach the top of the small hill and Hallie paused a moment to enjoy the view the height afforded her over Somerset.

From here she could see Baron Bankes's estate nestled in the gully below, it's glistening windows and sandstone walls standing out like a beacon about the green, lush lands. Slowly, Hallie turned, taking in the landscape of smaller hills, townships, rivers, and fields. A kaleidoscope of colors and one of the prettiest views to work by.

As much as she had loved Egypt, the heat, sand and

people, she had missed her homeland. The green, lush land that was prone to rain would've been welcomed every now and then abroad, certainly during a lengthy summer where the temperatures soared. Hallie hadn't thought to miss it, the cold and damp, but at times she caught herself doing exactly that.

With the stable hands' help, she set up a small tent to the side of the hill, well away from where the supposed Roman remains would be excavated. The men chatted, telling her of the area, of what their families had once known to have stood here and what they thought the ruins had been used for. Within an hour everything was in place and ready for when they started their excavation the following day.

"I'm going to be sketching here for the remainder of the day, so you may return to the estate if you wish."

Greg wiped his brow, leaning on a long hammer he'd been using to bang in posts that marked the trench that was to be dug out. "Are you sure, Miss Hallie? We should probably not leave you all alone out here."

Bruce nodded, twisting his cap in his hands. "Greg is right, miss. We should not leave you here alone."

Hallie waved their concerns away, having worked with minimal supervision in Egypt. She was well used to being alone and out on dig sites. Egypt was a lot more dangerous than England and she had nothing to fear here. "I'll be fine and back at the estate for dinner. I have every-thing that I need here now and truly, I do not need to keep you from your work a moment longer," she added, seeing that neither man looked at all comfortable with her staying out on the hillside alone. "Unless there is some threat to my person that I'm not aware of. Is that so?" she asked.

Both men shook their heads, seemingly opposed to

such an idea. "Of course not, Miss Hallie. We'll leave you be to your work."

Hallie pulled out her well-used, leather-bound sketchbook from her bag. She walked about the area in question that Baron Bankes had mentioned in his letters and glanced over the small sketches he had supplied.

There was a noticeable decline of the ground in certain areas that as a whole certainly looked like it could be where the outer building walls sat beneath the earth.

She picked up her small chair and sat, sketching the site, every stone that lay in the area now untouched for hundreds of years or even since the time that the fort supposedly sat here. For hours she lost herself in the drawings, moving about and drawing from different angles and degrees. At last she looked down at the many pages she'd filled in her sketchbook, happy with her progress.

A breeze blew across her skin and she glanced west, surprised to see the sun low on the horizon. She shivered at the evening air that started to settle over the land. Hallie stood, going into the tent and putting on her greatcoat, an article of clothing normally worn by men, but one she'd found indispensable when in England. After the years abroad in warmer climes, the damp, wet English weather was not something she was used to yet.

Before she lost light, Hallie packed up everything that could stay out on the site, stowing it away in the tent as best she could before starting back toward the estate. Lights were lit along the gravelled drive and the house was ablaze also, so very different to how the estate looked in the daylight.

She stopped just shy of where the woods ended and watched as carriages arrived before the double front doors, guests bundled out of the vehicles, their warn and wrinkled traveling apparel telling of their lengthy journeys.

Maybe the baron had arrived earlier than planned. Hallie skirted the woods, making her way around the back of the house, not wanting to be seen in her current attire and also too tired to attend any dinner or entertainment his lordship had planned for his guests.

Making the back servants' entrance she opened the door, scrubbing her hessian boots on the outside mat before stepping inside and closing the door on the cold night that had descended quicker than she'd thought it would. She would have to ensure the next time she finished up at the dig site that she gave herself plenty of time to return to the estate. She would hate to get lost and stuck outside in a location that she wasn't familiar with.

Hallie pulled off her gloves and stifled a scream as a shadowy presence leaning up against the wall stood straight and stepped into the light. She felt her mouth gape and she closed it, swallowing her surprise. "Lord Duncannon." Absently she remembered to curtsy and annoyingly she felt the heat of a blush rise on her cheeks.

She had not expected to see his lordship here. He'd certainly not mentioned traveling to Somerset when she told him of her plans. Whenever they were thrown together due to their mutual friendship with the Duke and Duchess of Whitstone it was awkward and hardly tolerable at best, and this chance meeting was no different.

"Miss Evans," he said, bowing. "Baron Bankes invited me to his estate for his month-long house party. I see you're already hard at work looking for historical artifacts."

His eyes took in her attire, his lips twitching when he noticed her breeches instead of a gown. His inspection of her prickled her pride and she raised her chin, well aware she was not the usual woman, certainly was not the type of lady that fluttered about in front of mirrors all day and cared for what was in the latest *La Belle Assemblée*. Women like those would suit Lord Duncannon and his esteemed family well.

"As you see," she said, moving past him and heading toward the servants' stairs. "Should you not be with your friends instead of pointing out my shortfalls, my lord?"

He ignored her question. "Are you not joining us this evening, Miss Evans?" he asked, turning but not following her.

Hallie threw him a dismissing glance, one she hoped he understood. She didn't want him following her coattails, nor did she particularly wish to be brought into the little upper-class party the baron was hosting. She may have a duchess as a best friend, but that was where her association with the *ton* started and ended. She was not part of that world and nor did she wish to be. If what had happened between them all those years ago proved men like his lordship were unworthy of her time, nothing would. "No, so if you'll excuse me I must return to my room. Goodnight, my lord."

❦

ARTHUR CHIDED himself for taking in her clothing and taking pleasure at the sight she made in the buckskin breeches and hessian boots. Not to mention her delightful shirt and jacket that accentuated her sweet form. Miss Evans disappeared up the servants' stairs and he rubbed a hand over his jaw. Just when he thought he was making progress with her, working toward being friends once again, he'd buggered it up by enjoying the sight of her instead of asking if her first day at the dig site was progressing well.

Idiot.

He inwardly groaned, the sight of her ass as it disappeared up the stairs embedded on his mind. A large whisky was what he needed and a cool bath. He shut his eyes a moment to gain some semblance of control. Always, whenever he was around her, the sensation that she was meant for him would not leave.

His family would never agree, she was poor after all, a bluestocking to her very core he had no doubt, but damn it all to hell, she was smart. An asset worth more than breeding and money combined. Especially since he needed neither in a wife. Not really. His family may have always thought these two things were priceless but he did not. Not after meeting Miss Evans all those years ago.

Now he wanted something entirely different.

Her.

He headed back into the drawing room, making his way over to Baron Bankes, his host for the month-long house party. One of the reasons why he'd accepted the invite was solely due to the fact that Hallie would be here. The baron had let it slip he'd hired her to excavate his Roman ruins and he could not come soon enough.

The baron summoned a footman for more wine, clapping Arthur on his shoulder in welcome. "How are you enjoying my home, my friend? I do believe there are some very fetching and available women here this month. Ladies that I know your grandmother would approve of." He chuckled. "We shall have a jolly time I'm sure."

Arthur smiled, taking in the room and finding little that tempted him. The one woman whom he'd never been able to get out of his mind was housed away upstairs and in no way tempted to join in with the activities downstairs.

A footman handed him a glass of red wine and Arthur took a satisfying sip, enjoying the oak and earthy flavors that bombarded his mouth from the well-aged beverage. "I do not see your historian here this evening. Is she here?" he queried, not wanting the baron to know he'd already seen her and her quick dismissal over joining them this evening.

The baron nodded, his cheeks ruddy from too much wine and the roaring fire behind him. Their host was a tall man, largely boned and with a jolly outlook on life. He was fond of the arts and history, which would explain why Miss Evans had been invited here to explore his ruins.

"Oh yes, she arrived yesterday. I sent word upstairs for her to attend whenever she was able, but I will not force her." Baron Bankes leaned in close. "Her father was a small gentleman farmer in Surrey, not a large landholder by any means, and I believe before he passed away they had lost their land and home due to debt and poor management. Miss Evans may not feel comfortable in our company, if you understand my meaning."

Arthur nodded, understanding only too well that she had to work for her living and in a line of business most unusual for a woman. "If you do not mind I would like to help her when I can out on the Roman dig site. As you know I'm the benefactor to the British Museum and historical finds are always most interesting to me."

"Oh yes, that tidbit quite slipped my mind. How are you finding the position?"

In truth Arthur had found the position uninspiring and with very little to attend to. To be the benefactor really only meant that when the museum required funds, he was obligated to open his purse. "Very satisfying," he lied, taking a sip of wine to lessen the sting of him lying to his friend's face. "Hence why I'm interested in Miss Evan's work."

Bankes nodded. "I will tell you something, but it must remain between us. I find the whole idea of a woman doing such a manual-labor, intensive job abhorrent, but the chit is very determined and seemed rather desperate for work. I could not turn her down." The baron laughed. "Let us not forget she's close to the Duchess of Whitstone and I must admit, I was swayed quite easily by her pretty face. One never knows, with such a woman under my roof, we may become better acquainted by the end of her stay." Bankes elbowed him and winked. "If you understand my meaning of course."

Arthur stared at him, unwilling to open his mouth lest he use it to shout expletives at the bastard for talking of Hallie in such a way. "She is a professional woman. I think your pretty words may be lost on her." He said the words in the nicest way he could without betraying the anger that simmered in his veins over what the baron had said. It would help no one, not even Hallie, if he allowed himself to say what he really wanted—that being for the man to stay the hell away from her unless he wanted someone feeding him with a spoon for the rest of his life.

"Bah, I think she would be willing. Hell, she spent years in Egypt without a chaperone. How virginal could she be?"

Arthur choked on his wine. "With all due respect, I know Miss Evans through the Duke and Duchess of Whitstone whom, might I remind you, are very fond of her. I do not think your speaking of her in such a way is becoming of you, nor respectful to Miss Evans and I must ask you to stop."

Bankes's eyes flew wide and his cheeks turned a deep, ruddy color. "I do apologize if I have offended you, Lord Duncannon. I never meant to be offensive. I was merely teasing, you understand." His lordship smiled at another guest across the room. "If you would excuse me, I must attend my visitors."

Arthur watched him go, glad of the solitude for a moment. He needed to gain control of his temper, which had been awfully close to snapping at his lordship's crude innuendo toward Miss Evans. The baron would need watching, and so too would Miss Evans. Under no circumstances, no matter what she thought of him in particular, would he allow her to come to harm or be made fun of simply because of what she did for employment, or because her family had fallen on hard times.

He'd not stand for anything untoward or cruel.

CHAPTER 5

The following morning Hallie arrived on the dig site with five stable hands instead of the two like the day before. They waited for her on chairs they had carried up to the locale and stood when they spotted her arrival.

"Miss Hallie, we're ready to do whatever tasks that you bestow on us. The baron has given us his permission to work here for the day and so we're just waiting for your instruction to start."

"Wonderful, thank you so much," Hallie said, relief flowing through her that she had others up on site, and not two men, but five. It was pleasing that the baron found her employment here worth the men's time away from their duties at the estate. To have them here to help with the digging—a labor-intensive job she'd never been fond of would give them great results and quicker than expected.

"We will be digging a trench in the eastern corner of the site." She walked the men over to the location she meant and pointed to the small decline in the ground. "Under here I believe are the outlying walls of the fort. If you look on the area from a distance and higher up, the sinking of the earth is more prevalent and obvious. We will dig across it. A good three meters on either side and three meters long. The soil is to be piled together and if I may use two of your men here," she said, moving to where she wanted the excess dirt poured, "I'll have them sift through this soil to look for anything of historical value that we may have missed."

Greg doffed his cap, excitement gleaming in his eyes. Hallie supposed for men who normally only worked with horses this would be a little adventure in their life. The possibility of finding an ancient artifact was in her estimation better than shoveling horse shit all day. "Very good, Miss Hallie. We'll start on that right away."

Hallie went and put away her lunch and drink that cook had placed in a basket for her in the small tent. She pulled a smock she had made over her clothing to lessen the impact on her attire. Thankfully the men had not said anything about her trews and the leather, knee-high boots she wore along with a shirt and jacket. To take part in such digs was not possible if one had to wear a gown and she refused to be hindered in any clothing suitable for her sex. Stepping from the tent, she pulled on her broad-brimmed hat and picked up a small trowel from her crate of tools and went over to where the men were digging.

They worked all morning, only stopping for a bite to eat and drink around lunch. By the time late afternoon settled over the land the trench was a good ten inches deep and a few meters both wide and long. With the trench only on its first day Hallie could already see the old Roman foundations to the fort starting to emerge from their thousand-year grave.

The men having finished for the day packed up their tools and offered to walk Hallie home. "I'll be along shortly. I need to draw today's findings and then I'll return to the estate. Thank you though," she said as they moved off down the hill, the mumble of their conversation fading along with the light.

Hallie pulled out her sketchbook, sat on a nearby chair and started to sketch. She lost herself in her drawing for a while, making sure to catalogue where little objects were laying and what she supposed they may be.

"I thought that I would walk you back to the estate, Miss Evans. A lady should not be out here alone."

Her hand stilled over the paper and she did not need to look up to see that it was Lord Duncannon. That he called her a lady made her teeth ache. She was no lady and in truth had never been. Certainly she never adhered to how a woman should go about society or anywhere for that matter. Her one night in his lordship's bed and her son born out of wedlock was proof of that.

"You do not need to do that, my lord. I'm more than capable of walking myself back to Baron Bankes's estate."

He came over to where she sat, and pulling up another chair nearby, he sat. "I know you are more than capable, but I wanted to come and see what the whole house party has been talking about all day. You're quite the latest *on dit.*"

Hallie inwardly cringed. She didn't want to be anyone's talking point and nor did she want society looking in on her life. If they found out that she had birthed a child outside the sanctity of marriage, she would never work again. No one hired a strumpet. At least, that is what they'd call her.

"This is merely an archaeological dig, my lord. Unless we find something of significant historical value, I fail to see how the *ton* will be very much interested. As you can see," she said, gesturing to the stone wall soaking up the last of the summer rays after centuries of being buried, "this is merely stone. Not gold or jewels or some ancient artifact made of jade."

He glanced at the wall, a small smile playing about his mouth and she watched him a moment. Allowed herself to enjoy his handsome face. A face that from the moment she had picked him up on the road heading back into Felday she'd thought too good-looking to be noble. And that was exactly what he was.

A little voice chided her in her mind. *You were not exactly noble either...*

Her friend Ava had told her numerous stories of his lordship's escapades in town. The gentleman was a jokester and did not take anything serious. Why the day they had met, the man had been thrown out of his friend's carriage, and all for a lark.

Not that she had found it amusing. To be expelled out of a carriage to face the freezing temperatures of an English winter was the embodiment of stupid.

"Bankes mentioned it may be Roman. Do you think that to be the case after finally seeing some of the ruins?"

She nodded. "I do. Fourth century and from looking at the ground prior to starting this trench I do believe the theory that this was a fort is correct. It could turn out to be a villa, but it does not seem to be big enough to be one of them."

He looked at her and she fought not to fidget under his scrutiny. "You're a wealth of information, Miss Evans. I do not believe I've ever met a woman who is as educated as yourself."

"My education abroad was a good one, not to mention working with Mr. Shelly in Egypt has supplied me untold information that you can only learn while on site. Textbooks can only teach a person so much."

"May I help tomorrow?" he asked, pulling his gaze

back to the half-dug trench. "I wanted to come up today, but I was waylaid." She sighed in relief at not having him look at her any longer. The man had the ability to unnerve her and she was much more her educated, quick-thinking self when he was gazing elsewhere.

"It's dirty work. I never took you for a man who liked to get his hands dirty." In fact, glancing at his gloveless hands, she noted his nails were well kept and perfectly clean. His skin soft and unmarked by the sun. Hallie glanced at her own chipped and dirty nails. The man was better kept than she, and she was a woman.

"I would like to. Between you and me, Miss Evans, a day up on the top of this hill digging in the dirt is a lot more enticing than being at the estate and having to pretend to want to be there."

She glanced at him. Why the sudden dislike of house parties and socializing? He was renowned to enjoy such events. Or at least, he used to be. Had he changed in the three years since she'd seen him last? "You may help if you wish, I will not stop you. But you need to dress with a little less finesse. I'd hate for you to ruin your superfine coat, not to mention those lovely cream breeches, my lord."

He glanced down at his pristine coat that was cut to his every measurement, the highly starched, perfectly tied cravat and buckskin breeches. He looked ready for a ball and not a day out in the woods or the tops of hills digging in the dirt.

He chuckled and the sound made her skin prickle in awareness. Would she ever be free of his pull? "I shall be dressed appropriately. What time do you leave? I shall walk with you."

"Be at the front doors by seven, my lord. We'll leave then."

The following morning, Arthur was ready and waiting for Hallie when she stepped from the front doors, a heavy woollen cloak about her shoulders and what looked to be a knitted hat covering her hair and ears. Her cheeks were flushed pink from her morning toilette. She looked adorable and sweet enough to nibble on.

He shook his head at his recklessness. Here he was, about to trek to a hilltop and dig in dirt all day, and all so he could try to sway her to like him back. He was a besotted fool.

He could understand why she was wary of him and kept him at a distance. His reputation preceded him everywhere he went, and for years his family was known to be at a loss to his inaction toward marriage. Granted, some of the stories circulating town about his escapades were true. The friends he'd had the day he'd first met Hallie had given him a wild reputation, but he'd parted ways with them years ago. He was a different man now and he needed to show her that.

He caught little glimpses of her as they walked through the forest they passed through to make the dig site. Her freckled nose that was a little red from the cold morning. Her lack of self-awareness of how exquisite she was humbled him. Her skin had been kissed by the sun and she had a lovely golden hue, nothing like his pasty-white self who had never traveled out of England.

Her indifference to him quite literally drove him to distraction. She was one of the very few women who didn't seem interested in his person. A dilemma that kept him up half the night, but would please his family to no end.

The Duncannons were famous for grand matches, either in relation to wealth or position. He was a viscount and Miss Evens was a gentleman's daughter with little means. He had no doubt that Ava had told Hallie that his family would expect him to continue on the tradition of marrying well. That did not mean that at times, like today when he walked beside one of England's most intelligent, beautiful women that she did not tempt him to throw all of his family's expectations aside and do whatever the hell he wanted.

Namely choose her.

"What is the plan for today?" he asked, pulling his greatcoat closed farther to keep out the chill, morning air. Birdsong had commenced in the trees as the dawn broke and from here he could see a few deer grazing on the estate's lawns.

"We'll finish the trench and then start troweling the soil, looking for buried artifacts. I'll have the other men sift through the soil we dig out to ensure nothing is missed. I'm sure there will be some mosaic or cobblestone flooring buried. One never knows how elaborate these Roman ruins are going to be until we start digging deeper. Either way, I do hope to find some pieces which would at least date the fort and also give the baron some information about the site."

"I'm looking forward to being put to work," he said, rubbing his hands together.

She scoffed and he glanced at her. "You find such a statement amusing, Miss Evans?"

"A little. It will be the first time that I've seen a viscount wrist deep in mud." She threw him a small smile. A little crumb of kindness that he'd lap up. "Please, call me Hallie or Miss Hallie as the workmen do. We're about to dig in the dirt all day together, formalities be damned."

So bold and different. He stood in awe of her a moment, unsure of himself and how he should go about getting her to see him for more than what opinion she'd formed in her mind. He may know how to have a good time, certainly, he knew how to bring pleasure to the women he bedded, but that did not mean he could not be genuine or care for just one person.

He wanted her, he wasn't fool enough not to admit it. But she was also completely wrong for him. Opinionated and brash were not traits usually associated with a Duncannon bride. His family would never recover from such a shock. A Duncannon did not marry a commoner and certainly not one who enjoyed digging in the dirt all day long. History showed those who married into his family to be meek and sweet natured. Mollycoddled society princesses that even thinking about, made his teeth ache.

Arthur's lips twitched. Hallie was none of those things. He liked her in spite of this knowledge and as she jumped down into the trench, kneeling before an odd-shaped rock, oblivious to the dirt that stained her breeches, that affection grew. He could not picture his last mistress ever doing such a thing or those of his set back in London.

"Please call me Arthur in return," he said, kneeling down beside her and picking up his own tool to remove the soil about the circular stone in the ground. "What do you think this is?" he asked, ignoring the fact she remained businesslike and professional around him, while his own insides were in turmoil. To be this close to her, the sweet scent of rose in the wind, drove him to distraction.

"I believe it'll be a pot of some kind. Probably one that housed wine." She dug a little of the dirt away. "See," she pointed, "it's not rock, it's terracotta."

He ran his finger over the smooth edge, thinking of those who had used it last and when. "All these years it's been buried, and now here we are, bringing it back to the surface for others to see and enjoy."

She smiled at him, and his gut clenched at the pure joy he read in her vibrant, green eyes. This was the love of her life. Digging in the ground and finding hidden, lost worlds. He would have to work hard to make her see anything else other than the artifacts she was determined to find.

"My thoughts exactly, Arthur. I may make an archaeologist out of you yet."

He chuckled, doubtful of the fact, but enjoying his day out with her in any case. This life was not for him, but he could see the attraction to being so carefree. With his many estates this type of existence would never be a course open for his feet to tread.

"For today at least you will." He paused. "Now, let's see how big this pot actually is," he said, continuing to chip away the dirt from their find. "Anything to do with wine and you have my full attention."

CHAPTER 6

The following evening Hallie was invited to dine and take part in after-dinner entertainments Baron Bankes was holding. She paced her room, continually going back to her wardrobe as if it would miraculously produce the latest designs from London for her to choose from. All of the gowns she had brought with her were pitiful and not at all suitable for dinner. Some she really ought to throw away, they were so tattered and worn.

She worked her bottom lip with her teeth. Maybe she could ask a maid to procure a dress from another female guest. If she asked nicely enough, maybe they would take pity on her and lend her a gown.

A light knock at the door sounded and she opened it, gasping at the sight of her friend. "Willow!" she said, pulling her into a fierce hug. "What on earth are you doing here?"

"We arrived this afternoon, you know my aunt the Viscountess Vance was invited and when Baron Bankes mentioned that you were working on his Roman fort excavation, well, I almost fell over myself to see you. Aunt wouldn't let me walk up the hill however, and I had to wait until tonight, but as soon as I'd heard you were home and preparing for dinner, I had to come see you."

Hallie pulled her into her room, marveling at Willow's beautiful gown. She was sent away to school in France just like her and their friends, and it was at Madame Dufour's Refining School for Girls that their friendship had been solidified. Of all of them, Willow had been the most fortunate. Her aunt had taken her in after her parents' deaths and her aunt happened to be wealthy, childless and titled.

Hallie devoured the sight of her friend, and the beautiful light-blue silk gown she wore, the long, elbow-length gloves and pretty pearl necklace. Willow was as beautiful inside as she was on the outside and a pang of hopelessness swamped her.

"You're not dressed yet, my dear." Willow walked over to her wardrobe, searching through her minuscule selection of gowns, a small frown settling between her eyes and marring her normally perfect visage. Willow turned toward her, shutting the wardrobe doors behind her with a decided snap. "Would you like to borrow one of my dresses? I have more than enough."

Hallie nodded in relief, only too willing to accept help. With the attire she had she would not be fit to be seen downstairs, nevertheless the dining room. "Thank you so much, dearest. I did not even think that I would be invited to dine and did not pack accordingly." Not to mention she was loathe to spend her funds on anything other than keeping Ammon clothed and well-kept at her cousin's. A new fashionable gown from London could keep her son clothed and fed for months on end, and so her attire had suffered and her lack of bother with it.

She supposed she would have to purchase at least one

gown if such situations like tonight came before her and there was no Willow Perry to save her the next time.

"Come, we'll go to my room and you can choose. I gather you've bathed already?"

"I have, and this dress is clean, although it's a day gown and not dinner appropriate, nor the latest in fashion."

Willow linked their arms and pulled her toward the door. "I have the perfect dress that'll suit your coloring. And you must tell me everything that you've been up to. I feel I did not see you enough in London and you escaped from there as soon as you were able. Please tell me that you're to stay in England from now on. I know Ava, Evie, and Molly along with I missed you dreadfully. What about your dig here? Have you been enjoying it?"

Hallie fought to remember every question Willow threw at her. She answered as best as she could, but also removed any mention of her child and the real reason she was so determined to escape London for employment. Not even Ava knew that she'd birthed a healthy and happy boy. Of course they knew of Omar, but not the child she'd birthed to him.

Nerves fluttered in her stomach at what her oldest and dearest friends would think of her should they find out she'd had a child out of wedlock, that her child was not only a bastard in society's eyes but also one of mixed race.

"You know London society has never suited me, and I wanted to visit my cousin before coming here. I'm going to stay in England for the foreseeable future, and this work, such as what I'm doing for Baron Bankes is what I want to do."

They made Willow's room and she ushered her inside, closing and locking the door behind her. "Well I for one am absolutely thrilled to have you here with me. I had thought this month-long house party would be a bore.

Just my aunt catching up with her old friends, but it isn't so. Did you see Lord Duncannon is here? Has he seen you?"

She nodded, seating herself on the settee before the fire. Willow's room was more opulent than Hallie's, but that was to be expected when Willow was part of their set and Hallie was not. "He helped me out on the dig site yesterday in fact, but I have not seen him today. I believe some of the gentleman were riding about the estate today, getting themselves out of the house and into some fresh country air."

"Aunt said the same thing," Willow said, her words muffled as she searched through the abundance of gowns lining her wardrobe. "Ah, here it is. I found it."

Hallie gasped at the sight of the dress Willow held up before her. It was simply the most beautiful piece she'd ever beheld. The empire-style-cut gown was a deep emerald green silk with a cream, very fine tulle overlaying it. Decorative cream satin bands and lace embroidery about the hem and bodice completed the ensemble to perfection. She went over to where Willow held it up for her to inspect it, letting the silk and tulle run over her hand. It was so fine and soft, Hallie wasn't sure she should be allowed near such perfection.

"This will suit your coloring perfectly. It'll compliment your beautiful green eyes and lovely olive skin," Willow said, laying the gown on the bed and ringing for a maid. "I'll have my maid do up your hair for you and with this gown on you'll not feel the least out of place amongst the baron's guests."

Hallie clasped her friend's hands, so thankful she was here. Her eyes smarted with unshed tears and she sniffed. "I'm so glad you arrived, Willow. I had hoped to excuse myself from such entertainments. I certainly did not pack for anything other than clothes suitable for working in the fields. You have saved me this night, my friend."

Willow chuckled, bidding the maid entry when a light knock sounded on the door. "What are friends for if not for such things? Now sit, my dear and let Jane do her magic."

Hallie did as Willow asked and watched with fascination how Jane was able to set her hair to the latest style and with very little trouble. Tonight may not be so terrible after all.

☙❧

ALL THROUGH DINNER Arthur fought to keep his mind on the conversation that Lady Portman was whispering to his left. The young countess recently married was hard of hearing and spoke very lightly in fear that she would be too loud. She was a delightful dinner companion, and yet his attention kept being pulled to another part of the table where Hallie sat beside a gentleman he'd never met before, and also Lord Hood, an earl and old Eton school fellow. Both of them were rogues if their less-than-hidden infatuation with Hallie's lack of gown around her bodice area were any indication.

When he'd first seen her in the drawing room prior to dinner he'd almost choked on his own tongue. Of course he'd seen her in London at balls and parties, but after seeing her yesterday, grubby and disheveled out at her dig site, tonight she was perfection. A woman who turned heads and could hold her own conversations with her wit and quick mind.

He'd wanted to go up to her and speak to her, but she seemed to be a little of an oddity here at the party and everyone wanted to converse with the woman who was researching the Roman ruins on Bankes's property.

Arthur welcomed the distraction of his friend and marquess, Noah, Lord Capell who came and stood beside him.

"The archaeologist among us is dreadfully attractive I must say," Capell said, his attention coursing over Hallie.

Arthur narrowed his eyes at his lordship's observation before looking back at Hallie. Warmth spread along his skin when she laughed and spoke to her companions who flocked about her. "She has always been, as you well know. If only she would throw me a crumb or two of that kindness I'd be most pleased."

Capell glanced at him. "You like her in a romantic sense? You've never said so before."

"Not to you," he quipped, taking a sip of his drink. "There is something about her that I like and cannot shake. No matter how much I try to dismiss the idea, whenever I see her I'm right back there again, admiring her intelligence and easy manners. Wondering what a future would be like with her at my side." He chuckled at his own nonsense. "I apologize for my less-than-stimulating conversation."

Capell chuckled. "Never mind that. This conversation is indeed interesting, but even if Miss Evans is the Duchess of Whitstone's favorite friend, not even that will make her suitable for your family, Duncannon. You ought to look elsewhere for a bride."

The idea of doing such a thing irked, but it was what his family would want. "I know, but putting my family and their ingrained prejudices aside, she wants very little to do with me in any case. We get along well enough, and she's friendly when we're in the same social circle, but she is also distant." He didn't elaborate as to why that was so. His sleeping with her and then running off the next morning, or so she thought, was reason enough.

Capell clapped him on the shoulder. "Maybe, and I say this with the upmost respect to you, and our friendship, but maybe she doesn't see you in a romantic light. Even so, surely you're not looking to marry. We're not nine and twenty yet."

The idea of Hallie marrying someone else, of being with her husband alone and behind closed bedroom doors made his blood run cold. He hated the idea of her being with anyone else other than him, and so if he had to marry her to keep her for himself, he would.

Arthur digested that way of thinking for a moment.

Marriage.

"You may be right." He glanced in her direction and caught her looking his way. His gaze hungrily took in her emerald silk gown and transparent tulle. Damn it she was beautiful, and that she was totally oblivious to the fact made her doubly so.

"Her little group of admirers seem to be moving on. If you wanted a chance to speak to her, may I suggest you go now."

Duncannon stepped toward her only to halt halfway when the gentleman who'd sat next to her at dinner came to her side and caught her attention. Arthur looked about for the footman carrying wine. He'd give her a moment with the gentleman and then he would talk to her. See if there was some way in which to create a comradeship with her that in time, he hoped would lead to more.

Perhaps even the state that in the past made him shudder in revulsion.

The marriage state.

CHAPTER 7

Robert sidled up next to Miss Evans and bestowed on her the best gentlemanly smile he could muster before the murdering wench. She inspected him, her gaze wary and he hoped he hadn't put her off at dinner when he spoke of the weather and the latest *on dit* floating around London. He didn't know really what one ought to talk about at these events, and certainly he did not want to talk to her at all if he could help it, but he did need to let her know that perhaps he knew more of her than she would like.

After all, his time here in Somerset was solely due to bring this bitch down and hurt the Duchess of Whitstone in turn through their friendship. To see both women fall from grace would be sweet indeed and his cousin would be pleased he'd accomplished revenge on them.

"Such a lovely party, do you not agree?" he asked, taking a glass of ratafia from a passing footman and taking a small sip of the sweet beverage. He caught Viscount Duncannon watching them with interest and he narrowed his eyes, making a mental note to be wary of the man. He did not need him sticking his nose in his business and halting his plan of bringing down the woman beside him.

"It certainly is," she replied, nothing more forthcoming.

A small smiled played about her sweet mouth as she took in the guests around them and he wondered if he could have a little fun with this woman before he brought her low. The idea of her mouth on him was not unpleasant and it would hurt her more should he play with her emotions a little before ripping away that footing from beneath her feet.

He leaned in toward her, closer than one ought. "Do you not ever wonder what secrets the guests at such events are hiding?" He took a sip of his drink, inwardly laughing as she stilled beside him. "Shall we guess as to what each guest may be keeping hidden? Secret lovers. Financial ruin. What else do you think we should include on our list, Miss Evans?"

"I should not know, Mr. Stewart. I've never taken the time to think about such things."

He met her gaze and did not miss the small flare of fear that entered her eyes. "Have you not?" he said, sighing for good measure. "Well, we shall have to think upon it I dare say. Do let me know if you come up with anything else. We shall make it our little game while we're here at Baron Bankes's estate. What say you?"

Miss Evans paled and Robert fought to keep a straight face. Oh, how delicious it was to torment her. She had supported and helped the duchess work out who was behind all the fires in Berkshire. Watched as his cousin died in her friend's home and did nothing to try and save him. He would bring this woman down, and through her the Duchess of Whitstone would be injured.

A young woman sat at the pianoforte and started to

play a country jig. Robert held out his hand to Miss Evans. "Shall we dance? It looks like some of the other guests are partaking in the impromptu event."

She looked at his hand as if it were a snake, but shook her head, placing down her glass of champagne. "I'm sorry, no. I'm feeling unwell and will retire. Goodnight."

"Oh, I do hope you're feeling better soon, Miss Evans," he called after her as she fled. "Maybe tomorrow night we shall continue our little game. I will ensure the baron invites you to dine with us again."

She threw him a wobbly smile over her shoulder, but he could see the fear lurking in her dark, green orbs. "Goodnight, Mr. Stewart."

He bowed. "Goodnight, Miss Evans." *And sweet, untroubled dreams, my dear…*

❦

HALLIE SWALLOWED the bile that rose in her throat as she walked from the room, trying not to bring attention to herself. What Mr. Stewart had said had been so shocking and unexpected that it left her with little choice but to leave. To play a game, to question her on her thoughts on what others present may have hidden in their pasts made her question his motives. He was too bold, too amused by his game, for there not to be a nefarious reason he wanted to know.

Did he know of Omar? Had he learned of her child?

She fisted her hands at her sides to stop their shaking and as unhurried as she could, made her way back to her room. She would have to apologize to Baron Bankes tomorrow for her departure without saying a word, but not for a moment longer could she stay.

Hallie started to pull off the silk gloves Willow had lent

her as she started down the long corridor to her room. Why would Mr. Stewart want to play such a game with her at all? His words told of someone trying to find out more information, and in this case, about her.

"Miss Evans," a voice called from behind.

Hallie shut her eyes at the sound of Lord Duncannon. Great, all she needed was for him to see and recognize her upset. He was too familiar with her, and able to read her like a book. She turned, attempted a look of pleasant interest that felt tight and unnatural to hold.

"Lord Duncannon," she answered, smiling a little. "Can I help you with anything?"

He stopped before her, his brow furrowed in concern. She considered him a moment, the sheer attractiveness that one man could possess didn't seem very fair in her estimation. Omar had been beautiful, dark-skinned, and his eyes the deepest brown with lashes that went on for days. Lord Duncannon was the opposite. His skin was fair, his eyes as blue as the ocean on a stormy day, his hair sun kissed and the color of wheat in the summer's sun.

She clutched at the gloves in her hand, aware that she'd started to undress before she'd made her room.

"Please do beg my pardon, but I could not help but notice you looked distressed when speaking to Mr. Stewart. You would let me know if he has insulted you in any way."

She nodded, swallowing the fear that the mention of the man brought forth in her. He had to know something, which made her wonder what was he going to do with that information and when.

"A sudden headache, my lord. Nothing more. I thank you for your concern."

He studied her a moment, his inspection thorough and a little skeptical. Hallie pasted on a smile, aware that if he were looking closely enough he would have seen through her like a pane of glass.

"If you're sure, Miss Evans." He frowned, seemingly fighting for the right words to say, or to ask if she were being truthful. "I will have a tisane brought up to you at once and a warming pan. The air is cold this evening."

She nodded, thankful for his kindness. After he'd left her in Felday, she had not thought he'd been capable of such emotion, but here he was, trying to comfort her without really knowing why. Hallie took in his finery, his strong jaw and aristocratic nose that could look down on people if he so chose. One thing he'd never done with her thankfully. Maybe he really had changed, or at least was trying to right the wrong he'd done to her all those years ago.

"I thank you," she said.

He nodded, stepping back. "Goodnight." Hallie watched him go, her mind whirring with what she should do. Not just about Mr. Stewart, but Lord Duncannon as well. Her secret was so very devastating, and there was a good chance that should anyone find out about her child she would never be offered the type of work she was now doing. To work in a great house as a lady's maid or a general housemaid could even prove difficult. No one liked to hire women who had not comported themselves in the manner in which was expected of them. Lord Duncannon may not look down on her now, but he would if he knew the truth. As much as she hoped that were not so, that he was honorable deep in his core, the fear that he too would turn against her would not shift.

She rubbed her brow, hopelessness swamping her. She could not let Mr. Stewart threaten her in such a way. Nor should she panic just yet. His game could have been just that, a silly little game that had hit home closer than he may know. For all she knew, the gentleman may not know anything at all.

Hallie opened her bedroom door and sank onto one of the leather chairs before the hearth. Tomorrow she would keep her wits about her, but carry on as if nothing had rattled her the night before. She would head up to the dig site at seven and continue her work and tomorrow evening she would attend dinner if she was invited and not scuttle off like a frightened bird before a cat.

Her future and that of her son's depended on her keeping a cool head and she would not fail him in this.

CHAPTER 8

The following day dawned with stormy, gray clouds and rain showers crossing the land. Hallie had fortunately made the excavation site before the first heavy shower passed over, and now with the ground damp, she helped the stable hands dig the last of the trench.

The hollow thud of horse's hooves on turf sounded and she turned to see Lord Duncannon pulling up a magnificent chestnut mount, his nose breathing out steam on the cool day and stomping one front hoof in protest at being halted on his morning run.

His lordship jumped off with little trouble and she admired the fact that he seemed so very good and accomplished at everything he did. His capable hands tied his mount to a nearby tree and he strolled toward her, his greatcoat billowing out from behind him like a cloak.

She glanced away, heat prickling her skin. Why she had this reaction with the gentleman every time she saw him was becoming exasperating. So what if he were the handsomest man she'd beheld in England? That did not mean she had to act or be silly over the notion. Nor did his being here mean that he was looking at her in any way romantic. He was, after all, the benefactor to the London Museum. If he did not take an interest in archaeological digs about England and abroad there would be something wrong.

"Lord Duncannon," she said, stepping out of the trench and walking over to him. "What brings you here today?"

He smiled down at her, pulling off his gloves. "I've come to help again of course." He strolled over to the tent and picked up the small trowel he was using the other day. "As I said before, I'd much prefer to be here than at the house party. They're playing charades and I do not feel like trying to figure out what or who people are. I'd much prefer to be here. With you," he added, his face serious all of a sudden.

Hallie reached out and pulled him to the side of the tent and out of vision from her workers. "My lord, I'm not certain why you're so very fascinated with the history of Baron Bankes's estate all of a sudden, but I must ensure that it's not because of me that you're here. We've known each other for some years, and well enough for me to speak plainly I think."

He raised his brow, crossing his arms over his chest. The action brought her vision to that part of his body. Her memory of their one night together many years before and what he felt like under her touch. Dear lord in heaven, she was going to hell.

"Do go on. I think I shall like to hear this opinion of yours."

She checked that the other men were out of hearing, all four of them still busy digging the trench. "What happened in Surrey will not happen again here if that is what you're hoping. Our night was a mistake. One that I regret and I hope you did not follow me here to Somerset in the hopes of having a bit of skirt to enjoy during the month-long house party."

A muscle twitched at his temple as he stared at her. "Is that what you think of me? That I'm only here to have you in my bed again."

The mention of being so once more sent an ache to settle deep in her core. She clutched her stomach, shaking her head, wishing that her body did not inwardly scream "yes" at the mention of exactly that. "I hope it is not. I was not myself that night and should never have propositioned you as I did. As you are well aware, I did not think we would see each other again. Certainly, I did not think that we would have friends in common."

He reached out, patting her shoulder and she narrowed her eyes. Disliking the condescending action. "Never fear, Hallie. I'm not here to seduce you, as much as I enjoyed our coming together the first time. No, I'm here to help as your friend and that is all. Your virtue is safe with me."

She studied him a moment hoping that were true, before walking back toward the trench. He was a complication she did not need, nor did she need him finding out she'd birthed a child by another man after being with him. He would think her a common whore who gave out her favors to anyone who passed her by. And that was not the truth.

Shame washed over her that she'd succumbed to his charm, good looks and too much wine that night in Surrey. That she had allowed herself to forget all her troubles and just give over to pleasure and passion to a man she thought never to see again. A reckless mistake she had regretted ever since.

Hallie rubbed the back of her neck, feeling his gaze upon her as she made her way back over to the workmen. Lord Duncannon followed her and soon was working near where he had found the remnants of a wine barrel the day before last. Every so often she caught herself watching him, his little nuances like how he bit his lip when he was trying to be careful, or how a slip of hair kept falling over one of his eyes giving him a rakish appearance.

She snorted. Like he needed to look any more rakish. The man was a veritable sex god on mortal legs. That she knew just how godlike he could be in the heat of passion did not help either. Of how soft that hair was as he kissed her down her stomach, her hands clasping those golden locks as he dipped farther on her body.

Hallie pushed her shovel into the dirt with more gusto than was necessary. She was not attracted or interested in him in such a way. Not anymore.

Now she just had to convince her body of the fact.

❦

ARTHUR COULD FEEL Hallie watching him. He'd be a liar if did not admit to liking having her eyes on him, watching him when she did not think anyone would notice. Today was the first time in years that they had broached the subject of their indiscretion in Surrey. He wasn't sure how it happened, and he supposed part of it was because she'd been so terribly sad when sitting next to him in the house that night. She'd just buried her father and he'd wanted to comfort her.

That comfort had spiralled into a hot and desperate coming together that had rattled him to the core. He'd left her bed early the next morning, walked to the inn to organize a carriage and had been practically abducted by his idiot friends.

It was any wonder she loathed him so much and did not offer the hand of friendship. He could not blame her, but he could try and change her mind about him. Tell her the truth.

He dug into the soil, looking out for anything that may surface and require delicate handling. Similar to Hallie, he would have to tread carefully around her. Earn her trust and see if they could move forward as friends and then possibly more.

His family would not like it, but then he wasn't controlled by them. From the moment he'd sat down in her small parlor in Felday he had felt a connection to her that he'd never felt with anyone else. An emotion he could not explain, and he knew, to his very core, that if he did not court her and see if what he hoped could be the start of something great, he'd regret it for the rest of his life.

His friends' actions and Hallie with her leaving had put paid to that idea. He shook his head. Hating the fact that they had missed an opportunity that may have been ever-lasting.

Hallie gasped and Arthur scrambled over to where she was digging. She started to remove more soil from the area she was excavating, taking her time to be careful. "Have you found something?"

"I think I have," she said. She smiled at him and his stomach clenched at the genuine pleasure written across her features. Hell, he loved seeing her happy, excited. "I think it may be gold. I caught a flash of color when I was digging."

He helped her remove soil from the area, and sure enough within a minute of further excavation the smooth top of a small, round-shaped artifact showed itself. They took their time removing the soil, and then within the hour Hallie had freed the buried piece of treasure and was holding it up before them. "I think this is a section of a legionnaire's helmet. How extraordinary."

Much like she was. He helped her to stand and for a moment they stared at the find. "The first of many great discoveries I hope."

She nodded, heading toward the tent and placing the item in a little box she had set up on a table. "Let us see what else this fort has to reveal, shall we?" she asked, slipping past him to go back to the trench.

"I'm right behind you, Miss Evans." Arthur settled down beside her. The remainder of the day did indeed sport new finds, other parts of the helmet and some arrowheads, although Hallie wasn't certain if they were from the fourth century or earlier.

Arthur contemplated his present circumstance. Should his grandmother see him now, Viscount Duncannon, boot deep in mud and digging in said mud for artifacts that no longer held any value to society, only the past. She would be appalled. And yet, never had he ever felt more alive and beneficial than he did right now next to Miss Evans. To be contributing to society, as small as it was.

CHAPTER 9

Hallie sat in her room later that night after dinner where thankfully Mr. Stewart did not deign to bring up any more games that they should play regarding people's past. Her friend Willow sat across from her, quiet and reflective as she stared at the flames in the fire.

"Willow," she said, catching her attention. "There is something I need to tell you, all of our friends in fact, but since you're here, I wish to confide in you if I can."

Willow's brow furrowed and she turned toward her, giving her full attention. "Of course. You know that you can confide in me. I will never betray your trust."

Hallie clasped her stomach as nerves over admitting to her secret that she'd never told anyone other than her cousin. She was not certain how any of them would take the news, or if they would look down on her, scorn her for her choice. "There are two things really, and I'm uncertain what you'll think of me when I tell you."

Willow reached across the space that separated them and clasped her hand. "I will never think less of you, no matter what you're about to tell me. I promise you that."

She hoped that was true, for to lose her friends over her secret would be unbearable. "You know how much I loved Omar, will always love him even though he's gone, but there is something that you do not know and I need to confide in someone before I shout it out at the top of my lungs for everyone to hear and be damned the consequences."

"Tell me what it is before I expire," Willow said, smiling a little.

Hallie took a calming breath and swallowed her fear. "Not long after Omar was killed I found out that I was carrying his child."

Willow gasped, wrenching back into her chair. "You were pregnant. What happened, Hallie?"

She stood, pacing back and forth between the hearth and her bed. "By then Mr. Shelly, the Egyptologist, was scheduled to leave and I jumped at the chance to return home. I needed to return home, to Berkshire, where my cousin lives and give birth. This all happened around the time that Ava lost her home to the fire. I went and visited her if you remember. Well, not that anyone knows it, but it was only a few weeks after giving birth to Ammon."

"You had a boy?" Willow asked, standing and coming over to her, clasping her hands. "You're a mother?"

Hallie nodded. "I am. He's the sweetest little boy, and my working here for the baron is so I can support him. I need positions like this so we'll be able to one day return to Surrey, to my cottage in Felday and I'll never have to leave him again. But there is a problem with that."

"What problem?" Willow asked, frowning.

"Lord Duncannon problem," Hallie admitted. "I've not been completely honest about his lordship either and after I tell you what happened many years ago I fear you'll think me a…"

"A what?" Willow clasped her shoulders to halt Hallie's pacing. "A what, Hallie?"

Hallie kept her attention on the fire, unable to look at her friend. "A whore," she admitted, shame washing through her that she'd been with two men in her life and both times married to neither of them. So unladylike even for a woman such as herself who thought women should have just as much freedom as men. Still, just like all the women of her acquaintance she was a product of her time and there were rules. Rules that she'd cast aside and now would have to pay the price for.

"You are not a whore. Tell me what happened, and please, stop pacing." Willow pulled her to sit back down before the hearth. "I want to know everything."

Hallie worked her bottom lip a moment before she said, "I first met Lord Duncannon by chance on the road to Felday, the day I buried Papa. He was cast off by his friends in a snowstorm and I gave him a lift to town so he may find a place to stay. But, due to the inclement weather, many people traveling through Surrey that day had halted in Felday for the night. There was no accommodation left in the town. Lord Duncannon asked if he could stay at my cottage and I couldn't see the harm in it and allowed him to." Hallie thought back on the night, the too many wines, the warm fire and cozy room, lit only by a single candle was a perfect situation for seduction and mistakes.

And oh boy, did she make one that night. The thought of his hands, strong and knowledgeable, certainly clever to make her even shiver to this day bombarded her mind. She let the memory take life in her mind as she told Willow all and everything that happened as if it were only yesterday.

"It started with a toast for papa, and spiraled out of control from there…"

Felday 1817

"I'M GOING to kiss you, Hallie," he'd said, brushing his lips just the slightest against hers. Without thought Hallie reached up and clasped his wicked, long locks and pulled him down for a kiss.

He moaned at her action and her body ached in places she'd not known could ache. What's more, Arthur kissed her back. He took her lips in a fierce way, and she scrambled to keep up with his desire.

She'd never done anything of the kind before, but a heady feeling came over her. A feeling that this was right and what she wanted, more than anything before leaving her home and starting a new life.

The action was scandalous of course, and when picking him up earlier today this was not how she thought her night would end, but in his arms, as his hand slid down hers, across her stomach and around to her bottom, nothing had ever felt so right.

"Are you sure?" he asked, kissing her throat and pulling the small ribbons on her dress apart, leaving the gown to gape at her neck.

Hallie nodded, kissing him again. "I'm sure," she gasped as his hand cupped her breast, his fingers finding her nipple and rolling it between his thumb and forefinger. Lightning shot through her veins and with a will of its own, her body purred against his like a feline seeking comfort.

Arthur stood, scooping her up in his arms and carrying her to her room. He lay her on the bed, following her down and kissing her, his intention as clear as her acquiescence.

"You're so beautiful." He rolled off her a little, lifting the hem of her dress, and pulled it upward over her body. Hallie sat up to allow him to take everything else off, and in her moonlit room she could see the need that burned in his gaze. He shucked off his breeches, his shirt his only attire, gaping at the neck and giving her a perfect view of his chiseled waist.

She reached over, taking the shirt in her hands and pulling it over his head. Hallie bit her lip at the sight that greeted her. His body was as lovely as his face, strong lines, taut and hers for the night.

Hallie ran her hand over the rippling muscles on his stomach, unable to stop her eyes from dipping to what stood erect between his legs. She reached down, running her finger along the tip and marveled at its perfection. "It's so soft and yet hard. I had no idea."

She felt his eyes upon her, and she looked up. "You're a virgin?" His words were breathless but controlled, and she nodded.

"Yes."

He frowned, his hand halting its path across her breasts.

"I don't want to stop," she said, moving over to him and wrapping her arms about his neck. "Show me what it's like before I leave all this behind. Just once I want to be with a man."

He pushed her hair off her face, clasping her jaw. "Are you really sure? I don't want you to think that I took advantage of you tonight. This was not my intention when I came here. I need you to know that."

She kissed him, slowly and deeply, just as he had before and he wrenched her hard against his person. "I know you did not, but I want to. I really want to."

Arthur kissed her fiercely, falling back onto the bed.

Hallie smiled through the embrace. Yes, this was what she wanted. This, all of this.

Her final memory before slipping off to sleep later that night, wrapped in his arms and hearing the thump of his heart against her ear, was of Arthur, and the perfect farewell gift he had given her. Multiple farewell gifts in fact.

Whatever next did the world have in store for her? She could not wait to find out.

HALLIE FINISHED TELLING Willow of her one night with Lord Duncannon, minus most of the details that were for her memories only. Her friend's eyes were wide, her cheeks as red as a Scottish lass who had stood in the sun too long.

"Well," Willow said, breathlessly. "You know Lord Duncannon very well indeed."

Hallie nodded. "I did not know he was a lord at that time. He introduced himself as Mr. Howard. When I met him again at the Duchess of Whitstone's ball, the night of the fire at Ava's estate I learned who he really was. Not that it would have changed what happened that night in Surrey, but I certainly would have been more prepared than I was when we did meet again."

"Which you did not think would happen. Am I right?"

"That's right. But we have run into each other again and its awkward. I think he likes me," she admitted, meeting her friend's startled gaze. "What are you thinking? You look surprised by that."

Willow threw her a concerned glance. "I'm just worried, that is all. Living with my aunt has been informative and not always in a positive sense. These lords are not to be trusted, and while there are a few who can be, the Duke of Whitstone of course, but most of the men of my acquaintance are rogues and go through women like a cook goes through dishwater."

"Eww," Hallie said, not liking the idea that she was being looked upon as dishwater or a just one of many on Lord Duncannon's bedpost. But then, she ought to think this way, for it would most likely be true. He was a renowned rake. His family also strove for him to marry only the best. She was surprised he spoke to her at all, she was so far beneath him, in his family's estimation at least.

But he did speak to her, helped her at the dig site and was trying to make amends. Hallie could not fault him for that. He was sweet and caring toward her. He'd already slept with her, so there was no reason why he should continue to work on their friendship, unless he was being truthful and trying to make things right between them.

"You need to speak to him, tell him that what happened in Egypt. Explain that what occurred between you both will not happen again and that he should concentrate on more eligible women who are actually interested in his courtship." Willow studied her a moment and Hallie fought not to fidget under her inspection. "Unless you are wanting his attention."

Nerves fluttered in her stomach at the thought of him touching her. She stood and went over to her desk, pouring two glasses of wine, having had the maid who turned down her bed tonight procure her a bottle before she retired for the evening.

Hallie handed a glass to Willow and swallowed hers down in one go. "Of course I do not, and I have already told him that nothing further will occur between us. I have other things taking up my attention. I do not need a man to get in the way of my life. I've had my fill of all that. I cannot ever see anyone coming close to how Omar made me feel."

She slumped down in her chair, laying her head against its back, knowing what she'd just said was far from the truth. Lord Duncannon had made her feel things as well, not just Omar, but she could not voice such things. To hope where there was no hope was a mistake she could not make. That road led to heartbreak and it wasn't only herself to consider now. She had a son as well.

"I think if you're honest with him he will leave you alone. He is the Duke of Whitstone's closest friend. Whitstone would not be his friend if he was not honorable."

Hallie nodded, having thought the same. "We did talk of what happened in Surrey today, at the dig site. The way he spoke made me believe he wants more."

Willow chuckled, sipping her wine. "I'm sure he does, but that does not mean he's going to get one."

"Of course not," Hallie retorted, ignoring the fact her body seized at the idea of having his hands on her again. The first time had been quick but so very satisfying. After being with Omar she was well aware of what her body was capable of and what she liked. To take a lover was not an awful idea, but the risks were too high. To have any more children out of wedlock was not something she was willing to do. Not even for another night in his arms.

"I'm glad of it," Willow said, standing and clapping her shoulder as she walked past to place her glass back on Hallie's desk. "I will leave you now to get your rest, but do not worry so, Hallie. Be honest with Lord Duncannon and all will be well. You'll see, he will understand you're no longer looking for that type of relationship. Your son must take priority and he will respect your decision."

"Goodnight, Willow," Hallie said as her friend left her room, closing her door softly behind her. She stood and went back over to her desk, pouring herself another glass of wine. By the time she finished the bottle she was not only a little tipsy, she was also in need of another drink.

Perhaps the library had some whisky she could take up to her room. Hallie slipped on her dressing robe, and checking the passage outside her door noted no one about nor any noise from downstairs. A few sconces burned along the walls, lighting her way, but as she came to the staircase, she spied a footman below, slumped on his chair asleep, only a single candle burning in the entrance hall.

She slipped past him and started for the library, thankfully finding it empty. The decanter was full and she picked it up, wondering if taking that to her room would look a little bit extreme. Instead, she placed it back down, bending to look in the cupboard beneath. A bottle of red wine sat there along with an array of glasses. She picked up the wine and turned for the door, her steps a little uneven as she moved across the room, trying not to run into any furniture and make noise.

A quick look about the entrance produced only the sleeping servant who had not moved. Hallie ran past him, taking the stairs as fast as she could. When she made the passage that led to her room her nerves settled. The wine had made her warm and relaxed and after admitting her two biggest secrets tonight she was in need of fortification.

Thank heavens Willow had seemed to take the news well. Maybe her other friends would also when she told them, and she would have to tell them. And soon. She wanted to live with her child and she would no longer live hidden away, frightened of what everyone would think. If they chose to turn their backs, that was their cross to bear.

"Drinking alone is never a good thing, Miss Evans."

Hallie stifled a scream and fumbled with the bottle, almost dropping it. She glanced up and through the darkened hall spotted Lord Duncannon, similarly dressed to how he was the night they were in Surrey together. His buckskin breeches fitted him like a glove and his shirt gaped open, yet again tempting her to sin.

She shut her eyes, forcing away the visual. "Spying on me now, my lord. If you keep this up, I'll start to think you're obsessed with me."

He chuckled and pushed off from the wall, strolling with a relaxed air that reminded her of a predatory cat slinking after it's meal. "Oh, I admit that I'm obsessed with you, Miss Evans and enamoured, in awe and many other things. If only you would put me out of my misery and be with me. Always."

She gasped and slapped her hand over mouth, wondering if she had drunk too much tonight and was now imagining all of this. Surely not. "You tease," she said, calling his bluff and meeting him in the middle of the hall. Sandalwood wafted from his skin and this close she could see that he'd recently bathed. The idea of him neck deep in water, rubbing soap over his skin and washing his body caused a shiver to steal down her spine. She clutched the bottle of wine between her breasts in the hopes of stopping her hands reaching out and touching him.

To know what if felt like to be with Lord Duncannon, to be the sole recipient of the gentleman's attentions was not something to remove from one's mind without sheer force. A force made impossible by the foxed state she was currently in.

"I've never been more serious." He stepped closer still and his chest brushed hers. Her breath hitched and she dropped her hands to her sides, bottle dangling from one hand. Her heart beat so loud she was sure he would hear it.

"I told you earlier today that what happened between us was a mistake and one I'm not willing to repeat." She studied his jaw, a small shadow of stubble marring the normally perfect visage. Bloody damn it, he was just so good-looking and so sweet. Her fingers itched to slide up his chest and clasp his jaw, pull him down for a kiss. Allow him to seduce her to the thought of them, a future that would never eventuate. If she allowed this madness to commence it would only lead to heartache.

She could not countenance that.

"I want you, all of you, Hallie. I have since the day you offered me a ride in Surrey. Did you not feel it also?"

She shut her eyes, willing the emotions that he wrought up in her to subside. To leave and never come back. He wasn't for her. If her lineage wasn't enough to exclude her to be anything to him, her actions in Egypt and the son she'd borne out of wedlock certainly would put paid to that notion.

"It makes no difference what I feel. We can only ever be friends." She started back to her room, needing to be away from him and all that he offered. To be loved by the Viscount Duncannon meant security and safety, both for her and her son. But it was a fickle dream. As soon as he knew the truth of her situation he would run for the hills. No man wanted to bring up another man's child. Especially if that child had not been born in wedlock.

He pulled her to a stop, whipping her around to look at him. "Why are you fighting this? I know you feel something for me, so if it's not too much trouble I'd like you to stop pushing me away. Can you do that?"

She ripped her arm free, glaring at him. Hating him for being so honest. It would be so much easier to deny him if he were not so sweet. "I do not feel anything for you, my lord. I'm sorry to disappoint you, but that is the truth."

"Really?" he said, a sarcastic tilt to his mouth. "Why do

I not believe that?" he whispered, leaning close and tempting her with his lips.

She bit her bottom lip, forcing her gaze away from his face. "You should. It's the truth. Goodnight." Hallie walked back to her room, the need to run almost impossible to deny. He didn't follow her this time and she was thankful for it. She wasn't sure she could deny him a second time. Not with her mind fuzzy with too much wine and also his own persuasive self.

His tempting words for a life with her.

CHAPTER 10

Hallie was late to the site the following day, a headache thumping hard at her temples. She watched from the safety of the tent as the men continued to dig, trowel, and sift through the soil in and out of the trench. She sketched some of the artifacts that had been found, and also the site itself, content with that line of work instead of the more manual-intensive jobs she would normally do.

No one wanted to see a woman cast up her accounts.

Lord Duncannon had not visited her on the site and she ignored the fact that his not being there made her stomach churn in an unpleasant way. Or it could be churning because of all the wine she'd imbibed the night before, having had several more glasses after leaving Arthur. Thankfully she'd fallen asleep and had not gone to his room to allow him to further their acquaintance.

Hallie rubbed her brow, her mind not as sharp or clear as it normally was. She would not drink again, she promised herself. No more drinking her worries into submission. She would face her fears and her life just as her father brought her up to face them. Head on and with her chin raised.

"Here you are," a deep, gravelly voice said before a head popped between the tent flaps.

Her heart gave a jump at the sight of him, all his blond, godlike features and a smile that would seduce a nun. "What are you doing here?" she asked, standing, clutching her sketchbook to her chest as if to ward him off like paper armor.

"Coming to see if you've changed your mind."

"I haven't," she retorted, stepping away to place the small work table between them.

He strolled into the tent, one hand idly running across the table top as he walked toward her. "Maybe you need a reminder of how very good it can be between us."

Hallie shut her eyes, no reminder necessary. She could remember every second of their time together in Surrey. Every touch and look, the way his lips took hers, demanding and yet, soft and supple.

"I know you're lying, my dear. Come, kiss me."

She halted and he continued to stroll about the table, catching up to her. "Kiss me, Hallie. If after our kiss you still do not feel anything for me other than friendship, I shall never bother you again. I promise," he said, making the sign of a cross over his chest.

Hallie pursed her lips, debating the offer. It would certainly allow her to tell him at least that his kiss did not affect her, even if it did.

"Very well, you may kiss me. Once. And that is all."

"And that is quite enough, I assure you," he said, quickly, hoisting her into his arms and taking her lips without hesitation.

The moment Arthur's lips touched Hallie's he knew what it was to feel right. The woman in his arms was his other half in this world. He was sure of it. She melted against him and he deepened the embrace, wanting to show her all that she made him feel, and she made him feel so damn much.

More than he had ever felt with anyone else. He'd known it the moment he'd touched her in Surrey she was different. His soul knew she was the one. Now, he had to convince her of the fact and his family, who would not be impressed that he was marrying a woman out of the sphere in which they circulated.

"You're so sweet," he said, lifting her to set her on her workbench. She gasped at the action and he took the opportunity to kiss her long and deep. His body roared to life when she kissed him back with as much passion as he remembered, spiking his need of her. It had been so very long since he'd been with a woman and especially a woman that made him feel so much more than just running through the motions of seduction.

He wanted more for Hallie. Wanted to make her happy both in these situations and in everyday life. He wanted to give her a home, security and, god willing, children.

Her hands clutched at his shoulders before slipping around his neck, pulling him close. He could feel her breasts rising with each breath against his chest and he ached to cup them. Arthur kept his hands on her waist, demanding them to stay put and not move. Not to push her too far. He needed her in his life, not to run away in fear.

Her tongue slipped against his and he growled. Damn it she tempted him like a siren's call. He stepped closer still, placing him hard against her body. A shame they both were fully clothed. He undulated against her sex, eliciting a gasp from her. Her leg wrapped about his, pulling him closer still.

Arthur's cock was as hard as a rod and he pushed against her sex, the action teased him and he fought not to spill in his pants like a green lad. Her raspy intake of breaths did odd things to him, and he increased his pace. Had anyone walked in, it would have appeared as if they were rutting like two wild beasts. He wanted to have her again, dreamed about it often for years, if he were honest with himself.

The sound of men's laughter outside the tent pulled him back to his wits and he wrenched out of her arms, stepping away. She jumped off the table, holding it for support just as Bruce pushed up the tent flaps and entered, taking his cap off when he spied them.

"Miss Hallie, we've found another gold artifact. Did you want to have a look at it before we trowel farther into the ground?"

Arthur watched as she fought to regain her composure. She checked her hair, and then looking about, grabbed her woollen cap she was fond of wearing and, slipping it on her head, walked out the tent without a word.

Arthur leaned upon the table, taking deep, calming breaths. Damn it all to hell the one kiss he'd asked for had progressed too fast that even now his head swam. He stared after her, hoping she would not dismiss him after his slip of etiquette.

There was something between them, and he needed to find out what that was. He had a sneaking suspicion that it was something akin to what his good friend the Duke of Whitstone felt for his wife.

He ran a hand through his hair, checking his clothing

before heading outside to join Hallie and her workers at the trench. Surely after a kiss such as the one they just shared she would agree that they had something special. Something that only came around once in one's life.

Something to hold on to and not throw away, no matter the obstacles.

LATER THAT NIGHT Hallie sat in the drawing room, listening to Willow talk of her day and that her aunt had given her approval to visit her dig site on the morrow. All of her friends' words were lost on her as her attention had been captivated by the very deadly and seductive Lord Duncannon, who spoke with a group of gentlemen across the room, including Baron Bankes.

After losing Omar she had sworn not to become affected or drawn into the games of men. But then, Lord Duncannon was unlike most men. That she'd known him before she left for Egypt also was a factor. Even then, when she hardly knew the gentleman, she had felt a connection to him. Lust, more than anything. Of that she was certain now that she knew what that emotion was.

And she was feeling that emotion again and more. A sentiment she didn't want to delve into too much right at the moment. To walk that path meant risking her heart, and she wasn't sure she could survive it breaking a second time.

She inwardly cursed at being weak. She needed to be strong, for her own moral compass and for her son. To be with a man again was a risk and she was certain that even as deadly sexy as his lordship was, he was not worth that price.

He laughed at something the baron said, and her heart

skipped a beat. She sighed, maybe he was worth that price…

"Hallie? Have you heard a word that I said to you?"

Hallie turned to Willow and fought to recall what her friend had been telling her. Something about lace… "I'm sorry, Willow. I was wool-gathering."

"You were not," her friend retorted. "You were watching a certain blond god across the room."

Heat bloomed on her cheeks and she shook her head, physically dismissing the idea even though her mind shouted, *yes, yes she was watching him and enjoying every moment of it.* "Of course I was not. I was merely taking in the guests, that is all. Lady Hayes looks very pretty this evening."

Willow cast a cursory glance at Lady Hayes and turned her disbelieving gaze back to Hallie. "Please, even I can lie better than that. You're slipping, Hallie. You used to be better at fibs."

She shrugged, her gaze unnervingly slipping back to Lord Duncannon. As if feeling her inspection, he glanced in her direction, his lips twitching into a rakish grin. Her stomach clenched. Whatever was she going to do about him?

"We're old enough to know that if you were discreet you could take a lover," Willow whispered, leaning in close to ensure privacy. "No one need ever know."

"No," she said, hating the idea. "I've already borne one child out of wedlock, I will not do it again. I'm content as I am. I'm independent, or will be very soon and in the next few months I'll be able to return to Surrey with Ammon and live quietly. I do not need anything to get in the way of that."

"Of course the decision is yours, but you must see that Lord Duncannon may be worth the risk."

"Maybe you ought to take him to your bed since you're so very fond of the idea."

Willow gasped, her eyes widening in shock. "It's not me that he's interested in, otherwise I probably would. I know my aunt wants me to marry well, but after all these years in society and no prospects I fear her dream is in vain. I'm destined to be an old maid. At least I'll have you for company."

Hallie chuckled. "You're incorrigible." She turned back to watch Lord Duncannon. He was deep in conversation with Lord Bankes about something and they both seemed absorbed in the subject matter. Probably horses or dogs.

"Have you kissed him since he's been here? I feel like you're not telling me everything." Willow raised her brow in question.

How could she tell her friend after all that she'd said about his lordship that she had kissed him and some other things. Allowed him to touch her while they were both guests of the baron, to slide up against her body in the most evocative way to tease them both.

She stifled a sigh at the memory of it. It was all deliciousness and a pastime that she could get used to. Even so, there were some things that Willow or any of her friends did not need to know and this was one of them. Nothing would come of their one kiss in the tent and so it would be silly to involve her friend or get her hopes up regarding his lordship.

"No," she lied, taking a sip of her wine. "And nor will it."

ROBERT SIPPED his whisky and watched Hallie and Lord Duncannon trade heated glances across the room. The silly chit was hot for the man, and he too was a willing participant if he were any judge. Pity his knowledge of Miss Evans would ruin her chances with his lordship. If Lord Duncannon did not turn away from an alliance with this chit when he knew her secrets, then his family would most certainly ensure it occurred.

"Miss Evans," he said, coming to stand beside her. "You're looking particularly pretty this evening. Is that another gown borrowed from Miss Perry?"

Her head whipped about to stare at him and he smiled at the disdain she held in her eyes for him. Good. For he had disdain for her as well.

"It is, Mr. Stewart. How very clever of you to notice. Are you so familiar with the female attire of this house party?"

"Only when it comes to you," he said, taking her arm and leading her away from Willow. Hallie frowned at his gumption. He smirked and continued on.

"I'm glad we're having this moment to better acquaint ourselves. I do love to be informed, to have information about other people. It's a little hobby of mine you could say."

"Really?" she said, her reply bored and uninterested.

"Yes, really, Miss Evans. Shall I tell you a little story that I heard while I was traveling through Rome last year?"

She shrugged, holding her hands at her front. He glanced at her hands, wondering if that was a little tremor he could see. "Of course, if you wish it."

He chuckled, enjoying this little game more than he thought he would. "That a certain unmarried woman from Felday had borne a child out of wedlock and to an Egyptian general. Can you imagine the scandal? Will you not ask me to whom I may be referring?"

Her skin visibly paled and she refused to look at him. "I will not ask. It seems to be of a private matter," she replied.

Clever girl, but not clever enough. "Well, as to that I can help there," he said, matter-of-fact. "It was you, my dear. Can you imagine such a rumor? However have you survived this long with that tidbit hanging about your neck like a noose?"

She didn't reply and he wondered how long it would be before he claimed any reaction from her. She was a cool one, this Miss Evans, but not cool enough to sneak out of this mess. He wanted her to make a fool of herself. To appear paranoid and unclear with her thinking. She had watched his cousin die without blinking an eye. To make the educated and well-respected Miss Evans pay for her indiscretions was his sole responsibility. His family and their honor demanded it.

"I shall not tease you any longer, Miss Evans. Me knowing your secret must come as a shock, I know, but I will be honest with you as to what I'm going to do with this information, which is more than you ever afforded my cousin. You and your friend did not give his lordship a second chance."

She pulled her arm free of his and stepped back. "Your cousin, sir? I do not understand."

"No you would not, I suppose, but I will explain it to you. Let me just say that I know everything there is to know about you, Miss Evans. I know of Ammon and where he lives. I also know that Omar, your lover, was from a very influential and wealthy family in Cairo. I'm sure they would be very interested in knowing that Omar, their only son, had fathered a boy child."

"You wouldn't dare," she said. He had to give her credit, where he thought she may succumb to the vapors or tears, she instead glared up at him, her mouth pulled into a hard, determined line.

"Oh I would. In fact I have every intention of telling everyone in London and here at this party of who you really are. That you're nothing better than a whore who, although I will credit you with a mind, is still just a woman looking for a hard tup."

"Why are you doing this to me?" she asked and he could almost feel sorry for her. She looked so very pathetic with the fear that lingered in the green depths of her eyes. How sad that as independent a woman Miss Evans was, she'd become pathetic at the first sign of a disagreement.

"My cousin, Lord Oakes probably asked the same thing, before you left him to burn to death. He did not deserve his fate and it was you and Miss Ava Knight who took his future from him. So now I will take your future from you, unless you do as I ask."

She glanced about the room. Robert did the same, noting they were quite alone. "What do you want?" she whispered, her voice trembling.

"Money. I want what you'll earn here at this dig and any other digs into the foreseeable future. I have a future too you see that I need to plan and work toward. You will help me in gaining all that I want."

"But if I give you everything that I earn, what will I have left to live on? I have expenses just like you, Mr. Stewart."

He shrugged. "Not my concern. You will do as I ask or I'll tell Lord Duncannon and your son's family everything you're hiding and let the dice roll where they will. You may either allow fate to choose your future, or you can. It's up to you."

She stared at him for a moment and he could see her debating, weighing up what he was demanding of her. He watched her with interest, already knowing that she would agree to his demand. What choice did she have? She had no choice.

Miss Evans nodded and walked away, placing down her glass and leaving the room. He smiled. "Just as I thought."

CHAPTER 11

Hallie fled the drawing room, and seeing people on the staircase and in no mood for idle chat, she headed for the back of the house and the servants' stairs that she used often throughout the day. Tears slipped down her cheeks and she swiped at them, not wanting anyone to see her upset.

What was she going to do? The one hundred and fifty pounds this dig was to be paid to her had been allocated to unpaid debts and stabilizing her and her son's future. She had wanted to purchase some new things for her son and help pay her cousin for his welfare for the past few years. The money was her safety and security when without work. To have to give it away to Mr. Stewart simply because she was involved in his cousin's reign of madness was in itself insanity.

Hallie slumped down on a settee in an unoccupied room, staring at the unlit hearth before her. He would ruin her, that she had no doubt. The hatred she read in his cold eyes was proof of that. To anyone looking at them they would not have seen his hidden loathing of her, but it was there, masked beneath a smiling mouth and charming voice.

Bastard.

She sniffed and dabbed at her face. How was it that men like Mr. Stewart even existed? She doubted he would try such a scheme with a gentleman. No, he only targeted women. Women like her who had a lot to lose and who had no family, no brother to defend them.

"Hallie?"

She jumped and turned to see Lord Duncannon standing at the door, the light from the hall behind him illuminating him but leaving his features too dark to read.

"Can I help you, my lord?" she asked, turning to look back at the hearth, not wanting him to see her upset.

"I saw you with Mr. Stewart and you appeared upset by his conversation. I wanted to ensure he has not injured you in any way."

She shut her eyes in part exasperation that Lord Duncannon was aware of her enough to know when she was injured and part pleasure that he cared enough to see if she were well. "Mr. Stewart was simply being a man. No need to worry about me, my lord. I'm perfectly capable of looking after myself." She sighed. Of course by paying Mr. Stewart her salary, she would keep his mouth closed for some months, or at least until she found further employment and then his threats would start again. How long did he plan on keeping this threat over her head?

Forever, probably. Who would not keep asking for funds and therefore not have to work themselves? A great many people she would imagine.

Lord Duncannon came into the room, shutting the door behind him before sitting beside her. She hoped that he could not see that she'd been crying or he would know she had lied and he could then possibly make a scene with

Mr. Stewart when not knowing all the facts. There was no knowing what the man was capable of if threatened. He would more than likely shout out to all who were present that she had slept with an Egyptian general and had his child out of wedlock.

"You're upset," he said, taking her hand and pulling her toward him.

How had he known? The man must have night vision to have seen that she'd been crying. His presence overwhelmed her, tempting her to lean into his warmth and care. To stay there forever.

"Nothing of concern, my lord. Please do not pry," she said, hoping he would let the subject drop.

"Hallie," he pleaded, reaching up and clasping her jaw, turning her to face him. "You would tell me if something was wrong. You know that I would help you with anything. I do not like to see you distressed."

She pulled her jaw free of his hand. His touch made her want things that she should not. Things that in the past now placed her in the predicament she now faced. The man was trouble, but in a completely different manner to what trouble Mr. Stewart brought her. One night in his arms was starting to be very difficult to deny herself, especially when to escape into that dream could remove her from the nightmare that Mr. Stewart made her live in.

"I'm tired, that is all, my lord. I think I shall retire for the night." She went to stand and he stayed her by touching her arm.

"Must you go? I've not seen you today. Lord Bankes asked me to ride out with him to his tenant farms and view some of his land. I could not refuse."

"There are more eligible and suitable women in the drawing room, Lord Duncannon. It confuses me still as to why you would waste your time with me. We do not suit."

The memory of Arthur in her bed that night in Surrey
bombarded her mind. She supposed that they did not suit
was not entirely true. They did suit very well when thrown
together in such circumstances. But the idea of forever,
well, that was an absurdity that she could not let herself
believe in.

His touch the other day at the dig site, the scorching
heat and need he made her body feel even now tempted
her. Tempted her when it shouldn't. Long after he'd
returned to working in the trench, she had burned for his
touch, to feel his unrelenting lips against her own. She was
doomed if such wants continued. A fault within her that
she wanted things similar to men. Wanting the same freedom, but unable to have it.

"I do not care what anyone thinks. I need you to know
and believe that you are the woman that I crave. The one
and only woman that I want in my bed." He shuffled
closer still, clasping her face with both hands. "I burn for
you, Hallie. I have for years. I know our history is as turbu-
lent as that first carriage ride you offered me in Surrey, but
you are the only woman that I've never been able to forget.
I do not want to regret not knowing if you and I can be
more than our history."

She stared at him, her mind tumbling to understand
what he was saying. "I'm not for you, Arthur. Your family
would never accept me, and if you knew me at all, I know
that you would not either." Hallie reached up and clasped
his hands, pulling them down to sit in her lap. "I would be
lying if I did not admit to wanting you. That at night the
longing in me to be with you makes me want to throw all
rules of etiquette aside and sneak into your room, but it
would not change anything. There are things in my past
that I cannot change and they are things that I do not
believe you or your family would understand. Please know

that I cannot give you what you want. I risk too much by such actions."

He frowned, his hands clasping hers in a relentless grip. "What has happened that makes you believe that? I know my family, once they meet you, they will adore you. You are a gentleman's daughter and I am a gentleman. I see no reason why I cannot court you at least."

Her breath hitched at the sweetness of him. To be courted and flirted with sounded heavenly, if she were not a woman who had taken a lover out of wedlock and birthed his child with no regrets.

"I'm past being courted. That time has long expired."

"Please," he begged, squeezing her hands. "Let me at least try to win you and if you do not wish to pursue a future with me, then I shall leave you alone. I promise you that."

Hallie stood and walked over to the window, looking out at the dark grounds that had only the smallest amount of moonlight to light anyone's way. She thought over his proposition. Not that she thought it could lead to anything, but then if Mr. Stewart thought she were being pursued by Lord Duncannon he may also leave her alone. He may, in fact, stop his threats.

She turned to his lordship, hating in part that she was using him to keep Mr. Stewart at arm's length. "Very well. I shall let you court me, but please know that I do not believe that anything can come of this union. Even so, it'll be nice to be flirted with by a handsome gentleman."

He grinned and stood, coming over to her. "You think I'm handsome."

She chuckled. "You know you are," she said, sucking in a breath as he stepped close to her person, his chest brushing hers and making her body ache.

"You're so beautiful." His breath tickled across her lips.

Hallie could get used to Arthur speaking to her in such a way. It had been a long time since she'd had such sweet words whispered to her. Even with everything working against them, his family and her past, still she could not help but fall into the dance of courtship.

She leaned into him and kissed him, inwardly smiled as he stilled a moment in surprise before hoisting her up hard against him and kissing her back. His lips took hers, and she opened for him immediately, wanting to feel his touch, the slide of his tongue against hers, his heat and desire. All of it just for her.

Being with him was delicious.

Their kiss, just like all that they'd shared went from sweet and tempting to hot and demanding within a moment. Only with Arthur did she ever have this reaction. This need that rose within her and left her aching and wanting more. Always more.

"We should stop. Anyone could walk in," she gasped, pulling away. He kissed down her neck, his tongue sliding against her collar bone. She clutched at his shoulders, her knees weak all of a sudden.

"God, you smell good." He kissed up to her ear, licking her lobe. Hallie shut her eyes, a shiver raking her body. Blast it, he was good at seduction. Good at making whatever woman was in his arms feel special. "It's hard to stop," he admitted.

With great difficulty, she pushed at his chest, separating them. He stepped back, disappointment written across his face. A disappointment she could well understand as she too was feeling it right at this moment.

"Are you heading up to the dig site tomorrow?"

"Yes," she said, checking her gown and making sure her hair was just as it was before they started clutching at each other. "Will you be coming up to help me? I'm hoping to start a second trench tomorrow."

He came up behind her, wrapping his arms about her waist and kissing her neck quickly. "I will be. I have some missives to write to my steward first, and then I'll be up there. I'll bring lunch if you wish to picnic with me."

The idea of having a lovely repast with him at the dig site, a place that she found pleasure just being near, nevertheless working at, made her heart beat fast. That Arthur not only liked what she did but supported her, told her that perhaps he was no longer the rogue he was reputed to be. Not all men would be so accommodating. Certainly not titled ones.

"I would like that. Thank you."

Arthur spent the morning writing letters to his steward regarding his two estates and then set about writing a letter to his grandmother. He'd been putting off sending her a missive simply because the last time that she had written him, she had gone on, to no end, regarding his continued bachelorhood and his lack of prospects or inclination toward marriage.

That had all changed. The kiss the other day at the dig site for starters, and now just last night had seemed to be a turning point with him and Hallie. That she was allowing him to court her was a big step for her, and a massive relief for him.

Now he had to write to his grandmother and explain what he was about and who he was courting. He was certain that once she met Hallie she would fall in love with her as much as he feared he was well on the way to doing.

He'd never felt such a connection with anyone before

in his life and to finally have her back in England and willing to see what may come of them was a desire he'd never thought would come to fruition.

"Ah, Lord Duncannon, may I come in? There is a book on botany that Baron Bankes mentioned and I'm most eager to look through it."

Arthur glanced up from signing the letter to his grandmother and nodded to Mr. Stewart, who stood at the threshold of the room. "Of course. Please, come in. I'm almost finished here in any case."

The gentleman scanned the bookshelves as Arthur wax-sealed his missives and stamped them with his family emblem. Out the corner of his eye he watched the man's progress, something about the gentleman not sitting right with him. Arthur could not exactly say what it was about him that he distrusted, maybe a gut instinct, but there was something decidedly off about the man. Hallie certainly did not like him, and his presence discomfited her, more than she would admit. He would bear keeping an eye on.

"What a delightful house party," Mr. Stewart said, his back to Arthur as he continued his search. "I do not think I've ever been to one with such congenial guests. Do you not agree, Lord Duncannon?"

Arthur had been to many house parties over the years, some with much more friendly and agreeable persons, but then Mr. Stewart may not have been to as many as he and so he nodded, showing his support. "It has been a most pleasant stay."

"Have you been up to the archaeological dig site yet? I must admit that I'm yet to look in on it, but I do believe the woman who's in charge of it, Miss Evans, is most accomplished."

"She is," he agreed, at least on this point Mr. Stewart was indeed quite correct. "They are starting a new trench tomorrow in fact. I'm sure in the days to come they will find many new artifacts to date and explain."

"Oh yes, no doubt," Mr. Stewart readily agreed. "I understand she spent some time in Egypt. How very exotic of her. The stories she could tell if only she would." He chuckled. "Do you not agree, my lord?"

Arthur set the letters on the silver slaver on the desk for the staff to post and leaned back in the leather wing-back chair. He steepled his fingers before him, watching Mr. Stewart stroll about the shelves. He narrowed his eyes, starting to doubt his sole purpose here was to discuss Hallie and not this book on botany at all.

The pit of his gut clenched at the idea that Mr. Stewart may like Hallie more than he was letting on and was looking to see if he had any competition. "I should imagine she would know a great deal about the area and the people. I know through mutual friends she was very much in love with the country."

"Maybe there is more to that than we know," he said. "Women, after all, are mysterious beings with many thoughts and dreams inside their minds."

Arthur stared at Mr. Stewart's back, the idea that Hallie had more of a life than work in Egypt had never entered his mind. He didn't think the culture allowed for balls like those he'd attended at Almacks with his numerous friends. That did not mean that they did not occur or that she'd had the ability to meet people. Men...

"Ah ha, here it is," he said, holding up the thick tome and showing Arthur. "I'm so glad Baron Bankes had not led me on a merry chase. A book such as this is just what I need in such a large and lonely estate."

Arthur stared down at the desk, thinking of Hallie and her time abroad. "I hope you enjoy your book," he said, standing. "Do visit the dig site, Mr. Stewart. I think you'll find it quite interesting."

The man did not reply, merely nodded. Arthur strode out into the entrance and started for his room. What Mr. Stewart had said gave Arthur pause. He'd never thought about Hallie in Egypt and her many years there must have been taken up with more than just archaeological digs. Of course their days were long and arduous and very much hard work, but that did not mean that was the only thing Hallie did when away.

Had someone abroad courted her? There were many Englishmen who traveled abroad, who went to Egypt and farther east to survey and learn of new lands. Had any one of them shown an interest in Hallie? Why else would Mr. Stewart say such a thing? The man was not to be trusted and Arthur could not help but think that he was hinting at something.

But what?

He rubbed his jaw, thinking over the prospect. It did not mean that Hallie had been courted by an Englishman at all. What if there had been a man from Egypt who had captured her attention? Had courted her?

And loved her as much as he was fearing he was starting to.

HALLIE THREW herself into work over the next few days. The new trench was well underway, a slow process by hand and she couldn't help but hope that one day such tasks could be made easier with some invention or contraption of some type.

Unfortunately Mr. Stewart had paid her a visit only yesterday, spouting on about what they had found and how very interesting it was to discover things that were lost. One of his particular comments about the past and how things never stayed buried for long was of particular interest and seemed to make him laugh at his own threats.

She had looked at him, wanting him to see how much she loathed him and his blackmailing. She could not trust him or that he would keep his mouth shut if she paid him. He was up to something other than taking her hard-earned money, and the pit of her stomach churned that he would not be satisfied with that compensation.

After an hour or so she had been glad to see him go and she was most especially pleased with the shower of rain that had passed through that had ensured his departure. For all of his spouting off of enjoying her type of work and being outdoors in nature, he didn't have a very fine opinion of the location or weather.

The rain unfortunately had continued to pass through Somerset and she had to abandon the dig site, heading back to the estate several hours earlier than planned. The men had laid tarps over the trenches to try to stop the soil from bogging up too much, but as the afternoon ticked away, the rain only seemed to get heavier.

Hallie ordered a bath, and with the help of a maid was able to remove her soaked clothing with little trouble.

"I shall take it downstairs to dry, Miss Evans. Will you be needing anything else before I go?"

"No, thank you," she said, walking to the door to lock it before she bathed. "I'll not be needing anything else tonight." Hallie locked the door and then thankfully alone, sank down in her hot bath. The servants had placed it before the well-lit fire and she lay back, relaxing in the little luxury this house stay afforded.

She smiled at the thought of being back at her cottage in Felday. The small house didn't have room for such a big bath. They would have to make do with a hip bath and one in the kitchen when the need arose.

Hallie picked up the soap that smelled of fresh herbs and cleaned the day's grime from her skin. Once this job was completed, she had hoped to do one or two more archaeological digs before collecting her son from her cousin and returning to Surrey. Mr. Stewart's threat now stopped her from following her plan.

Whatever was she going to do?

Maybe she could seek the gentleman out and ask him to rethink his threat. There were very few she could turn to. Of course Willow would help her, but then if society found out about her child and that she was unmarried, people associated with her would be tainted.

She could not tell Willow of Mr. Stewart's demand, for she knew her friend would defend her even if it were at her own peril.

Sadly the idea of burying Mr. Stewart in one of her trenches had come to mind. It would certainly fix all her problems and for a man to threaten a vulnerable woman, she doubted he'd be missed very much in this world.

A light knock sounded on her door and she sat up in the bath, the water splashing over the side. "Who is it?" she asked, thankful she'd locked the door.

"It's me. Duncannon. I need to speak to you."

She sat in the bath a moment longer, unsure if she wanted to speak to him. Every time she was around him, he made her feel and do things that she'd promised herself never to feel or do since losing Omar. Even so, she stood, clasping the towel off a nearby chair and wrapped it about herself, walking to the door. "What do you want?" she whispered, hoping no one saw his lordship whispering at her door like a lover after a midnight tryst.

"Can you meet me in the downstairs back parlor?

Everyone is in the front drawing room waiting for dinner to be announced, but I need to speak to you."

Hallie frowned. What did Lord Duncannon need to speak to her about? "I'll be down directly. I'll meet you there."

She listened at the door as his receding footsteps sounded on the carpeted passageway. Hallie dressed quickly in a clean afternoon gown. The bodice was a little snug and the cut of the dress was a couple of years old, but it was still reasonably unworn and suited her coloring.

As she made her way downstairs, she couldn't help but wonder what he wanted to discuss. She also couldn't help but debate whether she should confide in him about Mr. Stewart. She didn't have to mention her son, but she could mention what her past in Egypt had been, and that Mr. Stewart was threatening to expose. It would give her a good indication of what Lord Duncannon thought of her actions.

Her past as a woman who had fallen in love and slept with another man out of wedlock. If he was supportive and not offensive toward her, he may be someone she could turn to for help, to eventually tell of her boy. Lord Duncannon had powerful friends, many of whom could make Mr. Stewart keep his mouth closed and leave her alone for good.

The drawing room was dark, and yet a small candle burned on the mantel and the fire had been lit. Lord Duncannon came over to her as she entered and locked the door behind her, helping her to a chair before the hearth.

"There is something that I need to ask you and you may tell me to go to the devil, but I really do hope you're able to give me the truth."

"If I can I will." She looked up at him as he sat on a

nearby chair, working his hands in his lap. Nerves pooled in her stomach that perhaps Mr. Stewart had already been at work with his lordship and poisoning his mind against her.

"I'm nervous to ask you what I want," he admitted.

Hallie smiled to put him at ease and yet her stomach churned. What was it he wanted to know? Or worse, what did he suspect? "Ask me, Arthur, or you'll make me as nervous as you are."

He took a deep breath, meeting her with a steady gaze. "I wanted to ask you about your time in Egypt. What your life was like there."

Everything within her stilled. To ask such a question made it abundantly clear that Mr. Stewart had been whispering ideas into people's heads. Who else had he spoken to? What other suggestions had he made them think? Of course, she could be turning paranoid, but she highly doubted it. The man was bent on ruining her reputation. "It was a very busy life. We had multiple dig sites that Mr. Shelly was overseeing and every day a new artifact was found and catalogued. You're the benefactor of the British Museum, surely you would know as well as anyone how busy we were. The museum did take delivery of multiple artifacts from us."

"Of course," he said, a small frown between his eyes. She watched him a moment and could see he was struggling with some truth or a question that he wasn't certain he should ask. Or know how to breach. "Did you have much of a social life in Egypt?"

And there it was, the one question that she had been dreading. Even so, a little relief poured through her that he'd asked. She didn't have to tell him about Ammon, but she would not hide the courtship with Omar. She had loved him, with all her heart and no one would ever change that wonderful time in her life. "I enjoyed dinners and balls similar to those held in London at the Consul General's home in Cairo. Mr. Henry Salt had close ties with the ruler of Egypt, the Pasha Mohamed Ali, and the evenings were always interesting and pleasurable. Mr. Salt is an Egyptologist, and immensely clever. You know him of course."

"I have met him once or twice. He has given antiquities to the British Museum as well."

"Of course," she said, well believing that. "Just as in England, the ruler of Egypt had a militia, men who were under his rule and protected him. They too were often at these events, but always watching, not taking too much of an interest." Except for one of course. Omar, who had seen Hallie from across the room, and her world had stopped at the sight of him. His too, she knew.

Lord Duncannon's eyes narrowed on her and she could see he was weighing her words. "Did you..." He cleared his throat. "Were you courted while abroad?"

Hallie raised her brows as she thought back on that time. How the sight of Omar had made her heart skip a beat. He had not moved, merely watched, and yet his eyes had heated with interest at the sight of her and she had known, somehow, in some way, their lives would intertwine.

"My time in Egypt was very memorable and pleasant. I shall miss it forever."

He watched her and she could see in his eyes that he wanted no secrets between them. If he was serious about courting her she supposed they shouldn't have secrets, but something in Arthur's eyes gave her pause. A fear of hearing of her past may cause him to not like what he heard stilled her tongue. Stopped her from forming the words that she'd fallen in love in that wonderous, ancient land and regretted not a bit of it.

"I want us to be honest with each other, Hallie. No secrets."

"There is nothing that you need to know, my lord," she lied, hoping he could not read her too well or tell when she was trying to hide a secret. He was not ready to hear her truths, and in all honestly, she was not ready to tell him. Not really.

"What about you?" she asked, changing the subject matter. "You're well known in London and many mama's wish to turn your head toward their charges. Is there no one that your grandmother has chosen for you?"

He chuckled, leaning back in his chair, steepling his fingers. "I'm sure there are many, but none of them would suit. I've never been one for meek and mild," he said, giving her a pointed look that made her skin warm.

She wasn't fool enough not to know he meant her. He wanted to court her after all, but still, there were so many secrets between them. So many things that he'd dislike if only he knew the truth. For a moment she debated telling him everything anyway, laying her whole life in Egypt on the table, and letting the axe fall on her neck or not.

Lord Duncannon she was certain was above all a man of honor, but then, some were thin-skinned when it came to women and thinking they'd been duped by the fairer sex.

"I suppose that explains why you're courting me then. I'm neither of those things."

"No you're not." He came and sat beside her. His nearness overwhelmed her. Terrible as it was, scandalous even, she longed to be held, to be the whole focus of someone else. The way Lord Duncannon made her feel was reminiscent of how she'd felt with Omar and it was heady indeed.

He reached up, tracing her lips with his finger. "You're so beautiful you make my breath catch every time I see you."

Nerves fluttered in her stomach. "Even when I'm dressed in my breeches and covered in mud?" she teased, trying to lighten the mood. His steely gaze put paid to that attempt of denial and she swallowed.

"Even then."

She gasped as he took her lips in a fierce kiss, his tongue sweeping across hers. Her head spun a moment before she wrapped her arms about his neck and kissed him back. She'd wanted to kiss him again too. Every time she'd caught a glimpse of him on the grounds, strong and tall, muscular and lean, her hands itched to run across his body. To feel his warm skin against hers, his touch on her person.

"You drive me to distraction," he admitted, kissing her deeper still.

She pulled back, meeting his gaze. "It's the same for me too," she said, kissing him again and losing herself to him and to all he offered, for now at least.

CHAPTER 12

A rthur tried to rein in his need for Hallie, but her sweet gasps and her decadent kisses made his wits spiral. He clasped her face and took all that she was willing to give him. He'd longed for this woman in his arms from the very moment they had been parted. He'd dreamed about her constantly and with the few women he'd bedded over the years, all of them paled in comparison to her.

He did not care what his family thought of his choice, it was well and truly made. A wife without wits, a society doll that pandered to the *ton*, gossiped and took tea all day long made his jaw ache in distaste.

He found himself lowering her on the settee, coming over her. Hallie would never bore him, her mind alone was sharp enough to keep him on his toes. She loved travel and would be willing to visit foreign places without hesitation. Their life appeared before him, rich and full and he couldn't grasp it soon enough.

She was all soft curves and womanly flesh that made him ache. He settled atop her, basking in her warmth and acquiescence. He wanted this life with a desperation that scared him, and yet he could not help but feel she was hiding something from him. Her hesitation in answering him regarding her time in Egypt was telling.

Maybe Mr. Stewart was hinting at something after all. Was it so bad that she could not confide in him? He would never do anything that hurt her, he'd paid for that mistake for seven years, he wouldn't do it again.

One of her legs slipped about his and she pressed herself against him. He rubbed his hard-as-rock cock against her mons and she moaned through their kiss. Just as she was in life, in the private setting they were now in she was reactive, thrilling, and as sweet as he remembered.

It would be so easy to seduce her, but he would not. Not here. He needed her to trust him above anything else, and to see what they could be together. He would not rush her in this.

He pulled back, his breathing ragged and, looking down at her, he noticed her breath too was labored, her breasts straining against her bodice. The scent of flowers rose from her skin and he knew she'd bathed before coming downstairs. The image of her being in a bath, lathing soap and relaxing in water made him groan.

"I should escort you back to your room before anything further progresses tonight. We're in no rush."

She bit her lip, her eyes wide and a little cloudy with arousal. Her gaze dipped to his lips and he inwardly swore. Her thoughts stating otherwise as clear as the written word. The choice was impossible. He didn't want to leave. He wanted to hoist up her gown, slide down low on the settee and feast on her, every part of her person. Then, and only when he had her writhing in pleasure, and begging for him to take her, would he sheathe himself into her welcoming heat.

He shut his eyes, trying to blot out the image of doing exactly that.

"You should." She slipped her other leg about his, pulling him hard up against her core. Unable to stop himself, he slid against her flesh, the pleasure rocking him to his center. His body roared to have her.

She lifted her hips, grinding against him, taking her own pleasure when he didn't move.

"Damn it, Hallie. Stop."

A wicked grin slipped across her lips and his control snapped. He thrust against her, and she gasped into their kiss. The delicious friction was too much. He would not come here. Not in a drawing room at Baron Bankes's house party.

This time he found the strength to tear himself away and he stood, walking over to the window and hoisting it up. The cool, night air went someway in chilling his skin and cooling his need for her. He leaned over the sill, his brain demanding that he turn and finish what they both wanted.

And damn it all to hell he wanted her.

He felt her come up behind him and he straightened. She wrapped her hands about his waist from behind, holding him tight. "You make it hard to stop. I will tell you a secret and then you can walk me to my room."

Her hands slipped over his chest and his breath caught when her fingers dipped between the buttons on his waistcoat and slipped against his shirt.

"What is it?" he asked, curious and wanting to know everything there was to know about her. His grandmother would say he was a little obsessed with her, and perhaps he was, but his certainty that she was the one for him had never waned. Not even after all the years they were apart had it lessened.

"Even with all my plans to travel abroad that I had before meeting you in Felday, there was a small part of me that hoped you'd return that morning. That fate had placed you before me and that I should listen to its call. I think we both missed an opportunity that day, one that I'm unsure we can ever get back."

He turned, frowning down at her. "We can get it back, Hallie. The feelings that I had for you then have done nothing but doubled since that day. I will earn your affection and trust. I promise I'll never hurt you again."

She nodded, and he could see that her eyes had gone a little glassy with emotion. "I will hold you to that promise, Lord Duncannon."

"I hope you do, Miss Evans." *Always.*

HALLIE WOKE to the sound of heavy rain hitting the windowpane. She pushed back the covers on her bed and walked to the window, pulling back the dark, velvet drapes to see bad weather had settled in and didn't look to be going anywhere.

She sighed, debating what she should do. There was much work to do up at the dig site and she could still accomplish that in the small tent that had been erected for her workshop.

Finishing her morning toilette, she dressed in breeches, shirt, and jacket, and slipped on her greatcoat and broad-brimmed hat that she had used in Egypt. It would serve to keep the rain from dripping down her neck just as it stopped the sun from burning her skin.

The walk up the excavation site took longer than normal. The ground was already wet and boggy, her boots sinking half an inch with each step. The site was vacant of any workers and that suited her fine. She went into the tent, happy to see everything was where she'd left it last. Hallie lit a lamp and got out her sketchbook, needing to sketch their finds of the day before and explain what she believed they were.

For some hours she worked, drawing and studying while outside the rain relentlessly hit the canvas roof, lulling her with its calming rhythm.

The canvas flap of the tent flipped open and she jumped at the sight of Lord Duncannon, a warm swirl of pleasure blossoming inside her at the sight of him.

He sighed, the sound tinged with relief. "You're here," he said, more to himself as he stepped into the tent, shuffling out of his greatcoat. He ran a hand through his wet, dripping hair, leaving the golden strands on end. He looked deadly handsome and after last night she wasn't sure it was a good idea that they were alone together. He had left her unfulfilled, and all night she'd tossed and turned, wanting more.

To be teased in such a way without gaining release was not what she constituted as a gentlemanly thing to do.

"I am. I'm cataloguing our finds. What are you doing here? You're soaked through." She took in his clothing, his damp breeches and shirt that clung to his person and accentuated his every delicious curve of muscle on his abdomen. Hallie was unable to tear her eyes from his chest.

"You should probably stop looking at me as if you'd like to take a bite out of me before I let you," he teased, sending her a wicked grin. "I had not seen you about the house and I grew concerned. When your maid said that you had left before she had time to serve you breakfast, I came to check on you."

She chuckled. "Did you think I had run away, my lord? That your seduction last evening had scared me?"

He didn't say anything for a moment, simply stared at her a little mute before he cleared his throat, once again pushing back his hair. The action did little to cool her ardour. If she were honest with herself, she had started to think that she was a little preoccupied with him. More than was healthy. For both of them.

"It worried me that it had."

She looked at him quickly. "Why?"

He raised his brow, walking about her work table, picking up a few of her finds, inspecting them before placing them back down. "The thought of being with you again is what gets me up each morning and keeps me moving forward throughout the day. That the idea of not having you in sight, of having you by my side as we walk through this life scares me. That what I feel for you is stronger than what I've felt for anyone ever and that you may not reciprocate that emotion."

Hallie stilled at his words, having not expected such honesty from his lordship. Nor did she think that what he'd said would resonate so much within her. Last evening she'd wanted to keep walking along the corridor to his room, shut the doors on the world and become lost in each other's arms.

The stab of disappointment when he'd done exactly what he said he would had been profound. Even now, here up at the dig site, all she could think about was being with him like that again, and possibly more.

Her gaze flicked to the makeshift trundle bed that had been brought up for her, just in case she was caught here or in need of rest. Now it glowed like a beacon of pleasure. They were, no one would venture up here today with the bad, relentless weather.

Nerves pitted in her stomach and she busied her hand on her sketch of the small, round coin she had found.

"You have beautiful hands. Do you know that?" His hand that had been sliding across the wooden table top, slipped across the top of hers and slowly made its way up her arm. A shiver ran down her spine and she looked up, meeting his gaze. It was heavy with desire and she took a calming breath, placing down her pencil.

"You're touching my arm, my lord."

His teasing gleam entered his eyes. "I am."

She stood, her eyes level with his neck, his very nice neck that led to an even nicer abdomen that even now, years after she'd seen it last, still made her hands itch to touch. Hallie was sick of denying herself. It was obvious that he wanted her just as much as she wanted him. His breathing was deep and although slow, she knew to her very core he was trying to rein in his desire.

She didn't want him to.

Leaning forward she kissed the little dip at the middle of his throat, working her way along his shoulder blade. He sucked in a breath and she gasped as he leaned down, clasping her face and bringing her up to meet his kiss. It was deep and a little wild and sparked her desire.

She wrapped her arms about his neck and he lifted her off her feet, placing her on the wooden table, taking care not to ruin any of her work. He stood back, ripping at his cravat, never once losing eye contact with her. Hallie bit her lip as he threw off his coat and waistcoat before tugging his shirt free from his breeches and pulling it over his head.

He was simply beautiful, as perfect as she remembered him. All defined muscles and lines, his stomach taut and flexing with each breath. She ran her hand over him, marveling at his beauty. Heat pooled at her core and she ached to have him.

"Now it's your turn." He reached out and one by one, undid the small buttons that ran down the front of her shirt. Just like him she had breeches on, preferring to wear them instead of dresses when working at dig sites. He slid her shirt free from her breeches and glided it over her shoulders, letting it lay on the table.

His hand cupped her breast through her stays and she shut her eyes, reveling in the contact that she'd been starved of for so long.

"So perfect," he whispered, slipping her stays down her chest and exposing her to his view. She had not been so exposed to a man in years and the urge to cover herself was strong, but she forced her hands upon the table, letting him take his fill of her. Arthur leaned forward and kissed her breast, placing soft, sweet kisses against her nipple. His tongue slipped over her pebbled flesh and she cupped his head, holding him against her.

"I missed this. All of you." He made short work of the laces and, throwing them to the floor with little care, bared her to his view. Arthur grabbed her breeches at the front and pulled her off the table to stand. "Now these have to go."

Hallie reached down, slipping the buttons free at the fall and sliding them down her legs. She kicked them to the side before meeting Arthur's heated gaze that threatened to melt her into a liquid mess. She was as naked as a babe and yet, the pleasure on his face, the reverence that she read there, pushed away any doubt or fear.

Without help, she sat on the table, leaning back on her hands, waiting for him. "Are you going to join me here, my lord?"

He swallowed, the sound almost audible. "Arthur. Please, call me Arthur."

She grinned. "Will you join me here...Arthur?"

OH HELL YES HE WOULD.

He'd go to hell and back if only he could live the rest of his life with the woman before him. How had he let her go all those years ago? He should have told his friends to damn well stop the carriage and let him out. He should have forced her to take him with her to Egypt and never leave her side. Should have was a tormenting beast he loathed. So many mistakes that he could not take back.

Need riding him hard, he ripped at his frontfalls and pushed his breeches down and off. He stepped between her legs and a feeling of rightness swamped him. His cock strained between them, and he fought not to rush. To take his time and savor this moment. She wrapped her arms about his shoulders and he kissed her, tasting tea and honey on her sweet lips.

Reaching down he clasped one of her thighs, taking his time enjoying her warm, soft flesh, slipping his cock against her wet, willing cunny.

She moaned against his mouth and he nipped her lip. "You like that," he said, sliding against her heat again and gaining a moan of approval.

"Oh yes."

Her hand traced down his shoulder, down to his waist, before circling his member. Her hand slid down his phallus, teasing him with long, constant strokes and for a moment Arthur thought he saw stars.

He shut his eyes, enjoying the friction her touch

brought forth. His balls tightened and he reached down, stilling her hand. "You'll make me lose myself."

Watching, she guided him into her wet heat. She engulfed him, warm and tight. His body roared to take her, hard and fast, fuck her until they were both spent and gasping for breath.

God fucking damn it, she felt good.

Her mouth opened on a sigh and he kissed her, pulling her hard against him, their flesh touching from breast to legs. He thrust into her, and realized it would never be enough. He needed her more than ever before. She wrapped her leg about his hip, holding him against her with her foot. He fucked her, hard and fast. Heedless of where they were or the fact that anyone could come into the tent at any moment.

She was his, of this he was certain and she would be his wife if he could convince her to take him as her husband.

Arthur increased his pace, the feel of her willing body, her little gasps and sighs drove him senseless. He pulled back from kissing her, watching her as he took her. Her lips swollen and a little red from his kisses, her eyes cloudy with desire.

"Yes," she gasped, watching him, her hands tight on his shoulders as he thrust relentlessly into her heat. She threw her head back, her hair spilling down her spine. He leaned forward, kissing her neck in harsh little pecks. "Just like that. Don't stop," she gasped, her white, straight teeth biting her bottom lip.

Arthur did as she asked, dared not to do anything that would not bring her pleasure.

A mewling sound and his name spewed from her lips. He gritted his teeth, needing her to shatter about him before he'd take his pleasure. Sweat beaded off their skin, no matter the cool day. And then he felt the strong, pulling shudders around his cock, dragging him along to the road of pleasure. He wrenched free at the last moment, spilling onto the dirt floor beneath the table, his hand working his cock as he watched as Hallie caught her breath and composure.

She sat up, leaning once again on her arms, one leg swinging idly over the table. A satisfied smile played about her lips. "It should rain more often if that's how I'm to pass the time here when you visit."

He chuckled, stepping between her legs and pulling her close. "You do realize there will be no getting rid of me now."

She shrugged one perfect shoulder. "You're not so bad."

He clasped her face. "Neither are you," he said, kissing her again and losing himself once more in her arms.

CHAPTER 13

The rain unfortunately stopped overnight. The ground up at the dig site was still waterlogged and so Hallie continued cataloguing her finds and sketching them, making a journal and map of everything they had found and where on the map she'd sketched before digging up the trenches.

Once again she was alone on the dig site, and yet, when she was packing up her pencils and sketchbook it was not Arthur who met her outside to walk her back to the estate, but Mr. Stewart.

She greeted him with cool civility, having hoped she'd not be caught alone with him again. He was trouble, mostly trouble for her and she was still uncertain how she would survive if he wanted all her money that she earned.

"How is progress coming along, Miss Evans?"

"Very well, thank you," she said, buttoning up her greatcoat and slipping on her broadbrimmed hat and starting back down the hill toward the estate. She had left later than anticipated and in the distance she could see the lights at Baron Bankes's estate were already alight and shining through the many windows in preparation for the evening festivities.

"I thought while we had a minute to ourselves we should discuss if you've had any further enquiries about similar digs you may be interested in. You remember our deal of course or do you need reminding?"

She rounded on him, glaring up at the popinjay. He was a leach that society would expel, any level of society for anyone within half a mile of this man would know he was not good. Rotten to the core like fruit with a worm in it. "You would ruin my life, take everything from me simply because you cannot accept the fact that your cousin was a madman who killed people and almost killed my friend. How dare you, sir."

He grabbed her arm, squeezing her hard. She fought not to flinch under his assault. "I would dare, yes. My cousin was innocent and it was only because your friend fucked a duke that she wasn't caught out for the scheming, lying bitch that she is. My cousin wrote to me, I knew his character better than anyone. The things they accused him of were ludicrous. He would never do any of those things."

"Neither would my friend," she spat back at him, wrenching out of his hold. "And if you touch me again, I'll bloody your nose. Do you understand that, Mr. Stewart?"

He laughed, the sound condescending and repellent. "You owe me a debt that will be paid and will continue to be paid until I deem it appropriate for you to stop. Until then, remember I know all about your life in Egypt and the dirty little secret you have. Whatever will Lord Duncannon think when he finds out the woman he's cock happy for fucked another when abroad? Tell me, Miss Evans," he said, rubbing his jaw with his hand. "Have you always been free with your wiles?"

Without thought, she struck him across the face. The

crack of the slap ricocheted up her arm and she fisted her hand as pain spiked through her palm.

"I will give you that one, my dear, but you'll only get one. The next time you hit me, I'll hit back."

Hallie stood still and watched as he continued down the hill toward the house as if he had not a care in the world. *Bastard.* Tears burned her eyes and her vision of the woods swam before her. Whatever would she do? Could she tell Lord Duncannon?

Fear that what Mr. Stewart accused her of put paid to that idea. His lordship would think her fast if she told him the truth. As for her son, that would be the final straw and he would never think of her again knowing she had a child.

His family would be right in keeping him away from her. She wasn't pure, not from a great, well-to-do family, nor had she ever wanted to be. He would soon come to realize that his foolish dreams of them were unrealistic.

Not that she cared as to what his family thought of her, but she wouldn't put her son in a situation where he would be looked down upon, disregarded and treated unfairly. Not by Arthur and certainly not by his grandmother who was a formidable force in the *ton*.

Love had its limits, love for others at least. Her son and her love for him was not a price she was willing to pay to have the man she had started to think of more than she should. To see a life that they could have and dream. If only there weren't so many other factors that would tear them apart she would try for a life with him.

But she wasn't fool enough to follow that thought. Their affection was doomed and so too was their time.

Arthur found Hallie in the library the following day. She was seated on the floor behind a group of shelving. Baron Bankes had a well-stocked library that looked more like a book store with its many shelves lined up in a row at one end of the room. His lordship had taken most of the houseguests out for a walk down to the river that ran through his estate, but Arthur had remained scarce until they had left.

He watched her chew her bottom lip as she leaned over an old tome, her hair hastily tied back in a single ribbon, strands of her dark hair slipping over her face. An ache formed in his chest and he cleared his throat, making his presence known.

She glanced up at him and he had hoped to see pleasure on her features. Instead, all he saw was trepidation and regret. Unease slithered down his spine and he sat, stretching his legs out before him and crossing his feet.

"Lord Duncannon, please join me," she said, her tone oozing with sarcasm.

He glanced at her, meeting her eyes. "I had hoped we were past formal titles, Miss Evans. You were Hallie to me yesterday and I was Arthur. Can we not be that again?"

"What you ask is impossible," she said, closing the tome hard, eliciting a puff of dust.

He waved the dust away, coughing. "Nothing is impossible. Your travels abroad and the work that you did there is proof of that." She glared at the bookcase before her, not looking at him. Whatever was wrong? He mentally retraced everything that had passed between them since yesterday, and they had parted on good terms. Very good in fact.

She sighed, turning to face him. "You should court someone else, Arthur. You know your family would never accept me and I'll not ever conform to fit in to make people happy. I will only bring you pain in the long run."

He frowned, the idea that she was not good for him an illogical notion. She was perfect for him. Never with anyone else did he have intelligent conversations, she was sweet and honest, unafflicted by the *ton*, nor was she poisoned by its many barbs.

"I think not." He leaned toward her and kissed her cheek. She smelled of lavender, fresh as a spring morning. "I feel I'm falling in love with you, if I have not already." The despair that crossed her features at his declaration made his gut clench. "Why won't you let me love you?"

She shook her head vehemently. "Please trust me when I say that we cannot go anywhere. It's not fair for either of us if we continue this liaison."

"I'm not fickle, Hallie. I'll not leave you again. I promise." The day he'd left her in Felday was one mistake that he'd not make again. Ever. He would fight to keep her, fight to make her his wife. "Trust me, please," he begged, not the least ashamed to. He'd do more than that if only it meant she would give him a chance.

"You're so maddening," she said, giving him a small smile. The first today. The sight of it warmed his heart and he grinned back.

"What are you reading about?" he asked, looking down at the book she held in her arms, wanting to change the subject and make her forget whatever concerned her regarding them.

"It's a book on the Roman Empire. I was sketching another coin that I found yesterday and I wondered if it may have been locally minted, not brought in from abroad. If this book is saying what I think it does, the Romans did do this after their conquest."

"How much more do you have to do at the site? There are only a couple weeks left of the house party."

"Ah, but you forget I'm not here for the house party, you are. I'm free to stay as long as the dig takes. The original estimate was three months." A shadow entered her eyes, before she blinked and it was gone.

What was worrying her? There was something, he was sure of it, just as he was certain she was keeping something from him. In time he hoped she would trust him enough to confide in him.

"Whatever will I tell Baron Bankes to keep him from sending me away when everyone leaves?"

She chuckled, lifting her legs to lean on her knees. "That you're having an illicit affair with his archaeologist and you are unable to leave just yet."

"So we're still having an illicit affair? How daring of us." He reached out, needing to touch her. He ran his hand about her waist, wishing there were less clothes between them. He longed to feel her soft skin, to hear her sweet sighs of pleasure as he brought her to climax.

"If you will not listen to reason when it comes to us, then I suppose my only choice is to let you get your fill of me and move on. Is that not what most men do?" She reached out and cupped his cock. Arthur groaned at the contact and her boldness. Damn it, she was so perfect.

"I'm not most men." He placed his hand over hers and moved her hand downward, stroking his already hard dick. "For all the fun we may have together, I'm not going anywhere." She would see that was true soon enough.

HALLIE'S STOMACH clenched at the feel of him. All masculine perfection and hers to play with if she wanted. Even if it were not forever, she could certainly have him while he was here for the house party.

Their future was impossible, but here and now was not.

She moved and straddled him, easy to do since she was wearing breeches. His hands came around and clasped her bottom, pulling her hard against his engorged cock. Heat spiraled through her and she could feel herself grow damp. Hallie moved against him, seeking her own release and pleasure without taking him into her.

His mouth twitched into a wicked smile and she kissed him, reveling in his need of her, his promises of forever. Promises that she knew could never be, no matter if they pulled at a part of her that longed for stability, for protection for her son and herself.

"You feel so good in my arms."

She moaned through the kiss as a tremor of pleasure coursed through her. "So do you," she managed. Hallie undulated against him, their breeches the only thing that separated them. That they were doing this in Baron Bankes's library was not the smartest idea, and yet she could not leave. Not now. She wanted to take her pleasure and forget all her troubles for a moment at least.

"I want, you." Arthur broke the kiss. He kissed her jaw, working his way around her neck and up to her ear, biting her lobe. "Damn these breeches."

Hallie pushed harder against his manhood, as she undulated in his lap and his breath hitched. His engorged cock was delicious against her and she could take her fill without too much fuss. Nor did she care how much noise they made. Everyone was out, and those who had stayed behind had better places to be than the library. Spasms started low in her core and blossomed throughout and she threw her head back, enjoying the climax as it tore through her body. He kissed her sigh of relief from her lips, quelling the noise. Hallie sagged in his arms, laying her head against his shoulder as they both tried to regain their breath.

"That was very pleasurable," she mumbled against his shoulder, placing a small kiss at the base of his neck.

His rock-solid phallus twitched against her and she sat back, meeting his gaze. "Did you not find release?"

He shook his head, swallowing. "No, but I want you to come to my room tonight. Will you?"

Hallie nodded without thought. She would take all she could of him for the time both she and he had left here. All too soon it would be over and she would have to find new employment. Funds that would have to be handed over to Mr. Stewart. A little distraction before life's realities was just what she needed.

"I will join you when everyone is abed." The thought of sleeping in his arms warmed her soul and the night couldn't come soon enough.

CHAPTER 14

Hallie received a letter from her cousin later that day and she was relieved and pleased to hear Ammon was doing well and had started to learn his letters. A stab of disappointment that she was not the one teaching her son how to read and write pricked her conscience, but then she reminded herself that her working enabled him the comfort that he now lived in and supplied all the things he needed to learn and grow.

That was until the reality of Mr. Stewart and his blackmailing put everything she'd been working hard toward at risk. She could not allow him to use her in such a way. There had to be a way in which she could be rid of him.

She wrote back, telling them of all her finds and even drawing a couple of sketches of artifacts that she knew Ammon may enjoy, being a boy and liking military things. What boys did not?

After sending down her letter to be posted the following day, Hallie ordered a bath and prepared herself for bed, dismissing her maid early as she did not want anyone here later this evening when she snuck out to join Lord Duncannon in his room.

Her stomach clenched at the thought of being with him again. She hadn't thought to ever desire another man, but here she was, with the first man who had ever touched her soul and his wickedness, his determination to win her was a pleasure hard to deny.

A knock sounded on her door and she opened it to see Willow, her face stricken.

"Willow, come in. What is wrong?"

Willow looked up and down the passage and then, coming into her room, shut the door and locked it. "You will never believe the gossip I just heard before I retired for the night."

Dread lodged in her stomach and she clasped her abdomen. "Gossip? What is it?"

Willow's lips thinned into a disapproving line. "There is talk below stairs that a couple were caught *in flagrante delicto* in the library earlier today. Mr. Stewart says that he saw them with his own eyes. He did not know I could hear when he was telling Baron Bankes all the details otherwise I'm sure he would not have said a word." Willow paused for breath. "I know most who were out on the walk with the baron today, but there were several people who stayed behind. Lord Duncannon was one of them and so were you."

Her friend's direct inspection of her made her stomach churn. Hallie raised her chin, refusing to break under her friend's stare. "Mr. Stewart ought to be ashamed in telling such tales. I'm sure he would not like people talking about him if he found himself in that position." Hallie inwardly seethed. How dare he start such stories about anyone, not only her. It proved her unease correct about him. He was determined to bring her down, and not just financially.

"Oh, I'm sure he would not. Even so, it will not stop him from talking. He seems quite the gossiper."

Hallie yawned, hoping Willow would notice her need for sleep, even though she had no intention of sleeping, not for the next few hours at least. She wanted to see Arthur and tell him of what Willow had said. Perhaps he could speak to Mr. Stewart to ensure the man didn't spread rumors about them. That he knew they were in the library it was clear he understood what had happened between them.

Heat bloomed on her face over their actions and she cringed. If she did not have enough troubles already to worry about, now she had this to contend with.

Willow reached out and touched her arm, bringing her attention back to her friend. "I will bid you goodnight. I can see that you're tired. Goodnight, Hallie."

"I will speak to you in the morning. Goodnight." Hallie shut the door behind Willow and slumped against it. She glanced at the mantel clock that ticked just past the midnight hour. She would give it another half hour and then sneak over to Arthur's room.

Hallie sat in the chair before the fire to wait out the time. She watched as the flames licked the wood, it's flickering lulling her to sleep.

WITH A GASP SHE AWOKE, sitting up to the sounds of the maid opening the curtains and the sound of birdsong in the trees outside her window. A pot of tea and some toast sat on a silver tray on the small table before her, a pot of strawberry jam to the side that made her stomach grumble at the sight of food.

"Damn it," she mumbled, rubbing her face to try to

wake up. How could she have missed spending a night in Arthur's arms? She swore under her breath, rolling her stiff shoulders at having slept in a chair instead of a bed. A very comfortable bed with a hot, sensual man who only wanted to please her at her side.

Hallie quickly ate and dressed, her breeches, shirt, and jacket making her progress a lot quicker than had she worn a dress. As usual, she headed for the servants' stairs, wanting to slip away to the dig site without seeing Mr. Stewart or Baron Bankes, whom she was wondering if she'd ever be able to look in the face again, especially now that he knew some of his house guests were enjoying each other.

If he learned it was her and Lord Duncannon she would not be offered any work anywhere else. He would make sure of that.

She stepped out the back door, glancing up at the cloudless sky and breathing deep the crisp morning air.

"Good morning, my dear."

Hallie stifled a scream and clasped her throat, heart beating a loud drum inside her chest. "Lord Duncannon. You're up early."

"Sleepless night," he teased and she couldn't help but chuckle.

"I'm sorry about that. I fell asleep." She continued toward the back-gate entrance of the yard, and could see a carriage was hitched at the stables. Panic assailed her that Arthur being up and the carriage hitched meant that he was leaving. "Will you be joining me up at the dig site today?" she asked, hoping the carriage was not for him.

He shook his head, pulling on his gloves. "No, unfortunately, but then neither will you. I want you to come on a ride with me."

"On a horse?" She was never overly fond of the

animals, certainly not when she was on top of them and the idea of riding about all day wasn't something that tempted her.

"No, in the carriage. I want you to visit my estate. I'm neighbors with Baron Bankes, if you were not familiar. I have a proposition for you."

The mention of a proposition was intriguing and she studied him a moment wondering what he meant by it. She glanced toward the stables and saw Greg and Bruce waiting for her. Decision made, she went over to them.

"I'm going to visit Lord Duncannon's estate today. I'll not be needing you up at the dig site. We'll meet up there tomorrow at seven if you're free."

They tipped their hats. "Of course, Miss Evans. We shall be there tomorrow instead."

She smiled her thanks. Walking back, she gave Lord Duncannon her hand and he helped her climb into the carriage. She settled herself on the leather squabs, watched as Arthur joined her, seating himself beside her. The carriage was similar to what her friend and now the Duchess of Whitstone traveled in. Hallie didn't possess such a vehicle, having to travel about England by stagecoach, only having such luxury as this when she was with her friends who were well-to-do.

His lordship shut the door and rapped on the roof with his fist. The carriage rocked forward and he slipped off his gloves, placing them beside him. Hallie took in his strong, large hands. Without warning, his fingers entwined with hers and he held her hand.

She glanced at him, and yet he was studying the outdoors through the window, a serene expression on his face. Warmth spread through her at the sweet and innocent gesture, simply to hold her and be close without anything else insinuated.

Hallie wished it could be so easy as this. Just a joining of two people who liked each other, possibly even more than liked if her emotions were to believed. And if what Lord Duncannon had said in the library the other day was true.

"What is it that you wished to show me at your estate? What is this proposition you speak of?"

He smiled. "Well, as to that, I have a surprise for you that I think you'll be most pleased with." He shrugged. "I also wanted to show you my estate, my home."

She would be a liar if the thought of seeing where he lived didn't intrigue her. Was his home as warm as Arthur was turning out to be? A beacon of light that she couldn't help but warm herself against and chase away the chill of her worries?

They traveled in silence for some time and within an hour the carriage rocked to a halt, no sign of any home. Hallie leaned forward and looked out the window, seeing nothing but a dense area of trees in a shallow valley below. "Why have we stopped?"

His mischievous grin made her smile. "You'll see," he said, opening the door and helping her outside. They walked down the hill toward the trees and Hallie looked about, wondering what he was going to show her. As they entered the trees, the shadows chilled her skin and she rubbed her arms, wishing she'd brought a shawl. Arthur glanced at her and then, the gentleman he was, shuffled out of his coat and placed it about her shoulders.

"Thank you," she said, pulling him close and leaning up to kiss him. They were alone here, the servants on the carriage could no longer see them and his sweetness deserved a little something. Even if it were only a kiss.

He wrapped his arm about her waist and they continued on, coming to a low stone wall. "This," he said, gesturing to the wall and the others she could see, some taller as if they were an exterior wall to a castle. Hallie could see a fireplace, still blackened from the coal and past use. Beech and elm trees grew throughout the structure.

"It is the original site of our ancestral home. Cadding Castle was built during Henry the Seventh's reign and fell into disrepair when my great-great grandfather decided to build a bigger and much grander ancestral home, Cadding Hall."

Hallie ran her hand over the large stone blocks, could only imagine how imposing and large the castle would have been. She walked around the stone wall and into the center of one of the bottom rooms that no longer had a roof. She turned to face him. "It's very grand, but why did you want me to see this?"

"Well, as to that." He came about the stone wall and joined her, looking at the ruins with interest. "I'd like you to excavate the ruins. I want to rebuild the structure, but I would like any history of the site catalogued and preserved. I thought that if I had someone who knew what to look for, you may be able to help me rebuild it. Preserve it."

For a moment Hallie wasn't able to reply. She had not thought he would offer her such a proposition, but she could also not do the work for free. She would need laborers and equipment. This was a large job and would take months to complete. Did Lord Duncannon mean to pay her a salary, or was he hoping she'd do this for free?

"I'm honored, truly, but…"

"I will pay you handsomely. I'm not sure what the going rate is for an archaeologist, but I'll pay whatever you think is fair. Five hundred pounds, a thousand. Name your price and I shall pay it."

Hallie shut her mouth with a snap. "I do not need that much, my lord." The thought of such sums would help her secure her son and she would not have to look for more work unless the position was something that interested her. That is, if she could cheat Mr. Stewart out of what he claimed was his right to have.

While this was an interesting job proposition, she couldn't help but wonder if he were doing it to keep her close. Keep her in his bed for a little while longer. Not an awful idea, but still, being near him, day after day, night after night would only sink her further into that pit of emotions she'd hidden away for so very long.

"If I were to do this I need a promise, a declaration and contracts signed so everything is above board."

"Of course," he said, coming over to her and taking her hand. "I will admit to wanting you with me, but this rebuild has been in my plans for the estate for some time. I have the drawings already drafted, I just need someone to ensure the property or anything found here is protected from damage. Anything that was part of the original structure I'd like to include back into the build if possible. That's where you come in."

All of it made sense...but still... "I insist that I'll be given a cottage or a small building nearby to stay in. Our bed hopping has to end while I do this. I don't want to be talked about as your live-in lover who is being paid for her work at the dig site during the day and paid for my time in your bed during the night."

He ran a hand through his hair, looking about the ruins for a moment before he turned back to her. "Very well. I'll have you installed in a nearby cottage that my old groundsman used to live in and we'll keep our relationship purely business until after you've completed the dig here. But after that," he said, stepping up against her and wrapping his hands about her waist. Hallie relaxed against him, loving the fact that he made her feel so very at home, safe and adored. "I'm going to continue to court you, Miss Evans and nothing will stand in my way."

Hallie linked her fingers behind his back, wishing it could be so. "I think we have an agreement, my lord."

"And your price?"

She took a calming breath, thinking of her son and reminding herself Lord Duncannon said he would pay anything she asked. "I ask for one thousand pounds for the work I'm about to undertake, plus labor hire and tools." She held her breath as he contemplated her fee.

"Done," he said without question. "I'll have the money to you tomorrow."

She gasped and he took the opportunity to kiss her. Hallie forgot all about the dig, the money, everything, and gave herself up to his affection. She would have to tell him after she finished her work here everything of her past and let herself either live or die by the sword he could wield over her soul.

CHAPTER 15

True to his word, Lord Duncannon asked for a meeting with her in Baron Bankes's library the following day. They had spent a wonderful day at his estate, walking the grounds, seeing his home, the many family portraits and secret passageways.

He met her at the door and helped her into the chair before the baron's desk. "I have everything you asked for. I even had my steward write up a contract overnight and express it here this morning."

Hallie took the parchment from him and read through the contract, noting the amount to be paid, the support she asked for during the excavation prior to his building work to commence. Everything she'd asked for he had completed. She glanced up and saw another package tied with string. Her payment perhaps?

If Mr. Stewart found out how much he paid her, all of her negotiation and acceptance of this work would be for nothing. Overnight she had debated this dilemma and had decided that paying Mr. Stewart some of the money to keep him happy and quiet would be better than paying him nothing at all. It would still leave her ample money to finally take her son into her own care and move back to Felday. To be selective with the work that she wanted to do in future.

"It all looks very good, my lord. Quill please," she said, placing the contract on the desk, ready to sign. Arthur grinned, dipping the nip into the ink and passing her the quill. Hallie signed and with her scrawl of signature a little of the weight of having no security, having to rely on others for positions to keep the wolves at bay eased. This was the start of a new beginning. She sat back, meeting his gaze. "I'd like for the specifics of the contract to remain between us, my lord. No one needs to know the particular details of our agreement. Do you not agree?"

Arthur nodded without hesitation. "Of course." He pushed the package tied with string across the desk. "One last detail. Here is the one thousand pounds we decided on, delivered today as promised."

She picked it up, turning it in her hand, having never held so much money in her possession at any one moment. "Thank you. That is very generous."

He stood and came around the desk, dipping the quill once more and signing his part of the contract, then, rolling it up, turned and handed it to her. "Once you've completed your work here, I look forward to having you at my estate, Miss Evans."

She stood. "I do too." Which was true. She could not wait to be out from Mr. Stewart's watchful eyes and with any luck, with the money she would give him today, he would leave her alone for a little while.

"I must go, I'm already late heading up to the dig site."

"Of course," Arthur said, bowing. "Will I see you tonight?" he asked as she turned to leave. Warmth blossomed low in her belly and she bit back a small grin.

"When everyone is abed, I'll come to your room. I won't fall asleep this time. I promise."

He grinned. "I'll count the hours."

Hallie walked from the room, an absurd little smile on her lips and hope in her heart. There was more between them than just physical attraction. He cared, she was sure of it. But did that mean he cared enough to want her when he knew everything? More importantly was she strong enough to tell him the truth and risk her heart a second time?

LATER THAT DAY, Hallie sat in the tent at the dig site, eating a sandwich and waiting for a shower of rain to pass. Greg and Bruce had asked to return to the stables due to a mare who was in labor. Hallie had waved them off without hesitation and continued studying the small artifacts that had come out of the second trench. Half a statue that may be one of the many gods the Romans prayed to and more pottery pieces. The site was certainly of interest, but Baron Bankes had only wanted a small excavation to prove that there was once a Roman fort here. If her work here these past weeks proved anything it was that most certainly there was. At least she had proved the Baron and his family's thoughts on the site correct, even if she had not been able to make the site give up all its historical secrets.

"Miss Evans, just the woman I wish to see."

Hallie jumped at the sound of Mr. Stewart's voice, a voice that was both nasally and grating on one's nerves all at the one moment. "I hear you've been hired to work at Lord Duncannon's estate after finishing here."

She frowned. How had he found out? She'd asked

Arthur not to say anything, and yet, here was Mr. Stewart not two hours later querying her about it. "Who told you?"

He smiled, the action more like a grimace. "I have my ways, but that's not important. I will tell you that Lord Duncannon did not bestow the information."

As pleasing as that news was, still, having Mr. Stewart here meant he knew some of the agreement. "I suppose you want your share."

"Of course," he said, seating himself across from her at the table.

Hallie took in his hair, a little oily and slicked back over his head. He reminded her of an eel, slimy and untrustworthy. She stood and went over to a box that was hidden in one of the tool trunks in her tent. It was not where she left such valuables, but she also had learned to carry her valuables with her at all times. If she were up at the dig site, so too was her money. No matter how great or small that sum.

She quickly took out the two hundred and fifty pounds she had separated earlier, closing the money box and the lid to the trunk. "Here you are. This is what I've been paid, minus one hundred pounds that I kept for myself. I cannot work and not have any money, so if you wish to fleece me of my funds, you must accept that I will be keeping a little for myself."

He rubbed his jaw, not taking the money from her outreached hand. Hallie schooled her features, trepidation edging in on her at his continued stillness. "And the rest of it?"

She swallowed, frowning for good measure. "I don't know what you mean," she lied, hope that she may have tricked him fading.

He chuckled, the sound weary. "Ah, Miss Evans. I know you were paid one thousand pounds. So I would suggest you go back to the little money box in that trunk of yours, fetch out the six hundred and fifty pounds owed to me and do it quickly before I change my mind and take the one hundred pounds I'm willing to let go."

"How did you know? Tell me." She glared at him, all hope for her plans burning to ash before her. Her life with her son where they would not have to scrimp and save for every penny gone in a flash. That she would not have to take on multiple jobs such as what she'd done before Baron Bankes had offered her this position.

As much as she loved history, learning and exploring past lives through excavation, the position was hard work, hard on the body and tiring. Ideally she'd pick and choose the locations to explore and be paid fairly for it so she may be home most of the time, raising her son as best she could.

"I was in the library when you had your meeting with Lord Duncannon. Totally by chance as it was, but timely for me. Had I not been I would not have known you were trying to thieve from right under my nose. In future I will have to watch you more closely."

Anger spiked through her and she wrenched up from her seat, the stool she sat on falling down behind her. "Surely nine hundred pounds is enough for you that you do not need to keep blackmailing me. Is that not enough? I cannot do this forever."

"As I said before," he said, his tone bored and indifferent. Did the man have no heart? No moral compass? "You will keep paying me until I say otherwise. I'm looking forward to enjoying what this money can purchase me."

"You bastard. That is my life you hold in your hands. My son's future with me. His mother. You're taking that from me."

He pouted at her words and the urge to scratch his eyes

out grew. Hallie clasped the table's side lest she do as she wanted. "So very sorry for you, but you did assist the Duchess of Whitstone on snuffing out my cousin's life. When you look at it, this revenge is all very equal. You hurt my family, and now I shall hurt yours."

"I did nothing to your cousin. Any bad tidings that happened upon him were brought on by himself." The vision of Mr. Stewart blurred and she blinked, hating that she was upset and he was seeing her so. She went back to the trunk and counted out another six hundred and fifty pounds, slamming it onto the table. "Get out."

"Oh, do not cry, my dear. You're a tough, working woman. You should be pleased you're able to help your fellow man," he said, sweeping up the money, his eyes greedy little beads at the blunt in his hands.

"What is going on here?"

Hallie gasped and swiped at her eyes as Lord Duncannon entered the tent, confusion written across his features until he saw the wad of cash Mr. Stewart was holding. If murder had a look, his lordship was the essence of that word.

"Nothing," she blurted, "Mr. Stewart was just leaving."

"With your money." Lord Duncannon strode about the table and ripped the money from the gentleman's hand, the man's mouth pulled into a displeased line. "What are you doing taking the payment from Miss Evans?"

Bile rose in Hallie's throat and she thought she may be sick. She needed to tell Arthur of her past, no one else. He would hate her for lying to him. For others to know of her past before him. For giving him false hope.

Mr. Stewart adjusted his coat in an unhurried air. "In truth I've been blackmailing her. No point in not telling you everything if you wish to understand."

Arthur glanced at her, confusion and anger simmering in his blue orbs. "Why would you do that to her?"

"Because as I was just reminding her, she was involved in my cousin's death, Lord Oakes if you recall."

He frowned, before his eyes widened at recollection. "The bastard who almost raped and killed the Duchess of Whitstone?"

"The very one," Mr. Stewart said as if this was of such importance that it was worthy of such actions.

"Are you mad?" his lordship asked Mr. Stewart, staring at him as if the man had sprouted two heads. "This is not the behavior of a gentleman. You ought to be strung up for such underhanded, illegal business."

Mr. Stewart merely raised his brows, glancing at Hallie. "Perhaps Miss Evans would like to explain how it was that I've been able to blackmail her. Miss Evans," he said, "Do tell his lordship everything."

Hallie looked between them, warring with herself with the need to flee or stay and fight. The urge to flee rode hard on her heels, but she knew there was little point in doing that. Lord Duncannon needed to know the truth, she had just hoped he had not found out this way. Certainly not through the urging from Mr. Stewart, who seemed to be taking pleasure from both their pain.

She took a steadying breath, clasping her hands before her to stop herself from fidgeting. "Mr. Stewart has been blackmailing me because he knew of my past. My life in Egypt."

"I know of her life there, and yet you do not see me treating Miss Evans in such a way."

"You do, do you?" Mr. Stewart glanced at his lordship in surprise. "You know all of it? Everything?"

Lord Duncannon looked between them, doubt creeping into his gaze. "I thought so."

"You thought wrong," Mr. Stewart said, laughing and clapping his lordship on the back. Mr. Stewart headed for the tent exit. "I shall be off then, this little tête-à-tête has made me quite famished. I believe dinner will be served within the hour. Nothing like a little disagreement to warm the blood and make me salivate."

"Hallie?" Lord Duncannon said, pulling her attention back to him. "What happened in Egypt?"

Mr. Stewart popped his head back into the tent at the question. "She had another man's child, my lord. Thought you knew." He shrugged. "I must have been wrong. My mistake."

Hallie met Arthur's gaze and read the confusion and hurt within his stormy, blue orbs. She stepped toward him and he held up his hand, halting her progress.

"You're a mother!" A look of repulsion crossed his features and she raised her chin, not willing to be looked down upon, not even by the aristocracy.

"I am a mother. I can see by your face that this disappoints you, my lord, but if you expect me to apologize for my life I will not."

"You said... I thought you said there was no one in Egypt."

"I never said that, I merely did not tell you there was. You made your own summarisations on my situation. They were wrong." She was being unfair, and cruel, but then she had to protect herself now. No one else would do it.

He rubbed a hand over his jaw, looking out toward the dig site. "The child is not mine, is it? That night in Felday. You did not get with a child."

"No, my son is not yours. He's a man's named Omar whom I met in Egypt."

His lordship's eyes widened and he stepped farther

away, as if being near her was akin to being near someone who had leprosy. "Your child is half-Egyptian?"

She nodded, having no shame in that. "Yes he is. He's living with my cousin at present. Once I'm finished at Baron Bankes's estate I planned on traveling there to spend some weeks with him. He's only four, you see."

"I do not believe it," he stated, his face one of disbelief. "How could you not tell me such a truth? Were you ashamed?"

"I'm not ashamed of my son, but I'm also not a fool. I know that my options of positions like this or even as a servant in a great home would be compromised if they knew I had a child out of wedlock. I need money, my lord. I do not have a dowry or great estates that would earn my income and keep me well pleased and placed in life. That is the reason I chose not to tell anyone of my past. For capital reasons only, not moral."

"You allowed me to believe there was a chance for us. How could you do such a thing?"

She swallowed the lump in her throat at his words. So he was throwing her aside without hearing the whole story, her truth. Not even willing to see her side or to trust in the feelings she had thought he had for her. "I tried to dissuade you, to tell you that a future with me was not possible. You would not listen."

"I did not mean... It was one thing for me to overlook your status in society, the fact that you would come to the marriage with little compared to my wealth and property. That is what I thought you were concerned about. I did not care for that and would have ignored my grandmother's bouts of melancholy over our marriage, but I cannot overlook this. You are a mother. A mother to a child who is born out of wedlock."

"You're no better than Omar. We've been intimate and

a child could have been made. How is this any different? Is it that you're a lord and Omar was not, and that makes it alright?"

He ran a hand through his hair, leaving it on end. "It just *is* different."

Hallie sat back down at the table and picked up her small brush that she used to take the mud off of artifacts. "I guess we're done here then." She would not fight for a man, a life with a man who had double standards. If he would change his mind about her simply because she had birthed a child, he was not the man for her.

Tears pricked her eyes and she blinked for everything that she'd lost. If Omar had lived, she possibly would not be in this situation, even though his family too were against the union. Had, in fact, refused to consider such a thing. It was probably for the best. She would finish up here, return and collect her things tomorrow and go home. There would be other positions she would get, if Lord Duncannon did not tell everyone of her past. "Are you going to tell anyone?"

"Of course not," he said, staring down at the ground as if it would give him some magical insight. "I gather Mr. Stewart found out about your past. How much was he exploiting you for?"

"He had," she answered, seeing little point in keeping anything from him now. "He found out about my son, about Omar. He threatened to tell everyone everything so no one would hire me, not as an archaeologist, historian or servant," she told him, matter-of-fact, trying to keep her emotions in check. Her throat physically hurt at holding her feelings in order and she'd be thankful when he left.

She glanced at him and found him watching her, his face a mask she could not read. "In light of what you've told me, I see now that you will be unable to work at my estate. I will however give you the money, that's yours to do with as you will. Mr. Stewart will not get his thieving hands on that blunt."

"I do not want your money or charity, my lord. Please leave." She picked up the cash, handing it to him. "You know everything there is to know about me and my life and have said yourself that you're not interested in any of it. I think we both know there is little left to say to each other."

"I am sorry, Hallie. Had the circumstances been different…"

She nodded, not game enough to look at him. "Goodbye, Lord Duncannon."

"Goodbye, Hallie."

At the sound of his retreatment, she looked up and watched him walk down the hill, back toward the estate. She slumped back down into her chair, swiping angrily at the tear that snuck down her cheek. She would finish up her position here and then leave. She no longer wanted to be here, or anywhere near where Lord Duncannon was or his hypocritical ilk.

CHAPTER 16

Arthur returned to Baron Bankes's estate and, spying a footman, ordered his things to be packed and a carriage be ready within the hour. He paused mid-word to the sound of a woman's shrieking, authorative voice. He inwardly groaned, recognizing the voice of his grandmother.

What the bloody blazes was she doing here?

"I demand to see my grandson. Where is Lord Duncannon?"

God damn it. This was the last thing he needed right at this moment. His mind was a jungle of thoughts and denials of over what had just happened. Hallie was a mother! He could not wrap his mind around it. Anger thrummed in his veins that she'd lied to him, kept such important and personal details about herself secret. Did she not feel anything for him? Certainly it proved she did not trust him.

He started up the stairs for the first-floor drawing room. Guests of Baron Bankes's house party milled in the hall and some were also in the drawing room, all of their attention set on his grandmother and her demands.

"Where is Duncannon? He needs to answer to me and this news I received. Where is this vixen Miss Evans who thinks to make herself a countess?"

"My lady, you're mistaken," Arthur heard the baron say, trying to placate his grandmother with a soft tone. It would not help. The woman knew only one tone and that was abrupt.

"Miss Evans is employed here to do an excavation of my Roman ruins. She's in no way seeking marriage with Lord Duncannon."

Arthur made the door, seeing his grandmother wave a missive in the air. "This is not what this letter states. I demand to see him at once. Where is he?"

"Right here, Grandmother," he said, coming into the room. "Everyone leave, thank you."

"Have you offered for Miss Evans? The historian who has birthed a child out of wedlock? A child to a foreigner? An Egyptian no less." His grandmother clasped her chest, searching for a chair before seating herself down with the aid of two female guests who looked in no rush to leave.

"We will speak of this alone."

"Oh, no we will not. There is nothing to speak about," she said, her jowls vibrating with each word. "You're not marrying any hussy. The next Countess of Duncannon will be a lady of good birth and breeding. Why, any one of these young women present will do. I'll not have my grandson bringing the family name down for a common tart who should be working in St. Giles instead of digging up dirt in Somerset."

"Do not speak of Miss Evans in such a way, Grandmother. I'll not have it. No matter what your thoughts are on her past." *Or his.* Arthur glanced at the many faces who had heard everything about Hallie. She would return here to a pack of wolves, all waiting to take a bite out of her.

He turned to Baron Bankes. "Send word for Miss Evans's things to be packed up. You can see as well as I that she cannot stay here."

"I will do it," Willow said, stepping forward from behind some of the other guests, her disdain for him written plainly across her features. Willow's aunt looked at her charge, her face ashen with the news his grandmother had told them all.

"You'll not go near Miss Evans again, Willow. I forbid it."

"She is my friend, Aunt. I shall ensure she is protected before she leaves. Unlike some here, I do not forget my friends or those I care about," she said, looking directly at him.

Her words shamed him and he fought not to cast up his accounts. "Thank you, Miss Perry."

She turned to him at the door, glaring at him. "I do not do this for you, do not fool yourself on that account, my lord. Neither do I wish to ever see your spineless self again near my friend. Did everyone hear that?" Willow said, her voice peaking an octave or two. "Or do you wish for me to repeat it?"

Arthur watched her storm down the passage, her skirts flying about her ankles. Her steadfastness toward Hallie shamed him further and he inwardly swore. "Everyone. Out. Now," he yelled, startling the few about him. They scrambled from the room.

"I will ensure Miss Evans leaves today. We cannot have that sort in our homes. What will everyone think?" the baron said, clucking his tongue and shutting the door, leaving Arthur with his grandmother.

"How could you be so irresponsible, Arthur? You

know our family do not, ever, marry anyone that is not the finest, best bred, accomplished, and has a good dowry and from a respectable family. You will uphold tradition, and you will cease any contact with this Miss Evans. Whoever heard of a woman historian, or one who goes about digging up ancient piles of stone that no one cares about?" His grandmother rolled her eyes, clutching at her diamond necklace about her neck for support. "Your parents would turn in their graves should they see you now."

Arthur slumped into a nearby wingback chair, wrecked over what had just come to pass. He did not care that his grandmother was voicing her concerns, she could've gone on for months and she would not have swayed him from his choice of Hallie.

He shook his head. The thought that she was a mother unimaginable. She had never once slipped and mentioned her son or the man that she'd loved enough to bear him a child.

His hands fisted at his sides. The urge to punch something, anything, riding him hard. He hated the bastard, whoever it was who loved her. If the fellow loved her so very much why did he not marry her, bring her home and look after her and their child? Had he abandoned them in Egypt?

He groaned, having not thought to ask her why he was not with him.

"Are you listening to me, Duncannon?"

His head snapped up to look at his grandmother, her face a mask of disapproval. "What were you saying?"

"You're to leave and return to Cadding Hall tonight. Baron Bankes is as we speak going to set out to remove Miss Evans from his home. After I explained to him that for a baron to be around such a woman would not do his reputation in London any good, he saw the sense in this advice and will act accordingly."

Anger rode hard on Arthur's pride and still, the thought that Hallie would be kicked out as if her time here was worth nothing at all made him seethe. To be removed in disgrace simply because she had chosen a different way of life to those under this roof.

He stood. "I'm going to my room to pack." With nothing left to say to his grandmother or anyone for that matter, Arthur strode back to his room, ignoring the few who congregated about the drawing room door, no doubt listening in on his conversation.

A woman stepped in front of him and he reached out, grabbing her shoulders lest he tumble them both to the ground. He looked down into the steely-green eyes of Miss Willow Perry.

"How could you act such a coward toward Hallie? From what I can gather here today, you now know of her past and disapprove her choice."

His lip curled. He was not in the mood for a lecture. "There would be few who would not disapprove. Am I wrong?" he asked, glaring down at her since she continued to glare up at him. She sniffed her displeasure.

"Let me ask you this, my lord. How many women have you slept with in your life? I should imagine it would be many and yet women are not afforded the same freedom. Well," she said, jabbing him in the chest with her finger. "Hallie, Ava, me, hell, all our friends are not going to conform to a man's rule, even if this is a man's world. And if you're not man enough to accept and love Hallie for all that she is, then you do not deserve her."

"I guess I do not." The words rose up his throat and threatened to choke him. Still he could not accept what Hallie had done. What Willow said was true, he'd slept with a lot of women since first sampling a lovely lady's maid in his mother's employ before she passed. The idea, however, of his wife having been free with her body, her heart, left a sour taste in his mouth and he couldn't stand the thought of Hallie being with someone else.

To have had his child…

Yes, he'd slept with her, but he was going to marry her. If only he had been the only man to have ever entered her bed.

"Do not ever try and see her again, my lord. I'll not allow you to hurt her again."

"Is she back from the dig site?" Was Hallie back in the house already? If so, the baron was quick in having her services ended. The idea hollowed him out inside. Damn it!

"She is packing. The baron told her not half an hour ago that she was to leave due to everything your grandmother shouted out to half the *ton*."

"In my defense I did not know my grandmother was arriving today." His only relative wasn't even expected at the baron's home, so for her to be here, word of his attachment to Hallie had to have reached her side in London…

He clenched his jaw, thinking of only one person who would wish to cause her harm.

"Your excuses are not relevant. Leave her alone, marry a young, rich, *pure* debutante that has her maidenhead intact. One that your family are so famous for aligning themselves with and leave my friend alone. She deserves happiness and you and your toxic grandmother will only bring her pain."

Arthur stood silent, very little words coming to mind to retaliate against Miss Perry. How could he when everything she said was true?

He bowed. "I intended to, Miss Perry. There is no need to lecture me."

She scoffed, walking back up the passage toward Hallie's room. "Remember what I said or you'll not just face me, but Ava and our friends. And I can promise you, *my lord*," she said, his title full of sarcasm. "You think your grandmother is a tyrant, you haven't seen anything yet."

CHAPTER 17

A knock on the door sounded and Willow, who had been helping her pack, unlocked it and wrenched it open. Hallie couldn't help but look to see who was there, a little part of her hoping it was Lord Duncannon who had come to apologize and beg forgiveness.

Not that she would ever forgive him for his treatment or yet worse, judgement of her. Who was he to look down his nose at her simply because she had followed her heart? She doubted very much that he could say the same. There was little doubt that he had slept with many women, none of whom he was in love with, so who was worse? Certainly, it was not her.

Her maid over the past couple of weeks stood at the door, a missive in her hands. "Miss Evans, an express came for you this evening. I'm sorry it took me so long to bring it to you. I did not know you were back from the dig site." The young maid's eyes darted about the room, seeing her clothes and trunks out. "Are you leaving, miss? Do you need help?"

Her stomach pitched at the sight of the missive and she

all but forgot her troubles with the baron, Arthur, even her maid's question. Hallie took the missive and broke the seal, scanning the letter. Words of *illness, return home, post-haste* jumped out from the text and she stood motionless a moment, her mind a whirr of plans.

She started when Willow closed the door, speaking softly to the maid about a carriage and two footmen to help before coming over to her. "What is it, Hallie?"

"I must go at once. My cousin is ill."

"The one who looks after Ammon?" Willow strode back to the trunks and started packing them less carefully than she was before. "I've ordered you a carriage and a couple of footmen will be here soon to help carry the luggage down. We'll have you on the road to Berkshire before the hour is up."

"I do not think the baron will allow me to have the carriage all the way to Berkshire. I'll have to take the stage-coach from the nearest town."

"Leave that with me. I'll make sure you're safely delivered to Berkshire by tomorrow. I may only be a niece to a viscountess, but that doesn't make me entirely without merit. After what has happened to you today, you will not be dumped at the local inn to find your own way home. I'll not have it."

Hallie pulled her friend into a hug, so very thankful that she still had her true friends and that they would support her, no matter what. She should have trusted in that friendship when she found herself with child. No longer would she hide in the shadows, scared of what people would think of her or her choices. She would pretend to be the widow of Omar El Sayed, the mother of his child and everyone could go to the devil if they did not like that.

"Thank you, Willow. You are the best of friends."

"I am, and will always support you." They smiled at each other a moment before Willow patted her shoulder. "Come, more packing." She turned to a nearby trunk, throwing some of Hallie's boots into it. "Does the missive say very much about your cousin? How severe it is?"

"A severe fever and she's very ill. They're unsure if it's contagious. I hope Ammon does not get it. I would hate anything to happen to him. He's only a child."

"All will be well, my dear. I'm sure her friends have a doctor attending her."

Hallie tried to take comfort in her friend's words, but the mention of a fever that seemed to be affecting her cousin's mind made her fear the worst. What if she passed away? Whatever would she do then? She had not saved enough to keep her and Ammon secure in Felday. She had her friends, of course, to turn to, but they could not support her forever. After the atrocious way her truth came out here at the baron's estate, it was highly unlikely she'd ever gain such employment such as this again, or even work in a great house as a maid.

Her name was, or would very soon be, mud.

Hallie rubbed a hand over her brow, her hand coming away a little damp from perspiration. At least the baron had paid her in full for the work that she had done, and with no sign of Mr. Stewart she had not had to hand any over to him. Not that she had to worry about his blackmailing self any longer. Not now that everyone knew the truth.

The next hour was a blur of her trunks, missives to Greg and Bruce in the stable of her thanks to them, and where to forward her tools and paperwork, sketches and equipment that she had left up at the dig site. She had asked the footmen to take her things downstairs using the servants' staircase and to have her depart from the stables. She did not wish to see anyone from the house party, or the baron who had caved like a rock under pressure when Lord Duncannon's grandmother demanded he shun and fire her.

Hallie did one last turn about the room, ensuring she'd not left anything behind. She turned and picked up her pelisse and woollen cap that she preferred to wear. Willow watched her, her eyes a window of disappointment and Hallie took her hands, squeezing them. "None of that. I will do as you say and keep my thoughts positive regarding my cousin. I'm sure she will be well, and she'll get better even quicker when I'm there."

"I will miss you. We'll be leaving next week back to London, so please write me and tell me how your cousin fares and of course, yourself."

"I will. I promise." Hallie started for the servants' stairs, her steps slowing as she caught sight of Lord Duncannon waiting for her in the passageway.

"You're leaving."

It wasn't a question and she nodded, anger spiking through her blood at the sight of him again. What did he think he was going to achieve seeing her again? He'd made his opinions clear enough up at the dig site. She certainly did not need them to be repeated.

"I am. If you'll excuse me," she said, pushing past him and starting down the stairs.

"Hallie," he called after her. "If things were different..."

Hallie adjusted the small valise in her hand, ignoring him. She swallowed the lump in her throat that his words placed there. No more tears, no more heartache. She would return home, get her cousin healthy again and then return to Felday. Forget the Viscount Duncannon and bury everything he made her feel and want.

There was only one man in her life from this point onward. Her son. The rest could go to the devil. Sooner rather than later.

CHAPTER 18

Hallie reached Berkshire and her cousin's home the following afternoon. Thankfully Willow was true to her word and Baron Bankes's driver had taken her right to her cousin's door and helped unload all her trunks into the house.

The one, female servant her cousin could afford helped get her things inside. "How is Charlotte, Betty? Where is Ammon?" she asked, untying her bonnet and placing it on a nearby sideboard. Her cousin's home was larger than her cottage at Felday. Her only relative had married a gentleman farmer and after his death on the farm, had been left with the income from the land and the house. With no children of her own, she had been happy to help Hallie when she returned home, pregnant and with no support. Hallie owed her so much. In truth she would never be able to repay her kindness.

"She's upstairs, Miss Evans. Ammon is sitting with her. He wanted to tell her everything that happened at school today."

Of course, it was a Wednesday and Ammon would

have attended the local parish school. He was only four, and yet he was bright for his age. "That is good that she's up and talking. I had thought it was much worse than that."

"Oh, no, Miss Evans. It is merely a trifling cold." The maid glanced over her many trunks. "Are you staying for some time, Miss Evans? I will have the guest bedroom set up if you are. I do apologize, but we weren't expecting you."

Hallie frowned. They weren't? "Please, if you will. I'll be here for several days." Hallie started up the stairs. How could they have not expected her when they had written the missive?

She knocked on the wooden bedroom door and heard Ammon, his little excited voice telling of a story about a tree and his friend who had attempted to climb to the top. "May I come in?"

"Mama!" Ammon jumped from his chair and ran toward Hallie. She kneeled down, taking him into her arms and hugging him fiercely. His little hands clutched about her throat, and tears sprung into her eyes at having him near her again. No longer would she leave him behind. It wasn't fair on either of them. Somehow she would find work and be able to keep him close.

"Oh, I've missed you, my darling," she said, pulling back and taking in his sweet face. Eyes, the same as Omar's, stared back at her and made her miss him all the more. Miss what could have been. "You've grown. You'll be a young man all too soon."

Ammon stepped out of her hold, standing taller at her words. "Auntie thought so too. Miss Smith had to let down my pants. My ankles were showing."

Hallie chuckled, picking him up and going to sit on the bed, placing her son on her lap. Not wanting him too far away from her. She turned her attention to her cousin. "How are you, Charlotte? I received a letter saying you were very ill. Is this true?"

Charlotte shook her head, a confused mien on her face. "We never wrote to you at all, except a fortnight past about Ammon and what we've been up to. I have a cold, but not severe enough that you should return home."

"How odd." The pit of Hallie's stomach churned as she tried to figure out who may have sent the letter. "If you didn't send it, I wonder then who did."

"Ammon, why don't you go down to Miss Smith. I'm fairly certain she told me at lunch that she made a sweet treat for you today."

Ammon looked over his shoulder to Hallie. "May I, Mama?"

She leaned down, kissing his cheek. "Of course, my darling. I will join you downstairs soon."

He ran off, the sound of his small footsteps on the stairs making Hallie smile. "Sending Ammon downstairs, I assume there is something you wish to tell me, Charlotte?"

Her cousin's mouth thinned into a displeased line. "There have been some people in town, staying at the inn. They're Egyptian and I've seen them watching Ammon when I pick him up from the parish school. It's too coincidental. I think they know who he is."

A chill ran down her spine and the urge to run downstairs, pick up her son and keep him safe and in her vision at all times thrummed through her veins. "Does Miss Smith know to keep an eye on him?"

"Of course. She was the one who actually mentioned it to me first." Charlotte frowned. "Do you think they're here to take him away?"

"I'll not let them go anywhere with my son, but I also refuse to live in fear. I shall go to the inn today and see what their presence is about. I'll not have our family feel threatened, not by anyone."

"Good, very good," her cousin said, reaching out and clasping her hand. "I've grown so fond of the boy, I'd hate for anyone to take him away from us. Even if they are his father's family." Hallie nodded, trying to hide the fear that thrummed through her veins. If Omar's family was here, it meant only one thing. They knew he'd had a child and wanted him in Egypt.

ARTHUR SAT IN THE CARRIAGE, almost back in London, the houses on the outskirts of the city passing him by. He took little notice, his mind a whirr of thoughts, of regrets mostly on how he'd handled the situation with Hallie.

He'd let her down, turned his back on her when he should have stood behind her, a pillar of strength and support. He ought to be horsewhipped for judging her. Why was it all very well for men like him to bed whomever they pleased and whenever they wished? Hallie had not done such things, but instead had given her heart to a man in Egypt and had mothered a child.

He cringed, laying his head back against the squabs. No matter how much she hated him right at this moment, she could not hate him as much as he hated himself. He'd not just let her down, he'd let himself down too. The Lord Duncannon was not a gentleman who judged, not anyone. Life was for living, for loving and enjoying. From the moment he first met Hallie, her desire for life, to live and see the world told him of a soul that would not be tamed, and he did not wish her to be. He'd known that about her, it was one of the reasons he loved her, and yet, he'd thrown that back in her face, told her in a roundabout way that her life was scandalous and beneath his. That she would not make a proper wife.

"Fuck it," he said aloud.

His grandmother's eyes grew uncommonly wide, her face turning a ruddy red. "Arthur, I beg your pardon. Do not blaspheme in front of me. Not now or ever."

"Why not?" he asked, staring at her. He shouldn't blame his grandmother, she was a product of her time, a woman who had an opinion on everyone, no matter if it were wrong or right. "I've fucked it right up and will never be able to repair the damage I've done."

She sniffed, rolling her eyes and stared out the window as if the king himself was outside and keeping her attention. "I suppose you're talking of Miss Evans. The trollop."

"She's not a trollop. I'll not have you talk about her like that."

"I shall talk about her in any way I please. Unlike you, I did a little investigating on her before coming to fetch you from Somerset. Did you know that her child is the sole heir to the late Omar El Sayed family in Egypt? I had a very interesting letter from a gentleman who had taken an interest in Miss Evan's life. Another jaded lover no doubt, but he did impart some very interesting information. One tidbit that he'd written to her lover's family in Egypt telling them of the child. They are en route to collect the boy, or so I was informed last week."

Arthur's blood ran cold at his grandmother's words. "Was this letter informing you of this by any chance from a Mr. Stewart?"

"Why, yes it was. Do you know of him?" she asked, seemingly excited by the chance that they both knew the man. By god yes, Arthur knew him and when he got his hands on Mr. Stewart he would strangle him so he could not cause any more trouble. "You may not care, but Mr.

Stewart has been blackmailing Miss Evans for some weeks. Threatening to disclose her son, ruin her chances of earning an income all because he's the cousin of the late Lord Oakes, the very gentleman who tried to kill the Duchess of Whitstone. I doubt very much the duke would look favorably on anyone who aided such a man." Arthur watched as his insinuation was understood by his grandmother, her face paling. "Let us not forget that Miss Evans is the close friend of the duchess as well."

His grandmother's eyes narrowed. "Threatening me, no matter how vague you are being with words, will not work, my boy. You must admit your mistakes and move on from them. Miss Evans may have been a little diversion for you while in the country, but over my dead body will I allow her to become the next Countess of Duncannon."

"What if I want her to be my wife? Will you accept that and mute your viperish tongue? I would hate to have to send you to the country. And please, my dear Grandmama, understand my words are not a vague threat, but a promise of what is to come if you cause any more trouble."

"You're going to marry her! How could you do that to your family? The Duncannons do not marry fallen women. You'll bring the whole family down into the pits of scandal and debauchery."

He shrugged, having heard enough. "I love her. I have always loved her, even before she left for Egypt and I thought I'd never see her again. I find that I do not care about her past, only that I want to be in her future. If she and her son will have me." Never a bigger question to be asked. He would fight to keep her in his life, and if that meant he would become a father to her child, then so be it. He would not turn away from anyone whom she loved. Not even another man's child.

Some would call him a fool, turn their backs on him and some doors in London would be forever closed to them over his choice and yet he did not care. Let them close their doors, he knew there were some who would forever give admittance and that was enough. They were his true friends.

"I forbid it, Arthur."

He raised his brow at his grandmother's voice that brooked no argument. "When I drop you in London I'm going to continue onto Berkshire and win back the woman whom I adore, and nothing that you or anything that society says will change my mind. I'm happiest when I'm with her. I need nothing else."

She pointed a knobbly finger at him, her face pale. He was sorry for causing her such pain, but he knew the truth within himself. This was the right course. His body thrummed with expectation for his life to start and he knew who he wanted at his side when it did.

"I will never admit her to my home. Nor any children that you have. From this point forward you're dead to me."

He sighed, shrugging. "Well, that is a shame, Grandmother for I am the viscount and head of the family and as thus I control the money that supports the family. If you punish Hallie for a life lived to the fullest, I shall punish you in the same way. Is that what you really want?"

"How dare you, you insulant boy!"

The carriage rocked to a halt and Arthur glanced outside to see they'd pulled up before his grandmother's Mayfair townhouse. "I will write to you the details of my wedding. I expect to see you there."

His grandmother alit from the carriage, and huffing her discontent, stormed up the townhouse front steps. Arthur watched as she pushed the door open, not giving the butler time to get out of the way, making the man stumble.

Arthur shook his head, yelling out directions to Berkshire and settling back in the squabs. If they traveled through the night and changed the horses regularly he should reach Hallie's cousin's home by dinner tomorrow, perhaps a little later. His task to beg for forgiveness would not be an easy feat. Hallie would not be easily swayed that he was sorry, but he was. So sorry that his chest ached every time he thought of living a life without her.

He would not lose this war. He would win her and her love. For him, there was no other choice.

CHAPTER 19

Hallie walked into the taproom of the local inn later that afternoon, the venue eerily quiet and without its usual customers. She was thankful for the little brass bell that was above the inn's door, for not a moment after she'd walked into the room, filled with tables and a fire, well alight and filling the room with warmth and cozy ambiance, a short, but stout man walked in behind the bar. Hallie smiled, hoping her politeness would help her in making the publican disturb his guests and bring them down here to talk to her.

"Good afternoon, sir. I'm hoping to speak with some guests staying here, I understand. They're not English and perhaps have a thick accent. Do you have anyone who's staying her similar to that?"

"Oh ay, we did, miss, but they've rented the late Sir Garrick's estate just north of the town. If you follow the road that leads back to London, make a left about a quarter mile up and you'll come to the estate quick enough."

"Was there a woman who was part of that party?"

The publican rubbed his bearded jaw, pulling down on his tuft of hair as if stroking some sort of animal attached to his face. "No, there were two gentlemen, very well dressed, but no lady that I know of. They only stayed one night here before they were able to take up residence at the estate.

"Thank you for your help. I shall go there directly."

Hallie went back into the hitching yard at the inn and using a mounting block, jumped up on the back of her cousin's only mount. She patted the horse, hoping the beast didn't let her lose her seat. It was times like this that she wished she was as good a rider as Ava. Unfortunately, it was not a specialty of hers.

She made her way up the north road and turned left when she came to a well-worn road, the roof of the estate just visible over the tree tops. Nerves pooled in her stomach at the thought that the people there may well be Omar's family, his mother or father. They were such a wealthy and influential family in Egypt. Their presence here only meant one thing. They had learned of Ammon and wanted him.

Never one to deny people what they wanted, she of course would allow visitation to Ammon. Had Omar not warned her against contacting them, she would have done this herself, but he'd made her promise that their union be a secret. His family, he explained, would never understand his love for her or hers for him. Hallie had kept that promise, but perhaps with Omar's death, his parents had mellowed. Losing a child changed people, maybe it had changed Omar's family in regards to their thoughts on her.

It only took a few minutes before she pulled the horse up to the front of the house, tying her mount to the front step railings. The place looked deserted, no sign of gardeners or staff about the property. She glanced up at the building, a shutter on a window hung haphazardly from its broken hinge, and the steps looked like they'd not been swept for some months.

Hallie wrapped the brass knocker on the door, a hollow echo running throughout the house before the clipped footsteps of someone inside met her ears. She took a calming breath, ready to discuss and negotiate with Omar's family if need be, but she would not crumble under that great family's pressure.

The door swung wide and she stumbled back, fear spiking through her. "Mr. Stewart. What are you doing here?"

He stepped outside, his pace cautious as if she would bolt at any moment. The thought had crossed her mind, but the fact that she wasn't a fast runner and her horse was currently tied up behind where Mr. Stewart stood, the option seemed pointless.

"Miss Evans. I thought you would come. You're a clever woman, I will give you that."

She frowned, confused by the turn of events. She'd expected to see Omar's family here, but then maybe… "You made it appear as if my son's family were here from Egypt. Perhaps it is I who should say that you're a clever man. A cruel one too I should think."

He chuckled, the sound laced with menace. "Oh, I'm all of those things. I did do as you said. Made it look like your son's family were here to collect. But even I cannot get word to them quick enough that I found out where your son was, or have them here to take him away from you. I have, however, sent word to them, so I'm sure in the future your son will be well cared for. As for you, that's another matter."

"What do you mean?" She edged back and he followed like a lion stalking its prey.

"I hope you made your goodbyes with your son because you'll not be seeing him again." He clasped her arm, wrenching her toward the door. "Do come in, my dear. I've prepared a room especially for you."

Hallie tried to tug free, but his grip, punishing and stronger than she thought it would be given his wiry frame only tightened. "I'm not going anywhere with you."

"I'm not going anywhere with you either. I'll be leaving here today, but you, my dear will be well received downstairs in the bowels of the house. This place was owned by the late Sir Garrick. Their family is currently arguing who will inherit the house and lands. The disagreement shall go on for some months I'm sure, plenty of time for you to wither away and starve to death alone and in the cold. Just as you deserve since you helped snuff out the life of my cousin."

He pulled her toward a door that had it not been open Hallie would not have seen. It melded into the paneling of the room when closed and if he placed her down there, no one would hear or look for her in such a place. No one other than the publican knew she was here, and she'd not given her name.

Panic seized her and she twisted from his hold, slipping on the dusty parquet floor as she tried to run for the door. Her skirts, damn them to hell, caught on her legs and she fell to her knees. Mr. Stewart grabbed her from behind, hoisting her up against his front. "Shhh. Shhh, my dear. You'll only be hungry for a few days. After that you'll merely grow weak and tired. Eventually you'll not wake up at all. I could set the house on fire, give you an ending like my cousin, but I'll take pity on you and won't do that. I'm not that much of a monster."

He laughed at his own words and Hallie fought to remain calm. Not to panic. She stomped her foot hard against the top of his, and he let her go, swearing. Hallie took the opportunity to run, this time her focus on her feet and legs, making sure they remained upright and steady.

Pain sliced through her head as he clasped her hair, pulling her back. She landed with a thump on the floor, her head snapping back and sending her vision to blur.

He came over her, clasping her jaw and squeezing her mouth until the coppery taste of blood ran onto her tongue. She whimpered. "Do not attempt to escape again, bitch. I'll not be so kind next time."

Tears blurred her vision and he tugged her up onto her feet, pushing her toward the door that led down to the cellars and who knew what else. The staircase down was made of stone and looked to be a lot older than the structure of the house itself.

"Is your clever mind wondering if this is the home's original cellar?" He glanced at her, his easy smile and politeness back again instead of the deadly ire and loathing she'd read in them only minutes before. How a man could be so changeable was impossible to fathom and something she did not want to be around ever again. Not that there was a chance of that with her being buried alive down here.

"There once stood a castle here, during the eleventh century I believe. The cellar is all that remains and when the house was constructed they simply built over the existing footings. Perfect for you, my dear. As you're wasting away, you may study it if you like. I'm not so barbaric to leave you in the dark. I have supplied you with candles so you may see during your stay. Are you not pleased?" he asked, smiling.

Hallie clamped her mouth shut and kept her hands still at her sides lest she scratch his eyes out. The bastard was mad. As mad as his cousin. There must be some kind of disorder that ran through the family for these cousins to act out in such a mean and deadly way.

The thought of Lord Duncannon flittered through her mind, that she would never see him again. That her beautiful son would never know where his mama went or why. The stairs spiraled ever downward and even if she were to yell out for help until her voice was hoarse, no one would ever hear. This was in effect a tomb. Her tomb.

How fitting indeed since she'd spent her life studying the dead in places such as these and now she was going to be one of them.

Mr. Stewart had lit some sconces on the wall that showed them the way until the sight of a wooden door, leading into a room at the end of the corridor, revealed itself. Hallie rubbed her arms, the dark closing in about her, threatening to send panic to spiral through her mind. She would not succumb to panic. To panic meant death. Probably sooner rather than later.

Her cousin would send out a search party. She would find her way here. This was not the end. Mr. Stewart thrust her into the room, slamming the door closed. One candle burned in the corner and she raced over to it as the sound of steel locks sliding into the stone outside.

"Goodbye, Miss Evans. I do wish you a pleasant death," she heard him say, his voice muffled by the thickness of the door.

Hallie went about the room with the candle, searching the space for any way out, for more lighting. Fear turned her blood cold and she shivered. He'd left her one candle after all his talk of not leaving her in the dark, and nothing to light it with. She was going to die. Alone and in the dark. She leaned against the wall, her knees feeling all of a sudden less than steady and she slid down to sit on the floor.

The stone scratched at her back but she didn't care. There was no way out of this mess. She bit back a sob and fought not to cry. She was a strong woman, intelligent and brave. She would not give in, not now. If she was here in a week and still no one came, then she may lay down and wait to die, but until then, she would fight like hell to remain in this world. As unkind and unfair as it was at times, it still beat being entombed and buried alive like she was right now.

ARTHUR MADE it to the small village of Slough the following afternoon just as the sun started to drop in the eastern sky. He asked for directions in town and a young woman carrying a basket of bread and other foodstuffs pointed for him to continue along the road he was on until he came to the small, thatched-roof cottage on the outskirts of town that Miss Evans's cousin resided in.

At the nearby inn that he'd checked into earlier he had ordered soup, bread, and cheese to be packed and taken up to the residence just in case it was needed. He wasn't sure what was going on, or at least the severity, but the maid at the inn had mentioned a Mrs Nibley, Hallie's cousin had taken ill a week or so ago and was doing poorly.

Arthur came to the cottage that had a large front door and two windows on either side. It was quaint, but not as tiny as he'd thought it would be. The garden, mostly vegetables, looked well-tended, the windows sparkled clean in the afternoon sun. He knocked on the door, dread curdling his blood that Hallie would be displeased he had followed her. That she would not see him and send him away.

He could well understand that. He would not be

impressed if the situation were reversed. Her wrath he deserved more than anything, he just hoped that from that pain and disillusionment they could rebuild a life. Together as a family. He would not let her son's family take the boy away from her. Not after all she had done to keep him safe and protected.

His grandmother's words had haunted him this past day, and he could not help but fear that he was already too late. That Mr. Stewart's evil vendetta had already marked its victims and her son was lost to her. On a boat headed east. Arthur stood before the red door.

He took a fortifying breath and knocked. He fixed his cravat as the door swung wide, but instead of there being a servant or Hallie opening the door, a small boy looked up at him, his large brown eyes taking in his every feature and sizing him up. The boy was undoubtedly Hallie's, he could see her features in the boy's face, forever curious to know more. Something in the region of his heart squeezed and he kneeled, smiling to try to put the young boy at ease.

"Hello, I'm Arthur Howard, Viscount Duncannon. I'm wondering if Miss Hallie Evans is here."

The young boy shook his head, but opened the door wider.

Arthur stepped inside and took in the home. It was as clean and well kept on the inside as it was on the out. The small sitting room that the front door opened into had a large, roaring fire and comfortable-looking settee with a floral pattern on it. He went over to the hearth and stood before the flames, warming his back and hands.

The little boy ran off toward the back of the house and within a moment the steady beat of footsteps sounded on the polished wood floor. "Can I help..." a young woman's words faltered at the sight of him and she frowned.

He took her in, her modest morning gown that was a

little thread worn and covered in an unflattering apron. Her hair was askew and looked as if half the pins were missing. Even so, he could tell she was a relative of Hallie's. He was doomed to see people, it seemed, who reminded him of the very grave mistake he'd made. Of losing the woman he loved.

"I'm Lord Duncannon."

"I know who you are, my lord. Miss Evans is not here."

Her abrupt answer was more than he deserved, but he needed to speak to Hallie. To beg forgiveness. Promise her everything she'd ever wanted, if only she would be his. Be his wife.

"I'm looking for her. A matter of great importance that if you're willing, I thought to speak to you about." He glanced at the small boy and smiled as the little boy's mouth gaped up at him, watching the interaction with enthusiasm. Arthur winked at him, smiling as a small grin tweaked the boy's lips. "Alone if you're willing, Miss Nibley, I assume."

"Mrs Nibley." She glanced at the small boy, turning him to meet his eyes. "Go into the kitchen and help Miss Smith with the biscuits. I'm sure they're almost ready to go into the oven." She gestured for Arthur to sit on one of the settees in the room, before seating herself, adjusting her skirts and meeting his gaze. "What do you want, my lord?"

"First, I have come to apologize to Miss Evans, but to also tell her of what I've learned of her son's family. I believe they may be on their way here from abroad to take the boy. I need to warn her."

Mrs Nibley leaned forward, her hands clutched tight in her lap. "They're already here, and I do not know what to do. Are you in Hallie's confidence? You know everything?"

The question shamed him. He was in Hallie's confidence to a point, but then had shunned her like everyone else would eventually do at her past. He cringed. He was the worst of men. "I was, and I wish to be again, if she'll forgive me. But please tell me what you know. Maybe I can help before anything is attempted."

"We've seen men about town. Men that are undoubtedly foreigners. They have been watching Ammon for several days. The men had been staying at the local inn and Hallie went there yesterday. The publican told her of the house these gentlemen had rented outside town, on the north road to London and she went there. I know she did for I found my horse wandering the grounds the next day, but I cannot find her, or the men.

"There is no trace of anyone at the house. The property was the late Sir Garrick's. The family are arguing over the inheritance, and the house has not been lived in for months. It certainly would not have been leased to anyone, so for the publican to tell me that is where the gentlemen went makes no sense."

A chill went down Arthur's spine as he took in this information. His grandmother had said Mr. Stewart had written to Omar's family, but that could take months to reach them and then for them to act on such news. But they were here now. They had either found out about the child by other means, or Mr. Stewart was lying and was behind Hallie going missing.

"Where is this house?"

Mrs Nibley stood, striding to the kitchen, stripping off her apron as she went. "Miss Smith, I am taking Lord Duncannon to Sir Garrick's estate. We think we may find what we're looking for there."

"What are you looking for, Aunt?" the young boy asked, looking up at her with interest. Arthur watched as she reached down, cupping his cheek. "Is it Mama? She said that she would take me fishing before she leaves again."

Anger thrummed through Arthur's veins that if Hallie had been injured, had been taken away from her son and himself he would kill whoever removed her from his life. Mr. Stewart better be miles away from them, for when he caught up to the fiend, he would be lucky to survive the assault.

"Your mama will be home soon. I promise. Now, off you go and help Miss Smith. I'll be back shortly."

Using Arthur's carriage, Mrs Nibley gave directions out to the house and within half an hour they were pulling up before the large, imposing home that was in need of some repairs.

"This is where I found my horse wandering about yesterday," Mrs Nibley said, pointing to the overgrown lawns before the estate. "I have written to her friends from school for assistance after not being able to find her. I'm hoping they will be here within a few days to help look for her here or in London. It's so out of character for Hallie to do this. I cannot help but think these two men we've seen about town have taken her somewhere. Why they would take her and not Ammon though I cannot fathom."

Nor could Arthur. It did not make sense. He tried the door and found it unlocked. Pushing it open he called out. Hearing no reply, he stepped inside, looking about the large foyer. "Hallie!" he yelled, stilling to see if he could hear her. He turned to her cousin. "Let's search the house and then go from there. I'll start downstairs, you go upstairs and search the bedrooms and servants' quarters."

"Very good." Arthur watched as Mrs Nibley ran up the stairs. He turned for the first room on his left, a library, the books left as they were from the moment of Sir Garrick's demise. The house would not be worth anything if the family continued to argue over it for too much longer. He called out to Hallie as he went from room to room, checking in cupboards and in locked doors that sometimes had to be forcefully opened. The kitchen had a small cellar, but that was empty, save for a few blocks of cheese that had been left to rot.

He turned in the cellar, walking up to the wall and feeling it. It was made of stone, large gray blocks. The house was made of sandstone, but looking at these walls surrounding him, the house was built on top of an older structure. A much older one at that.

Arthur raced back into the foyer, yelling out to Mrs Nibley who started down the stairs at his yelling. "What is it, my lord? Have you found Hallie?"

"Has this house always been here or was there once an older structure in this area?"

Her eyes brightened. "Oh yes, you're right. This estate was built on top of the foundations of an old castle."

They stared at each other a moment before Arthur recognized the moment Mrs Nibley had the same thought as he. Her eyes widened, reminding him of Hallie and making him miss her even more.

"A castle often has a dungeon."

"Dungeon," Mrs Nibley said at the same time as Arthur, looking about.

"It's not in the kitchen," he imparted, before going to the stairs and opening the door beneath the central staircase. The space was empty, save for a few cleaning rags and an old dusty broom. He came back into the foyer, looking at the floor. Perhaps a trapdoor?

Arthur frowned, noting the dust on the floor had been disturbed more than what they had done. He stepped to the side, inspecting it from another angle and followed the disturbance toward the wall where it stopped. "What the hell," he mumbled, going over to the wall and feeling the wood paneling. He felt along the beading, not feeling any little lever or lock hidden in the wood.

"Push the wall," Mrs Nibley said, joining him and pushing farther along the wall as if she hoped the wall would open.

He did the same and to his surprise the wall released and a door opened along the beading, revealing another door. Arthur grabbed a nearby candle, lighting it quickly with the flint beside it and held it into the black void.

Stairs…

"Hallie!" he yelled, not hearing anything in return. "Wait here, Mrs Nibley. If I do not return within the hour, go to town and get help. I'm not sure how stable and secure this old structure is. Best that you do not follow me."

"Of course," she said without question.

Arthur stepped into the ancient part of the building and started down the spiraling stairs that were worn in the center from hundreds of years of use. The air was cool, musty and water seeped through the stone the farther down he went.

At the bottom of the stairs, of which he thought would never end, he came to an open space that led into a corridor farther into the ground. He shook his head, hating the thought that Hallie could be down here. It was no place for anyone. Even Arthur felt the shiver of the past crawl over his skin and whisper to remove himself.

Up ahead, out of the dark a door came into view. He lifted his candle, not seeing any light coming from the space. "Hallie, are you down here?"

A rustling sound and then two loud thumps sounded on the other side of the door. He stilled, his heart pumping loud in his ears, before he heard the faint feminine scream of his name.

He bolted to the door, taking care not to snuff his candle before unbolting it and pushing it open. No sooner had he opened it, was he engulfed in a fierce hug, arms wrapped so tight about his neck that he thought he may pass out from lack of air.

Arthur lifted her out of the cell, holding Hallie close, rubbing her back and trying to stem her fear he could feel thrumming through her body. Her skin was chilled, and she shook in his embrace. "I'm here. I have you," he said, kissing the top of her head, cooing calming thoughts of being out in the sunlight in a few minutes. Of seeing her son again.

"My candle snuffed out and I couldn't see. I couldn't see anything." Her sob tore at his heart and he swore revenge on the bastard who had done this to her.

Tears sprang to his eyes and he took a calming breath, needing to be strong. "Come." He wrapped his arm about her waist, and picking up his candle, turned back toward the stairs. "Let's get you home."

"I would ask you how you found me, but you're right, all I want is to get out of here, please. I just need to feel the sun on my skin and see my son."

"I know you do." They made their way upstairs and as they came closer to the foyer, the stairway started to come into view from the sunlight outside. "Almost there, Hallie. I'll not let anything happen to you. You're safe with me." He would keep that promise and he would find out whoever did this too her and murder the bastard.

CHAPTER 20

Hallie woke early the following morning, the sun streaming through the bedroom window and pulling her from sleep. She rolled onto her back, her hip sore from lying on the cold, stone floor of the dungeon for almost two days. The thought of still being there, of no one ever finding her made a cold tremor run down her spine.

She glanced about the room, thinking of Lord Duncannon, only to spy him sleeping on a chair beside her bed, his head laying back against the seat, his mouth open a little in slumber. Even dishevelled as he now was, still he was the handsomest Englishman she'd ever met and yesterday when she'd heard her name being called in his voice, she could have cried with relief. Well, perhaps she did a little.

As if sensing her watching him, he opened his eyes, his blue orbs heavy lidded, his hair askew and sticking up in places. The urge to run her fingers through his blond locks and tame his mane overwhelmed her, and she contemplated those feelings and what they meant, even now, after their terrible disagreement.

"You stayed."

He rubbed his jaw with his hand, sitting up to lean on his knees. "How are you feeling this morning?"

Hallie sat up and leaned against the bedhead, pulling the blankets up about her chest. "I'm sore, my hip is bruised from sleeping on the floor and I think I've pulled a few muscles. I had a little altercation before being placed in the dungeon."

Arthur growled at her words. "Who did this to you, Hallie? I need to know."

"Mr. Stewart." The thought of what that man put her through left no impediment in telling Arthur everything. He deserved to know who it was and how it happened. This was not a secret she could keep from him. Never again would she keep anything from him. "He hired two men who appeared to be foreign to watch my son. Enough so that it became obvious to my cousin and her servant. They wrote for me to return home, but I had already left by the time the missive arrived. I had also received a letter stating my cousin was ill the same day the baron asked me to leave his estate. All lies that Mr. Stewart had concocted to get me to return to Berkshire."

He cringed at the reminder of his failure. "And then?"

"The men being in Slough made us all think that Omar's family was here. I went to confront them at the inn, but I was told they had leased Sir Garrick's estate. When I arrived I realized my mistake. It was simply another threat from Mr. Stewart and a means to get me alone. I never saw the other two men that my cousin had spoken of, so I think they were merely hired thugs. Mr. Stewart locked me in the dungeon with no intention of coming back. Had you not found me..." A shudder wracked her body. The thought of being buried alive, far under the ground where no one could hear her shouts for help made her stomach churn.

"I will kill him."

Warmth seeped into her bones at his intention to defend her. She watched him a moment, he too was looking at her, the concern and warmth in his eyes made her wonder if he'd had a change of heart. That he'd found her certainly made it look that way. "Why are you here, my lord?"

He stood and came to sit at the edge of her bed, taking her hand. "Because I was wrong. I should not have judged you as I did. I should not have placed what my family thought, of what society would think above what I felt. I've fallen in love with you. You would not be the first woman to have had a life before marriage. I will never hold it against you. I promise on my life that I will not."

Hallie studied their intertwined hands. "Your family will never accept me. It is bad enough that I'm poor and have no great bloodline to bring to your family, but I have a child. One born out of wedlock and one who is of mixed race. I'm not certain you're prepared for what that will mean to you and your family. Progressive as you may be, or trying to be, society is cruel and there are those who walk among it who will never welcome you again into their homes, or offer friendship to my son when the time comes for him to take his place in that world."

"I will fight every day for the rest of my life to ensure Ammon is treated with respect that is due to him."

"Will you really, Arthur? Or are you merely saying everything that I wish to hear? Back at Baron Bankes's estate, you told me of all the reasons why it would not work between us. I'm no fool. I know one of the reasons is because my son is born out of wedlock and to an Egyptian man. I will not allow you to resent him in time if others turn their backs on us. If you were to ever do that, no matter the scandal, our marriage would be at an end. So if you really mean what you say, you must truly, wholeheartedly mean it."

"I do, Hallie. To my very soul, I shall never let you down."

She wanted to believe him, but he was a lord, a viscount. Marriage to her would mean so many sacrifices. To give herself to him, to allow him to become her son's father figure in his young life was a gamble she wasn't sure of. She fiddled with her bedding, unable to meet his gaze. So many thoughts ran through her mind, his past words, Arthur's declaration now. Denial of all that he made her feel. Refusal to accept that her heart had been touched once again. All of it confusing and muddling to her mind.

The door to the room flew open and Ammon ran in, jumping up on her bed and wrapping his small little arms about her neck. She pulled him into her, breathing deep the scent of his hair. To have him back in her arms, to see him again was the best medicine for her sore muscles and bruised hip.

"Mama, you're back. I thought you had gone away again."

"I'm here now, my darling and we'll never be apart again."

He pulled back and she pushed a lock of hair out of her son's eye. He had his father's eyes, a rich brown with golden flecks that would forever remind her of the hot, Egyptian land. As if remembering there was another person in the room, Ammon turned to Arthur, smiling.

"Good morning, Lord Duncannon. Thank you for bringing my mama home."

Hallie watched Arthur's reactions to her boy, and saw

434

nothing but sweet amusement and interest in his blue orbs. No calculation over what to do with him to remove him from view, to keep her son hidden from the social sphere they would circulate. Lord Duncannon simply looked at her boy, a sweetly mannered child who was happy to have his mother back and smiled.

"You're very welcome, Ammon. I told you I would bring her home, did I not?"

"You did. When Miss Smith explained to me what a lord was, I thought that you would not fail."

Arthur chuckled and Hallie smiled at their exchange. Her son, always the inquisitive boy, sat, legs folded on the bed and looked between them, his eyes narrowing in thought.

"You love my mama."

Hallie blinked to clear her cloudy vision that her son's question brought forth in her. Why she was teary over such a question she could not say. The fear that he would deny such feelings perhaps, or worse, state that he does.

"I love your mama very much, but I've been a fool these last few days and so you find me, Master Ammon groveling at your mama's feet, begging for forgiveness."

A grin tweaked her lips and she sighed.

"Mama, you should forgive. He looks sad and you always tell me that when people look sad we should try and make them happy. I think if you married him, he'd be happy." Her son nodded as if this was the very best idea.

"I think Ammon is correct. You should marry me and make me happy. And make you happy as well."

Hallie looked at her son, his sweet face alight with hope. As for Arthur, his eyes had clouded with uncertainty at her continued silence. She bit her lip, confounded if she should risk her heart a second time. The memory of Arthur pulling her into his arms after finding her in the dungeon swam through her mind. He'd come for her. Had saved her from a terrible, agonizing death.

"Promise me that you'll never let me down, Lord Duncannon and I'll marry you."

He smiled as Ammon yipped with joy, clapping his hands. Arthur pulled her son into a celebratory hug and the tears she'd been holding back fell unheeded. Never had she seen her son be embraced by a man, and not any man, but her man. Her future husband.

Arthur searched inside his coat pocket, pulling out a small box before holding it up to her. "Marry me, my beautiful, intelligent, loving Hallie."

"Yes, yes, yes," her son cheered, giggling.

Hallie glanced down at the yellow solitaire diamond ring. Never had she ever seen anything so beautiful. She sniffed, nodding. "Yes, I will marry you, my understanding, loving and protective Arthur."

She smiled as he pulled her into a fierce embrace, kissing her soundly, heedless of anyone about them. Her son made a disgusted sound and she heard him run from the room, yelling out for her cousin.

"Ammon seems well pleased," Arthur said, as she reluctantly let him pull back.

"And so am I. I'm sorry I wasn't more honest with you. I promise to never keep anything from you again."

He wiped the tears from her cheeks with his thumbs, kissing her softly. "I understand why you did. I will never hurt you again, Hallie. Nor Ammon. I give you my word as a gentleman and a man who's adored you from the moment you stopped your carriage and glanced out at me as if I were a madman. I fell in love with you that day, and nothing has ever changed that emotion in me. I love you so very much." He pulled her against him, holding her tight.

The familiar longing rose in her and she could not stop herself from kissing along his neck, up toward his ear.

"I thought you so handsome, so untouchable the first time I saw you. I think I too fell a little in love."

He groaned as she nipped his earlobe. "Only a little in love?"

"I told you that I would never keep anything from you again, or lie. I'm telling you the truth."

He pushed her back into the pillows, kissing her soundly. Heat thrummed through her and she could not help but wish they were alone, locked in a room and already husband and wife. "Hmm. Perhaps spare me those truths. A man does have his limits."

She chuckled, sliding her hand up under his shirt and feeling the corded muscles flex beneath her fingers. "You do?"

"I do, and let me be honest now, Miss Evans, you're pushing me to the edge of mine right now."

"Good, because you push me too." Not that she didn't love every moment of it.

EPILOGUE

Two Years Later, Somerset

Hallie heard the awful, loud bellow of an animal she'd not thought to hear emanating from their garden in Somerset. She pushed up from her desk where she was looking over the latest finds at the castle she was helping Arthur renovate and glanced out the window. "What on earth," she gasped, unable to believe what she was seeing.

A camel.

"What are you up to, my dear?" she mumbled to herself, watching with amusement as her son cautiously walked over to where Arthur was, standing beside him as the camel bent down to sit on the ground, two front legs first, followed by the back legs.

She rubbed her ever-increasing belly as the baby kicked, laughing as the camel gave out a mournful moan.

Hallie went to the doors leading out onto the terrace and pushed them open, going to stand at the balustrade. "Should I even ask what you're about, Arthur?"

He laughed, showing Ammon he had nothing to fear by touching the camel's neck. He called over a man she'd not seen standing aside. The owner of the camel she presumed.

Arthur kissed her as he came to stand beside her, wrapping his arm about her waist. "With our travels abroad planned in the next couple of years, I thought it necessary to show Ammon a camel. We'll be riding them, I have no doubt, when we get to Egypt."

She rolled her eyes, laughing at his forethought. "They have horses in Egypt, you know. Carriages too. We do not need to be riding camels."

He shrugged, his eyes dancing with amusement. "Where's the fun in that?" he said, throwing her a wicked smile that two years after their marriage still made her heart flutter and miss a beat.

Arthur had fulfilled all his promises he'd made to her that day in her cousin's home. He'd taken revenge on Mr. Stewart. Had hired a bow street runner and had the man arrested for bribery and kidnapping at a gambling hell one of Arthur's friends owned. A man Hallie had never met, but apparently had been friends with both the duke and Lord Duncannon since Eton.

Hallie couldn't help but feel sorry for Mr. Stewart living his days in Newgate prison. It would not be a place that she'd ever wish to be, but then whenever she had those thoughts, she reminded herself that all of what she had now would have been impossible if Mr. Stewart's plan had succeeded.

As for Ammon, well, Arthur had excelled as his step-papa. They were a pair to be seen about the estate. Always had their heads together, talking of books and horses, one of Ammon's favorite animals and one her new husband had gifted her boy upon their marriage. A gentleman always had a horse Arthur had declared.

Arthur lifted Ammon up on the camel and she clasped the railing. "I'm not sure that's a good idea. It's very high up there."

"No, Mama, it'll be fun."

With her heart in her mouth she watched as the camel stood, her son's eyes growing wide at the jerky action and height. "Hold on tight, Ammon."

Arthur came back over to her as the owner led him about the yard. "I have something to tell you."

Hallie kept an eye on Ammon, making sure he did not fall off. "What is it?"

"Ammon called me Father this morning at breakfast."

Hallie gasped, turning to look at Arthur. "He did?" Her vision blurred and she bit her lip, having never thought he would ever call anyone that term. They had been honest and told him of his father, of how brave and good he was. The letter Mr. Stewart had written to Omar's family did not evoke the response that he wished. In fact, the family responded with only one letter, disputing her claim and asking not to be contacted again. Hallie had been disappointed for Ammon who deserved to know where he came from as much as anyone, but she had expected that kind of reply. They had not welcomed her into their home when Omar was alive, it was unlikely they would now that he was gone.

"He did and that brings me to what else I have decided to do." Arthur picked up her hand, kissing it.

"Please tell me you're not going to keep the camel?"

He chuckled. "No, not that. But I have decided to have Cadding Castle bestowed to Ammon upon my death. That part of the land is not entailed and with it I shall include several thousand acres to support the estate. The castle will be rebuilt in a couple of years and I'd like to see it go to my eldest son, even if he is not mine by blood, he is mine in every other way. I want him to know that I love him as much as I will love the little child that we've created. I'll not see any of my children go without."

Hallie threw herself into Arthur's arms. How had she been so fortunate? "You're too good to me. Thank you, Arthur. Thank you for doing such a wonderful thing for our boy. If Omar were here, he would thank you for caring and loving Ammon when he could not."

He pulled back, clasping her face in his hands. "What is life if it is not for living, for loving and making those you love happy? I love you, Hallie, so very much. Ammon is not just your child, he is mine as well."

Hallie kissed him, deep and long. A heady ache thrummed in her veins and she wrapped her arms about his neck. If only they could go upstairs, disappear for a few hours... "I love you too. Thank you for being mine."

He threw her a wicked smile. "Thank *you* for saying yes. I always knew we'd be perfect for each other."

And they were...perfectly happy.

DARE TO BE SCANDALOUS

League of Unweddable Gentlemen, Book 3

After inheriting a small fortune, Willow Perry has everything she's ever wanted. Except a husband, that is. But not just any husband will do. She's looking for a grand love—someone who will challenge and excite her. It's just her folly that the one man who interests her is a notorious rake. He's as wild and passionate as Willow is sheltered and staid. Love between such polar opposites would be impossible … wouldn't it?

Abraham Blackwood has devoted his life to the pursuit of pleasure. He's perfectly happy to run his gaming den and ignore the expectations of society. But meeting the lovely Willow gives him another goal. Revenge. Making her pay for the sins her family committed against his will be easy. Ignoring how much he wants her—not only beneath him, but at his side, forever? That might prove to be infinitely more difficult.

. . .

When Willow discovers Abraham's true intentions, can the fragile bonds they've begun to form survive? Or will the cards remain firmly stacked against their happily ever after?

PROLOGUE

1826 London

W illow raced up her aunt's stairs, having been summoned back from her daily ride at Hyde Park. Sweat pooled on her brow, and she could feel it running down the line of her back beneath her gown. It was too soon. This day could not be the end of her aunt.

She ran as fast as her riding ensemble would allow and pushed open her aunt's bedroom door, coming to an abrupt halt at the sight of her lady's maid, the butler, and housekeeper, all of their faces masks of pity and sadness.

"Auntie?" She came and sat on the bed beside her, reaching for her hands. They were cold and limp in hers, and Willow squeezed them a little, needing to rouse her, keep her with her for just a bit of time longer.

"I'm still here, my child. I waited for you."

Tears pooled in Willow's eyes, and she clasped her aunt, her only family left in the world into an embrace, her throat as raw as if a hot poker had pierced her there, making each breath painful and hard.

445

"I'm so sorry. I went riding. I did not know that you were so poorly."

Her aunt shushed her, the action bringing on another bout of coughs that wheezed and rattled her chest. The hack sounded painful, and if her aunt's grimace each time she coughed was any indication, the infection was causing discomfort.

"I want you to go riding, even when I'm gone. You will have more time on your hands then. You won't have to trundle after me anymore."

That may be so, but Willow would have to trundle after someone. When her aunt passed, she would need to find employment, and soon. The thought brought her no pleasure, and her stomach churned at the prospect she would not find work. Not that her friends would leave her out on the street, but they had their own lives now, families to take care of, they did not need a friend latching on to them for charity.

"Never mind that," she said, not wanting to talk about what she would do after her aunt passed. The doctor had promised she had some weeks left, not one. Her decline had been so fast in the last few days. Too fast. Willow prayed for time to stop. For her aunt not to leave her alone in this world. "You'll be better soon, and we'll look back on this day and laugh. You'll see. Nothing to fear just yet."

Her aunt's lips twisted into a grin. "I wanted to tell you before I go what I've done." Her aunt squeezed her hands, suddenly stronger and capable as they once were. "You will have time, my dear. To finally do as you wish because I'm leaving you everything that I have. The London townhouse, my estate in Kent, my money. All of it is yours."

Willow stared at her aunt, knowing full well her mouth was gaping. "You cannot. I'm not a Vance."

"No one is. With no children and no one to take on the

title, I can do what I wish with everything else. The title and house in Norfolk will revert to the Crown, but nothing else."

"Are you sure, Auntie?" Willow asked. Surely there was more entailed than just the Norfolk property. She could not get everything.

"I will lose the house in Norfolk, but everything else is yours, my darling." Her aunt sat up a little, her eyes bright. "You have been a shining light in my world since Maurice died, the child that I never had. You are my sister's daughter, but you are mine as well. I want you to be safe, to be protected after I'm gone. Making you my heir accomplishes all this. I will rest easy knowing you will be protected."

"Oh, Auntie." Willow's vision blurred at her impossibly good fortune at a time when the loss of the woman before her would be too much to bear. "I love you so much. Thank you. It is too much."

Her aunt sighed, lying back on the bedding, a small smile about her lips. "I'm happy to." She reached up, touching Willow's cheek with her palm. "You will suit being an heiress, just try and keep some of the funds for yourself and not give it away to all the unfortunates. I know what a good heart you have."

Willow chuckled. Even now, as ill as her aunt was, she was making banter, trying to make her laugh. "I will try. I promise." Willow sat back as her aunt slumped into her bedding, her eyes closing with the exertion of having spoken the last few minutes.

She watched her, holding her hand. Her chest rose and fell, telling Willow she was still here. "I will miss you so much, Auntie. Thank you for loving me as you did. I will never forget your kindness."

The housekeeper came over to Willow and placed a

comforting hand on her shoulder. Willow could not stop looking at her aunt's breathing. In. Out. In. Out. In. She waited for the exhale. It never came. Willow stood, clutching at her aunt's hand. "Auntie. Auntie," she cried, louder this time, but nothing. No breaths. No words. Nothing.

She turned to the housekeeper who stared at her, tears in her own old eyes. "She's gone to be with God, my dear. Come away now."

Willow did as they bade, unable to fathom what had just happened. Her aunt could not be gone. It wasn't possible. She paused at the threshold of the room, looking back at her only relative — the dearly departed sister to her mama. The Viscountess Vance. "I will miss you," she whispered, before leaving the room. "Always."

CHAPTER 1

Twelve months later – The Season

Abraham Blackwood, Marquess Ryley, Abe to his friends and those who were fortunate enough to bed him, watched as his mistress energetically sucked and licked with enthusiasm on his phallus, her chocolate-brown hair cascading over his legs and tickling him with each movement. He leaned back in his chair, enjoying the slide of her tongue, the massaging of his tight, aching balls with her hand. She was a clever minx, and one he doubted he'd ever tire of — worth every jewel and penny he spent on her.

"Fuck, that's good." She made a sweet mewling sound that throbbed up his spine. He was close, could feel his balls tightening with his impending release. Lottie increased her ministrations as if sensing he was near spilling into her mouth. Another perfect reason he had her as his mistress. She encompassed good sense and was a fucking hot shag. She shifted a little, taking him to the back of her throat, and his seed released, hard and long into her mouth. The perfectionist and expert that she was, she swallowed, not spilling any over her swollen, pinkened lips.

"Hmm, delicious," she purred, sitting up on his desk and spreading her legs. He raised one brow, taking in her wet cunny. "You've been busy down there."

"Do you like it? It's all the rage in Paris. I thought it might be fun," she said, glancing down at her clean-shaven quim.

He licked his lips, not minding either way. Shaved or not, he enjoyed eating a woman to release.

A series of knocks sounded on the door.

Lottie sighed, lying back on the desk.

Abe reached out, running his finger along her wet folds, rolling his thumb over her sweet nubbin. "Fuck off," he yelled, kissing her inner thigh.

"It's me, Whitstone," came a muffled voice from the other side of the wood.

Abe groaned, settling back in his chair and watching as Lottie, aware that their playtime was over, shuffled off the desk and adjusted her clothing. "I'll meet you upstairs shortly. Be ready," he said, as she threw him a mischievous grin over her shoulder before opening his library door to reveal Whitstone, arm raised as if to knock again.

"Come in." Abe gestured to one of his oldest friends since Eton. Whitstone had protected him when other boys at the school would poke fun at his mama, a Spanish woman who had been fortunate enough to marry Marquess Blackwood when he was touring the continent. The young marquess had returned to England with a wife. Quite the scandal considering she wasn't a perfect English rose, as the marquess was expected to wed.

"My friend," Whitstone said, smiling at Lottie as she walked past His Grace, running her finger across the duke's chest.

Abe laughed. Cheeky wench.

Whitstone entered the room, closing the door. "I apologize if I interrupted you," he said, smirking.

"Drink?" Abe asked, standing and going to the decanter to pour a glass of whiskey.

"No, thank you. I have come here to ask for a favor and have little time. Otherwise, I would."

Abe raised his brow, downing his whiskey before pouring another. "What is it that you need?" He had little to do with society, not after what happened the last time he trod the boards at Almacks. Not that he'd ever be admitted to the place again, not after receiving a life ban for punching Lord Perfect, as he termed Lord Herbert, for being an ass. Something the man was afflicted with often.

"I'm not sure if you know Ava's good friend, Miss Willow Perry, but she's hosting a masquerade ball, a celebration to be back in society after the death of her aunt. She's become an heiress you see, worth over one hundred thousand pounds, and I want you there to keep her safe from those who may be looking at her as a bit of blunt to clear their debts. Ava is determined that Willow will marry for love and nothing else. Although..." Whitstone said, his tone bemused. "I'm not sure Willow thinks the same as the duchess."

Abe's lips twitched, well believing that what the duchess may think is well and good for her friend may not be what the lady in particular wants. The duke's wife could sometimes be, in every sense, a duchess used to getting what she wanted.

"You want me to babysit Miss Perry."

Whitstone leaned back in his chair, folding his legs. "You make it sound like a chore. Duncannon will be there also, and myself. We'll make a good night of it, but we must keep her safe from blackguards that may seek to ruin her to gain her inheritance."

Abe rubbed a hand over his jaw, the prickle of whiskers reminding him that he'd not shaved this morning. "What if she wants a little rendezvous in the garden? Are we to stop her from having a little fun?" Abe had fun often with the ladies of the *ton* who were free from the marital bed or looking to cuckold it.

Whitstone raised his brow, his visage one of censure. "She's a lady, Ryley. She will not be looking for a quick tup on the lawn."

His lips twitched, knowing how very fun a quick fuck up against a trellis or terrace railing could be. There was nothing sweeter than lifting the skirts of a willing woman and sliding into the tight quim that wrapped and pulled you in until you were lost. He thought about what Whitstone asked. There would be many women there, plenty of willing ladies under disguise for the masked ball who may be up for a little fun with the Spanish Scoundrel.

"Very well. I'll attend. When is it?" he asked, sitting back behind his desk. He had a masquerade outfit that would suit his heritage and, most certainly, his dark character.

"Tomorrow evening. Miss Perry is living in the late Viscountess Vance's residence on Hanover Square. That was her aunt."

Abe stilled at the mention of the name Vance. The surname raising ire and regret in his veins. Not regret that her ladyship had passed or that he'd not paid his last respects, but that he'd not been able to make the woman pay for her dealings with his sweet mama. Viscountess Vance had ensured his mother had never been accepted into society, helped along with Lord Perfect's mother too. A mean feat since his mother was a marchioness and much higher on the social ladder than lady Vance. Vance, however, had one thing that his mother never did.

English blood.

That this Viscountess Vance had a niece he'd not known of... Or perhaps he had, but had not paid enough attention when she'd been standing right under his nose.

"The night that we caught up with Mr. Stewart and threw the bastard into Newgate. That is where I've heard of Miss Perry. She was a school friend of the duchesses and Miss Evans. She was at your home that night, waiting with Ava and Hallie."

The duke nodded, sitting forward to lean on his knees. "They were all at a finishing school together in France. Madame Dufour's Refining School for Girls."

The duke took him in a moment, a small frown forming on his brow. Abe schooled his features, not wanting his friend to know of his loathing of the Vance family. Miss Perry's family.

"You seem curious about Miss Perry all of a sudden. You are going to behave yourself, aren't you, Ryley? Ava will tan my hide if you hurt Miss Perry in any way."

Abe chuckled, masking his features. No one knew how many nobs in London, how many families he'd paid back over the years for the wrong they did to his mama. Made her an outcast of society. Made her leave him and her life here in England to return to Spain. At least she was still living, and he saw her as often as he could. His father had never forgiven her for running away, and his sire had loathed her until his death only a few years ago.

A wasted life. For both of them. And he could lay it all at the door of Viscountess Vance and Lady Herbert, Lord Perfect's mother and their wicked tongues.

"You forget that I have a mistress and have zero toler-ance for society." The gaming den, Hells Gate, was profitable and diverting, and he sought out society little. Unless he stumbled across a willing lady in his club, a woman looking for a little diversion, only then was he up to being distracted, normally under her skirts.

Whitstone sighed, his shoulders sagging in relief. "Very good, you've put my mind at ease. So," he said, standing and clapping his hands. "Eight tomorrow night, Belgrave Square. Don't be late."

Abe stood and walked Whitstone to the door. "I'll not be late. You can count on me." He saw his friend out to his carriage and then started upstairs. He had a mistress to please, and he could use a little entertainment. No matter what he'd said to his friend, he would seek revenge on the late Viscountess's niece. If she were the last one in her ladyship's family that he could pay back, then she would be the one to suffer the consequences of her aunt's actions.

Abe frowned at his thoughts. His friendship with Whitstone and Duncannon was solid, but even he didn't know if it would survive his next step into society.

Certainly, Miss Willow Perry would not, that he was certain.

CHAPTER 2

E verything was in order for the masquerade. Willow
had a team of servants working for her, ordering
flowers, polishing the floor, cleaning windows, and ensuring
the gardens were manicured and well-lit for the dance.

After returning to London she had made some changes
to her life. Being an heiress allowed her certain freedoms
she'd not had before. She had hired a companion, a widow
who had a lenient mindset and liked nothing more than to
read and keep to herself most days, allowing Willow to do
as she wanted. Her two best friends, Evie and Molly, whom
she had invited to London for the duration of the Season
and beyond if they wished were also in attendance.

The house was certainly big enough for all of them,
and with Miss Sinclair watching over them all, when she
wasn't reading or strolling the gardens, the arrangement
was perfect.

Willow stood at the ballroom doors, watching as the
finishing touches were fitted to the room. She'd wanted the
night to represent magic and mayhem. Flower decorations
sat on every available surface, rich pinks, and stunning,

white forget-me-nots that showered the area with sweet scents. Groupings of candles, each of different sizes, sat in corners, and the three chandeliers were currently lowered, footmen and housemaids ensuring new beeswax candles were installed. Sheer netting hung over the curtains and across the ceiling, giving the room an other-worldly feel. A world where she was the master of her own fate. A heady feeling indeed.

"Oh my, Willow. This room is beautiful!" Evie said, walking into the space and twirling. Molly joined her, looking up at all the flowers and decorations her servants had been busy putting up the last three days.

Pride filled her, and Willow smiled. "I couldn't agree more. My staff have outdone themselves. I will be sure to congratulate them with a glass of champagne. They will enjoy that I should think."

"I think they would very much," Molly said, joining her. "I cannot wait for the ball. I've never been to a masquerade before."

"Neither have I," put in Evie, her eyes bright with excitement. "With Ava and Hallie with us, it'll be like old times."

"Except they'll have their husbands with them," Molly said, a little put out by that fact. "But then you never know what friends they will bring. Perhaps by the end of the Season we'll all have husbands."

Evie beamed at the idea. Willow smiled. After losing her parents so young in her life, she wanted nothing more than to have a family of her own. Her aunt had been her last blood relative, and now that she was gone, there was no one. A husband would be a suitable travel companion, assist her in seeing Paris or Rome. Give her what she truly longed for—a child.

Willow, Evie, and Molly were the youngest of their

friend set, and at seven and twenty, their time to find husbands was fast running out. The *ton* would have firmly placed them on the shelf and marked them as little or no consequence.

"I've ordered baths for you later today, and I've assigned you each a lady's maid to help you dress and have your hair styled. I hope you do not mind."

Evie gasped, clutching her arm so hard Willow thought it might stop the blood from flowing to her hand. "You've saved us both from another dreary year in the countryside with our families. As much as we love them, nothing ever happens in Oxfordshire or Hertfordshire."

Evie nodded. "The most exciting thing to occur in our village is church on Sunday. My brother has already laid bets at the local tavern on how long it will take for the vicar's new wife to fall asleep during her husband's sermon. His first wife, God rest her soul, was within seven to nine minutes, but this new one doesn't seem to have any stamina. We're guessing under five will be her limit."

Willow chuckled. "Come, I've had tea and sandwiches brought into the drawing room downstairs for lunch. I thought something a little informal would be nice. It has been so long since we've seen each other. At least a year."

"For me, yes," Evie said. "I had not seen you since Ava's Season-opening ball last year."

"Longer for me." Molly twined her arm with Willow's as they walked to the staircase to head up to the drawing room upstairs. "I've not been to town for a good two years at least. As you know, my parents are not in favor of London and so like to keep us hidden away in the country. Did you know that Mama tried to push me toward a local farmer as a potential husband? Under normal circumstances, I would gladly marry a farmer should I be in love with him, but he was my father's age. I could not countenance it. When I received your letter, dear Willow, I could not come soon enough."

"We're going to have so much fun," Willow interjected. "The chaperone I hired, Miss Sinclair, is, well, let me just say, a little flippant and inclined to forget her duties, so there will be plenty of opportunities to explore every part of this city, and the entertainments it has on offer."

"Like the gambling den, Hell's Gate," Evie supplied, a mischievous twinkle in her gaze. "Everyone is talking of it."

"Exactly like Hell's Gate," Molly said, smirking.

Willow frowned, having never heard of the club. "What is Hell's Gate? It sounds less than respectable."

"That's because it is," Evie said.

They came to the drawing room and entering the large, well-lit space, Willow couldn't help but be proud of her home. The windows that ran floor to ceiling lit the room with natural light, giving it a warm and homely feel. Willow closed the door. A tea service sat on a small table beside the settee. Her butler waited at its side.

"I'll serve the tea. That will be all, thank you, Thomas," Willow said, not asking what else her friends knew of this club until they were alone. Once the door closed, Willow set about pouring them all tea and handing each of them a sugar cookie.

"Now, tell me more of the club and, more importantly, how you know of it."

Evie waved Molly's curiosity aside. "Well, I'm surprised you do not. Remember when Hallie had all that trouble with Mr. Stewart? Well, he was caught at the Hell's Gate. The Bow Street runner found him there after the owner alerted the investigator that Mr. Stewart was a regular customer."

"Who is the owner?" Willow asked. She remembered the situation well with their dear friend Hallie, but she had not heard how it all went about that the would-be murderer Mr. Stewart was caught.

"That's the delicious part," Evie interjected. "It's Marquess Ryley. He owns the club, has done so for years. I heard Ava talking to Whitstone about it all, that's how I know. The Marquess is by all account quite wild, but a friend of Whitstone and Duncannon's, ever since Eton from what I understand."

How very interesting. Willow poured her tea, seating herself across from her friends. "And Mr. Stewart was caught at this club. I remember the night all of that occurred. I was with Ava and Hallie at Ava's London town-house." Vaguely Willow remembered seeing the men return that night, two familiar, one who was not. The one she'd not known had been dark as night, his hair ebony and disheveled as if he'd been woken from slumber. She remembered her breath had caught at the sight of him. Never had she seen anyone who looked as wicked as he did. As for his reaction to her, there was very little. His glance had slid over her as if she were not even there. Most disappointing. "What is it that happens at this club?" Willow queried.

"Well, as to that," Molly said, "anything that you want. Or at least, whatever a man wants. Gambling, dining, dancing, and of course, the fairer sex can ply their trade if you know what I mean…"

Willow raised her brow. "And a marquess runs such an establishment?"

"Oh yes, he's known in London as the Spanish Scoundrel. I'm surprised you've never seen him."

"Actually, I believe I may have, but I wasn't aware of his reputation or who he was. We were not introduced."

"Maybe not so surprising, he's a little wild. I would think Duncannon and Whitstone would try and keep their wives' friends at a safe distance from the gentleman. He's as wicked as they come, and cares little to the fact."

Even more interesting. Willow could do with a little excitement in her life, and perhaps Lord Ryley would be a diversion to kick off her first London Season as an independent heiress. "I've invited Whitstone and Duncannon to the ball this evening. I wonder if they will extend the invitation to their friend. What a coup my masquerade will be if Lord Ryley makes an appearance."

"He's very handsome. I'm sure if he deigns to wear a masque or not, you will recognize him immediately. Few would not," Evie put in, picking up another sugar cookie and taking a healthy bite.

Molly nodded. "Oh, I'm so excited about this evening. We cannot thank you enough, Willow, for giving us this opportunity to be here in London with you. We shall treasure our time in town with you forever."

"You're more than willing to stay for as long as you like. I'm not going anywhere, and if my newfound circumstances enable you to make grand matches yourself, then I will be well pleased. As for myself, I'm open to a little flirtation and courting if a gentleman so chooses." Willow smiled at her friends as more ideas for their life floated into her mind. "And if we become bored with London, or a husband is not forthcoming, next year we can always travel abroad, to Paris, Madrid or Rome. We can do whatever we like."

Evie slumped back into her chair, sighing. "That sounds wonderful. You're too good to us, Willow. We will never be able to repay you your kindness."

"You do not need to repay me anything. Had my aunt not bestowed on me her fortune, I should be at this very moment seeking employment as a companion. If with this new life that's been bestowed on me, I can make the lives of my friends easier, then I shall. This house is too big for me to be rattling around in alone in any case. Too many years it's been empty, without balls and parties, laughter and fun. I want us to bring all of that back and enjoy ourselves as much as we can."

"That sounds like a most perfect plan," Molly said, her gaze wistful. "And it all starts tonight with the masquerade. What fun we shall have. I can hardly wait."

"Ava and Hallie said they would arrive earlier than their husbands, to ensure everything was in place. We shall all have such a wonderful time, and be all back together again." The clock on the mantle struck the second hour, reminding Willow of how late the afternoon was getting and the time required to prepare for a masquerade ball. "We should be going upstairs soon. We have so much to do yet before this evening. If you wanted to rest before our early dinner, that might be wise. I believe the ball may go all night."

Evie rose from her chair. "You're right, we best not dawdle. Come on, ladies, let's be off. We have a mask to attend."

Willow followed her friends from the room, taking one last look in on the ballroom before heading upstairs. It was simply stunning and would be a night she was sure would be talked about for weeks to come. A perfect way to start the Season and to tell the world that Miss Willow Perry is no longer the meek, biddable niece of Viscountess Vance, but an heiress and a woman who's ready to live and enjoy all that life throws her way.

As society started to make their way into Willow's magic- and mayhem-themed ballroom later that evening, she was delighted to hear the gasps and exclamations as to its beautiful decoration. Her staff was to be commended, and she would ensure they had their glass of champagne, just as she promised them.

Willow stood between her friend, the Duchess of Whitstone and Countess Duncannon. Evie and Molly were already out dancing with two gentlemen who wore masks to cover their features. Willow had thought it would be easier to guess who some of the guests were, but it was proving more difficult than she'd first thought. Not that it mattered, only those who had produced their invitation were allowed entrance. Those who danced and enjoyed the festivities were an acquaintance of hers in some way or another. They were among friends.

"I must tell you, Willow before my maddening husband arrives, and you see for yourself," Hallie said, glancing at her. Hallie wore a golden mask, her dark hair perched high on her head in a motif of curls, an elegant gold chain running throughout the design. She had come as Athena, the goddess of wisdom and war. With her spear and shield, she looked as formidable as the goddess Willow imagined.

"Good gracious, whatever has Duncannon done now?" Willow asked, teasing her friend. It was very odd that his lordship would do anything against his wife, but something told Willow he might have this evening.

"Besides the fact he was determined to come tonight dressed as a servant to please his goddess, he is also bringing a friend that I've only ever met just once. And while I'm sure his lordship will be on best behavior, he is a little bit scandalous from all accounts."

Was she talking of Lord Ryley? The Spanish Scoundrel? Excitement thrummed in her veins that it could be so. "Who is to attend?" she asked.

"Abraham Blackwood, Lord Ryley. He's a marquess, and from all accounts, his name of scoundrel suits him well."

Better and better. "Evie and Molly told me a little of him this afternoon. He seems quite the gentleman," she teased. "Has he arrived? I would like to meet this Lord Ryley." To see for herself if all the fuss over this one man was worth it. Certainly, having a scandalous lord at her mask would create a little stir.

"They should not be long," Hallie said, glancing toward the ballroom doors. "Arthur was going directly to pick up Whitstone. Lord Ryley was already at our home when I left, so I should imagine they will all arrive very shortly." At the sound of tittering, an excited whisper went through the throng of guests. "Ah, they've arrived," Hallie said, a small smile playing about her lips as she glanced in the direction of her husband.

Willow's heart skipped a beat as she took in the sight of Marquess Ryley. Well, her friends were undoubtedly not lying or embellishing the gentleman's charms. He had many—too many—possibilities of wickedness to count on two hands.

He was all darkness, his hair as black as the domino that he wore. His skin was sun-kissed, his eyes intelligent and assessing as he took in the room. People looked at the three powerful lords who had arrived, some giving them a wide berth as they passed them by.

Out the corner of her eye, she saw Ava wave to her husband, the duke, who spying her, turned to the other two gentlemen before they started in their direction. Everything within Willow stilled as those obsidian eyes settled on her, running over her face before dipping to her bodice. Heat prickled under her gown, and Willow had the urge to go outside to cool off a little.

The gentlemen joined them, and the duke made the introductions. Willow dipped into a curtsy and stood back as the duke and viscount asked their wives for a waltz. Willow watched as her friends, with their grand loves, moved out onto the ballroom floor, making a concerted effort to keep from looking at the marquess beside her. All six foot something of looming muscle that he was.

"I must offer you my condolences on the passing of your aunt, Miss Perry."

His voice was made for sin, or at least it pulled forth all the ideas of debauchery and everything one could do with a person such as the marquess. Deep and husky and like nothing she'd ever heard before. Willow glanced at him, her stomach fluttering as if a million butterflies were in there. He was watching her, and she sucked in a calming breath.

"Thank you, my lord. My aunt is greatly missed."

"Hmm," he said, and nothing else.

Willow narrowed her eyes at the noncommittal *hmm*

and fought to come up with something else to say. The man was too overbearing, made her nervous, and yet she could not understand why. They shared mutual friends, he was a gentleman, even if he did not venture out into society all that much. The realization struck her as odd.

"I did not think you enjoyed such events, my lord. My understanding is that you very rarely enter society nowadays."

A muscle worked in his jaw, and her attention fixated on it. He had a lovely jaw, cutting and with the smallest shadow of stubble. Although she could not see all his features due to his mask, she could just make out high cheekbones, and his nose was perfect too, even if those eyes were as hard to read as a book with no words.

"I do not, but I have very persuasive friends as you well know." That was undoubtedly true. Willow knew that as well as anyone. Her friends had demanded they stay nearby during this ball to ensure her security. Now that she was an heiress, it made her more susceptible to men of little morals and even lesser fortunes.

Willow shook her head at the absurdness of it all. As if overnight, she had lost the ability to see suitors for who they were. If they were not interested in her before she gained her fortune, they should not bother with her now. She would marry for love and nothing less. With her newfound freedom, she could take the time to find a gentleman who loved her, shared similar pursuits, and wanted a family as she did.

"I understand well, but whatever would we do without them?" she said, making light of his words.

"Hmm," he said again, and she wondered if he had any other vocabulary when answering her. They stood there for several minutes, neither speaking and with each moment that passed, Willow looked to see if any alternate friends were about that she could talk to. The marquess may like solitude and be a man of few words, but Willow was not.

"I understand you own a gentleman's club, my lord, and that you spend most of your time there. I hear it's very popular with the gentlemen of your set."

His all-too-penetrating gaze landed on her. Willow looked up at him, oddly wanting to know more about him and what he did. She'd never met a man who owned such a business, and her time in society this year was to explore and learn, to see and do more things while searching for a husband.

"Pray tell me, Miss Perry, how do you know about my business?"

"Hmm, well," she said, using his elusive response that was really no response at all, "It's our mutual friends again, I'm afraid. They told me, as well as a few other snippets of information."

He raised his brow, his lips twitching. Had she amused him? A little light of hope bloomed inside her that she had. He was so very severe, dangerous looking. It would not hurt him to smile. Willow could imagine how very sexy a slow-forming smile would be on his lips. What it would feel like to be the recipient of such a gesture. To have those lips on hers. A shiver stole down her spine, and she pushed the thought aside, wondering where it came from.

"So you know what society calls me, or at least calls me when they're not standing in front of me."

She nodded. "I do, although I must admit to wanting to know how you came about such a name. Are you a scoundrel?"

He did chuckle then, a low and gravelly sound that made the hairs on the back of her neck rise. "I can be when it suits. Have you always been so inquisitive?"

Willow laughed, covering her mouth with one gloved hand when those about them noticed their conversation. "Yes, I suppose. I've always been active in my friend's lives, and I like to learn new things. I do not know much about you, but you're an interesting character that I'd like to know more about."

He shook his head, staring at her. "You don't want to know about me, Miss Perry. You'll only be disappointed if you do."

"I'll be the judge of that." Willow adjusted her mask, watching the couples on the dancefloor. "Thank you for coming to my masquerade. I'm sure your presence will make my ball the talk of the town for a few days, at least."

"And you wished to be the talk about town? There are other ways to do that, without the expense of a ball."

Willow supposed that was true enough, but a ball was always preferable to nothing at all. "Yes, I suppose, but where is the fun in that, my lord?"

He threw her a wicked grin, and Willow had the impression he was talking about something else entirely than what she was speaking of. She thought over their conversation and couldn't see anything untoward or leading by it—strange man.

"Perhaps you are right, Miss Perry. A ball is much more suited to your character, and the fun I speak of is not. We are different beasts, on very different paths. I will ensure my conversation remains intellectual."

A footman passed, and Willow procured a glass of champagne. She drank deeply, suddenly needing the sustenance. Lord Ryley was unlike any gentleman she had ever met. That he was friends with Whitstone and Duncannon did give him respectability, in her eyes at least, but still, he was an enigma to her, a man whom she could not figure out.

His short, elusive answers that were more like riddles did not help either.

"Please feel free to mingle, my lord. My friends will return soon from their dance. I do not wish to keep you if you have acquaintances here."

He didn't look at her, simply stared ahead into the crowd of guests. "I promised the duke that I would stay by you this evening. Keep you safe from gentlemen who may wish to force you into marriage by ruining your reputation. I will escort you to the retirement room should you need to go, or if you wish to stroll outside, but for tonight, my dear, you'll have to put up with my invigorating company."

Willow shut her mouth with a snap when she became conscious that she was gaping at him over his declaration. He was cosseting her like a child!

She glanced out to the ballroom floor and caught the duke and Viscount Duncannon sporadically glancing in their direction, keeping tabs while they danced. Those infuriating, maddening men! They would not get away with this.

"I do not need a man to take care of me, Lord Ryley. You may continue on elsewhere to enjoy the ball."

"Ah, you're angry. Let me assure you, Miss Perry, that it is because you're hosting a masquerade that your friends have decided that you need an escort. I have nowhere else to go in any case. No one present draws my attention. I would sooner be back at my club than scuffing the floorboards here, I assure you. But when friends ask for help, you step up and assist in any way you can."

The society tumult that happened every year when the Season commenced was a social whirlwind that some found impossible to stomach. Even Willow had felt the same a time or two when escorting her aunt about town. The sly, pitying—and some disdainful—gazes that the set her aunt had circulated with were forever etched on her mind.

Even so, hosting balls and parties, being present in the *ton*, was required if she were to marry and find true love like her friends. Granted, she may be more susceptible to fiends who would try and ruin her, but it was highly unlikely to occur. Not at events such as this.

She glanced up at his lordship, watching as he sipped his wine. His Spanish blood was prevalent in his heritage, and her fingers itched to run through his thick, dark locks. Locks that were disheveled as if he'd just rolled out of bed. His eyelashes were as opaque as a moonless night, but it was his lips that held her attention. They were full and looked as soft as hers. She studied him a moment, wondering what he would look like if he smiled, and not simply out of politeness, but out of happiness, of finding something funny that amused him.

Did he smile when at his club? If she were to visit his establishment, she could see for herself. If she found him as complicated as he was here, at least she'd know the truth of him in that small way at least.

"Just because people are wearing masks doesn't mean that I'm in any danger. Am I not standing next to the Spanish Scoundrel? Some would say that my friends have placed me directly in danger with you as my protector."

He coughed, looking at her sharply. "Afraid I'll pull you behind a door somewhere, Miss Perry, and take your virginity? You are a virgin, are you not?" He took a sip of his wine, all nonchalance. "I've never deflowered a woman before, but I could make an exception with you. You are lovely," he said, lifting her chin with his finger and staring at her longer than what was appropriate.

Willow gasped, pulling her face free of his hold. The scoundrel! Had he really just said that? "Thank you, but I think I shall relinquish the offer. I'm going to marry a gentleman for love. A marriage similar to what my friends have been blessed with." Not a union built on lust. An emotion she felt in spades the longer she stood beside Lord Ryley. He was too magnetic. Without words or touch, he could pull a woman to his side, all the while keeping himself distant and untouchable.

"Love is all very well for some, but not suitable for everyone, I find." He glanced at their friends who were finishing up their waltz.

"I know what you're doing, my lord, and it won't work. Not with me."

"Really?" he said, grinning and giving her a little sample of his hidden charm. "What am I doing?"

"Trying to scandalize me, but while I may be shocked at the words that you use, I've not been sheltered my entire life. I went to school abroad and have friends who are of independent thought and highly opinionated. We talk about everything, men like you no exception." After meeting Lord Ryley, she wanted to know even more, if only to cure her of her interest in him. He was certainly different from the other gentlemen of her acquaintance.

"Give me time," he said, throwing her a look that made her toes want to curl up in her silk slippers.

She wouldn't let him get in the last word. "You have the Season," she taunted, spotting Evie and leaving him where he stood. The skin on her neck prickled, and she smiled, knowing he was watching her walk away.

ABE DRANK down the last of his wine as he watched Miss Willow Perry flounce off. Her sweet, intoxicating scent of jasmine teased his senses, and he wanted to chase after her skirts and continue the amusing, if not highly inappropriate, conversation they were having.

She certainly was different, perhaps even innocent in what he planned for her. Still, if she were all that was left of the Viscountess Vance's family, then Miss Willow Perry would suffer the consequences for her aunt's atrocious behavior toward his mother.

He would ruin her, he decided. Financially perhaps with her newly inherited fortune. And mayhap her reputation too. Seduce her into thinking he was her future, and then rip it away like his security was ripped away from him as a boy.

No gentleman would want her if they knew she'd been plucked. After he'd fucked her each way and sundry, she'd never look for anyone else, and the gentlemen of the *ton* would not look at her either. It was an act of delicious revenge since Miss Perry's aunt had spread the rumors about his mother regarding her loose morals with the gentlemen of their set.

All lies he'd waited years to gain retribution for.

He watched Miss Perry walk out onto the dance floor with a masked gentleman. His eyes narrowed on the man, trying to garner who it was. Without thought, his gaze traveled down Miss Perry's gown of black and red silk. She was dressed as Boudica, and he could imagine what delectable flesh lay beneath the gown. For her common blood, she was a fine specimen of feminine beauty. Her golden locks, coiffured up high on her head, brought out her large, blue eyes, her lips pouty and of the softest pink. Abe inwardly groaned, wondering if her nipples were the same light shade.

"You told her, didn't you?" Whitstone said, coming to stand beside him, looking out toward Miss Perry.

"You knew I would, and as expected, she is not at all

impressed with you or Duncannon. I should expect a set down from her viperish tongue at some point. She certainly is very stubborn." Abe watched as Miss Perry's dance partner pulled her close during a spin during the waltz. He clamped his jaw shut, reminding himself that he was to keep an eye on her, nothing more. He certainly did not want any rumors circulating about town that Marquess Ryley was showing a marked interest toward a woman that he had every intention of ruining.

His blood pumped fast through his veins at the thought of seeing the only living relative of Viscountess Vance fall on his sword. A woman he had access to through mutual friends. He grinned, taking a sip of his drink.

"What are you planning? You look like you've concocted a scheme." Whitstone came to stand before him, cutting off his view of Miss Perry. "You're not to dally with Willow unless you intend to marry her. Do not cross me on that, Ryley."

He raised his brow at Whitstone's gumption. "We're friends, and I will always have your back, but don't tell me what to do. Not with anything."

Whitstone didn't move, simply stared at Abe. Abe stared back, not giving an inch. He didn't take nicely to bullies, and even though Whitstone was his friend, he still would not tolerate being told what to do. His mother had been bullied, practically forced to scuttle back to Spain. Never would he tolerate the same treatment or influence in his life.

"She's a sweet woman and Ava's best friend. Do not play with her."

"I have no intention of playing with her," he said, only partially lying to his friend. While he may not physically play with her, not yet at least, he would play with her security. He'd lost his mother and the security of her presence at a young age. It was only fair that Viscountess Vance's niece suffered the same fate.

"Thank you," Whitstone said, clapping him on the back and guiding him toward Duncannon. "Now, come with me. Duncannon and I are looking to invest in sugar and we'd like your opinion."

"Of course." Abe let the duke guide him over to Duncannon. He sporadically watched Miss Perry as her dance partner escorted her back over to where the Duchess Whitstone and Countess Duncannon stood. She smiled and dipped into a neat curtsy to the gentleman, bidding him a thank you. Her eyes met his over the gentleman's shoulders. His gut clenched as if he'd been physically punched, and he took a deep, calming breath. What the hell was wrong with him? Too little wine he'd imagine.

The way Miss Perry looked at him told him she'd be an easy mark. She may be annoyed tonight that she'd been manhandled by her friends, but with a few sweet words, and gentlemanly behavior, he'd gain her trust. And then and only then would he take his revenge.

He must have grinned a little as a light, rosy hue spread across her cheeks before she looked away, severing their moment.

Abe nodded to something the duke said, trying to gauge what his friends were discussing. The Season had only just commenced, and perhaps this year, to gain all that he wanted, he would have to partake a little more than usual.

Not the most terrible inconvenience to suffer. Not when at last he'd get what he'd always wanted.

Revenge.

CHAPTER 4

W illow sat before Ava and Hallie in the duchess's private parlor at their London townhouse and fought to keep her calm. "You had your husbands and their friend guard me the entire night of the Masquerade. What were you thinking, doing such a thing?"

Ava worked her hands in her lap, her face ashen. She should be ashamed. Never would Willow ever think to do such a thing to either of them. "I'm sorry, Willow. We were only thinking of your best interest."

"Really?" Willow said, raising her brow. "When you came to London before you married the duke... Did I follow you home when you left one particular ball only to find out later that you met with the duke in my aunt's parlor? I never chastised you over your actions that night now, did I?"

At her friend's silence, Willow turned to Hallie. "Nor did I impose on you every day at your dig site in Somerset to ensure you were always well-chaperoned. Which, if you remember, I should have since you had intimate relations with the viscount in a tent."

Hallie giggled and slapped her hand over her face. Willow glared at her friends. They were impossible! "Going forward, I think we can safely say that you will stop mollycoddling me as if I'm a child. We're almost the same age. I have a chaperone and two companions. Tell your husbands, the dears that they are, that they need to walk away and leave me to enjoy the little freedom I have before I marry."

"You're engaged?" Ava asked, sitting forward on her chair.

"Who to?" Hallie blurted a second later.

Willow sat back in her chair, sipping her sweet tea. "Oh, I'm not betrothed just yet, but I'm sure that will happen this Season. I know I'm unable to live as I am forever. Society would eventually shun me for such insolence, and I do wish for a family, and so the prospect is agreeable. But to meet a man that makes my heart beat fast, my skin to prickle, I must be left alone to have the opportunity to speak to him." The image of Lord Ryley flittered through her mind. He'd made her heart thump so loud in her chest she thought he might hear, and as for her senses, each time he touched her, it was as if a million little pins pricked her flesh, making the fine hairs stand on end.

Not that she would look at him as a possible husband. He was rude, abrupt, authoritative, and there was something about him that was raw, unkempt. Animal-like. A wolf perhaps. Unpredictable, and one never knew if it would bite or lick you.

Heat rushed up her neck at the idea of Lord Ryley licking her. Oh, dear lord, she needed to stop thinking of him.

"And Lord Ryley, Willow?" Evie queried. "Did you wish for Ava and Hallie to have his attendance on you cease?"

"I do, yes. I shall leave that in the hands of you fine ladies. And now there is something else I wish to ask you all."

"What is it?" Molly sat herself down on the settee between Ava and Hallie, her cheeks pink from standing in front of the window these past minutes. London was warm today, and Willow had planned on going for a ride in Hyde Park this afternoon. Not that it was the social hour, but she didn't care about that. She merely wanted Rotten Row all to herself.

Willow caught everyone's attention, needing to ensure they were all listening. "I want to do something a little scandalous, and I want you all to do it with me."

Hallie chuckled, sitting forward. "Do tell us what you want."

Evie nodded vigorously.

"You know as well as anyone that I've led a mundane life under the care of my aunt. And while I'll be ever thankful for all that she did for me and for leaving me her estate, I want to live. I want to sneak into balls we've not been invited to. I want to spend a night at Covent Gardens, and lastly, I want to visit Hell's Gate. Why should it be only the men who experience these places?"

"I think you're under an illusion if you think only men visit Hell's Gate," Ava interjected.

Molly gasped. "Are you saying there are women of the *demimonde* that frequent there?"

Ava chuckled. "And more."

"Has the duke ever been?" Willow asked, unsure what she thought of her friend's husbands spending nights in such a lewd and dissolute place. Not that it made her any less curious as to what went on within its walls, but she wasn't the one married here. A little voice reminded her she was female, however...

"He's not been since we married, but I do believe he used to visit quite often. Whitstone was frequently the talk of London if you remember."

Willow remembered well having spent some seasons in London with the duke before he earned back the love of her friend. "I want to visit there. We'll wear masks or dress like men, but I think it would be fun."

Hallie threw her a consoling smile. "While I would love to see the inside of Hell's Gate, I better not be caught there. I will, however, accompany you to parties and balls we're not invited to and Covent Garden. I see no harm in that."

"I agree with Hallie," Ava said.

Willow looked to Evie and Molly, both of who were wide-eyed and quiet. "Well, are you in or out, you two?"

"I'm in," Evie said, smiling. "I'm definitely in."

"I think I'd prefer to read a book at home if you do not mind," Molly stated.

While Willow did hope for all her friends to come with her, she could understand their choices. "Very well, each of us must make her choice." She turned to Evie. "It looks like it's just going to be us two."

Evie stood, bouncing a little on the spot. "This is going to be so much fun. I can hardly wait to see what the men of our acquaintance get up to while in London."

"I should say quite a lot," Ava interjected. "You must ensure that however you dress, you're unable to be identified. Maybe a gentleman with his mistress may be less obvious, a disguise such as that."

"That would certainly work." Hallie reached for the teapot, pouring herself another cup. "I'm sure Viscountess Vance has some old wigs that you could cut down into a man's design."

"You're taller than me, Willow. It's probably best that you dress as a man," Evie said with a decided nod.

All true, but the thought of being dressed in breeches, to be so exposed, did make her question her choice. Could she do this?

"Breeches are liberating, Willow. You'll enjoy wearing them." Hallie sipped her tea, grinning.

Exhilaration drummed through her veins at the thought of being so scandalous and secretive. She'd never once stepped out of the proper shell her aunt had encased her in. That could all change now. So long as she didn't get caught, behaved herself, her night at Hell's Gate would end perfectly well. Dressed as a man, no one would recognize her, and Evie with a mask would be even less recognizable. Her friend had been languishing in the country, so the *ton* hardly knew who she was. It was a perfect plan.

"When should we do it?" Evie asked, her eyes bright with expectation.

"Tomorrow? I think I can have my maid be ready by then." Willow chuckled and picking up her teacup, took a sip, cataloging everything she needed to prepare before their night out in London.

A side of London they'd never seen before and would never see again. One night would be enough, and she'd been happy with that.

"Sounds perfect," Evie said.

"Sounds absurd," Molly retorted, shaking her head.

Willow grinned at Evie. "You ready to play my doxie, Evie dear?"

"Oh yes. I most certainly am."

THE FOLLOWING evening Willow sat in the hackney cab they had hired for the evening, adjusting her cravat, and checking again the buttons on her breeches were indeed fastened.

"You look so handsome," Evie said, "a perfect lover for me."

Willow took in her friend's red, silk gown with a bodice that was so low that her breasts threatened to spill from her gown. Her little black hat and netting overlay disguised her face enough that no one should be able to recognize her. The blonde wig also helped, covering her dark locks.

As for Willow, her hair was braided under a man's wig. Her maid had been able to fashion it out of one of her aunt's old wigs. With a little makeup, they had attempted to make her skin about her jaw represent a shadow as if she were unshaven. Her breasts were wrapped tight behind a linen bandage. It was probably the most uncomfortable thing about her disguise. Her breasts weren't small, and to be so tightly wound wasn't natural.

"Are we going to gamble? I brought some pin money just in case."

"I think we must if we're not to look suspicious. Feel free to drape yourself over me during any games we partake. We must act the part."

Evie sighed. "I've always wanted to act. Of course, it's not open for women such as us, but even so, I do love the stage. We should spend a night at the theater. I know it's not a scandalous pastime, but we do not attend often enough."

"We will, I promise. Maybe later this week?" Willow offered, wanting to give her friends anything they asked, especially after Evie was so kind as to come with her tonight and put her reputation on the line.

The carriage rocked to a halt, and the door opened. A

man dressed in black breeches and a superfine coat reached into the carriage to assist them. Evie took the man's hand, and Willow reminded herself that he'd not slighted her by letting her alight herself. With her dressed as a man, the servant would not be expected to help her down. She took Evie's arm, slipping it around hers, and started toward the doors to Lord Ryley's club.

The muffled sound of music sounded from behind the wooden door, and another servant opened it, bowing to them as they passed.

Willow swallowed her gasp at the sight of the club. It was situated in what looked to be an old warehouse, industrial and cold. Yet, the chandeliers, the yards of colored silk drapes that hung from the ceiling across the room, giving secretive nooks that those who wanted privacy could slip away into made the room decadent and wicked.

A gray smoke haze floated near the roof, the deep timbre of men's conversation, and the tinkling sound of the women's laughter met Willow's ears. She stepped forward, giving Evie's hand a comforting pat as her friend stiffened at her side.

"Men are looking at me."

Willow narrowed her eyes, taking in those who would gawp at her lady friend. Many men were salivating at the sight of Evie. A shiver of unease slipped down her spine that perhaps this was a bad idea.

"Don't show any reaction to them. Lift your chin and stare them down. They'll soon realize you're not interested."

Willow spotted a staircase that led up to a second level. Glancing up, she spied a row of doors. Rooms perhaps where couples could become entirely familiarized with each other. They walked farther into the room, and Willow spotted a table free for *vingt-et-un*. She sat down, pulling out some notes from her pocket and bid the dealer to commence. Others joined in on the game, and twice she won a round against the dealer before losing all she'd accumulated by breaking over twenty-one.

Evie leaned over her shoulder. "Lord Ryley is watching us."

Willow stilled, her stomach roiling as if she were on a runaway horse. She glanced up and locked eyes with the very man that vexed her to no end. He was glaring at her, and a muscle in his jaw flexed as he continued to watch them.

She placed another bet on the table, ignoring the fact that her skin burned with his notice. "Do not look at him. He'll think we're hiding something."

Out of her peripheral sight, she noticed he moved farther into the room, and she chanced a glance and couldn't see him anymore. Willow sighed in relief, having thought he'd recognized her.

"Sir, I do not believe we've been introduced."

The deep, gravelly voice sounded behind her, and Evie gasped, standing upright. "Oh, hello, my lord. Ye do look very handsome tonight, I must say."

Willow glanced at Evie as her voice took on the familiar twang of an East London whore. She pushed down her fear and remembered to lower her tone. "We have not." She turned back to the game, gesturing for the dealer to start another round, ignoring Lord Ryley. Her mind raced for a name to come up with and…nothing. Nothing would come to mind.

Blast it all to hell.

Silence ensued, before his tall, muscular form slumped into a chair beside her. He laid money on the table. "You're new in town. Your name was?"

He frowned at her, waiting for a reply, and she swallowed. Why hadn't she thought of a blasted surname? "Frank Marsh at your service, my lord. Simply visiting town and wanting to enjoy a night out with my girl."

Evie tittered beside her, but Willow could feel Lord Ryley's inspection of her like a caress, slipping over her skin and leaving her breathless in its wake.

Lord Ryley nodded, a contemplative look on his face, before he leaned in close, catching her eye. "You will finish this game, Miss Perry, and then you will come to my office. It's the last door on your left when you make the second-floor landing. Your whore," he said, his gaze flicking to Evie. "Can wait with mine." He gestured toward a woman who stood to the side of the room, her black gown transparent and showing all her assets to anyone who looked. Heat bloomed on Willow's cheeks, and she fought not to gasp. "Evie will be safe with Lottie while we complete our little chat."

He pushed back his chair, leaving her gaping at his retreating back. Her gaze slid down his spine to land on his breeches. A perfectly shaped derriere that one could ogle to their heart's content.

"He's going to kill us," Evie squeaked, gasping as Lottie came over to them, smiling at Evie. Willow was taken aback by the woman's beauty, and a pang of jealousy spiked through her that this woman shared Lord Ryley's bed. Knew him intimately. Had his delectable, sinful lips on hers.

"This way, if you please. We have a retiring room you may use, miss."

Willow pushed back her chair and waited to ensure Evie was safe with Lottie before she turned and started in the direction Lord Ryley had gone. The gambling hell was full now. People jostled as she walked toward the staircase, women groaned and laughed as men made use of their assets.

Willow kept her eyes forward, her face a mask of indifference. The thought that she looked feminine and that had been why Lord Ryley had recognized her would not abate. Did everyone who cast glances upon her and Evie recognize them? His lordship certainly had.

She stepped onto the bottom step of the staircase, pausing. What did his lordship want to say to her? Was he going to scold her, scream and shout? She'd not put up with such treatment if he did. This club did allow women, and she was in disguise, even if not the most foolproof one it would seem. Even so, he could throw them out on their ears.

Willow glanced about, torn over her decision to run like the devil himself was after her, or confront him. Either one was not a welcoming thought.

❦

ABE PACED IN HIS OFFICE, stopping now and then to take a calming breath. Damn Miss Willow Perry to Hades and back. He'd not thought to see her again after his coddling of her at the masquerade ball the other evening. He'd made a conscious decision that he would not attend any more events with Miss Perry present. He could financially ruin her without having to see the chit. It was easy enough to have someone infiltrate whoever looked after her money, place it into high-risk investments that never had a hope of earning a profit.

He'd placed his man of business on doing that very thing only yesterday, so to see her today, bright-eyed and delectably dressed in breeches of all things was not what he'd wanted to see. Coward, perhaps he was, but to take a woman down was easier to do when one did not have to look her in the eye.

He checked his pocket watch. She'd been longer than five minutes. Where was she?

He wrenched his office door open, stepping out onto the balcony hallway and watched as Miss Perry and her friend all but ran toward the door. For a moment, he allowed himself to watch the perfect sway of her ass as she hightailed it out of the club. The idea of not having a private audience with her irked, and he leaned on the railing, contemplating going after her or chasing her down at the next social event she would attend.

She needed to know that to come here, she risked her reputation. After he was finished with her, there would be little to recommend her to any gentleman searching for a wife. She ought to take more care with her behavior.

His manservant and guard at the door opened it for the parting guests, and at the very last minute, Miss Perry turned and looked directly at him. His gut clenched at the challenging, haughty look she bestowed on him, and he smirked.

Taking down Miss Willow Perry would be a victory worth savoring. What a pity that he couldn't savor his victory between her legs.

CHAPTER 5

Their night out was a disaster. Willow stared at her reflection before her dressing table mirror, her eyes wide and bright, her male wig a little crooked, wisps of long, blonde locks slipped across her brow. Her cheeks were as pink as Evie's gown, and she couldn't have looked more feminine if she tried. She cringed. Any wonder Lord Ryley had recognized her. Studying herself now, she wondered how she had ever thought she could pull off this farce in the first place—an absurd notion.

Which begged the question, who else spied her and knew who she was? Some would call her foolish for partaking in such a venture, and they would be right.

Willow pulled the wig from her head, running her fingers over her scalp before she started to undo the braids. The feel of being free from the wig's restraint was delightful, and she sighed as she massaged her hair loose. She undressed quickly, slipping on a silk chemise, one of her indulgences since her aunt's passing, before climbing into bed.

Willow stared up at the darkened roof, the crackle of

the fire the only sound in the room. Her body felt tight and fidgety, and she rolled onto her side, attempting to find a comfortable position. The image of Lord Ryley glancing at her, his dark, hooded eyes that followed her every move would not leave her. Worse was the fact that somewhere deep inside, she liked having him watch her.

At the masquerade ball, his words that he was present to keep her safe from harm had sent a frisson of desire to shoot to her core. He was a handsome man, powerful and well-connected, and as sinful as the devil himself.

He certainly looked like the dark lord when he leaned over the railing at his club when she fled, his lips twisting into an amused grin.

Willow sighed, rolling onto her back, thumping the bedding at her side. If only she had a husband, she'd not be so fixated on a man whom she'd promised herself to dismiss as a likely candidate as a husband. There was little doubt he thought highly of himself and very little of others whom he deemed unsuitable as friends. That he thought women should be protected, swaddled in cotton, was not a becoming trait for a man. Not for a woman like Willow in any case. She enjoyed her independence and had learned long ago how to look after herself. Losing her parents young had achieved that and then being sent away to school in France.

Even so, the idea of Lord Ryley crawling up over the bed to lay atop her, bestowing kiss after delicious kiss on her exposed skin, sent an exquisite bolt of need to her core. He was a tall man, broad shoulders, and with muscular thighs. No doubt his many years owning a bawdy club had ensured he was athletic and fit. His height would typically suit her, being a tall meg herself. What a pity he was determined to remain scandalous and nothing else.

Willow slid her hand over her stomach, closing her eyes

as her fingers speared through the thatch of curls at the apex of her thighs. She rubbed her fingers against her skin, having read that for a woman to find pleasure, this is where they should touch.

As always, she found the caress to be pointless. It did hint of something more, made her feel tingly and relaxed, but never anything exploding or mind-numbing happened as she'd heard women whisper throughout her many Seasons.

Tonight was no different. Willow bit her lip, thinking of Lord Ryley's large hands, imagining them over her breasts, squeezing her nipples. She rolled her nipples between her thumbs and forefingers, gasping as the action shot a bolt of pleasure to her core.

Her interest piqued. Now, that was different. She'd never reacted to her touch in such a way before. The thought of Lord Ryley touching her, teasing and kissing her made her body hum with need.

And yet, after a time, nothing happened that was overly exciting. What was she doing wrong?

Willow groaned, rolling over once more, pulling the blankets up beneath her neck. There was no use. She would have to wait until she had a husband to find out what all the fuss was about. The image of Lord Ryley flashed through her mind, and she squeezed her legs together, wondering what a night with him would be like. A night in his arms so he could show her all that could be between a husband and wife.

"It would be delicious," she said to herself, knowing she'd never said a more accurate statement. The Spanish Scoundrel would be as wicked in a bed as he was in person. That she had little doubt.

Two DAYS LATER, after a summons from the Duchess of Whitstone, Willow was seated into a highly sprung carriage, luggage piled atop the vehicle, headed into the country. Evie and Molly sat across from her, chatting about their little sojourn to Hampton.

"Ava seemed very excited about the new estate. Do you know much about it?" Evie asked, looking out the window and taking in the passing streets of London.

"Only that the duke purchased it for her so they could be closer to London and also have the ability to train horses during the Season. You know how much Ava loves her horses."

"And so this is a house party? Or is it a small group of friends only that will be there?" Molly asked.

"I believe the duke will have some guests, but I understand it's only us that Ava has invited, and Hallie, of course."

Willow glanced down at her folded hands in her lap, refusing to give way to the hope that one particular friend of the duke's would be present. A silly notion. The man was busy, what with his infamous club, and no doubt numerous lovers to keep satisfied, so she doubted Lord Ryley would be present.

Still, her nights continued with images of him, of his dark, hooded gaze sliding over her, dipping to her lips whenever he spoke. Did he imagine kissing her as she imagined kissing him? Willow bit her lip, knowing she'd thought of little else but what it would feel like to be in his arms. A consummate lover who knew how to play a woman as well as any musician playing his instrument.

In under two hours, they were pulling up before the "cottage" as Ava had described her new home. Willow stepped out of the carriage, untying her bonnet as she took in the magnificent estate. The front door opened, and Ava stepped outside, waving.

"You're here. I'm so glad you could come." Their friend greeted them, hugging each in turn before ushering them into the house. "Come inside. We're about to have luncheon."

Willow couldn't believe the size of the house. It was as big as the duchess's main estate in Berkshire. "Ava, this is not a cottage." They entered the foyer, a large, marble staircase leading upstairs. Two footmen came to take their hats and gloves, and Willow handed them off, unable to take her observation off the home.

"It's lovely, isn't it? My darling husband spoils me."

"What does your darling husband do?" the duke asked, coming to stand beside Ava and wrapping his arm about her waist.

Evie chuckled at the duke's and duchess's public display of affection. Willow smiled at the genuine love that radiated off them.

"Only what is expected of him, my dear," Ava said, a teasing glint in her eye.

The sound of footsteps behind the duke caught Willow's attention, and she glanced over his shoulder. Her heart jumped into her throat at the sight of who strolled casually toward them. Lord Ryley took each of them in before his wicked gaze landed on her and stilled.

He bowed, all proper manners. Willow remembered to dip into a curtsy.

"Ladies, it's lovely to see you again," Lord Ryley said, watching Willow.

She raised her chin. He would not intimidate her, nor would she allow him to chastise her over being caught at his club. It wasn't a private locale. She could attend if she wished. No one other than his lordship knew she'd seen his gambling den in any case, so what did it matter?

Willow heard Molly and Evie mumble a reply, but she did not. Instead, she turned back to the duke and duchess. "After lunch, will you take us on a tour of the home and grounds? I understand you have horses here already."

"We do," Ava said, clearly excited to have some of her hairy children so close. "Would you care for a ride this afternoon?"

"I would love one," Willow said without thought. She loved to ride, and although she wasn't as good as Ava, she was the only other friend in their set who could keep up with the duchess. With Hallie expecting with Viscount Duncannon, she would not join in, and Evie and Molly rarely rode at all.

"Come," the duke said, turning toward a room off to the side of the foyer. "We were about to have lunch and would like you to join us, unless you would prefer to freshen up first."

"Lunch will be welcome," Willow replied, looking to Evie and Molly for their approval. They nodded, and so they started toward the dining room. Lord Ryley hung back, allowed the duke and duchess to pass, along with their friends, but stepped in front of Willow when she went to follow.

"Hello, Miss Perry. Or should I ask you what particular name you'll be using this week while here in Hampton?"

"Willow will do well enough, my lord." She slipped past him, and he came into step beside her. "Did you enjoy your evening out the other night?"

The tips of her ears burned, and she feigned igno-rance. "I do not know what you're talking about, my lord." His deep, evocative chuckle did odd things to her stomach, pulsed heat to her core. The man was a walking scandal, and he knew it.

"Come now. Your secret is safe with me. I was, however, disappointed you did not come to my office to discuss the matter. To enlighten me."

She gasped, meeting his eyes. Was he flirting with her? Or was she reading into his words more than she ought because she wanted him to flirt with her? Wanting him to touch her as the duke touched Ava. For so many years, she'd been the perfect companion, never stepping out of line or saying the wrong thing. Scandalous of her, but she was tired of always being proper. She wanted to live, explore, love, find a husband who joined her on life's journey. Have children and see the world.

"I can always revisit you, my lord." She grinned at him, and his eyes widened. A chuckle escaped her at his shock, and she was glad she was able to turn the tables against him. It was highly unlikely that he was ever on the receiving end of such banter, not from a woman of her status, at least. His dashing Cyprians perhaps like to tease, but virginal women who were once companions did not.

He reached out and pulled her to a stop before the door. Willow watched as the others prepared to sit, before turning a raised brow at his lordship. "Is something the matter, my lord?" she asked, her tone sweet and innocent, even though she knew her retort discombobulated him.

"You're never to return to Hell's Gate, Miss Perry. Ever. It's not a place for a lady of your constitution, and it's not safe for you to be in that part of town."

She patted his arm condescendingly. "Now, now, my lord. Don't make us be at odds with each other. Not when I was starting to like you a little. You have kept my presence at your club a secret from your friends, after all. Do not ruin it by telling me what I can and cannot do."

A muscle ticked in his jaw as his dark, consuming gaze stared down at her. If he were trying to scare her into submission, he would fail. There was nothing more she liked than a challenge, and although she'd never had one of the male variety before, there was always a first.

His gaze dipped to her lips, and without thought, she dampened them with her tongue. His nose flared, his jaw clenched, and fire simmered in her blood. He was attracted to her. No matter what he may say to the contrary, his reactions to her were telling.

Interesting…

"Should I tell our friends you were at Hell's Gate?" His deep voice held a warning any sane woman would heed. She was not one of them.

"A better question is, will you tell them? I can always counteract your words by telling the duke and viscount that you invited me into your office instead of bundling me into a carriage. One does wonder why you did that." She grinned, leaning close. "I hope you weren't thinking of dallying with me, that would never do."

Although after the last few nights that were consumed with images of him above her, touching and kissing her, a dalliance may be preferable.

"If I wanted to trifle with you, what makes you think I need an office, Miss Perry?" He pushed past her and went to seat himself at the dining room table.

She stared after him, the thought of such a thing making her skin shiver. Was it even possible? Were couples doing such a thing in public, and she'd never noticed? Extraordinary.

Willow sat herself to the side of Whitstone. She laid the linen napkin over her lap, taking in the place settings, and seeing who was present. The duke and duchess sat at the heads

of the table, Lord Ryley, directly across from her. He caught
her eye as he sipped his wine, and she read the challenge in his
deep-brown orbs that looked almost black under the candlelight. Sin camouflaged as a gentleman in a superfine coat.

"I understand Ava is taking you riding this afternoon.
We've brought down some hacks for everyone to use, so
you'll be quite safe."

She turned, smiling at the duke whom she loved as
much as a brother, if she'd had one. "Thank you. Ava's
been kind enough recently to help me in purchasing a
horse of my own. I've always loved riding, but as you know,
my aunt didn't like me too far away from her at any one
moment."

"I remember."

The first course of soup was served, and the delicious
scent of vegetables wafted up and made her stomach
clench, reminding her that she'd not eaten this morning.
They ate in relative silence for a time, the small hum of
conversation around the table sporadic, the subject matter
what the guests intended to do over the next week at the
house party.

"This is a wonderful idea having a home so close to
London. And one that has acreage. I should imagine you'll
have Ava with you more often now, Your Grace."

He smiled across at his wife, and she smiled back. A
pang of longing shot through Willow. She wanted a love
like that. All-consuming and grand. One of those loves
that people like Lord Byron wrote poems about.

As if drawn, her gaze slid to Lord Ryley seated beside
Hallie, Countess Duncannon. He was undoubtedly the
type of man that love sonnets were composed for, all those
long, dark eyelashes that were prettier than her own, his
skin a golden hue that made hers look washed out and

pasty. He was everything a woman dreamed about, trouble that would be hard to rid oneself of.

He was certainly not marriageable material. Too many scandals, too many lovers to contend with, and men like Lord Ryley would never be content to lay with one woman for the rest of his life. No. He would like his cake and to eat it as well.

Ava caught his attention, and he turned to her friend, his face changing to one of interest and pleasure at having Hallie by his side. How changeable men could be when they needed to be.

"Are you settling into your new home and way of life, Willow? If you ever need any financial advice you know you can come to Duncannon or me. Our doors are always open."

"Thank you, that is very kind. I do wish to look at investments in the next few months. The law firm which handles my interests believes it may be a way to grow my income. I haven't had time to look into it as yet. After the Season perhaps I will."

"Lord Ryley has multiple investments, both commercial and financial. You should seek him out while you're both here in Hampton, see what he suggests. I know he would never lead you astray."

To do such a thing would mean she would have to solicit his help. Not an entirely awful idea, which in itself was problematic. As much as she may long for his hands on her, for his kisses and whatever else he could show her, such a path would only lead to ruin and disappointment. To give herself to such a man would mean risking her heart, and she had that saved up for a gentleman who would be willing to give his in return. Lord Ryley was not one of them.

"Would you ask him for me, Your Grace? We're not the

best of friends I'm afraid, and I would find it uncomfortable asking his lordship for financial advice."

The duke frowned, turning to her. "Has he offended you in any way?"

His grace glared at Lord Ryley, and she touched his arm, bringing his attention back to her. "No. No, Your Grace. Nothing like that, but I fear we're just destined never to be friends, and that is all very well." She glanced at Lord Ryley, heat pooling in her belly at his smile toward Hallie when she spoke. "I have the impression that he disapproves of me for some reason. As if I've done something that has offended him."

"You must be mistaken, Willow, but I shall talk to him on your behalf and ensure all is well and that he is compliant in helping you in your investments. I have full faith that he will take care of you and not lead you astray."

She nodded, smiling at the duke, not wanting him to know that the thought of Lord Ryley leading her amiss left her breathless and warm. "Thank you, Your Grace. You two are too kind to me."

"No, we're not. We're friends, and that's what friends do."

The remainder of lunch was pleasant, and talk of her impending ride let her forget her troubles with the brooding marquess across from her. At least out on the estate with Ava, she would not have to deal with him this afternoon. One consolation she supposed even though the idea of not sparring with him left her more dejected than discharged.

CHAPTER 6

He was in hell. Literally. He rode behind the duchess, and Miss Perry, who in a trot rose and fell on her seat, her delectable rump all too visible to him in his current position. She wore a deep-navy riding gown, but instead of wearing a skirt and riding astride, she had donned a pair of matching navy breeches and was riding astride like the duchess.

Abe inwardly groaned. There was something wrong with him to be mooning over the chit whom he wanted to bring down, to topple from her lofty level that her aunt had placed her upon. Not fair, he knew, to make a relative pay for the sins of someone else, but it was his only recourse. The Vance family would fall. Their treatment of his mother had ensured she fell from grace. Miss Perry was part of the rotting London society he steered clear of. She was the only living blood relative of Viscountess Vance, and therefore she would fall.

That did not mean that he could not play with the chit for a little while before he brought her low. He had been going to stay well away from her, keep her at a distance.

Much easier not to know your prey, but there was something about Miss Perry that drew him in—aggravated and enticed.

The duchess and Miss Perry stopped under the shade of a tree to rest, and he joined them. His attention snapped to her long legs. They would fit about his waist perfectly.

He shut his eyes, dismissing the visual of them tangled in bed, sheets askew, her hair mussed from his attentions, her cheeks pinkened from release. Her mouth open on a gasp before he covered it with his.

God damn it.

He should go into the village tonight and find some release for his aching balls. He could not continue thinking of Miss Perry in such a way. In any way. She was his nemesis. The woman he would destroy. She was not the woman that stirred his loins. He wouldn't allow it.

Liar, a voice whispered in his ear.

"I'm going to go for a gallop. Did you want to join me?" Ava asked, glancing over the land.

"Not today, Ava. I'm not quite ready for that as yet," Miss Perry said.

"I will keep Miss Perry company, Your Grace. Feel free to go for your ride."

The duchess nodded to him, and then turned her mount, pushing it into a blistering pace. He adjusted his seat, his cock aching with his imaginings of them alone. A quiet settled between them, only the sound of birds in the trees and the slight rustling of wind through the grasses impinging on their solitude.

Abe studied her profile as she glanced in the direction the duchess had ridden, in no way inclined to speak to him it would seem. Her ignoring of him irked and he cleared his throat.

"You ride well, better than I thought you would."

"I've always liked to ride, but don't get enough time to do so. I'll be changing that now that I'm on my own."

He narrowed his eyes, disliking the idea of her being by herself. Her house on Hanover Square was one of the largest in London, and she was a woman after all. Anyone could take advantage of her.

Abe ran a hand through his hair, knowing he was hell-bent on being that person who took advantage of her. The one to bring her down to the level the Vances should be. He couldn't start to let his emotions get involved in his plan. Yes, Miss Perry was spirited, intelligent, and beautiful, but she was also a Vance. Hailed from a bloodline that was as vicious as a snake.

"I did not expect to see you here at the duke and duchess's estate. I wouldn't think that such an outing would be wild enough for you, my lord."

He clamped his jaw against a cutting retort that his life was so excessive, that he could not enjoy the slower parts of it. Such as they were now, out on a horse in the middle of the countryside. "I do not always live in London. I do have two country estates that I attend several times a year. I think you must believe me to be very idle indeed."

She shrugged, and the action brought his attention to her bodice. The tight, navy-blue spencer that sat over her riding attire, accentuating her breasts. He swallowed, his gaze traveling over her person. After the other evening, when he'd seen her dressed as a man, he'd thought that perhaps he'd been mistaken as to the size of her breasts, but he was not. They were full and lush and rose with every breath. A lovely handful. A wicked mouthful.

"I will not lie and say I have wondered how you fill your day, but I could not imagine the answer and so gave up on the notion."

He chuckled and stilled at the realization that he'd not

laughed in a very long time. And yet, here he was, sitting under an Oak tree with the woman he was determined to ruin, and she'd made him laugh.

She glanced at him, her eyes widening. The deep blue of her gaze watching him with something akin to shock.

"I not only run my gambling club, but I also sit in on parliament, and I have numerous investments that I manage. Speaking of which, the duke has asked me to assist you. He mentioned you may be interested in investing in such schemes.

"Schemes? I do hope any investments that I partake in are more than schemes, my lord."

Again, his lips twitched. This woman would be a worthy opponent and would keep him on his toes. Her downfall would be all the sweeter for it.

"They are, I assure you, Miss Perry." He adjusted his seat, curious about her past. "You were your aunt's companion. How long did you care for her?"

She sighed, glancing up at the clouds. "Eight years or so. I've been her companion since returning from school in France. As much as I loved my aunt, and I'll be forever grateful for her kindness toward me, I cannot help but be thankful that I did not live my entire life under servitude. It is not easy being at the beck and call to others all the time. My situation was better than most, being a relative, but it was not easy."

"I should imagine not." Not that he could really imagine at all. He'd always had servants, people doing his bidding. The idea that she was one of those people who had served men and women like him left him cold.

"Because of my past employment, I've decided to allow my staff to have rostered holidays throughout the year. Everyone deserves a little time away, to restore and remember that there is more to life than just work."

Abe frowned over his horse's ears, unsure he'd ever heard something so absurd or brilliant in his life. There wasn't a day that he did not work, did not overlook, and check in on all the little particulars that made up his life. He did not have time off, so why should his staff?

Miss Perry's take on the subject was interesting and worth thinking over. To drop all commitments, to leave and go elsewhere, a place to do nothing but relax both terrified and tempted him in equal parts.

"You saw yourself as being in service? You were a viscountess's niece, I do not think you were ever at risk of making your fingers bleed from too much embroidery."

"Have you ever sat all day and embroidered, my lord?"

He met her eyes, shaking his head. "I have not," he admitted.

"Then until you have, I suggest you keep your opinions to yourself."

Abe shut his mouth with a snap. Unsure how to respond to the set down.

For a moment, they sat atop their horses, the sight of the duchess on a faraway hill the only movement about them. "I cannot make you out, my lord," she continued. "You profess to work all the time. That you are busy and important."

He clenched his jaw at the sarcasm he heard in her tone, condemned to hear her out at least before he administered one of his own set downs.

"And yet you treat me as if when I lived with my aunt, I did nothing at all. She was a very private woman, disliked anyone knowing her business, and so it was left to me to take care of her all the time. Bathing, dressing, relieving of herself in the middle of the night all fell on me. For years, not months. I attended to her at balls and parties. I ensured she always had her favorite food for supper. I went on endless calls to her friends, day in, day out. Do not speak to me as if I do not know a day's work in my life. I know it well. Better than you, I should imagine. When last did you empty the piss pot from under your bed?"

He stared at her aghast. She emptied the chamber pot. Good god, her aunt was as bad as he'd always known her to be. Abe took in the defiant rise of Miss Perry's chin, and a little of his distaste toward her shifted. Maybe she was also a victim of her aunt. Not in the way that his mother endured, but in a demoralizing way. The way one eventually accepted their fate and lost their voice to say otherwise.

"I apologize if I came across as condescending. I see that I was wrong."

She shook her head, adjusting her seat. "My aunt ensured I was educated, and I thank her every day she sent me to France to learn, or I may have never known Ava, Hallie, Evie, and Molly, but I can also thank her for showing me that the staff that rush about for us are people too. They have lives just like you and I. They too dream for a better future. I see that now, and I will never go back to the way it was during my aunt's life. My servants are happier, always going about their work with a spring in their step. I did that because I understood their plight."

"You must be commended for your forward-thinking." Abe frowned at his own words. What was he saying? Complimenting her for being radical. Even so, the idea had merit and was worth considering implementing into his own homes. If it meant that his staff was more congenial, went about their chores in a more timely and productive manner, he would test the idea forthwith.

She threw him a small smile, and his chest tightened. Damn it. He didn't need to feel sorry for the chit. That wasn't why he was here, why he jumped at the chance to help her with her investments when the duke asked. He wanted her to pay for her family's betrayal toward his. And damn it, he would make her pay. Some way or another.

"Thank you, Lord Ryley."

WILLOW TOOK IN THE OVERBEARING, too-handsome-for-his-own-good gentleman seated beside her on his horse and reveled in his attraction. Never had she ever had this feeling that she felt when around this man. As if her body gravitated toward him, wanted to be near his person, his sphere. A sense of rightness that went against her morals.

The lord was a rascal, a rake by town standards, and he was undoubtedly not marriageable material. He was obnoxious and rude and had little idea of how to treat his staff.

Being unmarried as she was, even at her advanced age, some would say decidedly on the shelf, he wasn't someone she could dally with. Have a scandalous, clandestine affair.

As much as he tempted her to be scandalous, she could never do it. She chewed on her bottom lip, debating that fact in her mind. Placing all the pros and cons together and seeing what that sum equaled.

"I'd love to know what you're thinking right at this moment, Miss Perry."

His deep, curious voice broke into her musings, and she met his eyes. She grappled for some excuse as to why she was caught ogling him. "I wasn't thinking of anything. Merely pondering."

"Would you like to go for a walk? I believe there is a stream not far from here. The horses can be watered before we return."

She patted her mount, distracting her hands enough so they didn't reach out to test one of her pro theories that his lordship was a skilled kisser as she presumed him to be. "Yes, that sounds nice."

He pushed his mount forward, and Willow followed as they made their way down a small decline on the hill where even from where she sat, she could hear the tinkling sound of running water.

The stream was shallow, with round, pebbled rocks, some submerged, but most sitting just above the water's depth. Willow slid off her mount, throwing the reins over her horse's ears and tying them under its neck to stop the horse from stepping on it. She stood back, watching as both horses leaned down and nibbled on the grass before taking a drink.

The stream was narrow, with a large willow tree across the bank. Willow stepped into the water, ignoring the fact that her boots would be ruined after her little excursion.

The moment her foot stepped onto one of the smooth rocks, she knew she'd made a mistake. Her foot slipped out from beneath her, and she toppled, slipping forward. The ground rose quickly before her face, and she threw her hands out in front, wanting to protect herself as much as possible.

One would've hoped the godlike gentleman behind her would've reached out and plucked her from her impending doom. He did not. Instead, she landed with a splash, her gown instantly filled with chilling, cold water. She gasped, kneeling, checking her hands that stung like the devil.

"Willow," he shouted from behind.

Had it not occurred, Willow would never have believed it, but one moment she was kneeling in water, soaked through and decidedly embarrassed, and then next she was scooped up into the most muscular, warm arms she'd ever beheld. Her body sat nestled against his firm chest. Instantly her body sought his warmth, and she snuggled against him, taking the opportunity to revel in his hold while she could. It was unlikely that she would be in his arms again unless she started to feign falls all over the estate whenever he was about.

"Thank you," she said, surprised to hear her voice tremble a little. A shiver stole down her spine as he helped her to stand, rubbing her back vigorously to try to warm her.

"We should return to the house before you catch your death."

She nodded. He had the sweetest lips, or most sinful, she could not decide. What she did know was that he made her ache and shiver and long for things she knew nothing about. Something that she'd seen on occasion flicker within her friend's marriages. Willow had hoped for the same with her future husband, but alas, it would not be Lord Ryley. One had to protect oneself sometimes, and something about his lordship told Willow that to fall for the man before her would only end in heartbreak.

How many women had fallen at his knees, begging for another glance? How many had lain in his bed?

Too many to count.

His hands slowed on her back and she looked up to see his attention fully absorbed on her lips. Heat pooled in her core and her breath caught. Was he going to kiss her? "You have a mistress, my lord."

He stumbled back a step, his brow raised. "I beg your pardon."

She stepped back against him, clasping the lapels of his riding jacket. "Do you care for her? Enough that it will stop me from doing something that I've wanted to do for some time now."

He chuckled, but the slight tremor of nervousness could not be concealed. He was unsure. The thought was heady indeed. "No, but that does not mean I give you leave to do whatever it is that's circulating in that pretty head of yours."

His calling her pretty made her want to preen. She thought he was pretty too. Dangerous, but pretty. Willow took a determined breath, closed the space between them, and kissed him.

The word soft reverberated in her mind. Perfect, silky lips met hers, and her stomach roiled with longing. Never before had she ever kissed a man, and not just any man, but the Spanish Scoundrel. Unsure of what to do next, she pulled back, leaning on her tiptoes to kiss him again.

Still, he didn't move, simply stood there like a frozen statue one found in a museum. Willow chanced a look at him. His eyes burned with need, and she trembled. Would he kiss her back if she tried again? Something told her he would, but her nerve left her, and she stepped back.

"Oh no, you don't," he said, wrenching her against him, taking her mouth in a devastating kiss. A kiss that left her reeling and grappling for purpose. She gasped as his tongue slid against hers. "Oh," she murmured, having never felt anything so decadent in her life. His mouth worked hers, kissing her deep and pulling her tongue into a dance of desire.

He was as scandalous as he was rumored to be. He hauled her closer, his manhood pushing against her midriff, undulating and leaving heat to pool at her core. Fire blossomed over her skin, hot and prickly, and yet she could not stop. Could not get enough of him as he kissed her back, devoured her mouth as if she were the only thing keeping him alive.

His hands skimmed her back, lower still to cup her bottom, pulling her into his person.

Willow moaned as he dipped a bit, placing his

manhood at the apex of her gown, pushing against a spot that no one other than herself had touched before. For all the times she had explored her own body, never had she been able to make herself feel the need that coursed through her now, making her mad with a longing that demanded satisfaction.

"Sweet. So damn sweet," he murmured against her lips, kissing her cheek, her neck and beyond. Trailing his tongue against the ridge of her breast. With nimble fingers, he flicked open her spencer, exposing her further to his touch.

Willow leaned her head back, more than willing to have him ravish her. If ravishment felt as good as she did right at this moment, she should've married a long time ago.

She ran her fingers through his hair, relishing the feel of his thick, black locks. Without thought, she undulated against him, spiking pleasure to her core. She moaned, the sound foreign and breathy. Suggestive.

His hand cupped her breast, squeezing it before he pulled her gown and bodice down, exposing her nipple. He ran his tongue over his lip, and she shivered, wanting his tongue on her. Her breathing ragged, she watched as he dipped his head, first kissing her breast before taking her nipple into his mouth.

"Oh, Lord Ryley," she gasped, holding him against her. Madness overcoming her. She should stop him. They should stop this right now, and yet she could not. Could only clutch at him and hope he'd never stop.

"Abe, call me Abe," he said, the breath of his words warm on her exposed skin.

"Abe," she breathed, giving herself over to him. Completely.

CHAPTER 7

This was wrong. He was playing with fire, and he had no business doing what he was right at this moment with the delicious Miss Perry. Her nipple puckered in his mouth, and he gave it a teasing bite. She clutched at him, his to do what he wanted.

Here's your chance. Take her. Ruin her in this way and be done with it all. His name on her lips stopped him from picking her up, laying her on the bed of grass beside the small stream. That and the fact that the thumping of horse's hooves pounded against his conscience and the nearby turf.

He wrenched back, yanking up her gown and covering her breast. Her eyes wide and startled watched him, like a little bird that was certain it was about to be a cat's dinner. And Abe would've eaten her. Every last ounce of her skin he would've tasted, licked, savored.

She glanced toward the sound of Ava's return, more certain now, and quickly amended her hair, checking her riding attire. It was soaked through, dripping water at the hem, and yet, Abe was thankful for it. The disheveled appearance would give her cover for what had really tousled her person.

Him.

Ava came over the ridge, slowing her horse as she trotted toward them. "Here you are. I thought that you may have returned to the house." She was puffing from her ride, a light blush over her cheeks that matched the one of Miss Perry's. Abe reached out, offering his hand to the woman who left him entirely out of step.

"I fell over in the stream," Willow said to her friend, shrugging a little.

Ava chuckled, smiling at them, and thankfully not sensing anything untoward had occurred. "I'll have a bath readied for you on our return."

Abe inwardly groaned at the visual of Miss Perry naked in a bath, water cascading over her sweet breasts and cunny. "Let me help you mount, Miss Perry." She threw him a startled glance at his impatient request that was born out of frustration more than anything else.

She stepped out of the stream, and he cringed. He'd not even moved them from the water before he took advantage of her. Or had she taken advantage of him? She'd indeed kissed him first, had taken the opportunity while they were alone.

Not that he was complaining. He would kiss most women who offered themselves to him. He wasn't called the Spanish Scoundrel for nothing. He walked her to her horse, holding out his hand to hoist her atop the saddle.

She clutched the saddle and his shoulder and climbed on. The action gave him the most delightful glimpse of her derriere, and he took a calming breath, closing his eyes a moment to gather his spinning wits. The world wasn't the same, not after a kiss like that. His steps, more like strides toward his horse, didn't ease the need, the conflicting emotions that she wrought inside of him.

He hated her and her family.

Didn't he?

He was going to bring her down. Ruin her financially and now after that kiss, perhaps bodily as well.

Wasn't he?

Damn it. Abe hoisted himself upon his horse, waiting for the duchess and Miss Perry to precede him. They moved on, and he followed, not wanting to be part of their conversation. He was content to stay back, listen, and learn, plot his next step.

What that would be was anyone's guess. What he did know, however, was that one kiss would not divert him. After years of living without his mother, of having servants, stewards, and school headmasters raising him to be Marquess Ryley, he would not allow one kiss to throw him off. Make him question his morals.

He would need to start thinking with his mind more. Not his cock. Which right at this moment, was being led by a woman who had no business doing so.

WILLOW SAT in the upstairs drawing room, waiting for Lord Ryley. He had summoned her here this afternoon to go over possible financial investments that she could invest in to grow her inheritance.

The idea of seeing him again left her all fidgety and not herself. There was something about him that made her want things no woman of good birth should. Not that she could attest to being born high on the social ladder, but she had been brought up with manners and just as groomed as a duke's daughter.

After their kiss yesterday, her mind had been reliving, relishing the memory of his touch. How he'd forcefully pulled down her bodice so his warm, wet lips could suckle her breast.

Heat pooled at her core, and she crossed her legs, wanting to soothe the ache he filled there. With a disgruntled huff, she stood, striding to the window. Whatever would she do? He was not a man looking for a wife. She should be pursuing Lord Herbert, who had arrived for dinner last evening and was now a neighbor to the duke and duchess here in Hampton. He seemed quite fond of her, very accommodating and handsome.

Not as handsome as Lord Ryley, but very few were.

Lord Ryley was dark, sinful, and with a face made for debauchery. She closed her eyes, her skin prickling in awareness.

The door opened, and she jumped, turning to see who had entered. Anticipation ran through her blood, and she crossed her arms, swallowing her nervousness.

Lord Ryley came into the room and, spying her, shut the door and bowed. "Miss Perry. Shall we?" He gestured toward the desk that sat at the end of the room.

"Of course," she said, joining him. The desk had numerous books and papers, most comprising horse sketches and books on horse breeding and training manuals. This desk was most definitely Ava's little domain, or at least she had taken claim of the space.

His lordship sat and folded his hands before him, his gaze somewhere over her shoulder.

Willow frowned. Was he not going to look her directly in the eye? She watched him, her temper rising a little at his indifference to her. She would see about that!

He opened a folder that sat before him, lifting out a piece of parchment and placing it before her. "Here are some of the options I thought may be open to your deliberation. Some are based on mining here in England and Cornwall, coal mines to be precise. The second option is investing in cargo ships that travel to and from the West Indies or Jamaica. They deal in oil, salted skins, fur, sugar, that sort of cargo. You could of course invest in both if it pleased you."

Willow read over the neat script, the details of the mines, and the ships that would sail from London to Jamaica and beyond. She glanced at him, narrowing her eyes when again he watched something over her shoulder. Willow moved to the side, dipping her head to catch his gaze.

He relented, and triumph drummed through her when at last, she made him look at her, except her award was short-lived. His gaze was heavy, dangerous, and consumed her, making her mind blank regarding everything they were discussing.

How could he strip her bare, with only a look? Make her skin hot and clammy. Her female brain lose all concentration. "What do you suggest I choose?" she asked, not caring which one she invested in so long as he kept looking at her as he now was.

"The coal mine in Cornwall would be a good investment. I have money going into it as well."

She glanced back down at the report, her mind scrambling to make sense of what was happening between them. Willow bit her lip. Was this how rakes looked at women they wanted to bed? Was how Lord Ryley was looking at her how he looked at his lovers?

"You never answered my question yesterday," she blurted. The moment the words left her lips, she wanted to rip them back. But also, another part of her wanted to know the answer to her question. Before, he'd deliciously distracted her with his mouth.

He leaned back in his chair. Even from where she sat, she could see he debated telling her the truth. His gaze slid over her, and her skin prickled in awareness. Her breasts felt heavy and large, as if they were longing for his touch, his mouth once again.

Willow took a calming breath, clutching her hands in her lap to stop them from fiddling with anything.

"I have a mistress who lives with me. Are you glad to hear the truth?"

Willow wasn't glad at all to hear such things. He lived with his lover? Her mind screamed to get away from the man before her. While her body longed for his touch, to make him want her as much as she wanted him.

His jaw clenched before he swore, standing and coming around the desk. He wrenched her out of her chair and kissed her. Hard. Willow fought to keep her footing, to keep upright at the onslaught of his mouth.

She fell into the kiss, having missed his touch the moment he stepped away from her the day before. This is what she wanted. She wanted to live, to love and learn the ways of the woman, and she wanted to do all of that in this man's arms. If she were going to marry, what better way to learn the art of being a wife than in the arms of a rake?

At least by being tutored by such a proficient lover her husband would never stray. Would love and cherish her and no one else for the rest of their days.

His tongue fought with hers, and she threw herself into the embrace. The kiss was madness, a melding of mouths that was untutored and hard. The thought that he kissed his mistress like this doused her desire, and she pushed him away, moving out of his reach.

"You have a mistress and you're kissing me. What they say about you really is true, isn't it?"

He threw her a wolfish grin. Heat pooled between her legs, and she cursed him his good, undeniable looks. "Of course. I'll never be tamed, my dear. Not by anyone."

Willow reached around him, scooping up the papers and holding them against her chest. "I will look over these suggestions and get back to you."

He bowed, stepping aside to let her pass. "Of course. Let me know when you're ready to invest."

His deep, wicked chuckle followed her out the door.

THE FOLLOWING evening Ava had decided on an impromptu night of dancing. They were all gathered in the sizable ballroom, musicians having traveled up from London to play for them all. The duke had invited some friends from London. With their new estate so close to town, it was an easy distance to travel.

Willow stood to the side of the room, no sign of Lord Ryley, which suited her just fine. He was maddening if ever there were a man who was so. She spotted Ava talking to the tall and handsome Lord Herbert, her friend casting her amused glances every so often.

What was she up to? Lord Herbert glanced at her, and Willow studied him a moment. He was tall, blond, and the opposite of how Lord Ryley appeared. If Lord Ryley was dark and sinful, this gentleman looked light and pure. He had an air of innocence, much more suited to the future she'd planned to have.

Would he be different from all the other gentlemen

who kept mistresses on the side? That was yet to be determined. Willow inwardly cringed when Ava started toward her, Lord Herbert at her side.

"Willow, let me formally introduce you to Lord Herbert. Lord Herbert, this is my friend, Miss Willow Perry."

She dipped into a curtsy, and he bowed. "Miss Perry, lovely to make your acquaintance once again."

His voice was smooth, pleasant, safe. "It's good of you to come. I hear that you're neighbors to the duke and duchess here in Hampton."

"I am." He grinned, and Willow had to admit that he was charming, at least at the moment. Ava excused herself and he turned to her. "I understand you went to school with the duchess."

"I did." She smiled at the reminder of their school years, the antics and sneaking out that they tried whenever the possibility presented itself. Of how they all dreamed of their futures and what they entailed. To be where she was now, an heiress was not what she ever thought would happen. "She is one of the best people I know."

Lord Herbert glanced in the direction Ava had gone. "I agree. The duke and duchess are honorable."

"Have you known them long?" she asked.

"Since Cambridge with the duke. I've not known you for long, however, but I'd like to change that."

She glanced at him, surprised at his boldness. "You do?" She narrowed her eyes on him, debating if he were worth the effort. He raised his brow, his blue eyes dancing with amusement.

"I do if you're willing, of course." He glanced at the dancing couples. "Will you dance with me, Miss Perry?"

Without thought, she placed her hand on his arm, nodding. "Thank you, yes." He pulled her onto the floor, and she laughed as he twirled her into his arms. Perhaps this man was worth a little trouble. She was looking for love, for someone who would be faithful to her. Maybe Lord Herbert was that man. Lord Ryley certainly was not. That fiend hadn't even bothered to turn up yet.

CHAPTER 8

A be had ridden hard from London with the need to return to the duke and duchess's new estate, especially after he'd received a summons not to miss their dance they'd decided to host. He'd needed to return to town and check on the Hell's Gate. Tonight they were hosting a gambling event that had card players not only from England but abroad. He'd put up a large winning to those who registered, and the interest had been extensive.

That his oldest friend and his wife had decided to host a dance on the same night was bothersome but would not impact him too much. He had a team of people who were more than capable of handling the night. He could spend the evening with his friends.

He jumped off his horse at the front of the house, handing his mount to a waiting stable boy. He shucked out of his greatcoat, hat, and gloves, handing them over to the footman in the foyer, not bothering to go upstairs to change. All day, a nagging feeling of impending doom had crawled over his skin. Something was amiss.

What was amiss was evident the moment he stepped

into the ballroom. His lip curled. He should have expected to see what he now saw. Lord Perfect—or known within their society as Lord Herbert. A friend of the duke since before Abe started at Eton.

Lord Herbert was always eager to please during his school years. Willing to tell on anyone should he think they were doing wrong or he could get ahead by such information. As a grown man, he wasn't much different. Always sickly sweet to the opposite sex, keen to tell them what they wanted to hear and rumor had it, he was after a wife.

Miss Perry fitted his lordship's requirements perfectly. She was looking for a husband, was rich enough to satisfy the family, and for them to overlook her common heritage.

If she were to marry Lord Perfect, his revenge on the Vances would impact the Herberts also. A satisfying idea since it was Lady Herbert, Lord Perfect's mother, who had helped Viscountess Vance ruin his mama.

His conscience pricked at the thought of hurting Willow. Depending on how much he could persuade her to invest would depend on how much she fell from grace. A large sum could mean the loss of her Hanover Square home. Minimal staff and possibly having to find employment as a companion or lady's maid.

He stepped into the room, heading toward the Duchess of Whitstone and his friend Viscount Duncannon. He threw appreciative glances toward the women who looked his way, winking at Lady Sussex, who blushed and giggled like a young girl in her presenting year.

Thankfully he had a mistress, and his days of having to seduce married or widowed women were behind him unless they were unwilling to take no for an answer.

He never liked to leave anyone unsatisfied.

Abe glanced over to where he'd seen Miss Perry last and caught sight of her stepping onto the dancefloor with

Lord Perfect. He procured a glass of wine from a passing footman and continued, dodging the guests as he went.

"Duchess. Duncannon," he said, coming up to them and taking a fortifying sip of his drink. "What is Lord Perfect doing here? I would not think a sojourn into the country was his pleasure when there was more to be had flattering the ladies in London."

Duncannon chuckled, throwing him an amused look. The duchess whacked his chest with her fan. "Behave, Ryley. You know as well as I there is nothing wrong with Lord Herbert." She smiled at the gentleman as he pulled Miss Perry into a waltz.

Willow's laughter carried over to him, and he watched them. Her ease within the man's arms made his skin crawl.

"That is your opinion, and you are welcome to it, Your Grace." As for his opinion, he wanted to pummel the man into a pulp. His gaze narrowed in on Lord Perfect's hand. A hand that was far too low on Miss Perry's back.

"Miss Perry looks beautiful this evening. Her newfound independence suits her." Duncannon smiled at Ava and met Abe's eyes over the duchess's head, laughter lurking in his blue orbs. Abe did not appreciate the mocking.

"She does, doesn't she? I'm so glad her aunt thought of her and her security after her death. And did you hear, Duncannon that the wonderful Lord Ryley is going to help her with some investments? Are you not, my lord?"

Abe nodded, guilt creeping up his spine at the duchess's faith in him. "I have supplied her with suggestions. The choice as to what she invests in is up to her." Not that he'd given her high odds in earning back her investment. In fact, all the options he'd told her to consider were likely to fail and take down any investors who were foolish enough to put money into them.

He drank down the last of his wine. Revenge was never

pretty, and his mother deserved the respect that was denied her. He would take down the family that ruined her name in London and push aside the fact that Miss Perry had not been part of that plot. Not physically, but she was a blood relative, and the only one left. He would make them all pay.

That his mother had fled England, leaving him behind to face their taunts at school, Lord Perfect was kind to the boys he deemed his equal, but not Ryley. He had English and Spanish blood in his veins and was a lesser person in his lordship's eyes. The child had learned well from his sires, but Ryley was no longer the boy who had to fend off such insults. No longer in need of anyone's approval. He was wealthy beyond his means, women flocked to him, and men wanted to be in his inner circle.

The Lord Perfects of the world could go hang and their trouble-making parents along with them.

The duchess moved away, and Duncannon studied him a moment. "I've seen that look before. You have the visage of a man about to commit murder."

Abe took a calming breath, knowing the fact that Miss Perry danced with a man he loathed was not Duncannon's fault. His friend didn't deserve a sharp retort. "I don't understand why Lord Perfect would be invited in all honesty. We've never been friends, and the duke knows that. Perhaps he ought not to have invited me."

"No," Duncannon said, frowning. "Whitstone is loyal to you. I believe they invited him because he is their neighbor here in Hampton. Although, between you and me, I do believe they're trying to source a husband for Miss Perry."

"And they think Lord Perfect would do admirably. He's a popinjay and an ass. Two characteristics I wouldn't think are sought after in a gentleman."

Duncannon chuckled. "It is good then that you're not seeking a husband."

Abe refused to comment on such a statement. The situation was not at all amusing.

"Come now, Ryley. Even you must admit that he would suit Miss Perry. He's wealthy himself, so we know he is not hunting her fortune. He's merely ready to settle."

The word settle rankled. Abe watched as Miss Perry floated about the floor, seemingly enjoying her waltz with a man who made Abe seethe. The thought of Miss Perry settling with anyone didn't sit well either. Why, however, he could not say or certainly would not venture to understand. He was simply addled of mind after their two kisses. The memory of which made him burn and seethe in equal measure.

He called over a footman, taking two glasses of brandy. "Let him marry her. Maybe if the bastard is leg shackled, he'll fuck off out of London, and I'll never have to see him again." Abe clapped Duncannon on the back, ignoring his friend's shock at his words. "Now, let's get drunk."

❦

WILLOW SNUCK outside onto the terrace and away from the impromptu ball a little while after supper. The air was fresh, just the slightest chill that made her skin prickle. She took a deep breath, basking in the tranquil space and the fresh country air that smelled of grass and flowers.

Taking in the terrace, and spying no one outside, she strolled its length, looking out over the grounds, which were lit with burning oil lanterns.

Footsteps sounded behind her, and she turned. A small jab of disappointment marking her when she spied Lord Herbert seeking her out.

"Miss Perry, are you well? I saw you leave, and I was concerned."

She shook her head. He really was a caring gentleman like Ava had said he was. "Oh no, I'm perfectly well, thank you. I just needed some fresh air. Even though the ball is not large by London standards, the room has grown quite stuffy."

"I agree," he said, leaning against the terrace railing. "I have been away from England for some months, having only returned recently. May I say now that we're alone that I was saddened to hear of your aunt's passing. She was a close friend of my mother. I believe they had their coming out the same year."

"Really," Willow said, having not known that. She studied him anew. If her aunt had been friends with his family, he could not be a rogue or scoundrel looking to ruin her or marry her for her money. Perhaps his interest in her was honorable, and he was looking for a wife. "I did not know that, my lord."

"Yes." He smiled, and she had to admit he was very handsome. A lovely, wide smile and eyes that appeared kind and attentive. And yet even with all of these positives, there was nothing. Nothing fluttered in her stomach, nothing yearned or longed within her whenever he looked at her. She may as well have been looking at a brick wall for all the emotions he stirred inside. "Viscountess Vance and her friendship throughout the years have been a comfort to my mother."

Willow smiled, knowing that her aunt, for all her some-times opinionated ideals was kind at heart and always meant well. "She is missed to be sure. I'm glad you told me they were friends, perhaps we can be too."

He reached out, picking up her hand and bringing it to his lips. She prayed his kiss atop her glove would stir something, anything within her, but it did not. Willow inwardly sighed.

"Here is to our new friendship and possibly more." He grinned, and Willow smiled, her amusement slipping when she spied another lord coming onto the terrace. Or perhaps, stumbling onto the terrace would be a better term.

She stepped back, and Lord Herbert turned, facing Lord Ryley. The Spanish Scoundrel took in them both, the disgust at finding them together written clearly on his face.

He was drunk, a little less pristine to how he usually dressed, and she swallowed, hating that the mere sight of him made her blood pump fast in her veins. Made her skin prickle in awareness. Would he tell Lord Herbert of their kisses? The memory of which made her stomach twist into delicious knots. She licked her lips, scandalous as it may be, wanting to know what he tasted like when in his cups.

"Lord Ryley. Always a pleasure." Lord Herbert's tone seethed with sarcasm and distaste, and Willow took in both gentlemen. They glared at each other, reminding her of two dogs snarling and growling before a fight. Beneath all their finery, there was a core of hatred that was as palatable as the dress she wore this evening.

They hated each other, and it was an old hatred, not because of her, she would guess.

A little part of her was thankful for that. Another part couldn't help but wish that there were two lords as handsome as these two were who were fighting to win her hand. Her love.

Lord Ryley would scoff at the notion. He was decidedly not looking for love. Lust and sex drove that gentleman, and she would no longer be part of that. Two kisses were quite enough. It was time for her to find a man who would love her, who she could grow to love, and have a happy life. A man like Lord Herbert, for instance.

She pushed away the disappointment that Lord Ryley would never be the man for her. The Spanish Scoundrel was not marriageable material.

"Lord Perfect, I see you weaseled your way into receiving an invitation. How delightful to see you again."

Willow glanced at Lord Ryley, his tone just as sarcastic and lacking emotion as Lord Herbert's. And who was Lord Perfect? She cleared her throat, bringing Lord Ryley's attention to her. There was something about the way Lord Ryley was looking at Lord Herbert that gave her pause. If she were a betting man, she would say that he wanted to throttle his lordship. Whatever had happened between them to cause such hatred?

"I could say the same for you. Why are you not in your gambling den with the rest of the uncouth?" Lord Herbert stepped back, coming to stand at her side, watching Lord Ryley.

Lord Ryley took them in, his gaze landing on Willow and not shifting. She shivered under his inspection, the emotions that she hadn't felt earlier with Lord Herbert pumping through her like blood. Her body trembled and clenched, her stomach twisting pleasantly.

None of it would do. Lord Ryley would dally with her and leave her to rot after he'd taken his fill. She could not allow herself to fall under his wicked spell no matter how tempting the thought of it was. No matter how attractive the memory of his mouth moving over hers, his tongue sliding and invading her mouth was.

"Jealous you've never been there." Lord Ryley chuckled, the sound menacing. "I wouldn't think a gambling hell was a place Lord Perfect hankered to call upon."

"I've asked you repeatedly not to call me that," Lord

Herbert said just before Willow was about to ask who Lord Ryley meant.

"Gentlemen, please. I think name-calling is a little juvenile, don't you agree?"

"I never insulted the Spanish Scoundrel."

Lord Ryley raised his brow. "Have you not? I recall it differently."

They stared at each other, and Willow looked between them. Two bulls facing off from each other before they charged. "Shall we return indoors?"

Lord Ryley relented first, surprising Willow. He moved aside, gesturing for them to pass. Willow started toward the house, Lord Herbert by her side.

"Miss Perry, may I have a word before you return indoors?" Lord Ryley asked. His lordship glowered at Lord Herbert. "In private."

"It isn't proper for Miss Perry to be out here with you," Lord Herbert threw down, glaring at Lord Ryley.

Willow patted his lordship on the arm, gaining his attention. "I was safe with you, my lord. I shall be just as safe with Lord Ryley. I will return indoors directly."

He didn't move for a moment, and Willow wondered if he'd protest, but then on a sigh, he nodded and stepped back through the terrace doors, leaving her decidedly alone with Lord Ryley.

"What is it you wished to speak to me about?" she asked.

He leaned on the terrace railing, studying her with a quietness that left her discombobulated. How was it that a simple look was enough to make her nerves sizzle? How was it that a man she hardly knew could affect her so? It was disturbing and delicious all at the same time.

"Nothing at all. I merely wanted to separate you from

Lord Perfect. I always get what I want, Miss Perry. Even at the expense of others at times."

She huffed out a disgruntled breath, fisting her hands at her sides. "You're impossible." She started over to him, stopping a mere breath from his face. "I'm not your toy, and you playing with me before others is not acceptable. I was enjoying my time with Lord Herbert and you put a stop to that simply because you dislike the gentleman?"

He nodded once. "I did. I don't merely dislike him. I loathe him and his kind. Just like his mother, he's a nasty, conniving, gossiping prick."

Willow gasped, having never heard a man speak about another in such a crude way before. The hatred was old, and if she understood anything about Lord Ryley, which wasn't a lot, it was that a wound festered and rotted his core.

"Whatever you feel for Lord Herbert I can see it eats at you. Simply by the way you speak. You need to move on from whatever it was that he offended you with, or one day you'll look up, and no one will be around you who cares."

His lip curled in a snarl, and she took a step back. "Ah, but that's just it, my sweet Miss Perry. I do not care if no one is around to console me and my festering wound. If they walk from my life, they were never friends to begin with. And a word of advice, my dear. Do not talk to me as if you know anything about why I hate Lord Herbert. The wound is deep, but I shall have my revenge, you should heed my warning and take care."

She shook her head, his words not making any sense. "What do you mean by that? Why should I take care?"

"If you associate yourself with his lordship, you may be tainted by association. A friend of his is an enemy of mine."

"So, we're enemies now?" She took another step closer. It was wrong of her, but his scent of sandalwood and something uniquely Lord Ryley pulled her in. The memory of his mouth on hers, commanding a response that drew her in and made her yearn for more. "We were not so the other day," she said, hoping he'd remember their kiss, even in his drunken state.

His gaze dipped to her lips and a shiver wracked her spine. "No, we were not."

HER MOUTH, the memory of her kiss, almost undid Abe. He held on to the balustrade, fighting the urge to wrench her up against him and take her perfect, sweet mouth with his. He'd been uncommonly rude, arrogant, and cutting to her this evening, but seeing her with Lord Perfect had snapped some invisible thread that was holding his two halves together.

He shouldn't care what the chit did. She could go on and marry whomever she wanted, someone safe and spine-less like Lord Perfect. All tormentors were of such caliber. Even so, the thought of Miss Perry marrying such a man left a sour taste in his mouth. The idea of her in another man's bed made his blood boil.

Damn the wench and her wiles. Her ability to get under his skin must be a trait she'd earned being related to Viscountess Vance. That woman could always raise his hackles whenever he saw her.

"If you can give me a reason as to why I should keep away from Lord Herbert. A sensible reason, not some boyhood hatred you've refused to let go, I may do as you heed."

Abe listened halfheartedly to what Miss Perry said, his attention in his whiskey-fogged mind had diverted to her gown. The deep-pink satin suited her golden locks. The bodice hugged her ample bosom, and her slim waist was accentuated by the drop of the empire-style gown. The little cuff sleeves on her shoulder outlined her slender frame, the skin between where her gloves ended and her gown began begging for a kiss. His mouth.

"My lord? Did you hear anything that I just said?" she asked, catching his gaze.

With every morsel of control, he pushed off from the terrace railing, righting his cravat. "If he pleases you, by all means, marry him. It means nothing to me." He slipped past her, but she clasped his arm, halting him.

He stared down at her delicate hand, not quite believing she'd manhandled him into stopping.

"You're a terrible liar, Lord Ryley. And you know I know it."

He huffed out a laugh, harsh and condescending, hating the fact that a little part of him, a piece he didn't want to acknowledge, knew she was right. He didn't like the idea of her power over his person. Not a bloody bit.

"You don't know anything about me, other than the fact that I've taken advantage of you twice by kissing you. Do not read into my actions any more than what they are. I'm not for you, Miss Perry." He wasn't for anyone. What he needed was to return to London so the woman before him would stop bothering him so much. Saying things about him that he had to deny while knowing deep down what she said was the truth.

For all his ideals of bringing this woman down, of ruining her, there was something about her that thwarted his plan. Her ease with others, the fact that she had not had everything handed to her like so many of his ilk pulled at his honorable cord.

He reminded himself he'd been raised without parents

solely due to Miss Perry's aunt and Lord Perfect's mother. Servants and a tutor were the only security he'd had for years. His unhappy childhood could be laid at Miss Perry's feet and her family.

She watched him, her eyes bright with pity and regret. He'd have none of that. No one looked down at him, not for anything. He glanced at her hand before she became aware of her hold on him. She released him, but not before he read the awareness that ran through her. It vibrated through him as well. An unusual reaction that he'd never had with another woman before. He'd felt the rush of emotion for an impending shag, the desire as his mistress brought him to release, but never had he merely been within the same room as a woman and had his prick stand to attention.

Like it did now beside Miss Perry.

He leaned toward her, almost nose to nose. "I may not be suitable for a husband, but I'm more than happy to accommodate you in other ways. More pleasurable ways if you're so inclined."

Her mouth opened and need seized him. Damn her for being sweet enough to pluck. The memory of waking up in his large London home at the tender age of six years to see his mother's trunks being loaded onto a carriage floated through his mind. He'd begged her to stay, had clutched at her dress, and wailed at the idea of not seeing her again. It would be another twelve years before he did see her again, and that was in Spain where she lived.

She was happy there, had made a life for herself. One consolation he supposed.

Abe stepped back, starting for the door. He would not give in to her charms. She was a Vance. His enemy. She was allowing Lord Perfect to court her. Another enemy. There was no way in hell he'd let himself fall under her charm. No matter how beautiful, how loyal she seemed to be to her friends.

She was not for him.

"Have a pleasant evening, Miss Perry. I wish you well in landing your Lord Perfect." Abe stormed toward the door, ignoring her shocked gasp behind him. He wasn't called the Spanish Scoundrel for nothing.

CHAPTER 9

The next afternoon Willow sat and took tea with Lord Perfect. She frowned at her lapse in concentration and amended her thoughts to that of Lord Herbert. Lord Ryley and his inappropriate opinions on his lordship were wiggling their way into her mind and muddling her thoughts.

The gentleman wasn't too perfect. He was kind and knowledgeable, and from what he stated about his estates, was not after a wealthy wife. He seemed well-positioned to look after his affairs.

She took a sip of her sweet tea, watching him over the brim of the cup. He was discussing his estate here in Hampton, the extent and how many tenant farms he had. It was a sizable asset, or at least Willow thought it was. All she could hope was that his marked attention on her was heartfelt, and he wasn't playing her a fool.

Lord Ryley had not told her exactly why he disliked the man so much, but that Whitstone was his friend surely meant he wasn't so very bad. For all Willow knew, Lord Herbert may have cut Lord Ryley out of a possible mistress or won a game of high-stakes cards, fleecing him of funds.

"Do you have any plans for this afternoon, Miss Perry? I do believe the weather will be fine from what I could deem earlier for a ride."

Willow glanced out the window and caught sight of Lord Ryley talking to Whitstone out on the terrace outside. Nerves pooled in her stomach, and she tore her gaze back to Lord Herbert, not needing the distraction that his lordship wrought on her every time she saw him. Vexing man.

"I wanted to walk the grounds and catch up on some reading before the entertainments tonight. I do believe the duchess has some games planned for us."

Laughter caught their attention, and Lord Herbert glanced toward the terrace, his eyes narrowing on the duke. He turned back to her, watching her closely.

"Have you known Lord Ryley for long, Miss Perry?"

She shook her head. "Not at all. He is only a recent acquaintance."

"Hmmm," his lordship murmured. "I thought after his intrusion upon us last evening that perhaps I was stepping into a situation that I should not be part of."

Heat rushed onto her cheeks, and she sipped her tea to bide her time before answering. She had kissed Lord Ryley with abandon. Wantonly she'd allowed him favors that she should not have. The memory of his mouth on her breast ought to scandalize her. Make her feel uncouth and wanton, but it did not. If anything, her body simmered with awakening. A curiosity to learn what else he could make her feel. Which, unfortunately, was so very different from what Lord Herbert made her feel.

"Of course not. We simply have mutual friends, and he was concerned for my reputation being outside with a gentleman. That was all."

"If only it were the case," Lord Herbert said, placing down his cup of tea and leaning back in his chair, folding his legs. "May I speak frank, Miss Perry?"

Willow glanced about them, ensuring they were quite out of hearing of others before nodding. "Of course. Please."

He threw her a small smile before he said, "I want you to know that I'm at that stage in my life that I'm ready to settle down. Marry and start a family. You have probably heard this rumor about London or this house party, but I wanted to let you know that it is true."

Willow swallowed a sip of tea, having not expected him to be so forward, even so, it was refreshing that a gentleman was telling her the truth of his situation and not merely eluding to it like so many of them did. "I wish you good luck in finding your future wife, my lord."

He chuckled. "I want you to know that no matter what anyone may say," he said, glancing at Lord Ryley. "I am honorable and would never play anyone a fool. I would never lead any woman to believe I felt more for them than I did."

"That is an honorable trait to have, my lord. Thank you for telling me so."

"I tell you this because I do not wish for your good opinion of me to be sullied by Lord Ryley. I know it is wrong of me to name him so publicly to you, but his hatred of me is of long duration and somewhat jaded. He knows not what he speaks."

Willow narrowed her eyes at his lordship, before glancing at Lord Ryley. He looked up from talking to Whitstone, and their gazes clashed. Her skin prickled, and her heart thumped loud in her chest at his lordship's seductive, dark gaze. She wrenched her attention back to Lord

Herbert, ignoring the all-consuming man in her peripheral vision.

"Lord Ryley has not spoken ill of you," she lied, not wanting to further the rift that seemed to be between the gentlemen.

"That is sweet of you to say, but I know he dislikes me, and over the years, his actions within society have made me possibly dislike him just as much. We are not friends, nor will we ever be, but I hope that does not impact our friendship. I would like to get better acquainted if you're willing."

Was she willing? Before her sat a man who encumbered all that she was looking for in a husband. He was kind, well-respected by those closest to her in all the world. He was wealthy and titled, and so could not be termed a fortune hunter. Handsome too, with his dark-blue eyes and blond locks that were short and well-trimmed.

He may not light a fire in her soul, but maybe that would come in time. If he kissed her, perhaps then that would spark a reaction within her, similar to what occurred with Lord Ryley. She would not know until she tried.

"I would like that very much, my lord."

He threw her a broad smile and she felt a little giddy at his interest in her. She would give Lord Herbert time and see. To throw him over for Lord Ryley simply because his lordship had kissed her first was no reason at all not to see if someone else may suit her better.

Lord Ryley was not the marrying type. He was the type who stormed through a courtship, spinning everyone and leaving those affected by him heartbroken in his wake. She didn't wish to be left heartbroken by him. Ruined and left without a backward glance when something else more interesting, more alluring came along.

He'd said himself he wasn't made to be a husband, and she wouldn't try and make him into something he did not want to be. He would only end up resenting her, and that would never be palatable to her. A future with Lord Ryley was unattainable, but a future with Lord Herbert was a possibility. She would be a simpleton indeed to push him away just because Lord Ryley's kisses were so delectably naughty.

"Maybe this afternoon on your walk, I may join you?" he asked sweetly.

Willow could feel the heat of Lord Ryley's gaze on her, but she refused to look at him. He was an error of judgment on her behalf, a slip of common sense that thankfully had righted itself before too much damage was made. Lord Herbert, on the other hand, was safe, sweet, and willing to see where their courtship could take them. A much better option for her. "I would like that, my lord. Shall we meet on the terrace outside the library after luncheon?"

"I look forward to it, Miss Perry."

THEIR AFTERNOON STROLL had been pleasant. They had talked about London, her plans going forward, her desire to travel abroad, where Willow was doubly pleased to hear that Lord Herbert too was looking to travel in the next year or so.

Willow found they both liked horses, lived not far from each other in London. As they strolled the grounds of the duke and duchess's new estate, looking at the plants and the small stream that ran through the property, she could not fathom as to why Lord Ryley disliked the gentleman so much. He certainly seemed harmless. That his mother had been best friends with her aunt had put her mind at ease over his character. Even though she could not recall seeing her aunt and his mother together much in society.

Could the friendship have cooled a little over time? Or was it that their lives had simply moved in different directions? "You said that your mother was close to my aunt, and yet I rarely saw them in town together. Please tell me if I'm overstepping my bounds, but do you know why that was the case?"

Lord Herbert frowned, and she marveled at how handsome he was. Not in the dark, brooding kind of way Lord Ryley was, but in an ethereal, godlike way instead. Where Lord Ryley was dark, Lord Herbert was light. It was probably why she had gravitated toward Lord Ryley in the first place. A dark god, full of shadows and trickery always fooled its prey into believing they were something they were not.

Lord Ryley would no longer outwit her.

"You are right. They were not as close as they once were. I suppose their lives took them in different directions and social spheres. My mother, as you know, married an earl, but because they debuted the same year, they were always friends and did try to see each other as much as events allowed."

They strolled along, and Willow stared down at the grassy, soft lawn beneath her slippers. The air smelled of fresh pine and flowers, a light, cooling breeze took the sting out of the day's heat. Ava's new estate was very picturesque, and as they came around the west side of the house, they caught sight of the stables and new racing track Ava would use to train her horses.

"Understandable of course. My aunt only married a viscount, and I suppose even that rank can cause a chasm to open up between friends." Willow caught sight of Ava atop a horse, the duke at her side, glancing up at her with adoration. She hoped that her friendship with Ava and Hallie would not cease because they were now both titled and far above her, Evie, and Molly in rank. They had been friends for so many years, and she didn't know what she would do if she lost them.

His lordship strolled beside her, his arms clasped behind his back. She studied him a moment. "My friendships with Ava, Hallie, Evie, and Molly are the most important friendships of my life. No matter whom I marry, I shall never allow rank or wealth or opinions to come between that bond." Willow raised her chin, needing his lordship to know that should he ask her and she decided to marry his lordship, become a countess, she would not allow anyone, or any of his circle to influence or stop her friendship with Evie and Molly. Should either of her friends marry even a clergyman or gentleman farmer, she would continue to invite and love them as much as she did now, and the *ton* could go hang if it did not like it.

"That is a noble ideal, Miss Perry, but society has a way sometimes of coming between even the strongest of friendships."

Willow smiled noncommittedly and started toward where the duke stood watching Ava ride. "Shall we join Whitstone before we return indoors? Perhaps he can tell us a little more about these games that the duchess has in store for us all. She's been very secretive and will not say a word about it," she said, wanting to end their little stroll together. That he'd said what he did about her friendships rattled her. For all his kindness, his gentlemanly behavior, his words left her cold. Would he expect her to leave her friendship with Evie and Molly behind because of their position? It wasn't to be borne, but then, maybe he was speaking in general terms, not of what his own opinion was on the matter.

As they came up to the duke, she smiled in welcome and was pleased that the gentlemen became engrossed in talk of horses and the breeding of them. Willow slipped away unnoticed, needing the sanctity of her room. Why did having to find a husband have to be so very confusing and vexing? She was starting to think this whole idea of marriage was an absurd notion that was too much work.

And not the least worth the effort.

CHAPTER 10

A be had given Miss Perry some space over the last few days, but with each passing moment, the marked attention of Lord Herbert had started to irk. Why, he couldn't fathom. He didn't want to marry the chit. He didn't want to marry anyone.

His mother's parting words before she fled to Spain were to be careful of who he gave his heart to. She could have only meant one thing by that. That she'd given her heart to his father, and in her time of need, when she had needed him to stand up with her against those who ridiculed and taunted her, he had not.

Up to this time in his life, Abe had not felt the smallest inclination to give his heart to anyone. To let another in to know all his dark, ugly secrets. Until Miss Perry, that was.

Abe started at the thought, running a hand through his hair. What the blazes was he talking about? He didn't feel anything beyond mild amusement with Miss Perry. For all her pretty looks and ample bank balance, she held no special place in his life.

Did she?

He swore, storming, more than strolling toward the stables. He stood corrected. She wasn't just amusement, she was the sole reason he was out in the country for a blasted week. He needed her to sign off on a specific investment that would hurt her financially.

Abe had decided that he'd not let her invest all her money. He wasn't that much of an ass, but he would have her spend enough that it would require adjustments to her household.

His friends, if they found out what he intended, would call him a bastard, and maybe he was. But the Vance family was cruel, unforgivingly bitter toward his mother, and he'd not let them get away with it. The old Viscountess Vance had been crafty with loyal accountants who had not seen fit to invest in anything, but Miss Perry was different. From his investigations into her, he'd found out she had hired her own solicitor, more modern and forward-thinking than her late aunt's.

Solicitors who were easily persuaded into foolhardy investments suggested by a peer of the realm.

Abe came to an abrupt halt at the sight of Miss Perry walking arm in arm in the gardens with Lord Herbert. The pompous lord smiled down at her and even Abe had to admit that he looked genuine with his interest.

He wouldn't let that bastard have her either. Lord Herbert always managed to get what he wanted, but not anymore. He would too have his day, and at the hands of Abe, he would ensure that.

For the life of him, he could not see what Miss Perry saw in the pretentious fool. Lord Perfect, who didn't step out of line or do anything that went against his mother's will. If Miss Perry wished to marry into that lofty family, she would have to impress the old battleax. Women from far wealthier families than hers and with loftier connections had failed.

He stopped, debating with himself whether he'd interrupt them or not. To anyone watching his actions, he'd look like a besotted fool who'd had his love interest swooped out from beneath his grasp.

There was a first for everything, but he'd be damned if he'd let Lord Perfect have Miss Perry. Not that he wanted her from himself. Blast it, no, he did not, but the fiend currently walking with her, glancing down at her as if the sun shone out of her preverbal ass would not do either.

"Something amiss, Ryley?" Duncannon said behind him, startling him from his inspection.

Duncannon was a good friend, loyal to a fault at times, but could read him like a book, and there was little point in disassembling. "I'm vexed, damn it, and Miss Perry is the reason behind my ire." He started toward the stables again, Duncannon hard on his heels.

"Willow? What has she done to you, old boy?"

Abe halted, Duncannon running into him, sending him tumbling forward. Willow? Duncannon called her by her given name. He turned slowly, unsure what the emotions that were rioting about inside him meant by knowing they were on such intimate terms. "You call her by her given name, and your wife approves?"

Duncannon stared at him, eyes narrowing as he understood his anger. "I call all of my wife's friends by their given names most of the time. Has the fact that Miss Perry has not given you leave to use her name annoyed you, my friend?" Duncannon's knowing chuckle followed him, spiking his temper.

"Your mockery makes me question our friendship and what the hell I'm doing here."

"Wait," Duncannon said, clasping his arm. "This is

more than Miss Perry not giving you leave to use her name. You're jealous of Herbert."

"The hell I am," Abe sneered. "And anyway, what is he doing here? You know what I think of him."

Duncannon frowned, sighing. "Lord Herbert is only here because Whitstone does not like to cause trouble. You know we're loyal to you, have your back. There are many in attendance that we do not court close friendship with. Why this overreaction?" Duncannon held him fast, his grip tight on his arm. "You like Miss Perry. You like her more than you're even allowing yourself to admit."

"I absolutely do not," he stated, his voice curt and final. A lie upon his lips that tasted sour and wrong. He did like her. Liked her more than he'd let anyone know, even himself. Why, though, was the question? Was it because she was forbidden to him due to her family being his enemy? Her fortune, that many a gentleman would accept into their coffers? Or the fact that she'd been honest with him, had stated that she sought a husband, a love match, and he was found wanting?

He'd told her himself that he wasn't the marrying kind. The fact was not a lie. To be married to him would be on par with torture for a woman wanting a husband who remained faithful and adoring. Abe would never be either of those things. He ran a gambling den for crying out loud. A place where men came to escape their wives and duty to gamble and if they so chose, where they could bring their Cyprians and make use of his private suites upstairs.

"You do." Duncannon's words sounded astonished. Abe could understand that. He himself was feeling oddly out of sorts and not at all comfortable. "Well, well, well. This is a state that I had not thought would occur."

Abe wrenched at his cravat, annoyed at the stifling knot about his neck. "Don't be ridiculous."

"Willow seems quite taken with Lord Herbert. If my summarizations are correct, I suppose you'll have no issue with him courting her. He stated as much last evening when I was playing billiards. I do believe he intends to make her his wife."

A cold shiver raced down Abe's spine, and he started toward the stables, needing to be atop a horse and soon. Away from his insightful friend who was too loose with his opinions. A woman, Miss Perry...Willow...did not kiss him the way that she did and then turn about and marry someone else. The woman could not be so fickle, surely, unless she'd grown to like Lord Perfect. The idea repulsed him to his core.

"She can do whatever she likes," he threw over his shoulder, needing distance before he struck out and punched something, namely his friend's jaw for speaking the truth. Or at least speaking the truth to him and making him see the fact that he did not want to admit.

That Miss Willow Perry had wormed her way under his skin, and no matter how much he may try and remove her, she would not shift.

❧❧❧

WILLOW STROLLED WITH LORD HERBERT, his never-ending discourse regarding his home had been sweet and interesting at first, but after an hour of it, she had started to lose enthusiasm for the subject. She glanced about the gardens, spying Lord Ryley and Duncannon striding toward the stables. Duncannon seemed to have stopped Ryley, pulling him about to talk to him. She narrowed her eyes on the pair. Were they arguing?

Lord Ryley glanced in her direction, the disgust that formed on his features telling her all that she needed to know about the gentleman. It had been a mistake that she had kissed him, allowed him such liberties. Even if the memory of his mouth, hot and wet sliding over her breast settled an ache deep down in her core. He was a cad. She'd known it from the first, and it was her fault that she'd allowed herself to be swept up in his arms.

For all his help with her investments, there would not be a repeat of what had occurred between them. No more kisses. No more touches.

She glanced up at Lord Herbert as he spoke of his mother and how much he looked forward to their meeting. Willow smiled and tried to take an interest, but she'd heard the countess wasn't a woman to cross. A lady who had, on many occasions, harangued those she thought required instruction on better manners or decorum.

"We will be returning to town in two days. I look forward to introducing you to her."

If only she felt the same. Willow kept her smile in place, not letting it slip even though the thought of meeting Lady Herbert made her stomach churn. "I've heard of the countess. I look forward to meeting her too. I hope we can be friends."

Lord Herbert patted her hand, and Willow ground her teeth at the condescending way in which he did so. "Never fear, my dear. She will like you very much. You are her friend's niece, after all."

Would like her money she supposed, more than she would like Willow for herself. She had no title. Her aunt had married well, but none of her family on either side of her parents' line had. The countess would not like that no matter how much Lord Herbert may wish it so.

"I intend to head back to London the day after tomorrow. The Duke of Carlisle's ball is the next day, and I do not wish to miss it. It's rumored to be the ball of the season."

"Ah, yes," he said, nodding. "If you will, may I escort you back to London? I shall ride beside the carriage and ensure no harm befalls you and Miss Milton or Miss Clare."

She inwardly sighed. Vexed that she'd allowed Lord Ryley's opinion of Lord Herbert to taint him. He was sweet, caring, and was trying very hard to court her as a gentleman should. Not ravish her beside a running stream and then do everything in his power to avoid her since.

Willow needed to gain her sensibilities back. She would not lose her head to a gentleman who in no way wanted a wife and did not want her. "That is very kind of you, my lord. I would like that very much."

He pulled them to a stop, taking her hand from his arm and kissing her gloved fingers. His eyes held hers as his lips touched her skin. Willow attempted to appear flattered, but she wasn't sure if she succeeded. This was wrong. She knew it to her very center. Being with Lord Herbert did not fire any emotions within her at all. He was kind, could be a friend, but the word bland fluttered throughout her mind whenever they were together.

A marriage to him would be safe. Would give her the protection of his name and enable her to have children. Something she had longed for, for quite some time. She wished, oh how she wanted her blood to heat with every look from his lordship. For every touch or softly spoken word to make her shiver in awareness. But it did not.

Was it because she had not kissed the gentleman? Lord Herbert placed her hand onto his arm, and she realized he'd finished his little gesture and was escorting her back indoors. So lost in her own thoughts she'd not noticed. Hadn't reacted at all. The first time she'd seen Lord Ryley, without even having his dark, wicked gaze on her, she'd known of his presence. Had felt it like a physical caress.

Now, after she'd kissed the gentleman, she was even more aware of him. She frowned, knowing there was only one thing that she could do to remedy the situation. She needed to kiss Lord Herbert and see if, by kissing him, her reaction to him changed. After all, before Lord Ryley she'd not kissed anyone. Mayhap it was due to her lack of awareness and knowledge of men that stopped her from knowing if she could be with someone as their wife. It was possible that after kissing Lord Herbert that her body would become aware of him.

Her skin prickled, and at the terrace doors, she glanced over her shoulder and spied Lord Ryley pushing his mount out across the fields of the estate, his coattails sailing behind him, his dark, wild hair easy to spy amongst the green landscape and, damn it all to hell, her heart skipped a beat.

CHAPTER 11

Abe lounged on a window seat in the long portrait gallery in the Duke of Whitstone's new estate and stared out onto the manicured grounds below. His melancholy mood was unlike him, and he loathed that he'd been brought low by a woman. Or at least, one particular woman who had continued to stroll about the house with Lord Perfect as if he were the best thing that had ever happened to London in its thousand-year history.

That the bastard threw amused, cocky glances his way, practically rubbing his courtship of Miss Perry in his face wasn't to be borne. If the man did not stop, Abe would have to take the situation into his own hands. Namely, he'd punch the bastard fair on his aristocratic uppity nose.

Thankfully the window nook that he sat within shielded him from anyone else who thought to take in the gallery. Not that the duke and duchess had time as yet to update the images to those of their family members. The estate had been owned by the Earl of Glenmere, a family that had fallen on hard times and had lost their fortune. If he knew his friends at all, they were likely looking after the family portraits to eventually hand them back when they were able to procure them.

A lilting feminine chuckle caught his attention, and he stilled when he recognized it as that of Miss Perry. The deeper tone, however, eluded him, and he pulled the curtain aside a little and glanced down the gallery to see Lord Perfect standing before a large painting of a gentleman with his wolfhound at his feet.

Miss Perry, her profile as ideal as he remembered it, slammed into him like a physical blow, and he clasped the seat he sat upon to stop himself from joining the couple and putting an end to the little tête-à-tête they were hosting.

His lip curled at the image they made. That they looked like a perfect London pair did little to ease his temper. But what he saw next made his blood run cold. Lord Perfect, after he made her chuckle at something he said, leaned down and kissed her.

Not just a quick, sweet kiss either, but one where he drew her up against him and took her mouth like a man who wanted a woman in his bed. Abe stood, fighting the urge to break through their secret interlude. To pummel the basted to a pulp and wrench Miss Perry away from the one man who Abe would never allow her to marry.

He turned toward the window, fisting his hands at his sides, fighting for control. He would not interrupt. If Lord Perfect was the man she wanted, what was it to him? He was going to ruin her anyway. Make her pay for her aunt's wrongdoings. That she was possibly days away from being betrothed to Lord Perfect was indeed ideal. He could take them both down together, and much more easily as a couple. His contacts in London, his business dealings, could make it hard for Lord Perfect financially. The man, so like so many others, was not as perfect as they led everyone to believe, and he had vowels that Abe could purchase.

Thoughts and plans ran through his mind on how to ruin them both. Anger beat through his veins like an elixir of revenge. A gasp sounded behind him, and he jumped as a warm, well-rounded body slammed into his back.

He turned fast enough to clasp Miss Perry's arms and steady her before she tumbled onto her ass. He should let her go, to fall on her backside. It was the least she deserved after kissing the bastard Lord Perfect.

"Lord Ryley." She gulped, her cheeks a bright, splotchy pink as if she'd been caught doing something naughty, which she had.

"Miss Perry," he said, as blandly as he could. He stepped back, putting space between them. He didn't need another reminder of what her body felt like beneath his hands. He knew very well how delicious her curves were. How much he longed to have her in his arms once again so he could savor every ounce of her. "What are you running away from?" he asked, stepping past her and seeing the portrait gallery empty of the Lord Perfect.

"Nothing," she said on a rush, the blush on her cheeks reddening further. Not that he thought it was possible for her to look any more embarrassed, but there you go, she could. Her eyes darted about like a frightened deer, and he raised his brow.

"I thought I saw you before. Just outside in the portrait gallery and quite busy with a certain lord. Are you sure you're not running away?"

She bit her lip, and Abe stilled. Damn it. He wanted to kiss her. To kiss her so deep and long so she would have no other choice but to forget the pompous fool who dared to take such liberties with her.

"You were spying on me?"

He chuckled, seating himself back down. Abe kept watch of her, hoping she wouldn't flee. As much as he loathed himself for it, he longed for her company. Enjoyed their sparring and their kisses—when she wasn't handing them out to anyone else that was.

"Not spying, simply at the right place at a most opportune time." He crossed his legs, clasping his knee with his hands. "I am curious, though. Do you always go about house parties determined on kissing every gentleman that you speak to? First me, and now Lord Perfect. Does his lordship know that you've shared your delights with me as well?"

She crossed her arms at her front, accentuating her breasts in her pretty, green-silk gown. Abe inwardly groaned. Maybe it wasn't such a good idea that she was hidden away in here with him. Not after days of not being near her, not having the delight of teasing the little minx.

"Sounds like spying to me. You ought to be ashamed of yourself."

"Me?" he said, pointing at himself for effect. "I ought to be ashamed of myself? I'm not the one kissing random gentlemen guests with little heed to anyone who could pass you by or come upon you. I heard you and while I should have made my presence known I figured I was here first and so did not. You see," he said, glancing at the book at his side that he'd not opened the whole time he'd been sitting in the window alcove. "I was reading and then rudely interrupted with declarations of intent and disgusting sounds of a pompous fool kissing a woman that he is not worthy of."

Miss Perry gasped, staring at him, and Abe stilled, realizing that he'd said too much. May have given too much away as to what seeing her with Lord Perfect did to him.

Drove him to distraction where he wanted to harm the cad physically.

"If you must know, Lord Herbert is courting me. He's going to introduce me to his mother when we return to town. He's escorting me tomorrow, in fact."

Abe stood, having not known that the bastard was escorting her or that she was going home. Both tidbits of information sending his wits spiraling. "You're leaving? But I thought the house party was to continue up to Sunday. Are you so eager to rush back to town to meet his lord-ship's mother? I know I would not be."

"No? You do not like her, my lord? If I'm not to meet his lordship's mother, then maybe you'd like me to meet yours. You do seem so very put out that his lordship is courting me. Are you by any chance, Lord Ryley, jealous?" she said, leaning toward him and leaving not a whisper of space between their mouths.

That hers twisted into a knowing smirk snapped the little amount of control that he'd been holding on to. He wrenched her into his arms. She gasped, and he found himself watching her, realizing with some delight that the wench was enjoying his manhandling of her. His inability not to react to her taunting him with ideals and dreams of marrying another pleased her.

Abe wasn't sure if he liked that realization or not and didn't bother trying to determine the outcome of that thought when he took her lips in a searing kiss, eliminating all thoughts entirely.

THIS. This was what it was like to be kissed by a man who knew how to do it right. Willow stood on tiptoes and kissed

Lord Ryley back with as much enthusiasm and ability as she could remember from their last embrace.

He tasted of sweet tea and roguery, his wavy, dark locks in her fingers soft and supple in her hands. She dragged him down to her mouth, again and again, and she reveled in the feel of his tongue tangling with hers. Oh yes, this kiss was so much more than the one she had shared with Lord Perfect.

His had been closed-mouthed, stilted as if he was unsure if he could merely peck her lips or kiss her as Lord Ryley was now kissing her. Her back came up against the small partitioned wall between the windows, and he pinned her there. His hard, muscular chest teasing her nipples to hardened peaks. His large, strong hands slid down her back, eliciting a shiver down her spine before one hand clasped her bottom, pulling her hard against him.

Willow gasped, his straining manhood positioned at her aching core, and without thought, she moved against him. Sliding her sex against his, the annoyance of clothing, the muffled sensation making her impatient.

There were too many clothes between them. She wanted to feel him. To let him show her how it should be between a man and a woman. Between a husband and wife.

A moan rent the air, and she realized it was her as his hand slipped around her bottom to skim near the opening of her pantalettes. The burning need, the delicious ache between her thighs demanded soothing, to be stroked.

"You're wet for me, Willow." He kissed his way down her throat, taking little bites against her shoulder. "You know what that means, do you not?"

She shook her head, mumbling an incoherent answer that even she didn't understand. Not that she understood much at the moment. This was all wrong. He was wrong for her, even if he did feel so very right at the moment. Lord Ryley, the Spanish Scoundrel, would never marry anyone she was sure, indeed, not her. She wasn't connected enough, or wild enough for his lordship. From what she knew of him, of where he spent most of his time—In his gambling den—he lived hard and fast.

It was not what she wanted. She wanted to live, yes, but she wanted a family, a marriage of the truest sense. A life that would suit her. Lord Ryley did not suit at all.

She remembered his question. "No," she managed, sucking in a breath as his fingers skimmed her opening.

"It means that you like my touch. I'd wager you did not get as hot and wet when that popinjay Lord Perfect kissed you."

The reminder that she'd kissed two men in a matter of minutes slammed into Willow, and she shoved him away. He stumbled back, but where she thought to see smug understanding, she only saw a burning need in his eyes that matched hers. How could a man so unlike what she wanted make her feel so much that she would forget all propriety and damn it, Lord Herbert as well?

Willow took a calming breath, reaching up to check her hair and thankfully finding the pins in place. She couldn't keep allowing such liberties. Nor could she keep wanting to have them. If she were serious about finding a husband, she could not be ruined by the most infamous rake in London.

"No more," she said, holding up her hand when he went to step toward her. "We cannot keep doing this. Whatever this is," she said, gesturing between them.

"You like my kisses and my touch. Why stop when you do not have to?" He watched her, and she could tell he was trying to figure out what to do. What to say. There was little he could do or say that could help this situation. She needed to return to London if only to get away from the man before her.

As much as she may wish it, deep down in her soul, she knew that he could not be changed. Men like Lord Ryley did not fall in love and be loyal to their wives. She was deluding her hopes to think otherwise. Lord Ryley had spent far too many years disillusioned by the *ton* and having too much fun snubbing his nose at their rules of propriety. His opinion on marriage wasn't much better.

"I will not sleep with you, my lord."

"Abe, please."

She swallowed, having not thought he would give her leave to use his name. Not after denying him what he wanted.

Her.

A shiver raked her skin, and she rubbed her arms, chilled all of a sudden. "I cannot call you that." Not that she didn't wish to call him by his name, but it was too personal. Too intimate. Not as intimate as what they just partook in, but still, it was his given name.

"Yes you can. I want you to." He reached out, taking her hand and idly playing with her fingers. "We do not have to sleep together for me to give you pleasure." He flicked open the two pearl buttons at her wrist and slipped her glove free. Lifting her hand, he brought it to his mouth, kissing her palm. His hot kiss was similar to his kisses on her mouth, and she trembled, wondering what he would do after such a statement.

"So I'll remain a virgin?" she breathed, biting her lip to stop herself from stepping against him and forgetting all her own rules and dreams and giving herself over to the Spanish Scoundrel.

He grinned knowingly, and she wished she knew what he was thinking. She was not going to give herself to this man. Not without a proposal of marriage, and that most definitely was not going to happen.

"Yes, and let me show you how."

The pressure of his hold on her hand increased, and she knew he was a moment from pulling her against him again. Should he do so, she would not be able to resist. Not a second time. It had taken all her force of will to push him away when all she wanted was whatever he was willing to give her. No matter the consequences.

Willow wrenched her hand free, picked up her glove and left him staring at her, his eyes wide as she started down the picture gallery hall, determined to make her room without being ruined by a rake. Debauched in a window alcove by Marquess Ryley.

His chuckle followed her, and she strode faster. "See you back in London, Willow."

She cringed, hating that the sound of her name on his lips was like an elixir that she wanted beyond anything else. Even a perfect, safe marriage with a man like Lord Herbert.

CHAPTER 12

The London season was in full swing by the time they arrived back in town. Willow attended the Duke of Carlisle's ball, and every night since had attended one or another event. The opera, a night at Covent Garden, numerous balls and dinners. All of them pleasant, and all of them leaving her irritated and frustrated when they came to an end.

Stupid fool that she was, she'd thought when Lord Ryley had said he would see her in London that he'd seek her out. He had not. In fact, she'd not seen him at all.

Which was the sole reason she was now in a Hackney carriage and on her way to Hell's Gate. Without the chaperonage of her friends, who were at an event with the Duchess of Whitstone.

If her friends found out she'd played them by feigning a headache to stay home, they would never forgive her. But she had to know. She had to see if Lord Ryley was back in London and quite settled in, not seeking her out. If that were the case, then she could continue on her path with Lord Herbert. It would prove to her beyond any doubt that his lordship was the gentleman for her and not some scoundrel who played with women and then left them to pick up their scattered hearts afterward.

Willow scoffed. What was she saying? She wasn't heart-broken. Not at all. Lord Ryley had been a pleasurable experience, that was for certain, but that was all. She had not given her heart to him. A silly notion she would not entertain again.

She checked over her outfit, men's breeches, knee-high boots. The waistcoat and superfine coat fitted her to perfection that she'd had her modiste sew up for her. She didn't want him to recognize her tonight, and with a new wig of short-cropped black hair, Willow didn't think he would.

Arriving at the club, she paid the driver to wait and went inside. The sound of music met her ears, and a small group of musicians were set up in one corner, playing while the gathered gentlemen gambled. Very few paid her attention, too caught up in their card games or the women on their laps.

Willow strode about, looking for the one gentleman who'd occupied her mind far too much over the last few days. Why she couldn't fathom. Lord Herbert had been attentive at all the balls and parties, and she was certain that in a matter of weeks, if not days, he would offer for her.

Not that she'd met his mother yet, but she felt sure to very soon, or so Lord Herbert said.

Standing at the foot of the stairs, Willow bowed to a woman who walked past, eyeing her in the fashion rakes glanced at the fairer sex. After being kissed by Lord Ryley, Willow understood what the woman walking by wanted from any gentleman willing to pay her fee.

Lord Ryley's office was up on the second level, and she

turned, climbing the stairs. If she found him here, then at least she would know what he was about. What had kept him from seeking her out about town.

A couple ran past her, giggling and fondling each other before disappearing into a room and closing the door with a decided slam. Willow edged her way along the passageway, making sure to look like she was taking an interest in the gaming below stairs.

She stopped where the door she believed led into Lord Ryley's office was and leaned on the railing. The door was closed, and she frowned. She couldn't open it and glance inside, he would surely know who she was if she did that, but she could wait and hope that he'd come out.

A sultry laugh caught her attention, and she glanced toward the staircase, spying the same woman that Lord Ryley deemed his mistress.

Her long, dark locks flowed about her back unbound. Her lips painted a deep, glossy red, and she oozed sensuality. Willow sucked in a breath as the woman ran a finger along a gentleman that she passed before winking at him. Her gown was transparent and left nothing to the imagination.

Willow turned, staring downstairs as Abe's mistress knocked on the door behind her, before entering.

Thankfully she left the door open, and Willow shifted up the corridor a little to be out of sight, but within hearing.

"Darling, come downstairs and dance with me. It's not every night that we have musicians playing."

"Not tonight, Lottie."

Willow bit her lip at the grave, distracted voice of Lord Ryley. She heard a pouty sigh from the woman. Her stomach curdled at the idea that a woman as beautiful, as sinful as the Spanish Scoundrel, was the woman who shared his bed.

Despair tore through her. With a mistress as seductive as that woman was, it wasn't any wonder he'd not sought her out. She wasn't as worldly, or as beautiful, and it was only stupidity on her behalf that a small part of her had hoped that he'd change for her. That he'd fall madly in love with her and leave all this debauchery behind.

Willow glanced over her shoulder and, through the door, spied a mirror across the room. It gave her a direct view of Lord Ryley seated at his desk. He was bent over a stack of papers, his hair askew as if he'd run his hand through it too many times. The woman glided about the room, her flowing red gown doing nothing to pull his lordship's gaze.

A little part of her liked that he ignored the siren. At least she didn't have to be privy to his ogling his lover.

"Ever since you returned to town, you've been a bore." The woman rounded on him, coming to a halt before his desk. "Do you not want me anymore, Abe?" she purred, running a hand across the low cut of her dress. Lord Ryley. *Abe*…did look up then, a flicker of appreciation burning in his opaque orbs.

Willow blinked back the prick of tears at seeing him look at his lover with renewed interest. Damn him and his treatment of her. He was as bad as the *ton* termed him. Scoundrel fitted his character to a fault.

"You know I'm simply catching up on work, Lottie. No need to be jealous over what keeps you in the luxurious life you now live."

The woman's pout should be on the stage, not just for Lord Ryley's eyes. His lover sauntered around the table, coming to sit on the desk before him, scattering his papers. Lord Ryley leaned back in his chair, watching her keenly.

"Perhaps you'd like to have a little repast, my lord?" she said, spreading her legs and sliding her wine-red gown up to pool at her waist.

Willow felt her mouth gape, and she fought to catch her breath. He grinned, wickedly, as the word *bastard* reverberated around in her mind. She had come here tonight to see if he was simply distracted, and distracted he most certainly was, among other things. Namely, his mistress.

The sniffing he did about Willow's skirts in Hampton was merely amusement for him. She shook her head. She was a fool. Had been fooled. It was her fault. His reputation had preceded him, and she'd allowed his wicked kisses and ardent touch to sway her into allowing him liberties she should not have.

He would never change. His actions right now in his office with his mistress told her that, and she would not waste a moment longer wondering if he'd ever see the value in her, want to change for love. He didn't love her. He'd loved no one but himself.

Willow turned and glanced down at the gamblers, many of whom she knew, most of them married or betrothed. There were few who didn't have their mistresses with them. What was she doing here? This was not the life she wanted. No matter how much she may have enjoyed his lordship's touch. She had allowed herself to be caught up in his seductive game, but never again. Lord Herbert was kind, yes, a little boring perhaps, but he would be true to her at least. With a marriage such as the one that loomed before her with his lordship, Willow believed love could bloom. If nurtured in time, it would grow and thrive.

Lord Ryley's deep chuckle sounded in the room behind her, and she glanced through the door, not bothering to try to hide the fact she was watching them. His mistress was on his lap now, his arms loosely holding her about her waist.

Her feet would not move, no matter how much she didn't want to see what she was witnessing. Lord Ryley glanced over his mistress's shoulder and spied her. His smile slipped before he stood, causing his lover to fall on the floor before him.

"Willow," he said, striding around the desk.

Willow fled down the hall, heedless of the fact that she was the only one running out of this cesspit of rakes and bastards all. The sound of his Cyprian's protestations on being dumped on the floor floated to her ears. A small crow of pleasure ran through her that the woman had been dumped on her behind.

Not that any of this was the mistress's fault. Willow allowing Lord Ryley liberties was all on her. She'd let him play her the fool, and now she would have to live with that consequence. Or at least her fickle, stupid heart would.

"Willow. Stop."

She didn't halt, her small frame making it easier for her to weave her way through the crowd. A few gentlemen took an interest, laughing and ribbing Lord Ryley at having not known his interest lay with the same sex.

Willow ignored them all. Her course to reach the carriage outside and to run headlong into a marriage with Lord Herbert her goal. She made the doors, throwing them open and running full pelt toward the carriage. She could hear Lord Ryley's footsteps hard on her heels, but she wouldn't stop. She had to make the carriage. Had to get away.

Strong, immovable arms wrapped about her waist and hauled her to a stop. The feel of his chest, hard up against her back, sent a frustrating thrill down her spine, and she kicked at his shins as best she could, trying to remove herself from his hold.

"Get your hands off me, you rutting bastard." He stilled behind her and she did too. She'd never used such vulgar words before, but having said them aloud and to this very gentleman, in particular, was liberating. He deserved to be called out for what he was. How dare he play with her with so little regard? He knew she was innocent in the ways of men, and yet, still, he teased and taunted her with the possibility of more.

Even though she'd been a fool to silently hope, wonder if such a man could be changed by love. Lord Ryley was not that man.

"Tsk. Tsk. Tsk, my little hellcat. What has all your bristles upright?"

Willow wrenched free, rounding on him. She started at his closeness and gritted her teeth at having to look up to meet his gaze. The heat she read there did odd things to her insides, and she narrowed her eyes, reminding herself as to why she'd fled from his gaming hell in the first place.

"You, Lord Ryley. You and the way you treat women."

"Really?" he asked, crossing his arms, the action making her aware of his muscular frame and the fact he wasn't wearing a coat, only a shirt. Her gaze flicked to his neck, noting that too was without a cravat. He was half-undressed, and the awareness wasn't helpful.

"Yes. Really. You played with me in Hampton. Admit that you did. And now back in London, I'm to be tossed to the curb like all your past lovers." Why was she saying such things? She didn't care that he'd moved on. This was a good outcome for all of them. She was going to marry someone else, and all memory of the man before her would be eliminated from her mind.

The lie almost made her scoff aloud.

Damn him.

"We were never lovers, but seeing you in those breeches again, I can be persuaded to change my mind."

She gasped, stepping back. "You're a cad," she growled. "I would not touch you, not after I just spied you fondling your mistress. She looked more than willing. Why don't you go back upstairs and satisfy her, my lord? I'm not interested." Willow turned on her heel, calling out the direction to the hackney cab driver who turned to face the road, no doubt well absorbed in their public argument as she was.

"Oh, no you don't, Miss Perry," he said, his voice deep and menacing. He followed her into the carriage, rapping on the roof. The vehicle lurched forward and she glared at him. "What do you think you're doing. Get out at once."

He gestured toward the window. "We're moving. It wouldn't be safe, and anyway, we're not finished."

Willow laughed and hoped he heard the sarcasm in her gesture. "Oh no, we're finished, my lord. Not that we ever started." Which wasn't entirely true, but still, if he hoped for more fondling, more kisses, he would be mistaken. She'd spit in his eye before she did that again.

"Are you jealous of my mistress?" he queried as if he'd simply asked her about the weather.

She stared at him, anger spiking through her blood. "Jealous? No, but your actions confirmed to me what I already knew of you. I should have listened to everyone and kept away from you. I'll not be fooled a second time."

His jaw tightened, and he glanced away a moment. "Lottie is no longer my mistress, no matter how much she wishes to be. When I returned to town after the house party, I paid her enough to be comfortable for however long she wishes not to have a protector. Lottie is a playful woman and up for teasing if it means she gets what she wants."

Willow scoffed, leaning forward. "And she would have had you had I not interrupted?" Lord Ryley leaned forward, their breaths intermingling.

"She would not have had me, damn it."

"You lie, my lord."

"I do not lie, Miss Perry."

"Really? And I'm to believe that?" she asked, arching her brow.

"Yes, you should, because the only woman whom I've wanted lately is the little minx sitting across from me now."

WILLOW'S EYES widened before they narrowed, her distrust of him evident. His words slammed into him like a body punch, and he accepted them for the truth that they were. He did want Willow. Wanted her more than he'd ever desired anyone in his life up to this point.

She was everything he didn't need. A woman looking for love, a family, a secure, peaceful future. Where his life was chaos. Endless nights of debauchery, days of gambling, and endless idleness. All things he'd enjoyed up to the point he had met her. Now she'd thrown his life into turmoil.

He didn't want a wife. The thought repulsed him, but the idea of Willow marrying Lord Perfect, hell, anyone for that matter, repulsed him more. He'd never allow such an outcome. If she married, he'd lose her forever. Not that he'd won her at all. Even after all their kisses, their times together, she was prickly and distrustful.

Rightfully so since he'd embarked on making her pay

for her family's part in his mother's fall from society's grace.

"I don't believe you," she said. Her eyes stole to his lips, and heat tickled down his spine.

"Believe this, then." He wrenched her onto his lap, taking her lips in a searing kiss that rocked his axis off-balance. Kissing her was all he wanted to do, feel her sweet curves in his hands again as her mouth battled with his.

He growled as her tongue slipped against his own, and he clasped her nape, holding her to him, not ever wanting to let go. Their hands were everywhere, her little gasps as he explored her every curve, her lovely full breasts that were a perfect handful.

Abe had to feel her, satisfy his doubts that she wanted him as much as he wanted her. He wrenched her front falls open, reaching into her breeches and finding her deliciously wet. She moaned, kissing him deeper. The kiss turned scalding, their mouths fused, their tongues exploring, demanding more from the other.

He couldn't get enough. Would never have enough of her. "Damn it, Willow. You drive me to distraction."

Her fingers slid down his chest, his heart beating a continuous thrum of need. She shifted on his lap, straddling him, and for the second time this night, his world moved beneath his feet. Never before had he ever been on unsolid ground. He was a man who controlled everything, who his friends were, his estate, club, his lovers. But the woman in his arms was everything he disliked of the *ton*, his enemy, and yet, he could not let her go. Would not let her go, no matter how much he should.

She was so wet, her moisture coating his fingers and telling him that she wanted him as much as he wanted her. Even if she protested to his face that he was a cad. An ass. All true, but damn it, this right now, Willow in his arms felt right. Made him forget his past, forget all the wrongs done to his family until all he was left with was satisfying her. Making her happy.

"Oh yes," she gasped against his mouth. His cock strained against his breeches, and he cursed the fact she was wearing men's clothing. He wanted her. Wanted to fuck her, here and now, their location be damned.

"Tell me what you want, Willow." He would not force her, but a small part of him hoped she'd allow him to have her. To claim her as his.

"Just this. What you're doing now." Her plea, her eyes sleepy with unsated desire pulled at something in his chest, and he could not refuse her anything. He slid against her folds, sliding into her hot core with one finger while his thumb rolled against her bud of pleasure.

Her gasp, her undulating body against his hand, made his cock ache for release. He wanted her with a frenzy unusual for him. He wanted to satisfy her, show her all that could be between them. He cared…

Abe inwardly swore, knowing what she made him feel was the truth of his situation. He cared for the woman in his arms. That was what the difference was between her and his past bedmates. He wanted to make her happy, satisfied, and not just in a sexual way. He wanted to hear her laugh, see her more than just at balls and parties.

With his free hand, he pulled at her breeches, giving him more access to her. She tasted of vice, and his mouth watered with the thought of kissing where his hand worked her sex. Her kisses against his lips became frenzied and deep.

Abe took all that she was willing to give him. Her excitement slid over his fingers as he worked her, teased her swollen bud until, at last, she cried out against his mouth.

She fucked his hand, although he knew she didn't know that was what she was doing.

Need roared through him, overwhelming and urgent. He wanted her. Wanted to lay her down on the seat across from them, rip her breeches free and sheathe himself deep into her aching core. He worked her until the last of her climax ebbed from her body. She slumped against him, her head limp upon his shoulder.

Abe freed his hand, adjusting her breeches as best he could before wrapping his arms about her. He wasn't the type of man to cuddle after any sexual interchange, but with Willow, it was different. She made him want to hold her. To ensure she was satisfied and to let her know she was safe.

A sense of wellbeing, of calm, settled over him, and he placed a quick kiss to her temple, the sweet, berry scent of her hair making him grin. He held her close, rubbing her back as she regained her breath, content to stay like this always.

He frowned into the darkened carriage as they rolled through the streets of London. Who would have guessed that the one woman he'd sworn revenge on was the first woman who had captured his heart?

And he cared about her more than anything else, even seeking retribution for his mother.

CHAPTER 13

The following afternoon Willow sat in her private parlor and flipped through the latest designs from the *La Belle Assemblee*. She had ordered tea and biscuits, but she could not concentrate on the women's fashion magazine. It was pointless. That Lord Ryley was going to be calling on her to go over the investments as per their arrangement last evening after he'd dropped her home, made concentration impossible.

He'd kissed her so deeply, so passionately before opening the carriage door that she'd almost stumbled up the stairs to the front of her house. It was silly of her. The man was not looking for a wife, but dear heavens, what he'd made her feel last evening was nothing like she'd ever undergone before in her life.

She experienced a taste of the pleasure his talented hands could bring forth in her at Hampton, but that had been nothing compared to last night. The satisfaction had been searing, consuming, and left her wanting more, not less.

His hand upon her had brought her such pleasure that to remember it now made her stomach clench deliciously. She wanted him, and this afternoon she would seduce him. Here. In her private parlor while her friends were out for the afternoon with Hallie.

It was scandalous behavior, and she was taking a great risk in wanting him in this way, but she could not help herself. If she could not have him as a husband, she would have him in this way before she married a man who would love her back.

A light knock on the door sounded, and her butler introduced Marquess Ryley, a small line of disapproval on her old retainer's forehead. Willow thanked the servant. "Close the door please, Thomas. I'm discussing business and do not wish to be disturbed."

Lord Ryley glanced at her, brows raised, and she walked past him as her butler closed the door. She snipped the lock and turned to face Abe, but he was already upon her. He seized her in his arms, walking her back until she came up against the door. His heat, his delicious self, pressed into her, and her body yearned for him. For more of what he'd given her a taste of yesterday.

"I've missed you," he said, kissing her soundly, his tongue tangling with hers. Willow clutched at him, her body a riot of needs and wants. Of hopes and dreams.

"Me too." She slid her hand over his chest, taking her time in learning every flexed, sinewy muscle that moved under her palm. Willow slipped her hands beneath his coat, pushing it off his shoulders to fall at their feet.

He met her gaze, a wicked light in his eyes as she made quick work of the buttons on his silver waistcoat. That too, slipped from his shoulders to pool on the floor.

"Am I the only one who's going to be naked here this morning, Miss Perry?"

"Willow, please." She threw him a mischievous glance. "And no, you're not. I'm simply quicker at undressing you than you are me."

"Is that so?" His deep baritone held a warning that she wanted to poke. To see how far she could push him before he snapped. Before he showed her why it was that he was called a scoundrel.

"I'm winning so far," she said flippantly.

He drew her close, making short work of the small clips down her back. Her gown whooshed to the floor, and then her shift too was lifted over her head, leaving her with nothing but her stockings on.

The urge to cover herself ran through her, but glancing up and seeing the admiration, the heat in Abe's gaze stilled her hands at her sides. She raised her chin, watching him. Her skin prickled into goose bumps as he took in her form, admiringly.

He reached out, running a finger across one breast, circling her nipple, making it pebble into puckered flesh. She bit her lip, her breathing ragged. This is what it was like to be seduced. And by someone who knew how and she would enjoy every moment of it. If this was to be her only chance with a man other than her husband, at least it would be with one of London's most renowned rakes.

***

ABE SWALLOWED as he took in the sweet, shivering form of Willow before him. He'd come here today to go through the investments he'd propositioned her with. Investments which he was going to deny her now. He could not do it to her. Hurt her financially. Not because she was giving herself to him, but because she did not deserve it. She may be the niece of the woman who ruined his mother's place in London society, but she was innocent of any crimes against his family.

Now that she was here, his to claim, he knew there was only one outcome that would suit him now. Willow had to marry him. Had to be his wife. It was unimaginable the thought of seeing her as someone else's wife, and so it was the only course open to them.

She was the only woman he'd ever cared about. Thought and planned for. While it may not be love, what he felt, his affection for her was profound and more than he'd ever felt with anyone else.

He stepped closer to her, pushing her against the door and ravaged her puckered nipple with his tongue. Her gasp and rapid breaths told him she was hot, wet, and ready for him. The thought of sinking deep into her hot core sent a bolt of lust to his groin, and he nipped her breast in punishment of leaving him so hard.

Her fingers spiked into his hair, holding him to her, and he moved over to her other breast, reveling in the ample heaviness of her breasts. "So damn sweet," he said, kissing down her stomach, circling her navel before dropping to his knees.

He glanced up the length of her, caught her lust-filled gaze as he slowly kissed his way toward her glistening mons.

"What are you doing?" she breathed, her fingers massaging his scalp and sending a shiver of bliss down his spine.

"I'm going to kiss you here."

"Where?" she squeaked, holding him away from her.

He chuckled, reached out and slipped his finger over her bud, past her folds to tease her core. "Right here, love."

WILLOW WATCHED, entranced as Abe kissed her in the one spot she'd never thought anyone would ever go. Not with their mouth at least. She marveled at the sight of him as his tongue flicked out, teasing her at the same spot his hand had teased her in the carriage the day before.

Without thought, she lifted one leg and slipped it over his shoulder.

"That's it, love. Open for me."

She bit her lip, leaning back on the door as his tongue flicked and teased, his lips kissing her most private of parts. Heat coursed through her, a sweet ache settled at her core, and she wanted him to kiss her there. To run his clever fingers against her opening.

And then his mouth was there too, kissing, laving, teasing her to the point that she'd not thought possible to stand. She moaned and quickly bit her lip from making too much noise. They were at the door, after all. The servants could be standing on the other side.

He suckled on her, and a bolt of pleasure spiked through her. She clasped his hair, undulating against his mouth. All thoughts of propriety vanished. All that was left was the exquisite gratification coursing through her.

"Oh yes, Abe," she gasped, not caring how loud her words were.

He growled his approval, the tremor of his voice sending another bolt of heat to her sex. She could feel it again, a building up to the pinnacle of climax that she'd had yesterday. This time though, it was stronger, more carnal as his mouth worked her to a frenzy.

She moved on him, ground her body against his wicked tongue, and then his hand slid against her folds, his finger delving deep into her body. Willow clasped his shoulders as tremor after tremor ran through her core, spiraling up to burst through her body.

Bliss. Pure bliss.

And then she was in his arms. He carried her to the daybed on the other side of the room. Willow made short work of his breeches, ripping his front falls open and not waiting for him to slip them down before they tumbled onto the soft, cushioned bed.

She wrapped her legs about his waist, rubbing her throbbing sex against his phallus It was deliciously hard, shooting more tremors through her each time he thrust against her.

"Are you sure, Willow?" he asked, reaching down between them. "There is no going back from here."

"Please. I need you," she said, placing him at her core.

"Damn it. I can't deny you anything." He gave one sharp thrust and took her. She stilled as a stinging pain ripped at her core, and she cringed, having not thought it would hurt so much.

"I'm sorry," he gasped, kissing her deep and long. His tongue, the slow ebb of his kiss, took her mind off the full-ness of him, the little slice of pain she'd just endured. And then he started to move, a slight rock to begin as she became used to his invasion of her body.

The pain ebbed away and she was left with only a fulfilling ache that begged to be sated. Willow clutched him, unable to get enough, get close enough to the plea-sure he promised. Their bodies joined in a dance of desire, his every stroke lighting a fire within her core that sparked and teased her to burn.

Willow arched her back, the abrasive hairs on his chest teasing her nipples and sending a whole different type of gratification to course through her body.

"I've wanted to fuck you for so long," he gasped against her lips, catching her gaze. They stared at each other while he pumped hard and deep into her core. Willow reached up, clasping his face in her hands. His crude words ought to disgust her, turn her away, and yet if anything, they had the opposite reaction. She loved hearing that he wanted her so much. So much that he dropped his titled mannerisms and became just a man.

Hers...

"I've wanted you too." It was the truth of the situation, and there was little point in denying it. Lord Ryley was not for her, but today, right now, he was all she wanted, and she would take what he would give her. If only this once.

There was no future with the man causing her emotions to riot, her body to clamp and shiver deliciously beneath him. He was wild, and she wanted something tame. Not letting the thought take hold and dampen her emotions, Willow pulled Abe down for a kiss and forgot everything but what he was doing to her. All that he was gifting her with.

Heat spiraled at her core as he rocked faster into her. With each thrust, he teased her deep inside. The urge to beg, to plead for more sat on her tongue, and she threw her head back, gasping for strength to stand any more teasing that he wrought upon her.

"I'm never going to get enough of you," he gasped against her lips.

She kissed him, her heart skipping a beat at his sweet words before pleasure burst bright and strong through her core, shooting out into her limbs, her arms, everywhere. Willow cried out his name and reveled in the sound of hers on his lips as warm liquid spilled onto her stomach.

They slumped together, their breathing ragged. Willow ran a hand down Abe's back, eliciting a shiver. "That, my lord, was simply quite scandalous and marvelous," she sighed, lying back, spent and satisfied beyond imagining. Her legs felt of jelly, her arms weak, her body lethargic as if she could sleep for a week.

He rolled to her side, leaning up on one arm, watching her. His free hand reached out, circling her nipples that were hard buttons of sensation. "I fear, Miss Perry, that what we've done here today must be and will be repeated often. I simply must insist."

She chuckled, glancing at him quickly. "Is that wise, my lord? You said yourself you're not the marrying type, and you know that I'm husband-hunting this season. What if I fall *enceinte*? Will you marry me then?"

He stilled, and she grinned, knowing only too well that he'd not thought that far ahead. That their tryst today would only ever happen once, just as she planned. The only children she would bear would be her husband's, no matter how enjoyable sharing Lord Ryley's bed had been, this rendezvous would only happen once.

She sat up, patting his chest. "We have taken precautions today. Nothing will come of it. You're free to return to the lifestyle you adore so much, and I am free to marry whomever I choose. At least I can thank you for instructing me in the ways of the marriage bed. I must confess that I'm looking forward to married life a lot more now."

ABE GAPED at Willow before he realized she was dressing, and he was still lying on the daybed, his breeches halfway down his legs and his cock laying across his leg for anyone to ogle.

He shuffled to the side of the bed, shucking up his breeches and glancing about for his shirt. The thought of

Willow increasing with his child had not entered his mind before now, but now that it had the thought of it filled him with pleasure.

A most unwelcome emotion considering he never intended to be a father. Marriages were not an institution he held in high regard, and he would never father a child out of wedlock. Spying his shirt near the door, he strode over to it quickly, slipping it on, along with his waistcoat and jacket.

He turned, fixing his cravat, and his mouth dried at the sight of Willow, attempting to hook the small little tabs at the back of her dress. Warmth speared his chest at the sight of her, sweet and undemanding. She ought to be commanding, telling him that after taking her virginity that he would marry her, make her his wife.

The words that he needed to say to do the right thing lodged in his throat and would not come. She could fall pregnant, be the mother of his child, and still, he couldn't voice the possibility. Instead, he strode over to her, twisted her about, and started to clip together the small ties on the back of her gown.

Never before had he taken the time to stay, to help his lovers dress. He'd always left them where they slept and went about his business. No ties, no emotions. Nothing.

He was a cad through and through. He'd never really thought about it much, but his name, the Spanish Scoundrel, really did fit him very well. He was certainly acting the scoundrel right now to Willow.

"We shall discuss the investments tomorrow, perhaps. If you're free."

She waved his concern away, turning so he could admire her profile. The sight of her, her beauty, her alabaster skin kissed with the lightest shade of rose after their lovemaking made his stomach clench. Hell, she was a temptress, a woman who made him want to forget all his self-imposed rules and decrees. Made him want to throw them all aside and do whatever the hell made her happy.

"Oh, never mind the investments. I looked over them with my solicitor and we agreed on the Welsh Coal Mine. I've already instructed him to invest some of my funds into the scheme."

Abe stilled, a cold shiver running down his spine. For a moment, his mind worked furiously, and his gut clenched, threatening to cast up his accounts. "How much did you invest?" he managed to ask, hoping it was only a small sum.

"Thirty thousand pounds. I know it's a third of my inheritance, but I trust you and your business acumen." At his silence, she glanced at him over her shoulder. "Is that not enough, you think? Should I have invested more?"

Fuck!

"May I suggest that I visit your solicitor just to ensure that all is in order?" Abe prayed that she'd give him the details of the offices so he could travel down there immediately and stop the transaction. Damn it. He was a bastard for even thinking to do such a thing to her. She was innocent and didn't deserve such treatment.

Panic made his fingers clumsy on her gown, and he took a calming breath, trying to right her dress before leaving. He had to go. Now. If her solicitor was to place her money on the scheme he'd optioned for her, she would lose all that she invested.

"How many more clips do you have to do?" she asked, peeking over her shoulder.

Even with his mind in turmoil, his stomach in his throat, threatening to choke him, her looking back at him, her dark-blue orbs with a teasing light within them made him want to kiss her. To lay her down on the daybed behind them and while away the day making love.

Abe cleared his throat, stepping around her and starting for the door. He was rattled, his mind hazy after one of the best shags of his life.

What was he talking about? One of the best shags? It was the best shag he'd ever had, and she'd been a virgin. The idea of what they could do together when she became more self-aware, more open to other things that they could do made his cock twitch.

"The address?" he queried again, keeping his distance from her lest he pull her into his arms and ravage her a second time. To do so would be unforgivable. She needed time to heal after their afternoon together.

"Oh yes, I have a spare card here on my desk." She walked over to a small lady's portable writing chest, and opening a drawer, pulled out a small card. With a smile on her delectable lips that were a deep shade of pink after their many kisses, she came over to him, handing him the card. "Thank you again for helping me with the investments. I would like more advice, if you're willing, on others if you know of any."

He stared at her, feeling the lowest cad on earth. The Welsh mine looked like a winning investment on paper, and simply because he'd had the documents forged. He threw her a pleased smile that was as wooden as his heart. "My pleasure. I'll call on them directly to ensure all is in order."

Abe leaned down and kissed her, unable to deny himself one last taste of her before he turned and left, shutting the door softly behind him. He kept his calm until he made his carriage, and then he yelled out the direction and for haste.

His driver, sensing the urgency, made short work

through the London traffic to Willow's solicitor's offices on Harley street. Within ten minutes, the carriage rocked to a halt before a brown-brick building. Without waiting for his driver, Abe threw open the carriage door and strode as fast as he could without looking like a man on a full run. A gentleman stood at the front wooden counter, looking at him expectantly.

"I'm Marquess Ryley. I need to have an urgent meeting with...with..." He fumbled about in his coat and found the card in his pocket. "Mr. Turner, if you will. It's urgent."

The young man's eyes widened, and he bobbed his head so quickly, Abe feared for his health. "Of course, my lord. Right away, my lord."

Abe cooled his heels only a few moments before a short, stout man with a receding hairline wobbled out into the foyer. "Lord Ryley. It is a pleasure to meet you. Please come to my office."

Abe followed him and sat on the chair across from the older man, who picked up his spectacles and placed them on his nose.

"Now, what is it that I can do for you, my lord?"

Abe cleared his throat, now that he was here he was unsure how to start this conversation without making himself look like an ass. He resigned himself; there was no other way than to tell the solicitor the truth and hope it wasn't too late for Willow.

"A Miss Willow Perry gave me your address as my coming here today is in regard to the investments into the Cornwall coal mine that you're helping her invest in. I have reason to believe the documents were forged, and the returns on the investment were highly exaggerated. If Miss Perry were to invest in the mine, it will, as sure as I'm sitting here, fail, and she will lose the money invested."

Mr. Turner stared at him a moment, his face turning an awful shade of gray. "Are you well, Mr. Turner?" he asked. The last thing he required was for this man to keel over in front of him. Abe needed him to fix the problem that Abe had caused. He shook his head at his absurdity. What had he been thinking! Should Willow find out what he'd done, what he'd planned to do, she would never forgive him. Never trust him. And rightfully so.

"Miss Perry authorized the payment while staying at the Duke and Duchess of Whitstone's estate. The money has been invested."

For a moment, Abe felt as though his body was not his own, that he wasn't sitting before a man, and listening to him tell him that Abe hadn't just lost thirty thousand pounds of Miss Perry's inheritance. He ran a hand over his jaw, at a loss as to what to do.

The realization that his revenge was complete brought no pleasure. A pain seized in the vicinity of his heart, and he clutched his chest. This would hurt Willow, and that, in turn, would hurt him. He cared for her. While he would never forgive Willow's aunt for her treatment of his mother or that of Lord Perfect's parent, nor would he allow what had happened to impact what he'd started to feel for Willow.

Not that it mattered what he felt for her any longer for this would crush her. She would hate him. *Fuck it!* He took a calming breath when his vision swam.

He would not faint like a matron seeing her charge kiss a rogue. He had to fix this. Somehow, he would fix this.

"You must put a stop on the payment. The investment is not sound."

Mr. Turner frowned at Abe before he turned to his desk, shuffling through papers scattered atop it. "But I have a letter here from Miss Perry stating that you, Lord Ryley endorsed this particular investment. Indeed, there is paper-work here from your solicitors attesting to the soundness of it. What has happened in the last few days that all of this would change?"

Despair crashed over him, and he fought not to panic. The last few days, being away from Miss Perry, had thrown some truths Abe's way. That is what happened. Truths that he liked her. Missed her. Cared for her far above anyone ever in his life. That he'd just come from her bed, where for the first time in his life he'd lost control, allowed himself to enjoy, to savor the woman in his arms told him all he needed to know about how much his situation had changed.

He loved her.

Fuck!

"The documents were forged. They were forged at my instruction. It was a mistake, I grant you, and I had not thought that Miss Perry had proceeded with the investment yet. I just came from her home, where she divulged this information. Of course, hence why I'm here before you trying to fix my error. Trying to stop the payment."

Mr. Turner stood, leaning over his desk. "There is no stopping it now. It is done, my lord and now I shall have the displeasure of telling my client that due to a lord's folly she has lost one third of her inheritance." The older gentleman, as stout as he was, seemed to grow in size at his anger. "How dare you play her the fool in such a way? Such funds may be nothing to you, but they are everything for others. Please leave, I have work to do, one particular job of telling Miss Perry that you've led her on a merry dance for reasons only you understand. I highly doubt that she will be so understanding. Good day to you."

Abe wouldn't normally let anyone speak down to him

in such a way, but today he deserved the set down. Deserved to be called the bastard that he was—the scoundrel.

There was no coming back from this. Willow would never forgive him and he'd never forgive himself.

CHAPTER 14

Aweek after being told by her solicitor that her investment had failed, Willow sat in her library, having spent the past half hour pacing up and down the long room. Lord Ryley was due to arrive any moment. The mere thought of him made her blood boil, and she was ready to see him again after denying him these past days.

Thirty thousand pounds. She clutched her stomach, knowing she would never get that money back. Never have that security again in her life. What if she had risked all her inheritance? Not that she would be so foolhardy, but what if she had been interested in doing such a thing? She would've lost everything. Her home. The security for her friends who lived with her.

The bastard!

A quick rap sounded on the door, and her butler opened it, announcing Lord Ryley. His lordship stepped into the room, his hair, as usual, sat displaced atop his head as if someone had run their hands through it. His superfine coat fit him like her kid-leather gloves, and his

Hessian boots were polished to such a shine that Willow could see his lordships reflection in them.

"Please leave the door open, Thomas."

Lord Ryley schooled his features at her decree and came to stand on the opposite side of her desk. Willow gestured for him to sit before she also sat, adjusting the papers on her desk lest she stand, go about the desk and murder him in her library.

"Willow, I have wanted to see you. To explain. To–"

"There is no reason to explain, my lord. I understand perfectly well. You played me a fool and the green lass that I am, I fell for it. I should not have trusted you." Not just in the financial kind of way, but emotional as well. She'd given herself to this man. Allowed him liberties that she should never have allowed anyone. Not unless that anyone was her husband.

He sighed, running his hand through his hair. From the looks of it, he'd been doing that quite a lot today. Was he remorseful? She hoped so. If he was at least, it would show some kind of heart beat inside that chest of his.

"I'm sorry, Willow. I had not thought that you had already approved the investment. When you told me that you had, I did try to correct the action. As you know," he said, glancing down at his hands. "I was too late."

"Yes, well, when we spoke of it at the house party, I did not think I would need further tutoring on the idea. That you approved it, stated to the fact that you would be investing in the mine also, I had no reason for concern. What I did not know, of course, is that you were using me as a means of revenge."

He met her eyes, and she read the confusion in his dark, fickle gaze. "Who said that to you?"

"Lord Herbert explained there was some sort of scandal involving your mother that forced her to leave

England. That in some way you blame Lord Herbert's family and my own for her departure."

"Lord Perfect has no idea what he's talking about." Lord Ryley narrowed his eyes, contemplating her. "Did he tell you that his mother slandered my mother? Her best friend at the time. Called her all types of vicious lies simply because she was from Spain and not all peaches and cream as they so like their ladies of the upper ten thousand to be."

Willow took in this information and tried to tally it up with what Lord Herbert had told her. It did not make any sense. "That is not what he said at all. He told me that your mother left London due to having an affair with a man, not her husband."

"That isn't what happened at all, and I would suggest, madam, that you only speak the truth when it comes to my family. Unless you too are tainted as a liar like Lord Perfect."

"Very well," she said, leaning back in her chair. "Tell me your version of the events." Not that she deserved any of his treatment, his need to bring her down financially. Another part of her worried that he'd also set out to take her virginity to ruin her reputation as well. Not that he could hurt her any longer. She had ensured her future was secure before today.

"Lady Herbert disliked that my mother was regarded in the *ton* more highly than she was, especially since she was an outsider. A foreigner. They were friends once, yes, but that soon came to an end when jealousy imbedded its claws into Lady Herbert's spine. My mother was taunted and teased out of London and has not returned. I was left to be raised by staff and nannies before being sent off to school. Father fell ill at her leaving and never recovered. I place all of that dreadful time in my life at Lord Perfect's family and yours as well."

She shook her head, staring at him with pity. "Please explain to me how my family is involved?"

"Your aunt, Viscountess Vance, was in the thick of all this scandal. Throwing her opinionated self into the fray."

Realization struck Willow, and she stared at Lord Ryley with far greater insight. "And so you, all those years later, set out to ruin me financially because of something that my aunt did to your mother twenty years ago?" She barked out a laugh, unable to hold it in any longer. "You're mad!"

⚜

MOST DEFINITELY, he was mad. He was also shamed. Hearing Willow tell him that he'd taken revenge on her for something that happened twenty years ago made him look petty and idiotic. "They made my mother's life hell."

"Your mother now. Is she happy?"

He adjusted his seat, knowing his answer would make him look further like a fool. "She remarried a wealthy merchant in Spain several years ago. They are both very happy."

"And yet here you were, brooding and just waiting for your chance to strike like a Spanish viper." She leaned forward on the desk, watching him. Something in his chest hurt at the sight of her pain at her displeasure of him. He didn't want her to feel that way about him. At first, he'd wanted her to pay, but that had long changed. Had he known that she was going to move forward with the investment without further consultation with him, he would never have allowed it.

He loved her. For the first time in his life, his heart had beat outside of his chest for another. He wanted her to be his wife, but that right now seemed like a dream that would not come true. She hated him. Loathed him. He could see it in the blue depths of her eyes. He'd disappointed her.

"I'm sorry, Willow. I have hated them all for so long that I could not see past my hate. I should never have involved you in my scheme, but your aunt had been so cruel, so vindictive to my mother that I could not let it go. I was orphaned because of them all."

"No you were not, my lord. You were orphaned because your mother chose to leave you here in England instead of taking you to Spain. I do not know what story to believe, that your mother had an affair or if she was degraded by society due to the color of her skin, but either way, you choose to make me suffer for a crime that I wasn't part of. How could you do that?"

"The more I learned about you, the more time we spent together, I knew that I could not do what I had planned. Had you not moved forward on this investment, had you waited for our meeting, this would never have happened."

Willow gasped, and Abe cringed, knowing what he'd just stated was the wrong thing.

"Now you dare blame me for this? You're the one who gave me the investment, spouting on about how sound it was. How dare you blame me for your own scheme?" She stood, leaning over her desk. "I think you should leave, Lord Ryley. We have nothing further to say to one another."

He stood, coming to the desk and drinking her in, fear and panic rioting within him that his error could cost him her. "I can give you the money back, Willow. It's nothing to me."

She scoffed, shaking her head. "Of course it's nothing to you. You have multiple properties, a business that due to men's greed and need to sleep with women other than their wives, you'll always have an income. That money that my aunt gave to me was all I had. Was all I'd ever have from anyone. It keeps me safe and allows me to keep my friends safe from vultures like you, gentlemen like you who think some women are worthy of marriage and others are only worthy of lying on their backs.

"You and your hatred stole thirty thousand pounds." The disgust on her visage was as sharp as a physical blow to his gut. "You can give it back? How very fortunate you are that you have the luxury."

"Willow, please," he begged, uncertain of how to make this right. Damn it all to hell. He'd been a bastard. A fool, and now he'd gone and broken what they had been progressing toward.

A future.

"You should also know that I have been asked by Lord Herbert to be his wife, and I have agreed."

This time the air did whoosh from his lungs, and he clasped the desk to steady himself, hoping what he'd heard was untrue. "What?"

"I'm going to be married," she said, matter-of-factly, walking about the desk and going to stand at the door. "Good day to you, Lord Ryley."

He stared down at the mahogany wood, his fingers clenched, and fought to think, fought to understand how he could fix this. Change all that had happened the last week. He closed his eyes, forcing calm through his blood. Turning, he strode to the door. "Is that what you want?" he asked, hoping, praying that she'd say no. That she wanted him and not Lord Perfect.

"Let me answer this another way, my lord. I certainly do not want anyone I cannot trust and who would use me as a pawn for their own gain." She stared him down, cold and aloof. He'd never seen Willow so distant, and he hated the fact that he'd made her so. He'd made her like this toward him after all they had shared. Their bodies and their minds.

"Willow, please." He would beg if need be. He could not lose her.

"Leave. Now."

A footman appeared in the foyer, opening the front door. Abe glanced in the direction and spotted the very bastard who'd ruined his future, Lord Perfect, stroll into the foyer. Who was Abe fooling? He'd ruined his future. He'd pushed her away, used her, and made her lose a great deal of her fortune.

He had no one to blame but himself. Abe strode past Lord Perfect, the gentleman's lofty and amused greeting lost on him. It took all his effort not to look back. Not to run back to Willow and beg her to change her mind. To forgive him.

Instead, he crossed the threshold and strode to his carriage. Lord Ryley, The Spanish Scoundrel, never looked back. Not for anyone or anything. Not even his heart that he feared he'd left in the library of Miss Willow Perry's Hanover square home, Mayfair.

CHAPTER 15

Three weeks passed, and he'd not seen Willow. The time dragged like an endless clock that never turned the full face of the hour, merely clicked and taunted that he would not move forward. He'd buggered everything up with the one woman who'd captured his heart.

He leaned back in his chair in his study, a glass of brandy in his hand on the armrest. He swirled the amber liquid, lost in thoughts of her. Was she happy? The talk about town was that the wedding plans were going ahead with great gusto. Invitations had been dispatched. Not that he'd been invited, but he knew from the Duke of Whitstone who had been.

There had to be something that he could do to win her back. His treatment of her, his immovable stance on revenge had clouded his mind, and before he'd known the damage he would cause by acting against her, it was too late.

A knock sounded on his door, and he bellowed to be left alone before the door swung wide.

Light footsteps sounded, and he glanced over his shoulder, a small slither of hope piercing his heart that it may be Willow come to see him. Instead, the sight that filled his view left him grappling for words.

"Mother?" he said, standing and going to greet her. "What are you doing in London?"

She kissed his cheeks, clasping his face, just like she used to when he was a child. "I came to try and amend your mistake that I heard from Lady Herbert that you've done."

"What?" he frowned, taken aback. "Lady Herbert. What on earth is she writing to you about?"

"Well, as luck would have it, I've been traveling and was in Paris when I received her letter last week. She was concerned that her son, whom you like to refer to as Lord Perfect I hear, is marrying a Miss Willow Perry. A woman that has apparently caught the attention of the renowned rake and Spanish Scoundrel, Lord Ryley. You." She gave him a knowing look, stepping past him to seat herself on the settee. "A glass of sherry, if you please and then come join me."

Abe did as she bade, taking in his parent whom he'd not seen for several years. She was as beautiful as he remembered her as a child, tall, dark-haired, and golden-skinned as he was. Even at her advancing age, she was a beautiful woman and one who had not deserved the treatment that she received. Which meant her correspondence with Lady Herbert made no sense.

He handed her a glass of sherry, sitting across from her. Abe leaned back in his wingback chair, wanting to give an impression of being undisturbed, but it was false. His mother being in contact with Lady Herbert after all these years was not what he'd ever expected her to say.

"Why are you here, Mother? You swore never to return to London after what was done to you."

She sighed, taking a small sip of her drink. "It is time that you knew the truth of my leaving England, why I fled as I did."

"The truth? But you were shunned out of London due to being Spanish. Lady Herbert and Lady Vance mocked and ridiculed you."

"They did, you're right, but they did so on my behest. I needed a scandal so bad, so degrading that your father would force me to leave. And so, I, along with my two closest friends, came up with a plan. They would shun me, make up lies of my infidelity, and mock my heritage. It was the only way I would've survived, Abraham. Had I not left when I did, I would not be here with you now."

"What!" Anger coursed through him at the thought of his mother lying to him all those years. Of hating people that were now innocent of the crimes he threw at their head. The thought that he'd treated Lord Perfect the way he had since Eton, the way he'd ensured Willow had lost her money was all based on a lie made his stomach churn. "Tell me everything."

His mother stared at the burning wood in the fire, quiet a moment. "I married your father for love. We met when he was on a grand tour and visiting Spain. We married abroad and returned to England. You know all this of course. Not long after, we found out we were expecting you, and I was so happy. I had a husband I loved and a child on the way. I had friends, and life was marvelous for a time, but then it all changed. Your father became surly and mean at times. Little things would set him off, and I was at a loss as to why."

His mother stared at the sherry in her hand, lost in the past as she recounted the story to him. One that he was struggling to comprehend.

"Your father had syphilis, Abraham, and yet he

expected me to remain a true and loving wife. I could not do such a thing. Had I stayed, I too would have succumbed to the disease. I tried to reason with him, explain the risks that I would be taking should I remain a true wife, but he would not listen. He wanted me to stay, and he wanted his nightly pursuits in the bowels of London to continue as well. That is when Lady Herbert and Viscountess Vance helped me plan. My only regret was that your father refused to allow me to take you with me. Decided instead that you would be better off with a nanny until you could be sent to Eton."

"And so you left me here, alone, all those years. Allowed me to be raised by servants since father had washed his hands of me. Why did you not return after his death?"

"Your father ensured I was unable to return. For my silence on his affliction, I had to remain in Spain. Should I not do as he decreed, he threatened to never allow me to see you again. He promised that you would travel to Spain when you were fourteen and you did." His mother leaned forward, clasping his hand. "I wanted to take you with me, but you were the future Marquess Ryley, and your place was here in England. My friends have kept me abreast of your life, and antics within the *ton*," she said, looking down her nose at him. "But from afar, just as I was made to live apart from your life. So you see, my dear, there was a reason for my banishment, just not the one you believed. Now that your father has passed, and you're a man, you deserved to know the truth. Especially when that truth is stopping you from marrying a woman, I believe, who has captured your heart."

The mention of Willow filled him with regret, and he stared at his mother, unable to believe this tale that she told. Everything that he thought was the truth, the reason his mother had left him had not been because of Lady Herbert or Viscountess Vance, but because of his father. Because his father had gone mad with the venereal disease, had threatened his mother with the same affliction.

Anyone in that situation would flee or try to escape. Abe stared at his parent and read the fear in her dark-brown eyes that he would shun her. Hate her for lying, but he could not. He reached across the space separating them and clasped her hand. "I understand, Mother. I just wish that it hadn't been so for you. That father was true to you and never fell ill such as he did. Lady Herbert and Viscountess Vance were true friends in creating a scandal so bad that Father banished you. I suppose I owe them thanks instead of loathing, such as I've shown them. It seems I owe many apologies." One to Miss Willow Perry the most pressing of all.

He shook his head at his actions. However would he make amends, but then, he had not known the truth either, so mayhap forgiveness will be forthcoming from all he'd loathed for so long.

"Why, however, was Lady Herbert writing to you regarding her son's betrothal to Miss Perry? From all accounts, her ladyship is pleased with the union."

"Oh, she's pleased and adores Miss Perry, but she doesn't believe her son is marrying the woman he loves. He was enamored if you recall some years ago to Miss White. They were not permitted to marry as her father wanted her to be a duchess. She is now a widow and will soon be returning to town. Lady Herbert believes that when her son sees her again, his feelings for her will be as strong as they ever were. That he'll regret marriage to Miss Perry, and the union will decline because of his mistake."

Abe couldn't imagine ever regretting a marriage to Willow. The idea no longer scared him or made him want to cast up his accounts, but instead filled him with longing. With a need to move forward, have a fuller, richer life. With Willow.

"Does Lord Herbert know that his first love is a widow and returning to town?"

"He does," his mother said, standing and going to pour herself another glass of sherry. "But he's in denial, and you, my dear son, are reported to be as well. In denial about your feelings for Miss Perry, if you need clarification. When I heard of the predicament that you both were in, I knew I had to leave Paris and travel to London. Tell you myself that you must make Miss Perry cry off her engagement to Lord Herbert and soon. Lady Herbert tells me she believes this would be the best for everyone. We may be getting older, but we still see things as clear as air, and I trust my friend. She thinks you're in love with Willow, and she believes her son is in love with the Duchess of Markson. The solution is simple. Now you must make it a reality."

Make it a reality. As simple as that. Abe wasn't so sure. Willow was extremely unhappy with him and rightfully so. He'd acted a cad, a bastard to have made her lose thirty thousand pounds. He would be hard-pressed to forgive anyone such a crime.

"I will try and make amends, Mother. I cannot say that I'm not disappointed in you in not telling me the truth sooner, years ago, in fact. Why did you not?" he asked, needing to know.

She shrugged, coming to stand before the fire. "There was little point. You may have disliked Lady Herbert and Viscountess Vance, but they knew the truth and were willing to accept your anger at them if it meant that your father's secret was kept just that. No one in London knows that he was ill with that disease, and no one ever need know. All of that is in the past, and other than the woman you love marrying another, there really isn't a lot to repair."

Abe shook his head at his mother's trivializing of the situation. It was just like her too. Face a problem and find a solution. Pity her solution to her problem years before had led him down a road of revenge and hatred.

"I will make it right and save both Miss Perry and Lord Perfect from marrying each other. I shall not fail in this."

"Good," his mother said, smiling at him. He smiled back. Even with all that had passed between them, the time apart and the reasons why, both true and false, having his mother home in England made him happy. And now he needed one other thing in his life to make him complete.

Willow.

CHAPTER 16

Willow threw herself into balls and parties, nights at the theater with Lord Herbert. Every time she was with him, she marveled at his kindness, his understanding, but each time it became more and more prevalent that she did not love him.

She liked him very much. There wasn't a lot not to like about the gentleman, but he didn't make her heart race. Not even when on a carriage ride home from the theater, he'd taken her in his arms and kissed her again. Properly this time.

For all his ability, she may have been kissing the back of her hand for all the emotion it brought up inside of her. The streets of London passed the carriage windows, and she absently stared at nothing at all, wondering if this is how her life would be from now on. An endless parade of social gatherings and very little else in between.

"Willow, are you happy?" Evie asked, staring across from her in the carriage.

She rallied and schooled her features, knowing that what she was about to say was a lie. Since Lord Ryley, Abe, had left her library the month before, she'd slowly sunk into a life of lies. She smiled and danced, laughed, and allowed Lord Herbert to court her, plan their intertwined future. All the while her mind had been occupied with another. The scoundrel who had not only stolen her money but her heart.

"I'm very happy," she said, forcing the words through her lying lips. She bit back a sigh, wondering what Lord Ryley was doing at this very moment. He was probably at his club, women begging for any scrap of attention he may offer them.

Bastard.

Evie leaned forward, clasping her hand. Willow refused to look at her lest she see in her eyes that she was anything but joyful at the moment. For all of Lord Ryley's unforgivable actions, she missed him. Missed how he made her feel.

"You're lying, Willow. It's as clear to me as if I were looking through glass. What is wrong? Tell me. I'll not tell anyone else if that is what you wish."

Willow closed her eyes, slumping back on the leather squabs. "I'm not in love with Lord Herbert."

Evie nodded consolingly, her eyes full of understanding. "I know you're not, but I suppose you must decide if you're willing to let love grow between you in time, or not." Evie threw her a searching look. "Does your having concerns for your impending marriage have anything to do with Lord Ryley?"

The mention of his name sent a bolt of longing through her, and she bit the inside of her lip to stop her eyes smarting with tears. He didn't deserve any more of those from her. She'd cried enough over the loss of him. Over the fact he'd used her, seduced her into trusting him so he could steal from her and her security.

"I hate that man. Do not mention him again." She

didn't need any more assistance in remembering his every touch, how his voice sounded deep and seductive against her ear. How his kisses left her longing and spiraling out of control.

"You love him," Evie stated matter-of-factly. "Even after his treatment of you, you love him still. You will need to decide if you're willing to walk away from a future with Lord Herbert, who is everything you've always wanted. A nice, secure marriage to a man who adores you. A future where children will feature. Safe and secure just as you wanted. Against a future with Lord Ryley. A man hell bound, riddled with debauchery and someone I've concluded for some time that is as much in love with you as you are with him."

Willow gasped, looking up to meet Evie's eyes. "He doesn't love me. His actions toward me are proof of that."

"Yes, while I agree he acted in a way that begs the question as to whether he is intelligent, we also must not forget that his calling on you the day before you learned of his ulterior action was to dissuade you of the investment. He was going to right the wrong he intended you."

"Little good that did. I had already moved forward with the investment."

Evie came and sat beside her, turning to face her. "And knowing that he tried to stop the transaction by going to your solicitor. Mr. Turner told you that himself."

"Whose side are you on? You're supposed to be my friend, not supporting Lord Ryley." Willow cringed at her accusatory tone. Evie didn't deserve her annoyance, which should be fully focused on Lord Ryley and no one else. And herself for that matter. For allowing her disappointment and wretchedness over his actions toward her to cloud her judgment and agree to Lord Herbert's proposal the moment he made it.

"Willow, you know that I'm on your side, but I also have watched you these past weeks, and you're not yourself."

Willow exhaled, her lips set into a thin line. "What does that mean? I have been myself and I'm perfectly happy with my choice." Even though she was not. Evie was right, of course, but she'd given her word to Lord Herbert. To cry off from the betrothal now would be a scandal she'd never recover from. Her wedding attire was being made as they sat in the carriage on their way to the York's ball. Lord Herbert's mother had hundreds of guests attending their church wedding before hosting them an opulent wedding breakfast at their London estate.

Not to mention Lord Ryley had been noticeably absent from any social events the last month. Was what Evie said true, and somewhere in that dark soul of his he cared for her? One would think that if that were the case, he would try to win her back. Try to see her again and ask for forgiveness.

Not that she would give him any such thing. Fiend.

"No you have not, and as your friend, I'm going to tell you the truth, even if you do not wish to hear it. You're in love with Lord Ryley, and he is in love with you. Perhaps you both have not admitted as much to yourselves, but when we were at Hampton it was obvious to us all."

Willow scoffed, adjusting her seat as the carriage started to slow before Lord and Lady York's townhouse.

"Scoff all you like, Willow, but he made a mistake, a dreadful one, but is that error worth a life of misery, of half truths with a man you do not care for. A life half-lived because deep down, you'll know you married the wrong man."

The carriage rocked to a halt, and without waiting for the footman, Willow threw the door open and jumped from the equipage. Evie followed at a more sedate pace, but Willow needed time to think, to clear her head. Panic clutched at her skin. Her hands clammy and hot within the confines of her gloves. Damn her friend for being so honest. She didn't want to know what others thought. What others believed Lord Ryley thought of her.

None of it mattered. She was engaged to be married to Lord Herbert. Lord Ryley had stolen from her. He didn't deserve anything from her other than her disgust forever and a day.

By the time they arrived at the ballroom doors, and they had greeted their hosts, Willow forgave Evie enough to walk into the multitude of guests to make their way across the room to where they could see Ava and the Duke of Whitstone.

Ava stood beside the duke, her arm entwined with him and a knowing, loving smile on her friend's face as she spoke up to her husband, who had an equally adoring visage toward his wife. Something inside Willow snapped, and tears pricked her eyes.

She couldn't do it. She couldn't marry Lord Herbert and only be half the wife she longed to be. He deserved a marriage of affection, of adoration, not a marriage made up of half truths.

Willow deserved the same.

She kissed the duchess as they joined their friends, greeting the duke warmly, but her smile slipped as she caught sight of Lord Ryley across the room, a woman on his arm she'd not seen before. They were in deep conversation with a group of friends about them, ignorant of her presence.

"Never mind Lord Ryley," Ava said, looking at her with concern. A characteristic that all her friends were adopting toward her these past weeks. One that had started to irritate Willow. No matter that their intention was good. "He'll not disturb you tonight. He wouldn't dare."

"He may do whatever he likes. It's no concern of mine," she said, raising her chin and taking in who else was present. Lady Herbert was here she could see, along with Hallie and Lord Duncannon, who were talking to some of their friends farther along the room.

Evie held out a glass of champagne to Willow, and she took it, her mouth parched and in desperate need of fortitude.

As much as she tried, her attention kept snapping back to the one spot in the room it should not. Lord Ryley was busy with his friends, laughing and discussing something that interested him, which most certainly was not her.

His lack of awareness of her was telling. Evie was wrong. He'd never cared and never would. She was missing a man who never really existed. While she'd always known he was a rake, he'd been sweet, intense, and patient with her. But it was all a front—a lie. The whole time he'd been plotting her downfall, loathing her for her relatives and their actions toward his mother.

Lord Herbert may not be the man she would marry, but nor would Lord Ryley. In time her heart would heal, and it would bloom once again, ready to love, to give over to someone else.

Her skin prickled in awareness, and she looked up and caught the eye of Lord Ryley, his dark, heated gaze pinning her to her spot. Her heart gave a lurch, and no matter how much she knew she should look away, ignore him, she could not. All that they shared, the many kisses, his seductive words as he took her on the daybed bombarded her mind, and she bit her lip, hating that he could make her want him as much as he ever did. He'd tried to ruin her. Had made her lose a third of her fortune.

Still, she wanted him. Wanted him with a need that overshadowed everything she knew of the man and knowledge of what he did.

His gaze didn't leave her, not even when Lord Herbert bowed before her, kissing her hand and pulling her onto the floor for a waltz. And damn herself, for the simpleton she was, she didn't want Lord Ryley to look at anyone, unless that anyone, that someone, was her.

ॐ

ABE WATCHED Willow glide onto the floor with Lord Perfect, anger thrumming through his veins at the sight of it. It had taken him several weeks to accept the fact that she was to marry another. The whole of London was abuzz with the news and details of the forthcoming nuptials between the two.

He'd only attended tonight to see for himself that it was true. That they were a couple and he had lost her. It would seem so if her adoring gaze up at Lord Perfect and his, in turn, was anything to go by.

"Is that her?" Marigold said at his side. She clasped his arm, pulling his gaze away from Willow.

"Yes, it is her," he said, meeting his cousin's eye. She was his father's younger brother's daughter, an heiress like so many here this evening, but Marigold was sweet, pure and kind. The opposite to Abe. Perhaps that is why they had always been close. He'd spent many weeks at his uncle's estate when he wasn't in school after his father died and his mother was in Spain. She had heard the rumors that he'd been slighted by Miss Perry and had come to check on him immediately.

Abe was still trying to find out how that rumor had

started. The Spanish Scoundrel did not get slighted by the opposite sex, and he'd not let the rumor stand.

"She's very beautiful."

He nodded once, clamping his jaw. "Well, we have arrived and seen for ourselves that she is indeed happy with her choice. Shall we leave?"

"What? No," Marigold said, patting his arm. "You need to speak to her. Just to be sure this is what she wants, for it's as plain as day to me that it's not what you want."

He scowled down at his insightful relative. "I've never wanted to marry anyone. You know that." His mother's words to win Willow back reverberated in his mind, and he cast a glance in her direction. She was so lovely tonight. Her red, silk gown accentuating her unblemished skin and slight frame. So tall and luscious. Kind to a fault. Should she want him, he knew he didn't deserve her. Only a great man should have such an honor. He was not a great man.

"You're in love with her. The Spanish Scoundrel does not attend balls and parties just to look in on a woman to ensure she was indeed betrothed. You never cared for all this fanfare in any case. Since I've known you, you have turned your back on society, loathed and ridiculed its fickle ways. You promised your mother you'd try to repair this wrong. Here is your chance. Tonight."

Abe noted Lord Perfect's hand dipped low on Willow's back. He knew how that skin felt beneath his fingers. The warmth, the softness. Anger spiked through his veins and he fisted his hands at his sides. "I need a drink," he said, leaving his cousin and striding off in search of a good, hard whiskey or scotch, anything would do if it blinded him to the sight of Willow waltzing with a man, any man, if that man was not him.

CHAPTER 17

Willow excused herself after supper and went in search of the retiring room. After completing her tribulations, she sat for a time in the empty, opulent room and calmed her heart. Not because she had been dancing and laughing all evening with her betrothed, who really was a very sweet man, but because another was present. The very person that she'd sworn to forget, to curse forever.

But she could not. No sooner could she do those things than she could push away her friends. She cared for him. More than he deserved, but that didn't mean that she had to forgive him. How could she forgive him for his actions toward her? An innocent in all things relating to his mother, and he'd punished her for other people's sins.

It wasn't fair in the least.

Willow sighed and stood, starting back toward the ballroom. The house was large, and she turned down a passage, stopping halfway when the location didn't appear familiar to the one she walked through to get to the retiring room.

"Lost, Miss Perry?" a deep, husky voice said from a shadowed doorway farther along.

She lifted her chin, facing down Lord Ryley. "As a matter of fact, I am. Not that it is any of your business."

"I forgot to tell you the last time I saw you congratulations. You must forgive me my forgetting my manners at the time. I was confounded, to say the least."

She scoffed, not believing that for a moment. "You? Confounded?" She strolled up to where he stood, noting his cravat was untied and hanging loosely about his neck. Had he just finished a clandestine meeting with the woman he'd brought to the ball? Had he just taken her in the darkened room behind him? Her stomach rolled at the thought, and she took a calming breath to stop herself casting up her accounts all over his shining Hessians.

"How are the wedding preparations coming along? Your grand match is all that London is talking about."

Willow knew that as well as anyone, and the pressure now to go through with the marriage was immense. Even though, deep down, she knew she could not. Lord Herbert was not whom she wanted. The blasted fiend before her was.

"Very well, thank you. Thomas has been very involved."

A muscle worked in his jaw and not for anything could she tear her eyes from him. Her gaze slid to his lips, lips that she'd dreamed about, longed to feel against hers, and she cursed herself a fool. What woman lusted after a man who had set out to ruin her? To bring her low financially and perhaps socially as well. Not that he'd made it known to anyone that they had lain together.

"Thomas?" He cleared his throat. "I suppose it is only expected that you would call him by his given name."

Willow met Abe's gaze, wondering why such a thing

would aggravate him if his caustic tone were any indication. "He's to be my husband," she lied, knowing she'd flee London—England—even before she went through with such a future. Not that Lord Ryley needed to know that. The scoundrel.

"Hmm," he said noncommittedly. "I suppose you would." He turned and went into the room behind him and left her standing in the passage.

For a second, she debated turning about and fleeing his presence, but the need to see him more, to hear his voice, if only to disagree with him forced her hand, and she stepped into the room.

He stood beside an unlit fire, leaning on the mantel and staring at the fire that had been set, ready for tomorrow. "Where is your lady friend?" Willow asked, having expected to see her dressing or fixing her hair at the very least.

He glanced at her curiously, a small frown between his brows before he chuckled. "Are you suggesting I was in here having a tryst with the woman that I brought to the ball?" He strode over to a decanter of whiskey and poured himself a glass, downing it in one go. "Sorry to disappoint you, my dear, but that is my cousin recently returned to town. I simply accompanied her as she wished."

Willow refused to allow the relief pouring through her to amend her features. She held fast to her face of impassivity.

"Why do you ask about my affairs in any case, Miss Perry? You're to be married, am I not allowed to court whomever I please, like you? Move on from our little incident in Hampton such as it was and the one again in London."

"You may do whatever you want, just as you always

have," she said, reminding him of his scheme all along to ruin her. And he had ruined her in a way. Certainly, no one else lived up to him now or made her feel an ounce of the emotion that she always felt when around Abe. The urge to stomp her foot at having to have fallen for a man who was so wrong for her in so many ways. He'd wanted to make her pay, damn it.

Which he succeeded in doing, a little voice mocked in her head.

Willow ground her teeth, coming farther into the room. "I was surprised to see you here, that is all. Even accompanying your cousin as you say, you've not been in society the past month. I thought you would've scuttled back to your hell hole you love so much." Irritation tore through her at his treatment of her. Of his plan to bring her down. How dare he? How dare he make her care for him while all the while wanting nothing more than to make her pay?

"Oh, I've been in my hell hole as you state, my dear. Still," he shrugged, "I have been part of this society longer than you, and whether I like the lifestyle or not, the people in this ballroom are my friends and keep Hell's Gate profitable. It never hurts to show interest, even when I do not have any. It is the same for women who warm my bed. They're all the same. After a tumble…before they fuck you over."

Willow gasped. Did he mean her? "Are you implying that I used you, my lord? That I gave myself to you only to marry another?" She could not have heard what he'd just said. Surely he was simply baiting her.

"Isn't that what you have done, Miss Perry? Or have I been mistaken this past month?"

Willow stormed over to him, standing nose to nose with the vexing, impossible man. "You sought revenge and used me while working toward your goal. If anyone pushed me into the arms of another it was you. Why don't you just admit it, Lord Ryley? You're jealous. You're so jealous that someone other than yourself can call me their own. Maybe what everyone is saying about you is true."

"And what truth is that," he said, his voice low with a dangerous edge to it that made her shiver. She was walking a delicate line with Lord Ryley. He wasn't tamed, and certainly wasn't a gentleman most of the time. There was no telling what would happen if she kept poking his temper.

"That you love me. That you regret pushing me into an investment that took a third of my money. That you want me still." Just as she wanted him. After all that he'd done to her, still her body yearned for his touch. If only he'd admit his wrong. Admit that he was sorry. To beg for forgiveness.

His lordship on his knees, begging for mercy, would be a lovely sight.

"You want me to admit to wanting you?" he said, stepping toward her and pushing her back against the small table that ran behind the settee.

"And everything else," she whispered, the backs of her thighs hitting the table. His intoxicating scent of spirits, of sandalwood and something else altogether, lewdness perhaps, consumed her and heat pooled at her core.

"Oh, I want you. I want you on your back right here and now." He scooped up her gown, pushing it up her legs so the cool night air kissed her skin. "I want you to break off your engagement to Lord Perfect. I want you to be mine."

She should stop him. Shove him away. But she did not. Silly, silly woman that she was. His nearness consumed her, and then what he'd said, his words, flittered through her mind. He wanted her for himself? She was engaged, and this was wrong. For all that Lord Ryley thought of Lord Herbert, he did not deserve for his fiancée to be kissing another man.

And that is exactly where this interlude with Lord Ryley would end if she did not leave right now.

With all the self-will she possessed, Willow pushed Abe away, stepping out of his reach. "I should not be here, and you should not be trying to seduce me."

"Why ever not? I want you as much as I ever did. You cannot marry Lord Perfect. You do not care for him, Willow. I can see that you do not, and all of London knows it as well."

All of London knew that she did not care for her betrothed? Heat bloomed on her cheeks, and she took a calming breath, reminding herself Lord Ryley wasn't always correct about things. "What do you know of feelings, Lord Ryley when you care for nothing but yourself?"

"That isn't true. I care for you. More than I ever wanted to or thought I could, but I do."

"What?" she asked, turning to face him. Never had she thought to ever hear such words from the Spanish Scoundrel. The way he looked at her, sincere and as if his future hung on her response, made something in her chest twist.

He cared for her?

Dare she hope that his feelings ran deeper still, to love? For as true as she was standing before him, she loved him. Loved that he vexed and teased her. Loved him enough to overlook his stubbornness and foolhardy schemes. She could understand the reasoning behind it. Had she known her mother at all, she would never have wanted her run out of London simply because of her ethnicity.

She would have fought back as well and sought to make those who had hurt her family pay.

Her aunt had been one of those people, and although Lord Ryley's revenge was misplaced, there was honor pushing him forward to seek it.

"I owe you an apology, Willow. I owe Lord Herbert one as well. There are things that I was not aware of that have come to light and have consequently changed my opinion on things."

Willow took a step toward him, needing to know what had changed. "How so?"

"Come," he said, taking her hand and leading her to sit on the settee beside him. The muffled sound of a cotillion drifted around them, and only the candles burning in the passage illuminated the room. The sitting room was dark and private and dangerous. She should not stay. She should leave, return to her betrothed, and tell Lord Ryley to call on her tomorrow and explain himself.

Instead, Willow sat, turning to face him and drinking in his exquisite visage that looked at her with emotions she could only dream would last forever.

"My mother is in London. She arrived several days ago, and with her arrival, so too came the truth."

Willow frowned, wondering what that could mean. "What truth?"

"Well, as to that," he said, explaining to her everything he had learned.

She sat and listened as Abe told her of his mother's plight all those years before. Why she was made to leave without her son, and the reasons why she could not return. The more she listened, the more Willow realized that Abe had been living under a miscomprehension. One that his mother should have told him the truth of years ago.

"Did your mother know of your plan to seek revenge when the opportunity arose?"

"No," he said, sighing and leaning back in the settee. "She knew my dislike of her friends, or enemies as I assumed it was the case, but because I simply ignored their existence, there was little concern on her part. She was in Paris when Lady Herbert wrote to her and asked for assistance."

"Lady Herbert. What? Why was Lady Herbert requesting assistance?" Willow asked, sitting forward. A wedge of dread knotted in her stomach, and her mind raced as to why her ladyship was asking such a thing.

"She believes that your betrothed is not in love with you. That he's in love with another. She wrote to my mother because she believed that you also did not love her son. That you, in fact, loved Lady Ryley's son instead. And so, a marriage between Lord Herbert and Miss Perry would be a disaster if it proceeded."

Willow stared at Abe, unable to take in all that he was saying. "But Lady Herbert has been so very helpful with the wedding plans. She's so excited."

"Of course she would be, Willow. You're a perfect woman that any man would be proud to marry. I know I would be."

She blew out a breath, meeting his dark, hooded eyes that burned with a need that echoed her own. "You don't want a wife, Lord Ryley. You made that abundantly clear, and should I marry you, I would not like to share."

He chuckled, leaning forward and taking her face in his hands. Willow could feel herself falling for his charm. He only had to touch her, and she was lost. No longer in control.

"The last month has been hell, and I've come to realize that I don't want anyone else in my life other than you. You are the sweetest, most honest and most loyal woman I've ever met, and somewhere between seeing you in breeches at my club, or beneath me on a daybed here in London, I fell in love with you. I love you. I want you to break off your understanding with Lord Herbert and marry me. Be mine."

Willow sucked in a shaky breath. Her hands fisted about the lapels of his coat, and she realized sometime during his speech, she'd reached for him. The idea of being his filled her and a sense of peace settled upon her. The feeling that this was right coursed in her every nerve.

"You're certain that Lady Herbert will not be devastated if I cry off? Lord Herbert has been very attentive."

Abe's eyes narrowed, his face becoming hard. "The blaggard has kissed you again, hasn't he?"

Willow grinned, unable to stem a small chuckle at his annoyance. "They were nothing like your kisses, my lord. I may as well have been kissing my hand."

He scowled at her a moment before he audibly sighed. "I suppose one must kiss one's betrothed. It would be strange not to."

Willow shuffled closer to his person, wrapping her arms about his neck. The scent of sandalwood intoxicated her senses, and for the first time in weeks, she felt herself again. Alive and happy. So very happy. "Do you have anything that you'd like to ask me, Abraham?" she teased, wanting him to say what she'd longed to hear from almost the moment she knew he was an unattainable rake.

He closed the space between them, kissing her softly on the lips, leaning his forehead against hers. "Marry me?"

She nodded, tears pricking her eyes and making the vision, the perfect lovely, unforgettable vision of him, blur before her. "I will marry you. I promise to love you always. To be faithful and honest and forever yours."

"I do too," he said, kissing her again, this time, no sweet, short embrace, but a kiss that fired her blood and made her wish she'd closed the door when entering the room. But there would be more of these to come. Tonight merely marked the beginning of their life. Their start of forever.

EPILOGUE

Four months later

Willow sank into her bath before the roaring fire at Blackwood Hall, Abe's ancestral home, and where they had moved to after their wedding in London, a week after she cried off from marrying Lord Herbert.

As Abe had said, Lord Herbert seemed more relieved than devastated that she wanted to end their understanding, and only today, they had returned to Blackwood after attending Lord Herbert's wedding to Her Grace, the Duchess of Markson. The woman he should have always married had the bride's father not been set on her marrying a duke and not an earl all those years before.

Willow lay back in the jasmine-scented water, closing her eyes, her hand moving to touch the small, hard swelling on her stomach that wasn't noticeable to anyone but her. Now that they were home for the foreseeable future, certainly through the winter months, Willow would tell Abe of the child. She had snuck away in London to their doctor and had her prognosis confirmed. With everything well, she felt ready to let Abe know that he was going to be a father.

The crackling fire warmed her arm as she lay it on the side of the tub. Emotion welled up inside her, and she could not remember ever being so happy. She was married to a man she adored, her friends living happily in her townhouse in London where she had asked them to remain after she married Abe. Neither of them wanted to move back to the country, and the house would otherwise be empty. It was a perfect solution to have her friends there. Hallie was still in town and promised to keep them out of trouble.

Willow smiled at the thought of Evie and Molly, the last of their friends who were yet to marry. She felt certain they too would meet the men who would sweep them off their feet. Next season she would ensure they were courted and adored and married by Season's end.

"Well, this is a delicious sight if ever there was one."

Willow chuckled but did not move. The water soothed her aching muscles after all the traveling they completed that day. "How were the tenant farms? Everything in order?"

"Everything is well. My steward has it under control as usual."

Willow opened one eye when she heard a rustling beside the tub. She sat up as a muscular, hairy leg stepped into the tub, followed by another. She gasped as he sat and joined her, water toppling over the sides and splashing on the Aubusson rug.

"Abe, the mess!"

He grinned, shrugging. "It'll dry," he said, reaching out and pulling her over to his side. Instead of laying on him, like she so often did when they bathed together, she straddled his legs, placing her aching core against his manhood.

The water made him slippery, and she clutched his shoulders, running her hands over his chest that would forever catch her attention. From the moment she'd agreed to become his wife, he'd bathed her in love. Sometimes to the point that she worried about him should anything happen to her. Whether he would be okay, so deep was his affection for her.

His mother had stayed on in London and had taken her place back within the *ton*, which made Abe happy. As for his club, he still ran the establishment, but it had changed to a men's only club, become less *demimonde* and more *beau monde*.

His wicked gaze made her forget everything else, and she leaned forward, kissing him, taking from him whatever she wanted. Over the last few months, she'd become quite bold in her seductions of him, enjoyed teasing him throughout the day, and making him wait.

Today had been no different. Throughout the carriage ride home, she'd thrown him hot little glances that promised pleasure. His tongue meshed with hers, and she sucked on his, mimicking what she liked to do with his hardened member.

Abe groaned, his hands a vise about her head, keeping her against him. She reveled in his passion, taking all that he offered and matching it twofold. Willow undulated against him, his hard, large member sending spikes of pleasure to radiate through her body.

"God, I love you," he said, kissing his way down her face, her neck, before lifting her a little to take one erect nipple into his mouth. His tongue flicked out, teasing the bud, and she watched him, her breath ragged. Willow bit her lip, grinning at what his touch did to her. Made her feel.

So much joy. So much love.

"Your breasts are so perfect." His hand ran over her other breast, his thumb and forefinger rolling her nipple. Willow moaned, rocking against him as his mouth teased her flesh.

"You're not to come yet, my love."

And then she was lifted and spun about in the tub. His large, muscular arms sliding down hers to set them against the edge of the bath. On her knees, Willow looked over her shoulder, wondering what he was up to. His body leaned against her back, his cock settling between her aching folds, and realization dawned.

They had never made love this way. Was it even possible?

He kissed her back, slipping her hair over one shoulder. His tongue traced her spine, and Willow closed her eyes, unsure she could take much more of his teasing. It was delicious and all-consuming.

"Stop taunting me, Abe," she gasped as he slid against her core again, just enough to keep her wanting more. And she'd never get enough of her husband, that was one thing she was certain.

❦

ABE WOULD NEVER GET ENOUGH of Willow. She was his world, and he adored every little tidbit of her. His balls were tight, his cock hard. Her heat slid around him as he teased them both. He groaned at the delicious friction, wrapping his arms about her to clasp her breasts.

They hung heavy in his hands, and he tweaked her nipples, eliciting a sweet gasp of need from her lips.

He reached for his cock, guiding himself into her, taking her inch by sweet inch until he lodged himself fully.

Her tight core clamped about him, and he thrust hard once to tease her.

She moaned, undulating her ass, seeking his cock, and he sucked in a breath, not wanting this to end. Damn, she made him want. Always a need that was never sated, no matter how much they came together in such a way. From the moment they'd married, it had been like this, and he hoped it would never end.

He adored her and only lived to make her happy.

She was wet, coating his cock even in the water, and he thrust again, picking up his pace. They hadn't had sex like this before, but he was certain she would enjoy it. If her moans and sweet little gasps were anything to go by, she was enjoying his tupping of her from behind quite a lot.

Abe leaned back, clasping her hips and thrusting hard and deep. With one hand he reached around, sliding it against her cunny and teasing her little nubbin that he loved to suckle, to kiss and lick. Later, he promised himself. Next he would bring her to release on his face.

The thought of the act made him harder still, and he groaned.

"Oh Abe," she gasped, reaching down to place her hand on his, holding him against her mons.

Her sexual demands only excited him more, and he continued his relentless pace, knowing how she liked to be fucked hard and fast. Deep and sure. His cock swelled as he took her. Leaning down, he kissed her neck, the sensitive, sweet spot under her ear.

She mewled, gasping, and then he felt it. The tightening, pulling sensation around his prick. Her release spiked his, and he joined her in the kaleidoscope of pleasure, taking her until at last she relaxed in his arms, sated and satisfied.

He disengaged and helped her to slip about to face

him. He held her against his chest, his hand idly running up and down her back. Her skin was so soft and smelled always of flowers. Today it would seem the water had been spiked with jasmine. A scent he now forever associated with her.

"That was different," she said, turning a little to kiss his chest before she placed her hand over his heart, one finger idly playing with his chest. "I liked it."

He liked it too. He kissed her temple, holding her close. "I thought you might, and I have other things planned for you this evening. Other enjoyable delights that I know you'll enjoy."

"Hmm," she mumbled, meeting his gaze. "I'll look forward to it, and speaking of other things for this evening. I wanted to tell you something."

"You do?" He glanced down at her expectantly. "What is it?"

"Well," she said, sitting up a little to see him more clearly. "When we were in London this week, I went to the doctor."

"Are you well? Is there anything the matter?" he said, interrupting her and sitting up so fast that water sloshed onto the floor once again. The poor maids would be cursing them later for this mess. His hands searched her body as if he would find something ominous, and Willow clasped them, holding them still.

"Nothing is wrong, Abe. Everything is perfect, in fact."

"It is? Then why did you need to consult a doctor?"

She didn't reply, merely grinned at him, and waited for him to understand. To know what she wanted to tell him. It only took a moment, and his eyes widened, his mouth gaping for words that wouldn't come.

"We're going to have a baby. I'm pregnant."

"Damn it," he said, clasping her shoulders.

For a moment, Willow wasn't sure what to say. Was he happy or did *damn it* mean he was disappointed? "You're not pleased?" she asked when he merely stared at her like a stone statue they had in certain parts of the garden.

"Oh no, I'm more than happy, Willow. I'm beyond all thought and coherent sentences, but I'm beyond happy."

Tears blurred her vision, and taking one hand, she slid it to cover the small bump that sat low on her belly. "The doctor thinks I'm several weeks along. Do you think it's going to be a girl or a boy?"

Abe let out a half laugh, half snort. "I hope it's a girl. I'd love to have a daughter who is as sweet, as pure, and good as her mama."

Pleasure filled her at his words. Such poetry she could get used to. "I'd like a boy so that he can grow up as handsome and noble as you."

"The Spanish Scoundrel. Would you want a son knowing his father held that title?"

Willow reached up, running her hand over his jaw, knowing how much the title irked him once they were married. Some still referred to him like that, and he loathed the connotations that came with the name. "I fell in love with the Spanish Scoundrel, and you were not so very bad. Personally, I think your reputation was exaggerated more than necessary."

"Really?" he said, one eyebrow arched.

Heat pooled between her legs at his wicked glance that promised retribution for saying such a thing. He stood in the bath, more water splashing to the floor. Willow looked at him with exasperation before he lifted her up, hoisted her in his arms, and stepped from the tub.

"Not so very bad, you say?" he said, only a few short strides to the bed. He hoisted her onto the mattress, and Willow laughed as she bounced. "We shall see about that."

Willow reached for him as he came down upon her, a willing recipient for anything that Abe, the Spanish Scoundrel, was willing to do to her. Not just tonight, but always.

For all days.

Dear Reader,

Thank you for taking the time to read *League of Unweddable Gentlemen series box set, books 1-3*! I hope you enjoyed the stories.

I'm forever grateful to my readers, so if you're able, I would appreciate an honest review. As they say, feed an author, leave a review! You can contact me at tamaragillauthor@gmail.com or sign up to my newsletter to keep up with my writing news.

If you'd like to learn about book one in my Royal House of Atharia series, To Dream of You, please read on. I have included chapter one for your reading pleasure.

Tamara Gill

TO DREAM OF YOU

The Royal House of Atharia, Book 1

After months spent in hiding, Princess Holly is finally ready to take her rightful place as ruler of Atharia. All she has to do now is survive her murderous uncle's attempts to steal the throne for himself. But when a mysterious gentleman washes up on the shores of her beach, she's shocked to realize she needs his help almost as much as he needs hers …

When Drew Meyers left his estate, his plan was to escape the arranged marriage, his scheming father brokered for him. The storm that nearly killed him was not part of the plan. Neither was meeting her. Holly is everything he ever wanted, and he will do anything to keep her safe and get her home—even if doing so means he'll be forced to let her go forever…

A union between a princess and a lowly future duke is forbidden. But as intrigue abounds and their enemies circle, will Drew and Holly defy the obligations and expectations that stand between them to take a chance on love? Or is their happily ever after merely a dream?

CHAPTER 1

Sotherton Estate, Suffolk, 1805

My Lord Balhannah,
Drew…
I write to you today from necessity and desperation, and I hope you
shall heed my words and help me due to our friendship. There is no
doubt in my mind that in the coming days your father shall demand
that our marriage takes place forthwith. In fact, as I write this, my
father is readying the coaches to travel two days hence. I assume a
marriage license has already been procured and contracts signed, unbe-
known to us of course…until today.
Know that as much as I admire and care for you as a friend, I do not
love, nor do I wish to marry you, as I'm sure you do not want to
marry me. You see, my heart has long been given elsewhere, and I will
not, not even on pain of disinheritance, give up the man I love.
When we arrive at Sotherton, please do not be there, unless you wish
to break my heart and give yourself to me before God, when you know
that I shall never love you how a wife should love a husband. If you
can provide me with time, my love has promised to come and collect
me at Sotherton, where we shall run away to Scotland and be

married. I'm sorry to be so frank with my words, but I'm desperate to get this letter to you and, with it, stress how much I do not want such a union.

Please do whatever you can to dissuade this marriage from going ahead.

Forever your friend,

Myrtle

Drew placed the missive from Myrtle into the fire in his room and went to the window. He pulled back the heavy brocade velvet curtains to gauge the weather. A perfect spring day, and from his window, he could see the sea and the cove where his small sailing raft was kept.

Absently he listened to his valet, Jeffries behind him go about his duties in his room. He could not stay here. Not with Myrtle so heartsick over their impending marriage. With his decision made, he turned and faced his servant. "I'm going sailing and may even travel down the coast to visit Sir Percival's at Castle Clair in Kent. I will meet you there. Please pack me a small bag to get me through until we meet again. Nothing too fancy, mind you, we'll be mostly hunting or taking our leisure about the estate. Maybe only two dinner jackets."

Jeffries stared at him, his eyes wide with this change of plans. Drew raised one brow, waiting for him to comprehend he was serious with his demand.

"Of course, my lord." Jeffries started for the chest of drawers, pulling out cravats and buckskin breeches before walking into Drew's dressing room to collect a trunk. "Will His Grace be aware of your travels, my lord, or are we keeping this excursion a secret?" Jeffries asked, from the small room.

Drew went to his chest of drawers and pulled out the oldest buckskin breeches he owned. He stripped his perfectly tied cravat from his throat, along with his waistcoat. Rummaging through his cupboard, he couldn't find his old woolen waistcoat that was warm and what he liked to use for sailing. "I cannot locate my..." Drew smiled when Jeffries passed it to him, a small smile on the man's face. "Thank you," he said, slipping it on, along with his coat.

Drew walked over to his desk and scribbled a short note to his father. Folding it, he handed it to his manservant. "Have this sent from London when you move through there. The duke may travel to town and demand answers, he will try to find me, but he will not succeed. Under no circumstances are you to tell him where I've gone. I will send a word in a week notifying you, God willing, of my safe arrival." His father was ruthless when it came to having his way, the marriage to Myrtle no different. He would lose his allowance, Drew had little doubt, but what of it? It would not be forever. Myrtle would run away and marry, and then Drew could return home.

Thank heavens Miss Landers was also against the union and only needed time to ensure their marriage would never happen. And time is what he was buying now.

Jeffries handed him a small black valise. "Yes, my lord."

Drew pocketed some blunt and left, leaving via the servant's stairs and the back door, two places his father's shadow never darkened. He ran a hand through his short locks, pulling on a cap to disguise himself further.

The brisk, salty tang of sea air hit him and invigorated his stride. Drew walked through the abundance of gardens his mother had so painstakingly cared for before passing last year. Memories of running about the garden bombarded his mind. Of hidden vistas and large oaks that any young boy enjoyed frolicking around whenever he could. His mother had designed the garden to incorporate hidden vistas perfect for children. Plants that camouflaged the old Roman ruins on the south side of the park, so it wasn't until you were almost upon them did the ruins reveal themselves, the long-lost castle of the Sotherton dukes who came before them.

Drew had spent hours playing on his own within the walls of this green sanctuary. As much as he disliked having the idea of a wife at this very moment, he couldn't help but look forward to the day his children would run about the beautiful grounds and enjoy what he always had.

The crashing of the waves echoed through the trees. Stepping free of the manicured grounds, Drew stood at the top of the small cliff and looked down on the beach's golden sands below. Many years ago, he'd had a small boathouse built to house his sailboat, and as the tide was high, it would be no problem pulling it out and dragging it the short distance to the water.

Taking the winding path down to the shore, it didn't take him long to haul the boat into the shallows and throw his bag under the little compartment that would keep it dry. The sky remained clear, with only the slightest sea breeze. It would help him travel down the coast to where his friend and closest confidant Sir Percival lived. The trip should only take a few days, and he couldn't get far enough away from this estate. To be forced into a union, not of his choice, or Miss Lander's, was reprehensible. The year was 1805, for heaven's sake. His father really ought to get up with the times. Step into the nineteenth century and embrace the new era. He was a grown gentleman, fully capable of making his own decisions. For his father to demand he marry, simply because he'd stumbled across an heiress, was offensive.

Drew pushed off from the shore, releasing the sail. The wind caught the sheet and pulled him out to sea at a clipping pace. He steered south and smiled. His father would forgive him in time, he was sure of it. The duke was never one to hold a grudge for long, and no matter how mad he'd be at finding out Drew left, he would get over it in time.

Want to read more? Purchase To Dream of You today!

LEAGUE OF UNWEDDABLE GENTLEMEN SERIES AVAILABLE NOW!

Fall into my latest series, where the heroines have to fight for what they want, both regarding their life and love. And where the heroes may be unweddable to begin with, that is until they meet the women who'll change their fate. The League of Unweddable Gentlemen series is available now!

LEAGUE OF UNWEDDABLE GENTLEMEN

THE ROYAL HOUSE OF ATHARIA
SERIES

If you love dashing dukes and want a royal adventure, make sure to check out my latest series, The Royal House of Atharia series! Book one, To Dream of You is available now at Amazon or you can read FREE with Kindle Unlimited.

A union between a princess and a lowly future duke is forbidden. But as intrigue abounds and their enemies circle, will Drew and Holly defy the obligations and expectations that stand between them to take a chance on love? Or is their happily ever after merely a dream?

ALSO BY TAMARA GILL

Royal House of Atharia Series

TO DREAM OF YOU

A ROYAL PROPOSITION

FOREVER MY PRINCESS

League of Unweddable Gentlemen Series

TEMPT ME, YOUR GRACE

HELLION AT HEART

DARE TO BE SCANDALOUS

TO BE WICKED WITH YOU

KISS ME DUKE

THE MARQUESS IS MINE

LEAGUE - BOOKS 1-3 BUNDLE

LEAGUE - BOOKS 4-6 BUNDLE

Kiss the Wallflower series

A MIDSUMMER KISS

A KISS AT MISTLETOE

A KISS IN SPRING

TO FALL FOR A KISS

A DUKE'S WILD KISS

TO KISS A HIGHLAND ROSE

KISS THE WALLFLOWER - BOOKS 1-3 BUNDLE

KISS THE WALLFLOWER - BOOKS 4-6 BUNDLE

A MARRIAGE MADE IN MAYFAIR

SCANDALOUS LONDON - BOOKS 1-3 BUNDLE

High Seas & High Stakes Series

HIS LADY SMUGGLER

HER GENTLEMAN PIRATE

HIGH SEAS & HIGH STAKES - BOOKS 1-2 BUNDLE

Daughters Of The Gods Series

BANISHED-GUARDIAN-FALLEN

DAUGHTERS OF THE GODS - BOOKS 1-3 BUNDLE

Stand Alone Books

TO SIN WITH SCANDAL

OUTLAWS

ABOUT THE AUTHOR

Tamara Gill is an Australian author who grew up in an old mining town in country South Australia, where her love of history was founded. So much so, she made her darling husband travel to the UK for their honeymoon, where she dragged him from one historical monument and castle to another.

A mother of three, her two little gentlemen in the making, a future lady (she hopes) and a part-time job keep her busy in the real world, but whenever she gets a moment's peace she loves to write romance novels in an array of genres, including regency, medieval and time travel.

www.tamaragill.com
tamaragillauthor@gmail.com

Made in the USA
Middletown, DE
24 March 2021